THE
GOOD
ADVENTURERS

by

Sandra George

Los bienaventurados los que tienen hambre y sed de justicia....
5 Mateo: v. 6

The good adventurers are those who hunger and thirst for justice....

Open Door Publishers, Inc.
Malta, NY

See, I have placed
before you an open
door that no one can shut.
Rev 3:8

Open Door Publishers, Inc
P.O. Box 2871
Ballston Spa, NY 12020 (518) 899-2097
http://www.opendoorpublishers.com

Printed in the United States of America

First Edition

First Printing 2012

ISBN: 978-1-937138-18-9

DEDICATION

I dedicate this novel to my husband, John, with whom I have shared many good adventures. The book would not have become a reality without his ongoing support, not only as a resource, but also, as my original editor and an always-encouraging presence.

ACKNOWLEDGEMENTS

I thank Russell Barton, writing workshop teacher; David Sparenberg, author, poet, teacher, and professional editor; Duncan Searl, professional editor; and my publisher, Open Door Publishers, Inc., for their editorial assistance. Additional thanks also go to Lillian Johnson, Peggy Graham, Jean Brugger, Isa Cann, and Ingeborg Cann, avid fiction readers, who reviewed the book, adding many useful comments, and to Kathy Knight, who corrected my imperfect Spanish.

I thank the John W. Peterson Music Company for permission to use the hymn "Chariot of Clouds," © 1972, and Jerod Ruleaux, Commercial License Administrator for Oregon Catholic Press, for permission to use the song "Alabaré, alabaré, alabaré a mi Señor" by José Pagán, Manuel Alonso, and Santa Biblia Reina-Valera Actualizado for permission to use "bienaventuredos los que tienen hambre y sed de justicia."

NICARAGUA
Political Map

HONDURAS

N

Puerto
Cabezas

REGION AUTONOMISTA
ATLATICO NORTE

NUEVA
SEGOVIA   JINOTEGA

Ocotal

Wiwli

Somoto
MADRIZ

ESTELI

Jinotega

La Cruz de
Rio Grande

Esteli   MATAGALPA

Potosi   Rio
Grande

El Sauce   Matagalpa

Nuevo
Amanecer

CHINANDEGA

Muy Muy

Chinandega   LEON

BOACO

REGION AUTONOMISTA
ATLATICO SUR

Leon   San Benito   Boaco

Santo
Domingo

Caribbean Sea

MANAGUA

Juigalpa

MANAGUA   MASAYA

Bluefields

Masaya   Grenada   CHONTALES

PACIFIC OCEAN

Jinotepe   GRENADA   *Iago de
Nicaragua*

Nueva
Guinea

CARAZO

Rivas   *Isla de
Ometepe*

Punta Gorda

RIVAS

RIO
SAN JUAN

San Juan del Sur   Penas Blancas

San Carlos

COSTA RICA

0   75Km

Copyright © 2011-12 www.mapsofworld.com

(Updated on 1st May, 2012)

LEGEND

–·– International Boundary
– – – State Boundary
▣ National Capital
▪ State Capital
• Other Cities

BOOK ONE
ANNE

CHAPTER ONE

Guatemala City, Guatemala – January 1991

Vicente Carranza, driver for the Escuela Rosada del Idioma Español, the Rosada Spanish Language School, watched the *indios* terrify the *Americana*. It was not the first time he had witnessed such an event. Privileged ones undone by poor peasants were a treat for drivers fortunate enough to work at the airport in Guatemala City. Most drivers dealt with *ricos* in full control, some nice, some arrogant, but always expecting excellent service, as though *guatemaltecos* were created to provide for their comfort. He, on the other hand, was privileged from time to time to observe these *ricos* intimidated by fear.

As the *Americana* bolted toward him, he glimpsed her full breasts through her torn white blouse. He felt his hardness grow observing the tall woman, frantic and vulnerable. She was dressed like the pictures of rich city women he perused in glamour magazines while waiting for a plane's arrival. He guessed the mane of golden hair straggling over her eyes had once been neatly clipped to her head and felt a malevolent satisfaction in seeing it in such disarray.

"You saw! Why didn't you help!" she panted, braking to avoid crashing into him. Beads of perspiration moistened her upper lip; her hips and breasts were trembling, warming his blood.

"Tranquilo. Tranquilo. Yo te ayudaré," he purred in mock concern, cradling her arm within his hand and leading her to the van. She accepted the direction without protest and once inside lowered her head into her hands and moaned, "I kicked away a crippled child."

Thirty minutes earlier, two stocky porters with totemic dark faces speaking an unfamiliar language had approached the woman as she stood by the baggage chute at the airport, awaiting three bulging black bags stuffed with provisions for a year's sojourn in Central America. Anne Harrison assumed the words spoken by the little men in rumpled green uniforms and oversized visor caps were one of the twenty-three Mayan dialects spoken in Guatemala and that, like her, they spoke Spanish as a second language. She hunched forward hoping a correct reading of their facial expressions would enhance the communication between them. Being tall was a handicap in a land of short people, something she had discovered during her past visits to Nicaragua where she had to look down on everyone, including her petite cousin Evelyn.

The fatigued dull eyes of the porters punctured the balloon of euphoria she had carried from Boston. Impassivity and defeat shrouded their faces, the same impassivity and defeat she had observed in the parents of poor inner-city students during an ill-fated senior year university internship twenty-three years ago. Unknowingly, the dispirited little men spiraled her back to where guilt and regret remained.

Anne drew in a breath, then fixed her eyes on the baggage chute. She pointed out her luggage to the porters and followed them toward customs. As she expected, the line was long, but eventually she reached a custom booth where a handsome young light-skinned man flashed straight white teeth as he asked in English for her passport. Anne thought he was probably Ladino, a mixture of Hispanic and Mayan, favoring the Hispanic side as he lacked the high cheekbones and darker skin of the Mayan. He reviewed the passport, stamped it, slipped in a ninety-day visa, and asked her to place her bags on the table next to his booth. The porters obliged and with a quick zip of each bag and a cursory look at their contents, the inspector said, "Welcome to Guatemala. Have a good stay."

They continued into the airport terminal, like any terminal in the United States, except for the shops selling colorful Mayan crafts and clothing. She stifled a desire to enter one of the shops; the representative from the language school where she would study Spanish during the next six weeks would be waiting.

Anne followed the green-clad porters toward the exit congratulating herself for choosing to study Spanish in Guatemala, known as the Land of Eternal Spring. A colleague at Malden Community College who traveled extensively informed her that Nicaragua had no decent Spanish language schools and that the language schools in Antigua were top quality. They would prepare her for life in Nicaragua more completely than Spanish courses tucked haphazardly into an overcrowded teaching schedule. Brimming with anticipation, she followed the porters onto the red stone tile surrounding the terminal building. US coins jingled in the pocket of her tailored slacks, to be handed out to the beggars she expected. A puff of spring-like air brushed her face. It was 9:30 p.m., Guatemala time, and she had remembered to turn back her wristwatch an hour. As always, she was prepared.

Uniformed ambassadors from hotels and travel agencies hoisted signs announcing the names of passengers for pick up. Anne searched for the sign *Escuela Rosada del Idioma Español* as she followed the porters over a ribbon of black asphalt snaking through the airport illuminated only by a few widely spaced street lamps.

"A dónde vamos?" she asked the porters.

"Estacionamiento," one said.

"Parking lot," she murmured, noticing silhouetted figures materializing under the glare of the lamps. She quickly identified the figures as beggars and they were soon buzzing around her like hungry mosquitoes. Stretching forth calloused hands they pleaded, *"Quetzales, Señora. Por favor, quetzales."*

Anne obliged, plopping American coins into the open palms, but once examined the coins were refused.

"No good. *Quetzales, Señora. Por favor, quetzales."*

She carried no *quetzales*, no Guatemalan currency. The Spanish language school had advised her not to change money at the airport, insisting they offered a better rate.

"No tengo quetzales," Anne declared to a haggard old beggar who cocked his shaggy dark head upward and held out the American coins in a dirty palm.

"Entonces, dólares," he said.

"I have no dollars," she apologized.

"Dólares. Dólares," he insisted through his rotten teeth. Anne shrank back from the sour smell of his body.

"No tengo dólares," she repeated warily, if falsely, for the American bills she carried did not include any singles. She had a few tens and twenties in the carry-on, none of which she intended to part with. The remaining five thousand in larger bills were stuffed into a plastic bag in her underwear for safety. Evelyn claimed that sum would support her adequately for ten plus months in Nicaragua.

As the pleading crowd bunched nearer, a growing sense of unease gripped Anne. She looked around to see how other passengers were coping with the onslaught, but they were invisible, swallowed by other crowds of beggars. The porters growled, "Go away!"

Cowed, the beggars faded off into the open expanse of asphalt leading to the shadowy parking lot.

"*Señora!*" a porter shouted pointing to a sign on the hood of a faintly visible white van declaring, *Escuela Rosada del Idioma Español*. They jogged forward, Anne briskly following until an old woman holding out a bouquet of limp flowers appeared before her like an apparition.

"*Para la señora,*" the woman croaked frog-like through quaking lips. Her skin shivered as loosely as partially congealed gelatin.

A startled Anne gingerly accepted the decaying blossoms. *A welcome gift from the school,* she thought.

"*Dos dólares,*" the crone hissed.

"*No tengo dólares,*" said Anne realizing her mistake. She held out the flowers in return. The woman slapped her hand away. "*Dos dólares,*" she demanded, encircling Anne's wrist with surprisingly strong fingers.

Startled, Anne whipped her arm free, sending the faded flowers floating toward the ground. As she turned, the woman's claw-hand snatched the sleeve of Anne's white blouse. "*Gringa basura,* garbage,*" she spat contemptuously.

Sudden fear sliced through Anne and she shot forward, hearing the tear of the cloth and feeling the woman's spittle on her arm. She uttered a strangled cry for help toward the porters, but they continued on their forward march without response. Safely distant from the witch-woman, she slowed her gait to swallow bile in her throat and wiped away the spittle. The two upper buttons of her blouse had popped revealing her bra, and a section of cloth swung loosely from her arm like a flapping flag. She pulled the stray halves of her blouse together as she walked rapidly toward the van, longing to disappear into its cocoon of safety.

"Shit!" she cried out when something grasped her left leg. A small boy with twisted legs joined like a pretzel at his ankles was lying on his stomach, his arms encircling her calves. When she tried to move, the deformed child thrashed fiercely scraping his little belly on the asphalt. Other children drifted out of the darkness like phantoms pointing and murmuring, and Anne's mouth went dry. If the deformed child brought her down, the children, eyes wide in delicious anticipation for her treasures, would pounce on her like jackals. With a surge of adrenaline, she reached into her pocket, snatched a handful of American coins and flung them upward, sending the children scattering after them. Kicking fiercely until the pretzel child fell back, she leaped over his tiny body and sprinted forward, her carry-on bag swirling behind. The two porters and the driver next to the Spanish school's van stared in her direction, and at that moment, she hated them for not coming to her rescue.

"I kicked away a crippled child," she moaned as the driver helped her into the van. For a few moments he observed her heaving breasts and listened to her strangled gasps waiting for her to regain control.

"Señora, tenga que pagar," he finally said, flashing an inauthentic toothy smile. He was taller than the porters with only a hint of indigenous features. She looked into suspicious eyes that declared, *Don't trust me,* as he jabbed a finger toward the porters. "Pay," he said in English.

Anne rooted around in the carry-on for two five-dollar bills. She saw him slip one bill into his pocket before approaching the porters, but dared not challenge him. Her heart pounded as she pressed into the soft upholstery of the cavernous van. With a tissue she dabbed at the mascara streaking her cheeks. Then she blew her nose and bound back the cascade of blond hair that had burst the confines of its clip, inhaling short deep breaths until the agitation had melted into a manageable apprehension.

"I am called Vicente Carranza, Profesora Harrison. I take you to Antigua," the driver stated in broken English as he started the van's ignition. They pulled out of the airport and into Guatemala City, a cosmopolitan capitol of two million people bathed in the artificial lights of street lamps. Unlike Managua, the capitol of Nicaragua, Anne could not see the visible signs of Guatemala's endemic poverty strategically hidden from the main streets and centers of commerce. She saw no earthquake ravaged buildings serving as homes to impoverished families or begging street urchins.

They had passed through the city into the countryside before Carranza began to speak in a mixture of Spanish and English. *"Mucho* danger in the city," he said.

"Sí," she responded feeling vulnerable and aware of the tension in her voice.

"In Guatemala we have much war, much crime, much danger. We must be careful not to stop on the road. *Banditos* are everywhere. They kill just for fun."

Although her Spanish was basic, at best, Anne understood the driver's comments, but more importantly, she comprehended the glee in his tone. Why was he trying to frighten her? She felt the pounding in her chest. Did she have anything to fear from this man?

"*Pero* I am a tiger," he boasted. "You are safe with Vicente."

Anne saw his smug, thin smile in the rearview mirror. "Safe with Vicente," he said after watching her squirm with his comments on war, crime, and danger in Guatemala. Her wariness morphed into anger. He was a weasel, although probably not a dangerous one, and what the hell could she do about it anyway? She was exhausted from the demanding day and closed her eyes, but her body refused to relax. The forty-five minute trip from Guatemala City to Antigua seemed interminable.

***

Arturo Coronado, owner and director of the Escuela Rosada del Idioma Español, awaited the arrival of Professor Harrison. Usually an underling would welcome a student arriving at 10:30 p.m., but he wanted to give a special welcome to this lady who had attended the same university in Boston his daughter Carlita was presently attending. Also, she was an evangelical Christian, like he, sent by the Christians United Churches denomination in the United States, which contracted his school to teach their missionaries and volunteers Spanish.

A small, trim man with shiny black shoes and neatly slicked black hair, he was dressed in an immaculate white suit, his appearance suggesting the vestiges of wealth, even though his inconstant father had lost most of their wealth before he drowned drunk in a watery ditch. Now the family's only real estate was the country house where Coronado, his wife, and four children lived and the grandiose colonial-era pink stucco building in which he operated the school.

When he opened the door to his student, Anne Harrison, and led her into the living room, he observed her eyes falling upon an austere portrait of General Rodrigo Arturo Santos Coronado García, which was dramatically framed over a massive fireplace dominating the room. A red sash flowed down the general's uniform, replete with silver and gold medals.

"My grandfather," Coronado declared proudly. "He was awarded many medals for his bravery against the criminal insurgents that have plagued our country for over thirty years."

Anne had read enough about the political history of Guatemala to know Coronado was referring to the ongoing civil war in the countryside where Mayan peasant farmers were accused by the government of being sympathetic toward the leftist rebels that had waged war for decades. The Mayans had suffered the destruction of many of their villages by government soldiers and the loss of thousands of their people.

When Coronado's eyes fell upon her blouse, clumsily fastened with a safety pin, then shifted to the flap of its torn sleeve, Anne made an awkward gesture of flattening the wayward cloth against her arm, but offered no explanation. He shook her hand and arched his chin slightly upward, noting she was too tall for a woman, yet she was elegant in a Grace Kelly sort of way. He had always liked Grace Kelly and was sad when she died.

As the pair walked through the house toward Coronado's office, Anne observed the elegance of her surroundings. The Escuela Rosada, as it was known among Antiguans, announced its opulence whenever a student stepped through the intricately carved mahogany door onto white polished floor tiles. Coronado enjoyed their pleased reactions as they took in the richness of his house, feeling a swell of pride over their admiration.

"The door into your office is exquisite," Anne said softly, looking at a Mayan village scene delicately carved in its midsection. Her intriguing green eyes shone like emeralds summoning the amorous interest within Coronado that always surfaced in the presence of an attractive woman. Fine lines spiraled outward from these jewels, the only indication of Anne's forty-one years, a year younger than he and the age of his wife Carla. Unlike Carla, however, there was no wrinkling around the lips, no sagging at the chin, and no thickening around the middle. Coronado thought, *"Like me, she is a perfect specimen of middle age."*

"The Mayan are extraordinary craftspeople," he declared to Anne. "Weaving is their specialty, but they are woodworkers as well, and Central American hardwoods are the best in the world." Coronado spoke in the near perfect English he had acquired at boarding school in the United States prior to the loss of the family fortune. "You will find Antigua to your liking, Profesora Harrison." He motioned her to an overstuffed leather chair in front of his antique mahogany desk.

"A magnificent piece of furniture," she said as she examined the desk's soft curves. "It reminds me of my grandfather's writing desk."

"A Harrison, I presume," said Coronado. "Like the president."

"The president?" she asked curiously arching light brown brows slightly.

"William Harrison or, perhaps Benjamin Harrison."

Anne chortled. "Oh! No. No. My father's name is William, but we are not related to any president." Pausing, she added, "You appear to know American history."

"I attended a private boys' school in Vermont," he explained. "I like all things American, including history."

She tilted her head slightly to the right. He knew she was observing him with interest. Throughout Antigua he was known for his charm and dark good looks and he had conquered more than one of Antigua's upper-class ladies. Quickly her gaze left him to float around the office with its brooding Spanish colonial-era furnishings. Her eyes settled on the portrait of a Spanish flamenco dancer, blood red rose in her hair, a white and red-layered skirt billowing outward, her chin uplifted.

"Lovely," she commented.

"Ah, yes. She was a relative. My paternal great-grandfather was born in Spain and made his fortune in Guatemala. At one time our family owned half of Antigua," Coronado declared, leaning back in his chair tenting his manicured fingers. He waited for her to speak, but she was silent, so he turned his attention to a manila file folder on his desk.

"I see from your application that you teach English at a university," he said as he shuffled papers in the folder.

"Not quite, Señor Coronado. I teach at a two-year community college."

"Ah," he said disappointedly perusing the application more carefully. "But I see you received a master's degree in English from Scotia University in Boston. My daughter, Carlita, is in her freshman year there." He paused awaiting comment, but she seemed to have no interest in conversing.

"I see that your place of employment is in Medford, Massachusetts. Isn't that where Tufts University is located?" Coronado asked pushing on.

"Yes," she said. "We are not far from Tufts."

"My daughter Carlita considered Tufts. They offered her admission. She is a scholarly young woman."

"You must be proud of her," Anne commented hoping that would end talk of his daughter. In their brief time together, Anne had sensed a self-important posturing in Arturo Coronado. He smiled and declared, "Yes, I am."

Anne wanted to be taken to the family with whom she would stay and climb into bed, but he continued to speak returning to the application. "I see you have been sent to our school by the Christians United Churches denomination."

"Yes. When I decided to come to Guatemala, I asked them for a recommendation and they recommended you," Anne replied, aware of the weariness in her voice.

"Will you be staying in Guatemala following your time with us?"

"No. I am going to Nicaragua," Anne said.

"Nicaragua?" Coronado looked surprised. "This is not possible. Nicaragua is an unstable country. They are always at war."

The remark dismayed Anne given Guatemala's ongoing civil war. She considered rebutting him, but she did not want to prolong the conversation, so she offered an explanation hoping to satisfy his obvious curiosity. "My church helps to support a rural church there."

"Ah! I see. We have many fine evangelical churches in Guatemala seeking ties with our brothers in North America. Has your church considered affiliating with a Guatemalan church?"

"My cousin Evelyn lives in Nicaragua."

"*Claro.* Your cousin is a missionary at this church," said Coronado. His conclusion was wrong, but she made no effort to correct it. He cleared his throat, then asked, "And you too will work with this church in Nicaragua?"

Anne, growing more irritated, forced herself to answer politely. "No. I will be teaching English at Managua University. I am on a one-year sabbatical. Right now, I am very tired, Señor Coronado."

Coronado perceived her sudden impatience. The charming banter of earlier had evaporated. He assumed that in spite of his best efforts she had not recovered from whatever unfortunate incident had torn her blouse.

"Let me assure you that you have nothing to fear in Antigua," he said speaking to the unarticulated incident. "Some of our students have told us life in Antigua is like paradise. Here we have almost as many guards as residents. People from all over the world study safely in our language schools. You must be careful, of course. Even in America you need to take care."

"Yes," Anne agreed, her fatigued mind wandering back to her internship as a student teacher in the Boston slum.

Coronado realized from the glaze in his student's eyes that he had lost her to another world. She nervously twisted what appeared to him to be a wedding band on her right hand, raising his curiosity. Was she divorced or widowed?

"Profesora Harrison?" he asked in an insistent voice designed to recapture her attention.

"Yes, sorry," she muttered emerging from her reverie. "I'm tired."

"I see," he acknowledged. Placing palms down on the desk, he pushed to his feet and cleared his throat again. "Well, we have arranged for you to stay with one of our choice families, unfortunately a Catholic family, but there are few quality evangelical homes in Antigua available for hosting."

"I will be fine," Anne agreed, too weary to protest the prejudice implied in his remark. She did not like Arturo Coronado anymore than she liked his driver Vicente, and all this negativity worried her.

"Like you, I am evangelical," Coronado announced as he took her arm and led her to the door. "Once I was Catholic, but in the 1980's our Bishops in Latin America adopted the theology of liberation. We were told God prefers the poor. We were asked to allow *indios* into our churches. I would not allow my family to sit next to *indios*," he declared, indignation ringing in his voice. Anne tensed. "These so-called Christians that believe in liberation theology side with the rebel criminal gangs in some areas of our countryside."

"Is there a point to all of this?" Anne asked, not bothering to disguise her irritation. Surprised by her sudden rudeness, Coronado frowned.

"It is time to go," he said frostily, shooting forth his hand for her to shake.

"Yes," she agreed, brushing her hand across his quickly.

As he watched the van disappear into the darkness, he murmured to himself, "Even if she is *evangélica,* she is just another arrogant American."

***

Vicente stopped in front of a white stucco house connected to a row of similar white houses lined along the cobblestone street of Avenida Verde. The street was rimmed with black lanterns hanging languidly from tall iron posts. Under one, a shadowy figure rested, a rifle at his side.

"Guard," Vicente explained in English as he unloaded the luggage and held his hand out for a tip. Anne gave him her remaining change, a few nickels and dimes.

He looked at it. "No good American coins," he said. She shrugged her shoulders. "Look in your pocket for your tip," she replied, and he understood.

"Pero, Señora," he protested.

"No more," Anne snapped as she lifted one of the suitcases. Vicente's mouth fell open.

"Two bags remain," she added, motioning in their direction with her head. He seized them irately and followed her toward the house. A portly, balding man in a silk maroon dressing gown was waiting at the door. Vicente plopped the luggage before him and stomped away. Anne's host looked at the driver curiously. Peeking over his shoulder was a thin woman with long gray hair winding down her white silk robe.

"I am Roger Gonzáles, and this is my wife María," the man said in English as he pumped Anne's hand. "You are tired. Tomorrow we will talk."

He grasped two of the suitcases plopped at his feet and led Anne into a small room with the typical masonry walls of middle-class homes in Central America. After pointing out the attached private bath, he and María murmured their goodnights. Anne dropped her suitcase and she lowered herself down onto the bed covered in a multicolored Mayan spread. She sat still allowing the room where she would be living for the next six weeks to introduce itself. There was a small woman's dresser minus mirror upon which sat a pitcher with water, a glass, a vase of brilliant yellow and red flowers, and a fat white candle. Her eyes slid to the room's one window curtained in gauzy white that fluttered on a gentle entering breeze. A straight-backed wooden chair stood next to the window awaiting clothes and clutter. There were no wall decorations except for a simple wooden cross.

Siding the bed were two caned-top wooden end tables with wooden lamps perched on them. Anne kicked off her pumps and fell backwards onto the mattress. Within seconds she fell into a heavy sleep until church bells summoning inhabitants to early morning mass nudged her awake. The sun poured through the window, highlighting the bright white walls and shiny rust-colored floor tiles. Stiff from the lumpy mattress, Anne yawned and stretched.

"Ugh," she said to her reflection in the mirrored metal cabinet above the bathroom sink. Splotches of remaining make-up spotted her face and the residue of mascara and eye shadow were smudged over her eyes giving her the appearance of someone who had been punched. She turned on the faucet and scrubbed until she blushed pink. Emerging from the bedroom dressed in light blue slacks and a fresh white blouse, she walked down a short hall into the living room furnished with a small oatmeal sofa, two walnut rockers, and a coffee table with books lazily scattered. The sunlight flowing into the room from a nearby window heightened the bright colors of a Mayan tapestry hanging on the wall. It depicted quetzals, Guatemala's national bird, their vivid plumage spreading outward. A ceramic statue of the Virgin Mary stood reverently in her corner shrine, hands folded, dark eyes looking blankly forward. Nearby a bookcase stacked unevenly with books and magazines hugged the wall.

"*Usted está bien?*" asked her host Roger Gonzáles as he entered the room, still attired in his maroon dressing gown, his thinning hair in disarray.

"*Sí, gracias.* I slept soundly," Anne responded.

A smile graced his plump face. "*Bueno.* I speak English this morning, but only this morning," he said. "May I call you Ana?"

"Of course."

"My wife speaks only Spanish, Ana. We welcome students into our home from all over the world. Next week we expect three more, one from your country and the other two from Germany. We find this interesting."

"I'm sure it is. Are you retired, Señor Gonzáles?"

"Call me Roger," he urged. "I am semi-retired. My sons and I export ornamental flowers. My youngest son, Sergio, manages the business in Antigua working with growers in the countryside. My oldest son Roger runs the Miami office. My wife and I lived in Miami before my heart attack brought us home. Do you have children, Ana?"

"Yes, I have twins, a girl and a boy. They are twenty-one."

"Ah, twins, a double blessing from God." He turned to go. "Excuse me. I must dress for breakfast. María has placed a coffee carafe on the dining table. Help yourself."

Anne ambled into the dining room where, in addition to the long mahogany dining table, were a refrigerator, a microwave, and a cabinet for dishes. Spread across one wall was a large wooden crucifix where Jesus, head lowered, hung in silent suffering. Anne peeked into the kitchen to see María and a small dark Mayan girl preparing breakfast.

"*Buenos días,*" chirped María. Her gray hair was neatly pulled back in a chignon, her brown dress covered with a white apron. She entered the dining room carrying a platter of scrambled eggs and the girl, whom Anne guessed to be about twelve, padded behind carrying a bowl of fruit, her head submissively lowered. The child placed the fruit bowl on the table and scurried into the kitchen returning with a bowl of beans and a pitcher of orange juice. Roger, now dressed casually for the day, entered the room. Anne waited while her hosts mumbled a prayer and then crossed themselves. Roger announced, "*Buen provecho,*" and they began to eat.

"Why do you want to learn Spanish?" he asked as he sipped his coffee. Anne observed the sagging flesh around his full face and guessed he was over sixty.

"I will be teaching English in Nicaragua for a year," Anne explained.

"Nicaragua?" Roger asked, arching his bushy eyebrows as though in disbelief.

"Yes. My cousin Evelyn lives in Nicaragua, and my church contributes to the support of a rural Nicaraguan church." Anne scooped a forkful of eggs and added, "We are Protestants and the Nicaraguan church is our mission church."

"Here we call you *evangélicos*," Roger said amiably. "We welcome many students into our home who come to Guatemala to work as *evangélico* missionaries. Is your cousin a missionary?"

"No. Evelyn's husband was the pastor of the church that my church supports. He was killed during the Contra War," Anne said quietly lowering her head.

"*Triste*," uttered María indicating she understood English in spite of her husband's claims.

"War is terrible," declared Roger. "War is here in Guatemala too. Many innocents are killed."

"Yes, too many innocents," agreed Anne with a weary sigh. "Evelyn also lost her daughter Jasmina to a landmine last year."

"*Dios mío!*" exclaimed María. Her pixy face was all compassion.

"It was a terrible time. The child was three," said Anne almost inaudibly through a surge of emotion she had not expected. She cleared her throat and spoke again.

"Evelyn works in Managua arranging trips for people who come to Nicaragua on educational and humanitarian delegations."

"She is an admirable woman," Roger remarked.

As they chatted Anne felt comfortable and safe in the presence of the friendly couple. Time slipped by until Roger announced, "Ana, in twenty minutes your class begins. The school is a fifteen-minute walk." Observing her hesitation, he added reassuringly, "We saw your torn blouse. You are safe in Antigua."

"The director of the school said as much," Anne conceded with an audible gulp. "I think I overreacted in the airport."

María touched her arm gently. "Safe," she whispered in English.

Anne reluctantly left the table, gathered a notebook and her bag, and paused warily at the front door of the Gonzáles house like a bird poised for flight. Roger had given her directions, and she knew no swarm of beggars

19

would assail her. Still her apprehension lingered. Roger and María watched like concerned parents until she had gingerly edged away from the safety of the threshold onto the cobblestones of Avenida Verde. With a hopeful wave they slowly closed the door and disappeared from Anne's view.

For a moment she stood perfectly still looking toward the lamppost where she had seen the guard last night. No one was there. A warm sun, soft as spring on a Massachusetts morning, splashed over her. She looked upward to the towering cone of one of the volcanoes that dominated Antigua, its purple-blue haze defusing into a pale blue sky. Straightening her back, she walked cautiously down Avenida Verde toward Antigua's main commercial street with its mix of modern and colonial-era buildings, as well as ruins left behind by the city's many earthquakes. Unlike Nicaragua, they did not serve as homes for the homeless, but as prized tourist attractions.

At a small park, Mayan women lined up at a row of public *pilas*, the familiar concrete troughs with corrugated washboards that she had seen in Nicaragua. Peering over the park's crumbling stonewall, Anne saw an expansive oak tree and scrub grass where multicolored textiles were spread to dry. All of the washerwomen glanced at her briefly with uncurious eyes, except one young woman who looked up and smiled. The smile lifted her spirits and she returned it with a broad grin deciding she would visit that park after class.

Quickening her pace, Anne entered Antigua's jeweled center, the Plaza Mayor, dotted with tourist shops, cafes, and restaurants. Other tourist-students were moving in the various directions of their language schools. Soon she spotted the pink building rimmed with brilliant red bougainvillea and signed *Escuela Rosada del Idioma Español*.

Nothing had frightened her during the journey to its door. Confidence regained, she entered.

CHAPTER TWO

After morning class, Anne returned to the park where she had seen the Mayan women washing clothes hoping to mitigate the unpleasant airport encounter with Guatemala's indigenous with one more pleasant. Much to Anne's surprise, the young woman who had smiled at her earlier was still there gathering her now dry clothing from the scrub brush and carefully folding them into a pile for transport. Her roped black hair fell in one long braid down her back. Once again she returned Anne's broad grin with a timid smile. Encouraged, Anne walked toward her when she heard a grunt and felt the brush of something against her arm. Startled, she pivoted to face a shoeless ragged man, his right arm crooked as a gnarled tree branch, his crazed eyes bulging. He began to sing in grunts and groans while stretching forth his left arm, palm up. Repelled by his filth and deformity, Anne backed away. In response to her disgust, he hobbled behind the trunk of the expansive oak tree that had caught her attention earlier that morning. There he grunted to another wretch, and the second beggar supported by a crude cane made from a stick hopped forward on one leg, the other being a sunburned knee-length stump. His contorted mouth twisted upward through a brown-spotted, deeply wrinkled face, and he was silent as he thrust forth his open palm.

Shocked by the intrusion of these repugnant creatures, Anne's mind spiraled to the deformed pretzel boy at the airport and she froze like a disoriented explorer in unfamiliar terrain. Succumbing to an overwhelming desire to flee, she turned on her heels and ran. Minutes later, in the safety of the small bedroom within the Gonzáles home on Avenida Verde, she calmed a racing heart with deep breathing and realized what she had done.

Anne had meticulously prepared for life in impoverished and sometimes dangerous Central America. She had read the tortured histories of Nicaragua and Guatemala. She had spent weeks deciding which clothes and books and food products she could not live without during a year's sojourn in the region. In all of these preparations, she had been in control, but she had lost that control at the airport when she had kicked away one of Guatemala's abandoned children. A day later she had allowed fear and revulsion to steal her composure once again. Her preparation, determination, and intelligence were useless in the face of such fear and revulsion. Sitting on the lumpy bed, she sunk her head into her hands and prayed for God's forgiveness for her callousness toward the hapless, unfortunate creatures from which she had fled. In the year to come, she would certainly witness more of these kinds of tragedies experienced by those under siege in their own lands. Would she be able to bear the intensity of that witness? *Oh, God, how can I cope with so much misery? How can I overcome my fear of it?*

Anne lay stretched on her bed reflecting and remembering her last trip to Nicaragua in 1987. She remembered Evie and Rudy's tiny adobe house in Los Ríos, the mosquito netting flowing around her bed like a thin veil of safety from ravenous insects. She remembered listening to inaudible mutterings and footfalls outside. She remembered the hot humid blanket of fear weighting her body to the bed as she listened to the unfamiliar night sounds. Peeking through a small-screened window into the moonlit blackness, she saw shadows stealthily creeping about. Were they Contras? Were they even human or tricks of the moon casting illumination on the limbs of trees feathering in the wind?

No Contras arrived that night. They came a week before Christmas at dawn leaving behind Rudy's decapitated body alongside three *compañero* defenders of Los Ríos.

In Massachusetts, Anne's church, the Christian Community Church excitedly awaited the arrival of Rev. and Mrs. Rudolfo Gutiérrez and their one-year old daughter Jasmina. Rudy was scheduled to preach on the Sunday before Christmas. Instead, a despondent Evelyn and Jasmina arrived on Christmas Day. With sadness, Anne watched Aunt Jane and Uncle Roy shower their daughter and granddaughter with a desperate kind of love. They pleaded with Evelyn to remain with them pointing out the opportunities for a better life for Jasmina in the United States, but Nicaragua called to Evelyn, and two weeks later mother and daughter went "home."

Even in her sorrow, the joy that sparkled in Evelyn's violet eyes when she spoke of Nicaragua profoundly affected Anne. She longed for that kind of certainty about where she belonged. There were times she burrowed under her blankets reluctant to leave the escape of sleep to face the staleness of another day. By the time Evelyn had left her weeping parents, Anne, newly divorced and finally tenured at Malden Community College, had decided to join her cousin in Managua for a year. Hoping to absorb Evelyn's spirit into herself, Anne began to make tenuous plans.

Jasmina's heart-wrenching death by a landmine two years later forced these plans into fruition. A stricken Evelyn again returned, this time with her friend Pat Butler, a compassionate woman the age of Evelyn's mother. The tragedy seemed beyond bearing, but within days, Evelyn felt the call to Nicaragua. Before departing, she and Pat specified plans for Anne's visit the following year. Anne would request a sabbatical year to teach English at Managua University. Pat, a Christians United Churches missionary and director of financial development at MU, would make the necessary arrangements in Nicaragua.

Anne's mother Lynn warned her against romanticizing life in Nicaragua. With her usual frankness, she declared that Anne did not possess the emotional strength to endure the role of tragic heroine like Evelyn.

"Was Mom right? Am I foolish to be here?" Anne wondered, aware she was floating on a sea of insecurity. The pretzel boy. The deformed beggars. Could she handle this?

The following day, Anne commanded the courage to purchase clothing and shoes to take to the wretched park dwellers along with a grocery bag of food and bottles of water. She timidly held out two shirts and two pairs of pants that the beggar with the crooked arm snatched from her hand and pressed awkwardly to his body like a bundle of rags. The one-legged beggar hobbled behind him. He smiled through rotten teeth while nodding his head up and down making grunting noises. She placed a grocery bag of fruit, cheese, and bread at her feet and backed away. The two beggars bent over the bag and peered in. Immediately the crooked-arm beggar dropped the clothes and snatched two mangos from the bag, handing one to his companion. They stuffed the soft fruit into their mouths like starving dogs diving into garbage, juices oozing down their chins as they chewed. Observing the repulsive, yet poignant sight Anne felt her throat tighten as she realized that in her battle between compassion and fear, compassion had won this time.

Most mornings after classes Anne found beauty in the Parque Central, Antigua's jewel abutting the Plaza Mayor, which was dominated by a magnificent cathedral. Strolling onto cobblestone paths lined with majestic oak, cedar, and rosewood trees, she inhaled sweet fragrances of jasmine and roses shimmering in pure mountain air. Lithesome bodies of Mayan children, the boys dressed in multicolored blouson shirts and the girls in long skirts, baskets of handicrafts perched on their heads, scurried through the park seeking customers. No signs of desperate poverty were visible in the Parque Central as they were in what Anne thought of as the Park of the Wretched where lived the deformed beggars. Anne assumed Antigua's numerous police and paramilitary kept them out, preserving a little paradise for wallet-bearing tourists like herself. As guilty as she felt over the practice, she was also grateful for the unmarred beauty and serenity.

Toward late afternoon, Anne routinely settled onto a bench in the center of the park before the stone women of the Fountain of the Sirens. Their graceful bodies arched upwards, trickling soothing water songs from their lovely lips into the glittering wide pool at their feet. Attentive to the fine lines accompanying her own aging, she admired their unchanging, symmetrically perfect stone faces and their smooth, elegant necks, and she remained in their presence until the soft rainbow light of dusk leisurely lay on the water. When the light faded into monochrome, she knew it was time to return to the Gonzáles home for good conversation over the supper table, followed by homework and a walk.

A week into her arrival, she had fallen into a pleasant doze before the stone sirens, when a husky male voice roused her.

"Esquivel, a revolutionary poet forced into exile," it declared. Fog melted into a vague outline of a man sitting next to her. Willing herself into focus, she saw a wide smile set in a square suntanned face with a slight dimple in the right cheek and a mop of unruly sandy hair, silver streaked at the temples.

"Gregory Garner," he introduced, stretching out a hand that she accepted hoping she wasn't blushing. "It appears I woke you. I'm sorry," he added apologetically. Noticing that her book of Guatemala poet Julia Esquivel was dangling precariously at the edge of her lap, Anne scooped it into her free hand. "I must have dozed while reading *The Old Weaver*," she said.

"A beautiful poem. You are a lover of poetry I presume."

"Yes, I am," she stammered as she slid her hand from his, straightened up from a slouch, and introduced herself. "My name is Anne Scott, uh, I mean, Anne Harrison."

"Pleased to meet you Anne Scott, Anne Harrison," he said mischievously.

She giggled self-consciously. "I'm unaccustomed to using my maiden name. Recently divorced."

He shook his head empathetically. "Yes. Divorce. One of the many complications a change in love presents," he said and paused slightly before speaking again. "Yet, I still welcome love. And poetry is the language of love."

Anne smiled. "I agree." Their bodies were an inch from touching. She sidled away.

"Are you a tourist or a Spanish student?" he asked.

"Student," she said.

"Me too, although I know Spanish. Did a Master's in it. But they make me take a course every five years. In-service training, they call it."

"They?"

"The military. Marines. I'm in Language and Cultural Affairs."

"Oh," said Anne. "What do you do in Language and Cultural Affairs?"

"I try to prevent our military personnel from being seen as ugly Americans by orienting them to the social and cultural life of the country they are assigned to," he explained.

"A worthy task," she said. "Where are you studying?"

"The Escuela José Rodríguez."

"José Rodríguez?" Anne asked. "Yes, of course you would be studying there. That school is known in Antigua for providing Spanish to US military." She paused, and then added. "And to secret intelligence personnel."

"Secret intelligence personnel?" laughed Garner. "You mean spies? You have been reading more than poetry. James Bond, perhaps?"

The tease broke Anne's reserve. Her eyes involuntarily fell to his left hand in search of a wedding band. She knew he noticed her unsubtle gaze and blushed at being caught, but he was kind enough not to comment. They were flirting and she loved it.

"How about a coffee and pastry?" he asked, nodding in the direction of the cafes on the outskirts of the park in the Plaza Mayor. She agreed. They stood up simultaneously and she judged him to be over six feet tall with a physique worth noticing.

Side by side they strolled on the cobblestone path toward the cafes. A frisky dog scampered between them and looped around a cedar tree with abandon.

Garner was dressed neatly in gray pants and a subdued Mayan shirt of geometric blue and black design. His run-away wavy hair seemed too long for a military man. "So why are you studying Spanish?" he asked.

"I will be spending a year in Nicaragua," she responded.

He stopped abruptly and announced enthusiastically, "Nicaragua is my next post."

"The US is sending Marines to Nicaragua?" she asked, not bothering to conceal her surprise.

The question clearly surprised him. "A few advisors," he responded, observing her curiously.

"Damn!"

"That's quite a reaction," he said calmly.

"How many so-called 'advisors' are being sent?" Her voice had taken on the sharp edge of anger.

Garner shrugged his shoulders. "I don't know." He looked bewildered.

"Another American invasion of Nicaragua," she declared.

"A few advisors requested by the new government is not an invasion," he said.

Anne drew in a deep breath. They walked in silence, he waiting for her to speak, hoping her unexplained anger would dissipate.

"My cousin lives in Nicaragua," she said finally in a calmer voice.

A silent sigh of relief passed through Garner. "So, that's why you're going to Nicaragua. It's not exactly a hot tourist spot, at least, not yet, although with the Sandinistas gone, foreign investment and beach hotels will soon arrive. Has your cousin lived there long?"

"For about eleven years," Anne answered flatly.

"During the war," he noted. "Is she a missionary?"

"Why do you want to know?" Anne responded rudely.

Taken aback again, he raised his hands in mock defense. "Just making conversation," he declared, thrusting a hand into his pocket to withdraw a pack of cigarettes. He stopped to light one while she kept on walking. He briefly pondered if he should continue to engage this puzzling woman and decided she was attractive enough to give it a try.

"Most of the people who stayed during the war were missionaries," he explained, jogging a few steps to catch up with her. She turned her head away from the smoke, and he slid the cigarette-bearing hand behind his back. She was one hell of an attractive woman, but what was troubling her? An enjoyable flirtation had become strained.

Catching his perplexed gaze, a slight shudder shook Anne's body. All her senses urged caution. She suspected he was not really military. No Marine would be allowed to brandish such unruly hair. If he were not military, he was probably in intelligence, and even harmless flirting with a CIA agent would betray Evelyn. The CIA had trained the counter revolutionaries, and it was from US supported military bases in Honduras that the Contras had sent men into Nicaragua to plant landmines that murdered innocents like Jasmina. A more intimate knowledge of Gregory Garner, pleasant and appealing as it might be, was impossible. He presented too many unanswered questions.

"I really don't have time for coffee," she said suddenly. "I have to go."

"What did I say?" he asked.

"Nothing," she said as she scooted off.

"Anne," he called after her.

She kept on walking away. *"Adios!"*

"Quickest rejection I've ever had," he muttered aloud. He was certain her behavior represented more than a mere rejection of him. She had become almost hostile once he had revealed his assignment to Nicaragua, and he intended to find out why. He sucked in a long, satisfying drag from his cigarette and continued toward the cafes.

***

Surrounded by rose walls, the courtyard of the Escuela Rosada del Idioma Español served as a communications center and a place of respite, where students gathered around wrought iron tables to study, chat, and drink fresh juice and coffee. Open to the sun, it was studded with small trees, plants, and colorful flowers in large ceramic pots. On one wall hung a bulletin board sprinkled with student messages, ads from local eateries, and notices of evening events in Antigua. On this day, a white letter-sized sheet of paper announced in black bold letters an important meeting regarding security. A busload of Japanese tourists had been robbed a few kilometers from Antigua, and rumors had swept through the school. Everyone knew something was happening "out there" - the sharp reports of arms could be faintly heard in the distance. The attack on tourists, however, had occurred nearby and that was cause for anxiety.

Arturo Coronado had summoned his forty-two students to the courtyard not to address the attack on the Japanese. He was unaware his students knew anything about it. Looking splendid in his impeccable white suit, he focused steely eyes on them, cleared his throat, and began to relate his reasons for calling them together. "Yesterday a German woman was raped and murdered in the picnic area on the hill overlooking Antigua near our beautiful cross," he reported with business-like flatness.

A collective gasp arose like steam from a teapot. Coronado raised his hands for quiet. He disliked frightening his students, concerned they and others would be discouraged from coming to Antigua for language study, but the police had ordered him to issue a warning following the murder. Guatemalan officials did not want foreigners wandering off controlled territory. If too many met with misfortune, the tourist industry would be ruined.

"She was alone," Coronado continued. "You are safe if you do not climb up the hill alone, and do not go there at night or in the early morning." He had a chary look about him, as if he had left something out of his warning.

"What about the bus of Japanese tourists hijacked outside of Antigua?" shouted a young man. Surprised and furious that they knew about the Japanese incident, which the local press had not reported, Coronado clasped his hands behind him and began to rock slightly betraying an outward appearance of calm. Now he had to describe the unfortunate attack and still assure his students that they were safe. A multi-ringed hand shot to his throat, which he cleared again.

"That bus was hijacked many kilometers from Antigua. Antigua is safe," he declared.

"What happened to the passengers?" asked the same student.

"The passengers were robbed." Coronado hesitated before he told them the rest, concluding he had no choice but to be truthful. "Two were killed," he added. A nervous murmur waved through the courtyard.

Coronado raised his hands again for quiet. "Do not be concerned. The bus was hijacked many kilometers away from Antigua. Antigua is safe. You may return to your classes secure in this knowledge."

"Were the hijackers Mayans?" another student asked, much to Coronado's consternation. He answered carefully.

"We have criminals in Guatemala like in all societies. And it is true that some of our Mayans are bandits. But the Mayan vendors in Antigua are harmless creatures. You must buy their colorful textiles to share with your friends. And take many photos. They love to have their photos taken, especially the children." Oblivious to his patronizing tone, Coronado knew that the craft-producing Maya were intrinsic to Antigua's charm as a tourist destination, and his students must not see them as a people to be feared. As for the insurgent and criminal *indios*, Guatemala's best hope lay in forcing them back into their holes in the hills. During the 1980s officials had tried and failed to eliminate the problem. Now they were paying the price for that failure.

With a glacial smile, Coronado bid a stiff farewell to his students, leaving them to talk anxiously among themselves. Following the disturbing news, Anne skipped class to sit before the stone women in the park where her anxiety melted away. She continued to read the exquisite poetry of Julia Esquivel, which celebrated the suffering indigenous people of Guatemala. She read until the shadows of evening fell on the pages.

***

"Go into the street!" Roger Gonzáles shouted, pounding on the bedroom door. Anne shot awake to a shaking house and the ominous swishing of water in the flower vase on the bureau. Throwing on a robe, she dashed through the living room, dodging tumbling books, and stumbled outside behind Roger and María into an unknowable blackness. Around them swirled the turbulence of people - some shouting; others crying. Suddenly Roger bent forward, and Anne, knowing he had heart disease, desperately tried to catch him, but he slid past her and knelt placing both palms on the ground. Moments later, he looked up and announced, "It is over."

Hearty moans and sighs of relief waved through the crowd of huddled neighbors. The relief prompted high spirits, and they called out friendly greetings to each other as they reentered their houses.

"We haven't had a real earthquake since 1976," Roger assured Anne. María brought out a rum bottle and Roger splashed the liquid into small glasses with a shaky hand. They drank and spoke quietly until their emotions had calmed enough for sleep.

In her bedroom Anne gingerly turned on the light and mopped up the water from the flower vase, now lying on its side. The bureau's candle was on the floor, and the wall cross hung crookedly. Anne sank onto the bed, but despite the rum, the trauma of those few uncertain moments sat like a heavy iron ball in her stomach. Her breathing was shallow as she thought of the impact of her death upon her twins, Lynn and Danny. At 21, they acted as though they no longer needed or wanted her consistent presence in their lives. That is why she was so surprised by their negative reactions when she announced her intention to join Evelyn in Nicaragua.

Would high-strung Lynn crumble emotionally? Would Danny retreat into the cool distance of denial modeled by his father and grandfather? Were her children angry with her for going to Central America because they feared she would be killed? Anne had never considered this, except on a superficial level, giving limp assurances that she would be safe. She had instead assumed their hostility reflected unresolved anger over her decision to leave their father and their resentment of her admiration for Evelyn. But maybe they were really afraid she would be killed. She wondered if she should have given them more time to become adjusted to the divorce before she left for Nicaragua. She had assumed that as young adults, they were involved in their own lives, disinterested in the lives of their parents, and Keith could handle their numerous requests for money and their miniscule hints for guidance. But maybe she had been wrong.

Near the end of Anne's second week in Guatemala, Roger led a young couple and another young man into the living room to become acquainted with each other and with Anne. Petra, a statuesque German woman with luminous skin, planted a kiss on both of Anne's cheeks, while the man, Holger, a monk-like crown of dark brown hair perched atop a round face like a wig, looked on smiling. They were dressed in T-shirts and jeans, the universal uniform of backpackers, but Holger looked awkward in the informal clothes, like a priest without robes. The third newcomer, a lanky American with a high freckled forehead edged by thinning light brown hair, in spite of his youth, shook Anne's hand enthusiastically. "Tim Haverford from Texas," he introduced.

"Señor Gonzáles say you live near Boston," Holger said to Anne in thickly accented English. "We want to go to Boston, but we visit Negarahfulls instead."

"Negarahfulls?" repeated Anne.

"In New York, where water falls from the mountain."

"I think he means Niagara Falls," drawled Tim leaving no doubt about his home state. He grinned broadly from his boyish face, circling a cowboy hat in his hands.

"We board the bus in New York City to go across the United States and down to Mexico. We speak Spanish but not good so we come to Antigua to study for two weeks. Then we will see more of Guatemala," Holger continued.

The couple held hands, gracing each other with loving glances, and Anne envied their affection. It had been over twenty years since she had felt the euphoria of new love and, at times, she ached for it. A thought of Gregory

Garner flittered through her mind like a butterfly, displaying its beauty for only a second, yet long enough to capture one's attention.

Petra's pale blue eyes fell on Tim's wide-brimmed hat. She had never met a cowboy, but she had seen a few from the glass windows of a Greyhound bus.

"Are you cowboy?" she asked him.

Tim chuckled. "Real cowboys don't own expensive hats like this," he confessed. "I'm a missionary. My church is sending me to Nicaragua."

"You are priest!" Petra concluded, astonished by the idea.

"Not a priest. I'm an evangelical missionary," he explained. Tilting his head toward Anne, he added, "Señor Gonzáles told me she's a missionary too. Missionaries bring the Word of Christ to the people." He gave Anne a knowing smile and then returning his attention to Petra he asked, "Have you received Christ in your heart?"

The young woman's hand migrated to her mouth where she nibbled absently on the nail of her forefinger while looking questioningly at Tim.

"Tim, did you know that per capita there are more Christians in Nicaragua than in America?" Anne asked moving Tim's attention from Petra toward her.

"But as you must know, ma'am, they don't follow Jesus," he replied.

"They don't?" Anne asked sharply, her voice implying a challenge. Tim furrowed his forehead.

"You must know, ma'am, that they live together without getting married. They drink rum. And too many believe in communism. The Saving Waters Christian Church in Dallas sponsors the Young Adults in Christ. We YACS will build a church in Managua. The communists no longer run the country, but their poison remains in the hearts of too many Nicaraguans. God has called us to bring Christ to the Nicaraguan people." Finished, he smiled proudly.

Anne glared at him. Observing her hostile reaction Tim said in a less confident voice, "Señor Gonzáles said you are going to Nicaragua as a missionary too, ma'am."

"I'm going to Nicaragua to teach English at a university," Anne responded coolly.

"But Señor Gonzáles said you have a church in Nicaragua," Tim insisted.

"My church in Massachusetts has adopted a poor rural church as a mission focus, and I'm bringing a donation from my church to rebuild their chapel. I am not a missionary."

Tim's face brightened. "So you will build a church? Praise God!" he exclaimed as he slapped his thigh with the cowboy hat.

"Not the kind of church you have in mind," said Anne ungraciously.

Before Tim could respond, Holger interrupted. His dark eyes under straight brows communicated that he comprehended the tension between Anne and Tim. "It is good to help poor people," he said. "In Germany, we help Turkish immigrants who have few clothes or good places to live. The world is cruel to the poor." Anne wondered if Holger had Turkish blood and was speaking about the experiences of his own family.

Their conversation came to an abrupt halt as Roger and María entered to show the new students to their rooms.

Over the next two weeks, Anne abandoned her afternoon sojourns in the Parque Central to join Holger and Petra in enjoying the sites of Antigua. At the Mayan markets set up on Antigua's streets during the weekends, Indian children targeted them, chirping stilted English "Hellos," followed by, "Sell cheap." Vendors spread merchandise on colorful blankets, and tourists and student tourists flitted from weavers to belt-crafters to woodworkers to jewelry-makers. Anne, Petra, and Holger snapped photos, passing out quetzales for the privilege. When they tired of the markets, they explored Antigua's colonial heritage, venturing into cathedrals and ruins of churches, monasteries, schools, and mansions, always finishing their expeditions at a dessert café on the Plaza Mayor where Anne's eyes subtly searched for Gregory Garner.

On the morning of their departure, the three temporary friends promised to write, but Anne realized their friendship built on a shared sojourn in a foreign country would soon fade. When they left, backpacks jostling with each youthful step, Roger said in a worried voice, "I tell them, do not travel alone. There is danger in Guatemala."

Later during dinner he elaborated on his concern declaring, "The countryside is not safe. Bandits and rebels are everywhere."

"I will pray for them," offered Tim waving a fork in Roger's direction.

"And we will say Rosary tonight," María added softly.

"God will protect them," said Tim with certainty.

Roger nodded and the conversation ceased until he restarted it moments later with a question designed to dispel the somber mood. "How are your classes?"

Anne started to reply but Tim spoke over her. "Spanish is easy," he said. "I grew up hearing it spoken all around me. Mexicans are everywhere in Texas. My teacher Eduardo and I spend time together after class speaking Spanish."

"Yes, that is helpful," noted Roger.

"I bought Eduardo's wife Teresa a two-burner stove and a propane tank," Tim announced proudly. "Teresa was cooking in a communal kitchen on a wood-fire grate behind the building where they live. Now she has a cubby kitchen in the basement and keeps the stove and tank under lock and key."

"It is generous of you," Roger declared.

"It is my obligation as a Christian to care for the needy," Tim stated enthusiastically. "Eduardo and his wife are good Christians. Eduardo takes me to church with him at night. Their praise songs are filled with the Holy Spirit."

"*Claro*," said Roger with feigned interest. Tim reached for another serving of refried beans. His appetite was enormous. María's eyes were always on the disappearing food when Tim was present at meals.

"Eduardo's family lives in a building on the corner of Avenida Cerro," Tim continued. "They live in one room. A bad place."

"They live in a good place for Mayans," corrected Roger.

"Eduardo told me he is Ladino. Is he Mayan?" asked Tim.

"His father is Ladino, but not his mother. He grew up in the Mayan barrio at the edge of Antigua. Officially he is Ladino, but everyone knows his Mayan roots. His father sent Eduardo to school and found him the apartment. So you see, Timoteo, Eduardo is fortunate to live on Avenida Cerro."

Anne heard defensiveness in Roger's words.

"I do not think he is fortunate," remarked Tim. "The family lives in one small room."

"They have electricity and an indoor bathroom," María said quietly.

"The owner of the building is a friend of ours and he makes a good place for the Maya," Roger added, but Tim would not be dissuaded.

"There are roaches everywhere, and the building stinks," he said.

Roger stared at Tim. "Mayans do not value our standards of cleanliness," he said coldly.

"Have you been there?" asked Tim.

"No," responded Roger tersely.

"Would you like to visit? I am going over later," Tim pursued.

"No," responded Roger in a firm and elevated voice.

Tim finally understood he had upset Roger, although he did not know why. To Anne's surprise, he turned toward her and asked in English, "Would you like to visit Eduardo and his family?

CHAPTER THREE

Life was slowly pouring out of Juancito. Unless Eduardo Cayoa could find money to take his two-year old son to the doctor that treated the Maya, he and Teresa would lose him. But where to find the money? Eduardo's father, the usual source, had moved to Costa Rica and broken off contact. Eduardo's friends were as poor as was he. The American Tim recently bought them a stove and a propane tank that he could sell, but by the time he found a buyer, Juancito might be gone. Would Timoteo be generous again so soon? Eduardo's rheumy eyes gravitated to his wife Teresa sleeping fretfully on the double bed, the ghostly Juancito in her arms.

"*Papá. Tengo miedo.* I am scared," said Eduardcito, tugging at his father's shirt. Eduardo gathered the six-year-old into his arms.

"*No te preocupes.* Juancito will get better," he comforted the boy hearing the desperation in his own voice as he remembered the quick, wrenching death of his first son Felix after a fever. Eduardcito whimpered, burrowed into his father's body, and drifted into a sleep punctured by muttering and shivers. Eduardo stroked the fine black hair of the boy lamenting that in spite of all he had accomplished, he could not protect his children from the cruel vicissitudes of life. With the small soft body nestled against him, Eduardo fell into a shallow doze until an urgent knocking woke him. Placing his sleeping son on the twin bed, he opened the door to face Timoteo and an American woman, whom he immediately recognized.

"*Buenas noches, mi amigo,*" greeted Tim as he took a proprietary step into the room. "I have brought someone to meet you."

The tall slender woman hesitated on the threshold. Eduardo knew her as one of the new students favorably noticed by the male teachers at the school. "You are welcome to my home," he invited, his mind grasping the possibility of money for the medical clinic.

Anne knew him immediately and felt a twinge of shame for thinking he was the school janitor because of his Mayan features. A stale dark scent filled her nostrils as she stepped onto the pitted linoleum floor of the cave-like shabby room.

A scratched wooden table with two chairs occupied its middle, and a bureau with a small black television set stood in the corner. Her eyes fell on a twin bed hugging one wall on which slept a little boy; a double bed against another wall held a disheveled looking woman cradling another child. The woman opened her eyes and stared groggily from a dark broad face drenched in weariness.

"My wife Teresa," said Eduardo. The woman, her deep-set black eyes rimmed red, gently laid the child on the bed and rose to greet them. Eduardo offered the visitors the two table chairs while he and Teresa sat on the edge of the double bed next to the sleeping child.

"Tim tells me you are an excellent teacher," Anne said to Eduardo.

Eduardo accepted the complement proud of how far he had traveled from the Mayan barrio to being acknowledged by a woman from America. He was fortunate to work at the Escuela Rosada del Idioma Español, and he knew he had his father to thank.

"I am a language teacher too," explained Anne and began to speak to Eduardo like a colleague. They conversed for a few minutes, and Eduardo concluded that she would be approachable for money for the doctor. As he pondered how to present the request, Tim interrupted his thoughts.

"Eduardo, I wanted Anne to meet you and your family because you are good Christians," he declared.

Eduardo smiled modestly.

"Anne will build an evangelical church in Nicaragua, praise the Lord," Tim continued.

Anne started to object to this stretching of the truth, but Tim slapped his hands together and spoke over her. "You see, Eduardo, God leads Americans to do good works."

"*Sí. Americanos* are good to us," agreed Eduardo.

"Americans who follow God's Word are good," corrected Tim as he tossed a side glance at Anne wordlessly informing her that she had a way to go before she would be considered a good Christian in his eyes. "Come, let us form a prayer circle and praise God for the blessings He bestows upon us," he declared and stood up.

Observing Eduardo's bloodshot eyes and Teresa's dull stare, Anne said, "The children are sleeping. Perhaps, this is not a good time, Tim."

"There is never a bad time for prayer, Anne," Tim responded eyeing her reproachfully.

"*Sí*. We pray," agreed Eduardo forcing enthusiasm.

"I think Eduardo and Teresa are very tired, Tim," Anne persisted.

"No one is ever too tired to pray," Tim insisted. He snatched her hand and stood upright pulling her with him. "We will form a prayer circle," he announced. Eduardo and Teresa sluggishly joined the circle as Tim began to pray in a mixture of Spanish and English.

"*Gracias, Jesús!*" he exhorted. "*Gracias, Jesús!* I will praise, praise, the Lord for His goodness and mercy. Praise the Lord! *Alabaré, alabaré, el Señor por su bondad y misericordia. Alabaré el Señor!*" His thunderous baritone reverberated in the room, echoing off the walls. Anne poked him in the side and pointed toward the children.

"They're sleeping," she whispered sharply, but he continued the booming exhortations. Eduardo mouthed praises along with Tim while Teresa and Anne nervously watched the children. Tim praised God for home and family and friends and country and food and work and government leaders, the crescendo rising with each praise.

Eduardcito was the first to awaken, a whimper escaping his contorted face. Teresa broke from the circle to wrap her arms around him. Then baby Jauncito awoke and began to howl, capturing Tim's attention. The praising ceased as Eduardo rushed to Teresa and swept Eduardcito into his arms freeing his wife to cradle the howling toddler. The child's bright red face and raspy crying alarmed Anne who gently ran her fingers over a hot and clammy forehead. "This child is burning with fever!" she exclaimed.

Teresa patted and cooed to her child through a cascade of tears. Anne laid a hand on her arm and said, "We must take him to the hospital, Señora." But Teresa shook her head.

"He will die there," protested Eduardo.

"We will go with you," offered Anne. "We will pay."

"No, never!" Eduardo cried, surprising both Anne and Tim with his objection. "A clinic on Avenida Sur is where they look after Mayans. It is a Christian clinic."

"Fine. Then we will go now," Anne, insisted, her voice urgent. She withdrew a fistful of quetzales from her purse and held them out to Eduardo. The big black eyes of the little boy in his arms widened at the sight of so much money.

"They are not open today. Tomorrow morning we will go," declared Eduardo quickly snatching the bills from her hand.

Anne raised a hand to her forehead in frustration. "Señor Cayoa, your child is very sick. He needs help now," she said urgently.

"No. No," repeated Eduardo.

Anne looked pleadingly at Teresa's anguished face. The young mother choked, "Only the Mayan Clinic is good for us."

Anne understood. Even though she had lived in Guatemala for less than a month, she had seen the blatant discrimination against its indigenous population. In medical clinics that treated Ladinos, this little Indian child might receive poor care. Snatching her purse and pulling out a small bottle of pills, she said, "Acetaminophen. I will cut off a corner of a pill and give it to Juancito to bring the fever down until tomorrow when you go to the clinic." She gave Teresa three pills emphasizing the small portions. Acknowledging Tim's superior Spanish, she asked him to repeat the instructions.

"Gracias, Hermana," Teresa sniffled. With a spoon, Anne crushed the acetaminophen into a fine powder, diluted it with water, and gave it to Teresa to maneuver into Jauncito's mouth. When the medication took effect, Juancito's howls dissolved into whimpers and he fell asleep.

"Is he okay?" asked Tim, grateful Anne had taken charge.

"I don't know," Anne answered honestly in English not wanting Teresa to hear her doubt. "There's nothing more we can do."

"Then we'll go, but first, I want to show you the new stove," said Tim. Overwhelmed by emotion, Anne had no interest in seeing a stove. Instead, she felt the child's forehead again.

"Dios le bendiga, Hermana, God bless you, Sister. I lose Felix. I no lose Juancito," Teresa cried fervently.

"He will get better," Anne said, silently praying it would be so. She grasped Teresa's hand feeling the ineffable connection that exists between mothers – a willingness to die for their children. You have children, *verdad?"* Teresa whispered hoarsely.

"I have two children, a boy and a girl," said Anne.

"Dios le bendiga. Juancito will be well again. You have blessed him."

Reluctantly Anne released Teresa's hand and hunched over to hug the tiny woman, noticing the slight swelling in her belly. Another baby was on the way. *Dear God! What a dreary future awaits this family,* she thought dispiritedly. Education guaranteed Eduardo work, but it was no guarantee of upward mobility. Anne hoped they would be one of the few who worked their way out of poverty into a house with bedrooms on a street like Avenida Verde, but she knew it was unlikely given Eduardo's ties to the Mayan community.

Reluctantly Anne followed Tim and Eduardo down a flight of stairs onto the ground floor where they passed the malodorous communal toilet and made their way to a cubby safely secured with two padlocks. A shelf on one wall held four plastic dishes and two pots. On a rough table rested the prized two-burner stove connected to a propane tank on the concrete floor. Anne knew Tim was pinching pennies, yet he had purchased the tank and a stove for Teresa to lessen the burden of her day. The complexity of people drove her crazy. After a few polite words about the new kitchen, Anne and Tim emerged from the dank building. Although the only light available to them was the moon and a dim street lamp, Anne felt she had left the darkness to walk in the sunlight.

"They are so poor," she lamented.

"In the Lord, no one is poor," Tim declared.

"The poor are all around us, Tim."

"In material things they are poor, Anne, but with the love of Jesus, Eduardo and Teresa have found Salvation. God brought you and me into their lives when they needed a stove and money for a doctor. You see, God provides."

"But the little boy may die. These people live on the edge because they are not valued by those in charge of this country," Anne countered.

Tim sighed in frustration. Obviously, Anne had not been born again and, therefore, did not know Salvation. If she had any faith at all, it was weak. Perhaps God had sent him to help her see the light. "Anne, the poor will always be with us. It says so in the Bible."

"So what is that supposed to mean?" Anne snapped.

The angry words annoyed Tim, but she was around his mother's age and he knew he must approach her with as much care and respect as he would his mother.

"You see, Anne, when a Christian is born again and has Christ in his life, anything that happens to him, even death, is God's will." He spoke with deliberate patience, as though to a child. His patronizing tone increased Anne's anger and she challenged him.

"Are you saying that if poor little Jauncito dies, his death is God's will? Teresa's desperation is God's will? Eduardo's inability to earn enough money to afford a doctor because he is Mayan is God's will? If that is what you are saying, Tim, your version of Christianity does not agree with my understanding of a loving God." Realizing she was losing control and that objective discussion would be useless, she lifted her hands and let them fall. The physical movement diffused her anger. "This is too controversial a subject for us to discuss. I admire what you have done for Eduardo and his family and thank you for taking me to meet them."

Tim fell silent. Nothing more was mentioned about the Cayoa family that night.

Juancito did not die. The infection that had caused his fever was treated with antibiotics at the medical clinic that served the Maya.

"Hallelujah! I told you God provides," proclaimed Tim triumphantly. Rather than provoke another controversy, Anne simply smiled and muttered: *Gracias a Dios.* They spoke no more of church or Christianity, both sensing the futility of such a conversation and at the end of her fifth week in Antigua, Tim departed for Nicaragua. Relieved of her efforts at self-censoring in his presence, Anne enjoyed the time alone with Roger and María. She appreciated their warm caring personalities, but it bothered her that the material comfort of their lives contrasted sharply with the daily struggles of the Cayoa family. Both Roger and Eduardo were intelligent men of integrity and María and Teresa were loving mothers, yet their lives were lived in stratified inequality and Roger and María seemed to regard the Mayan people as their inferiors.

Anne realized she was the American equivalent of Roger and María, while her cousin Evelyn had chosen to live poor with her husband and her child. Only, unlike the Cayoa family, Evelyn had chosen that life. Anne recalled nights holding a feverish Lynn or Danny assured that the prescribed medicine of the pediatrician would soon take effect, and if it didn't, the pediatrician was only a phone call away. Eduardo and Teresa had no such assurances for their children, and neither had Evelyn for Jasmina when the family was in Los Ríos with Rudy. Anne remembered how she had glibly admonished her children when they had cried, "It's not fair!" But they were right. Life is not fair. Still Anne knew she could never live like Evelyn, and she could not judge the Gonzáles family because of their advantages and prejudices, the same advantages and prejudices she reluctantly acknowledged were intrinsic to the society in which she was raised.

A few days after Tim's departure for Nicaragua, she was awakened in the middle of the night by what sounded like bursts of gunfire. She swung out of bed and padded to the living room to peer out of its broad windows. To her surprise she found Roger there, slouched forward in the sofa, his hands cupping his face, his elbows resting on his knees.

"What is happening?" she asked.

"*Es el sonido de la guerra*," Roger replied solemnly. "The sound of war." He looked up, his mouth turned down at the corners and Anne noticed the ridge on the bridge of his nose where his glasses had trenched. Without them, his dark eyes were almost glassy like purple marbles.

"Are they close?" she asked.

"No."

"Then why can we hear them so clearly tonight?"

"The wind carries sound."

"You are worried."

Roger Gonzáles studied the American woman, a nice lady, a knowledgeable one judging from her comments about Guatemala, more knowledgeable about politics in his country than most of his student guests. Still, she had little understanding of what was really happening, not only to the Maya, but also in the lives of Ladinos like himself.

"*Sí, estoy preocupado*," he sighed. "This terrorism is a monster."

"Are you speaking of your government or the rebels?" she asked. His face suddenly pained as though she had struck him.

"Forgive me, Ana, but I speak of your government before I speak of mine," he said defensively. "Your CIA helped Guatemala's large landowners overthrow our democratically elected President Arbenz in 1954 because one of your fruit companies felt threatened by his land reform program. He had a vision of sharing the land, uplifting the poor, making our class divisions less. Your government authorized the CIA to agree to a *coup d'état* and replace Arbenz with a military junta that spilled blood across our country. You know nothing of how that coup so long ago still affects our lives. Our hearts have been broken ever since."

Anne regretted her comment.

"The war started after Arbenz was deposed," Roger continued. "We have lost over 100,000 people. Once we had hope. Now, we despair that it will never end. The German couple is foolish to travel in the countryside. I worry for their safety, especially for Petra. She is a lovely, young woman." He gulped a quick breath and stood up to retie the belt of the silk maroon dressing gown around his rotund belly.

Moving toward the window, Roger looked out as he said, "We have a legend – the legend of *la siguanaba*. It tells of a beautiful woman with lovely long hair who lives near the fountains and rivers. A seductress, she captivates men with her beauty, but then her features change into those of a horse and she carries men away and they are never seen again. My country is like *la siguanaba* —beautiful, captivating. The rolling green hills of the Central Highlands and the clear blue of Lake Atlitan are like no other place in the world. But Guatemala is not as it appears on the surface. In one instant you can be killed or carried off by bandits, soldiers, rebels. Language schools like yours, Ana, will not take their students outside Antigua except during the daylight, and even then, it can be dangerous. I would never leave this country of my birth, but I am glad that two of my children are living in America. Money goes further here, but what use are comforts when you must live with fear?"

In a rush of tenderness, Anne gently touched his shoulder. During the six weeks she had lived in his house, they had not spoken of the war, the government, or the insidious social strata in Guatemala. When she raised these subjects, neither he nor María responded and she sensed their unease and did not press. Now Roger cupped his hand over hers and they briefly broke through their cultural and political barriers to cross into the land of shared humanity, with all its vulnerabilities. After a few moments he pulled away and said softly, "It is late," and left the room.

Anne continued to gaze out the window, anxiously listening to the staccato gunfire. They were partly responsible for this violence – she and Roger. The war may have been precipitated by the CIA and Guatemala's elites, but the basic struggle between the haves and have-nots had been going on since the Spanish Conquest. Roger knows what an unfair system he lives in and he knows he has acquiesced by his silence. He knows about the horrendous massacres in rural Mayan villages and is aware of the ongoing violence and discrimination against Mayans in his country. He fears what could happen to him and his family if he speaks out. He knows what he can live with and cannot live without. And what about her, the beneficiary of a rich country? What can she live with and cannot live without? She, like so many others, had written to politicians to stop funding the Contras in Nicaragua and after a while, they had done so, but her heart had not been broken like Evelyn's or Roger's; she had been spared such sorrow and she felt a sliver of guilt to have been so lucky.

A week later, Anne bid farewell to the *familia* Gonzáles and reluctantly climbed into the white van of the language school for the ride to the airport, placing her safety once again into the hands of its smirking driver, Vicente. As he approached the airport, Vicente glanced in the rear view mirror at the woman in the back seat whose hands were clenched so tightly the knuckles were white.

When they arrived at the terminal building, Anne waited in the van until Vicente had removed her luggage and secured two porters to carry it. Then she tipped him – generously this time - and bounded toward the terminal door, porters loping behind her. Vicente laughed aloud.

CHAPTER FOUR

Managua, Nicaragua – February 1991

Newly arrived passengers struggled their suitcases through customs jostling and overlapping in a chaotic ragtag line. Porters and carts at the Augusto C. Sandino International Airport were nowhere to be found. People elbowed Anne to push her aside, and one man came close to walking off with one of her suitcases before she smacked him with her carry-on bag. After an hour in stifling humid heat ripe with the sour odor of sweaty bodies, Anne finally shoved her way to an inspection counter and struggled to lift her bags onto it. A harried customs agent carelessly riffled through clothing, books, and papers. He shoved them back and zipped the suitcases, leaving slivers of paper and swatches of clothing snagged in the zipper. He tossed the bags onto the floor in a heap and Anne kicked the luggage through the terminal door. Perspiration-soaked, rumpled and exhausted, she gasped like a beached fish, sweeping the back of her hand across her forehead and showering salty sweat into the air. *Now what do I do?* she thought.

A broad-shouldered Nicaraguan in a yellow guayabera shirt approached with a purposeful stride. He nodded in her direction before he snatched her two largest suitcases. In a surge of angry adrenaline, she lunged at him. The man jumped back declaring in a voice ringing with indignation, *"Profesora, yo te ayudaré.* I help you."

Anne peered into iron black eyes above a crooked nose in a rough brown face topped by a crown of coal black wavy hair, the face of Dr. Ramon Morales, Rector of Managua University, her soon-to-be boss. Mortified, she fell back stammering in English, "I didn't recognize you."

His brows furrowed and his querulous eyes telegraphed he did not understand her words. He nodded his head for her to follow and strode off carrying the two suitcases with the brisk dignity of one accustomed to being in charge. An embarrassed Anne followed meekly, clutching the remaining suitcase and carry-on. For a second Evelyn appeared in Anne's line of vision, a flash of white, red, and black that was quickly swallowed by a crowd of travelers and their greeters. Anne quickened her stride until she caught up with Dr. Morales. Passing him, she pushed on toward where she had seen the fleeting glimpse of Evelyn. When her cousin reappeared in the crowd Anne landed her suitcase with a thud on the tiled floor and flew at Evelyn encircling the smaller woman with her long arms. They clung together speaking in the breathy half-phrases of reunion while Dr. Morales watched smiling at the giant *Americana* hovering over the tiny woman he knew as Evita Gutiérrez.

When they parted Anne dabbed at her eyes with a tissue before sputtering another apology to Morales, this time in Spanish.

"No es importante, Profesora Harrison. Bienvenido a Nicaragua," he said, offering a crushingly firm handshake. "In two days, we will have a luncheon to introduce you to Managua University," he explained in slow, carefully articulated Spanish.

Morales had waited an hour for Anne's overdue flight from Guatemala thinking of the pile of paperwork on his desk demanding attention, but protocol and respect for Evita commanded his presence at the airport to greet her. Pat Butler had assured him of Anne's pedagogical competence, but even if she proved to be a disappointing teacher, she spoke English as a first language. The Cuban, Dino Fuentes, MU's only English teacher, was a native Spanish speaker, and Pat often claimed Dino to tour English-speaking visitors and potential donors around campus. Both Pat and Morales were so satisfied with Dino's performance that Morales wanted the young man to spend more time soliciting funds and less time teaching English. MU was in deficit and the new administration of President Violeta Chamorro had already declared that they would not willingly provide universities with the six percent of the annual budget written into the 1986 Nicaraguan Constitution. He needed Dino to raise money.

Morales carried Anne's two heaviest suitcases toward the parking lot in a military stride, propelling the two women into a light jog as they followed. Despite their rapid pace, ragamuffin children swarmed around them, pleading for córdobas, and Anne handed out the Nicaraguan currency she still had leftover from her last trip in 1987, the year Jasmina was born.

"We do not respond to begging. It teaches dependency," Morales said brusquely, looking back at her. Anne glanced furtively toward him and continued the distribution until the money was gone, hoping he would not be upset with her. He made no further comment.

Heaving the suitcases onto the truck bed of Evelyn's new silver pick-up, Morales said, "We look forward to your help, Profesora Harrison. You will find our students grateful. *Hasta pronto.*" He shook her hand again and hopped into a bright red sedan. Anne and Evelyn watched the car disappear from view.

"He doesn't like me. I made a mess of our first meeting," Anne sighed.

Evelyn laughed. "I'm sure he thought you feisty, and he likes fighters. He grew up poor and had to fight to get where he is. He's quite brilliant and will work you hard with no excuses for anything."

"What have I gotten myself into?" Anne asked rhetorically, yet cheerfully.

Evelyn smiled, her violet eyes twinkling. Silky black hair cascaded down her back as though each strand knew its place. The orderly strands delicately feathered over a cotton white dress, trimmed in red, reminding Anne of the elegant Spanish dancer on the wall of Arturo Coronado's office.

"You've gotten yourself into a wonderful year. Welcome to my adopted country, my cousin. I have a surprise. Actually, I have two surprises," Evelyn declared happily.

The women climbed into the truck and Anne declared her agreement with Evelyn's choice of vehicle. "It's much more practical," she said, stopping herself before uttering *than the Jeep.* She could not say aloud the name of the vehicle in which Jasmina had died. Whenever she heard the word *Jeep* her body tensed. If Evelyn understood her reluctance in uttering the word, she gave no indication of it.

"Doug found it for me," she said. "He who holds great affection for Jeeps thought a pick-up would be, as you said Anne, more practical."

Anne smiled thinly as she thought of Padre Douglas Michaels, the imposing priest who had assumed a fatherly role in Evelyn's life.

They rode through a grim Managua of crowded streets, manholes without covers, and cavernous potholes, passing oxen and cattle feeding at median strips before wandering off among the vehicles. Horses pulling carts of firewood trotted past cars minus doors or windows or both rattling as though held together by wire and duct tape. Rusty buses heaved forward, people hanging off their sides like mountain climbers clinging to a precipice. A few late model vehicles were sprinkled in the mix, but the majority were barely drivable. Venders wearing merchandise on their bodies – sunglasses, calculators, Nicaragua stenciled T-shirts - darted through traffic hawking their wares as did people selling oranges, water in plastic bags, and live squawking chickens. Forlorn beggars in wheelchairs and zombie-like old men and women stretched out their hands pleading, *córdobas, por favor*, whenever traffic slowed or stopped. Unconcerned about dependency, Evelyn carried a change purse in the ashtray to plop coins into the outstretched hands.

Squalid and semi-squalid wooden and cinder block buildings - businesses and residences - lined the road. Earthquake-gutted structures used as homes displayed the family laundry hung over the damaged building's jagged edges to dry. Patches of land on corners or between buildings sprouted makeshift dwellings of plastic, surrounded by open sewers and semi-naked children. Ragged waifs swarmed around cars trapped at traffic lights to perform their "service" of wiping a dirty windshield with an equally dirty rag for *una córdoba.*

Anne rolled down the window of the air-conditioned truck to inhale the humid scents of earth and animals intermingled with sharp carbonic odors of vehicular exhaust. The smell sent a wave of nostalgia through her, resurrecting memories from four years ago when she and Evelyn, Rudy, and baby Jasmina had chugged through the same chaotic streets in Evelyn's Jeep. Anne shivered even though she was sweating.

"Managua is heartbreaking," she said, rolling up the window.

"Yes," Evelyn sighed. "The poor were the focus of the Revolution, but there wasn't time to change things before money was diverted to fight the Contras."

The women sped up the highway. In the distance loomed the majestic Momotombo volcano, its peak touching gauzy clouds in a brilliant blue sky. Soon they passed through Las Palmas, a community of upscale homes cocooned behind concrete block walls and metal gates. President Violeta Chamorro was the community's most famous resident, her house located near a park of root-protruding chilamate trees. At a rotunda they circled away from the most populated areas of the city.

"Where are we going?" asked Anne, noting that they had passed the Barrio Bella Sol where Evelyn lived.

Evelyn smiled. "That is my first surprise. I've rented the Bella Sol house for the year and found a house in San Linda in the Managua Sierra where it's cooler." She reached over and gave Anne a pat on the leg. "I remember how you suffered in the heat and humidity of the city during your last visit."

Anne offered God a silent prayer of gratitude. "Thank you, Evie," she sighed.

San Linda was twenty minutes from Siete Sur, an intersection at the western edge of the city with a collection of small shops and a bus station with routes snaking outward to all parts of Managua like the tentacles of an octopus. From Siete Sur they climbed into the rolling hills. The wide skies and deep ravines splendid with thick green foliage beginning to fade into dry season brown reminded Anne of the beautiful Central Highlands of Guatemala. Twenty minutes later, they arrived at the iron arched entrance to Lower San Linda. They entered the community slowly, passing the Santa María Roman Catholic Church, the truck jostling over an unpaved road past wooden shanties and simple cinder block houses intermingled among malinche trees ablaze in fiery orange. Like soldiers awaiting inspection abundant proud oaks lined up along the dusty road.

"Lower San Linda is predominately Sandinista. Its inhabitants are working class, mostly poor," declared Evelyn. "I found the house through a colleague of its owner, Francisco Sánchez, who worked in the Sandinista government. A small forest separates us from Upper San Linda where the diplomats, professionals, and businessmen live."

She stopped the truck in front of a four-foot high stone wall. A gaunt, shirtless man scurried to swing open a metal gate.

"*Hola, Renaldo*," Evelyn greeted as she drove through and stopped. A pudgy young woman exited a small boxy cement house and rushed toward them.

"Annie, let me present our neighbors," said Evelyn introducing Renaldo Aguilar and his wife Anita Guadeloupe de Aguilar.

"Our names are alike," declared the woman looking like a little girl with her short cropped curly black hair as she stood on tiptoe to place a kiss on Anne's cheek. Her husband appeared old enough to be her father. He uttered a quick greeting from a ragged worn face as he solemnly shook Anne's hand. Then without another word, he carried her suitcases toward the house that was to be her home until the end of December. The house was constructed of concrete blocks, blanketed with whitewashed stucco and covered with the kind of zinc roof ubiquitous to Nicaraguan homes. Set back seventy feet from the road within a grove of mango, lemon, and papaya trees and banana palms, it was hugged by red poinsettia bushes. A brick patio at the front leading to the front door was surrounded with hibiscus and ferns. A hill sloped up behind the house where palm trees waved as though welcoming the arrival of Anne and Evelyn.

The setting is perfect; I could stay here forever, thought Anne.

"Señora, we go into the house," Anita announced, taking Anne's elbow. They entered a spacious room divided into three sections: the living room or *sala*, the dining room, and the kitchen. At the kitchen sink, Anita turned its single faucet and cold water spurted in myriad directions.

"Inside water," she announced. "Señora Ana, you have the most beautiful and cleanest house in Lower San Linda. Señora Evita and I scrubbed away everything bad, even *las cucarachas*."

On a yellow tiled counter next to the sink was a portable two-burner stove attached to a large propane tank on the floor similar to that of Teresa's in Guatemala. An apartment-sized refrigerator abutted the wall near the sink. The unstained wooden cupboards were bare of dishes, except for two cups, two plates, and two glasses.

With Anita in the lead, the women migrated into the *sala* where two lizards scurried up faded yellow walls toward rectangular windows set two feet from the ceiling. Furnishings were four teakwood rockers with caned backs circling around a coffee table that looked as though it was made from a packing crate. A wooden shelving unit separated the kitchen from the *sala*. The dining space contained a dining table and six straight-backed wooden dining chairs. A narrow hall leading off the main room led to three bedrooms.

"Firm," Anita commented, patting the mattress in the first bedroom. Off the room was a primitive bathroom with a wobbly sink and cement shower stall. The second bedroom also contained a bed and a few shelves, but the third bedroom was empty.

Anita led Anne to the end of the hall where she opened the back door to the laundry with its *pila,* which was smaller than the *pilas* Anne had seen at the Park of the Wretched in Antigua. The laundry area had a concrete floor and was open to the back yard, enclosed only by a steel black fence with a gate. A tall water tank stood outside the gate. Anne soon learned it was essential during the frequent shut-offs of water pumped from Managua's antiquated pumping station.

"Is it not a beautiful house, Señora?" asked Anita standing by the *pila,* her face brightly lit with a broad smile.

"Yes, it is very pretty," Anne agreed making a mental note to have the dingy yellow walls repainted.

"I take care of it." Anita pointed to dull maroon tile floors as they reentered the main part of the house. "I make them shine like glass."

Anne was confused. "Is Anita our maid?" she asked Evelyn in English.

"Anita and Renaldo come with the house to give employment to the locals. The house is rented only to foreigners. Anita is its maid and Renaldo its gardener," explained Evelyn. "She's superstitious and when I told her your name was Anne, she declared that it's a sign from God that she will work for us. They live across the street deep in the woods behind a grove of trees and have two little boys, Hernández and Camilo."

Anne smiled at Anita. "*Gracias* for the tour."

"*De nada.* Now I make you *limonada,*" she announced and rustled into the kitchen.

"She is a take-charge sort of person," Anne noted dryly.

Later in the day, Anne unpacked the luggage from which she extracted three porcelain six-inch high unicorns and one awkwardly carved from wood, and carefully set them on the dining table. "Uncle Roy made the wooden one," she said.

Evelyn lovingly caressed the thick horn of the wooden unicorn. "I miss him," she said softly in a voice full with remembrance.

"I know," Anne whispered, yearning to add, *come home, Evie,* but knowing better than to suggest it. She wouldn't come home now, not after all that she had sacrificed for her life in Nicaragua, even though her family would have given anything to have her back.

Anne had silently admitted long ago she resented the good fortune that had blessed Evelyn with such a family. Anne's father was always preoccupied with work and her mother was present sporadically when she wasn't volunteering for one cause or another to escape the presence of her cold and distant husband. When her mother left her father and moved to California where she remarried Anne was not surprised or even particularly sad. Anne knew her mother loved her, although she was unsure about the love of her father, but neither of them were as devoted to her as was Evelyn's family to Evelyn.

Uncle Roy and Aunt Jane had affectionately named their violet-eyed child Evelyn after her paternal grandmother and Juanita after her Mexican maternal grandmother. From the first time Anne had laid eyes on her baby cousin, Anne had taken the beautiful Evelyn Juanita into her own heart.

As a little girl, Evelyn, created imaginary stories about unicorns, all of which culminated in the imagery of her unicorns flying free, soaring over continents and into space. Uncle Roy read his only daughter and three sons bedtime stories. He claimed that once Evie had heard her first story about unicorns, the mythical creatures had become an important part of her life. Anne remembered him good-naturedly complaining about having to build a bookcase to house the collection of unicorn statuettes that she requested whenever asked what she wanted for her birthday or for Christmas.

When she was ten, Evelyn wrote a play about unicorns, and Anne, then fourteen, suggested they perform it for the neighborhood. Of course, Anne appointed herself as the play's producer. She relished recruiting actors. She cast Evelyn as Baby Unicorn, selected herself to play Mama Unicorn, and convinced a local boy who had a crush on her to play Papa Unicorn. At her request he asked his father, an amateur woodworker, to build four wooden trees for the set. Anne recruited Evelyn's older brother to play Monster Hunter and asked her mother, Lynn, and Evelyn's mother, Aunt Jane, to sew unicorn costumes and to provide cookies and juice after the performance. Evelyn wrote the script, but Anne reviewed and edited it. As editor, producer, and director of the play, she was, temporarily at least, a member of Evelyn's family.

The play was performed on the circular front porch of Anne's parents and was well attended by neighborhood children. Evelyn's fourth grade teacher brought a few kids from the local elementary school and watched her precocious student's modified version of *Little Red Riding Hood,* minus the grandmother. Evelyn sang a song she had written while strumming on a toy ukulele. In the story, Monster Hunter, a stand-in for the big bad wolf, saw Baby Unicorn go alone into the forest in spite of being warned of its dangers by Mama and Papa Unicorn. Monster Hunter rubbed his hands together in malicious anticipation of capturing a live unicorn, but just as he crept up behind Baby Unicorn, a swarm of dancing unicorns swooped down and carried the Baby Unicorn into the sky where she prances from star to star illuminating them one by one to brighten the blackness of the night sky.

Like Baby Unicorn, Evelyn had ventured into the forbidding forest of war-torn Nicaragua. Anne knew that the early hopeful days of the Revolution had brought her cousin much joy, but she also knew that Evelyn had not entirely escaped Monster Hunter. She could not escape the darkness of her losses. Rudy and Jasmina would never brighten her life again.

Stroking her father's unicorn, Evelyn repeated, "I miss him." Anne looked on, her eyes filling with tears.

At three in the morning, Anne dashed for the toilet to vomit her first meal prepared by Anita Guadeloupe. She gargled with mouthwash she had carried from Massachusetts and glanced toward the shower. In a far corner, a gargantuan brown spider with long hairy legs plodded methodically along the cement wall. Stuffing her hand against her mouth to squelch a scream, she backed out of the bathroom returning to bed after carefully examining the walls for spiders.

With the lessening of insects during the dry season, Anne, much to her relief, did not need to sleep under mosquito netting, but she lit a mosquito coil by her bed to discourage the few mosquitoes buzzing about in her room awaiting an opportunity to sample her blood. She dozed periodically, listening to the music of cicadas as her mind replayed the day's events. When shards of light trickled in announcing early morning, she caught sight of a gray animal with a long tail as it scurried by the window onto the roof. The pitter patter above her was followed by a cacophony of crowing roosters. Abandoning any thought of additional sleep, she tiptoed into the living area, put on a pot of coffee, and settled into an uneven rocker to sip a cup.

As she shifted her weight to find a comfortable position in the rocker, her eyes landed on one of the high windows of the *sala* where she spotted a long form stretched out on an overhang of the roof. The advancing light of morning illuminated the creature that Anne quickly identified as an iguana. Curious, she pulled a dining chair to the window and climbed up for a better look. A stream of sunlight bathed the roof, spotlighting the green iguana's rough skin, pointy scales, and long fingers and nails. Anne estimated its length as five feet, half of which was the outstretched tail.

"What a magnificently ugly, totally fascinating creature you are - the exact opposite of a sweetie pie - so that is the name I will give you, Sweetie Pie, " she said to the unmoving iguana. Feeling lighthearted, Anne climbed down and resumed sipping her coffee, listening to the crowing roosters, clucking hens, barking dogs, and grunting pigs.

Through the commotion of morning sounds she heard birds chirping their dawn greetings, and in response, she flung open the front door and peered through the screen at a village alive with morning activity. Warm wind tickled her face as she filled her nostrils with the scent of heat and earth and floral fragrances. A man on horseback trotted by the gate of the Casa Sánchez, followed by a farmer parading mooing cows to pasture. From the other direction, oxen lumbered toward the woods with rough-looking men hunched atop the empty carts. That evening Anne would see them emerge from the woods, their carts piled with logs.

Evelyn was singing in the shower in a clear soprano voice. She had always loved to sing. When she was twelve, her parents had upgraded her toy ukulele with a guitar, and she had taught herself to play. Nostalgically, Anne remembered vacation nights around a beach campfire on Cape Cod where Evelyn had serenaded them.

"Good morning. Have you met Hairy?" Evelyn called cheerfully as she entered the kitchen wrapped in a towel.

"Harry?"

"Not Harry. I call him Hairy because of his furry legs. He's our resident spider," explained Evelyn.

"Did you say, resident?" asked Anne.

Evelyn laughed. "Hairy lives on the wall of the shower. Tarantulas eat insects, and they will not harm humans unless provoked. So don't worry, *mi prima.*"

"I was afraid you would say that," Anne grumbled, not anxious to shower with a tarantula. When she finally summoned enough courage to enter the cement stall, she eyed Hairy suspiciously, hoping they could co-exist.

That afternoon the cousins, accompanied by Anita, went into Managua to the Mercado Oriental to buy household furnishings and supplies. Assaulted by the stench of animal waste at the open-air market, Anne moved gingerly, her stomach fluttering ominously. Pigs, chickens, and emaciated dogs roamed freely, as did ragged urchins scurrying through animal droppings and urine like sand and surf on a beach. They stopped only to beg, little hands tugging at the skirts of the Americans pleading, *córdoba, una córdoba,* they cried, one finger raised to emphasize their plea. Menacing red eyes identified the glue sniffers among them. Evelyn handed out coins to the urchins, including the glue sniffers.

"This place is nauseating," Anne gasped tasting bile in her throat.

"It's the dirtiest, smelliest market in Managua, but it's the place to go for a bargain. One can buy anything, legal or illegal. Renaldo used to sell charcoal here. Anita told me this is where she met him.

"I've never been to such a nasty place."

Evelyn smiled. "I owe you an apology for not warning you. I wanted you to see the desperation of the children to understand what I've decided to do. This is my second surprise." She stopped walking and Anne followed suit. Looking up at her cousin, Evelyn announced, "I will open a children's home to rescue the youngest children. For the older kids, it's too late. Violence and drugs are already ingrained in them. Unfortunately, they are tomorrow's criminals. Seeing children suffer is the worst thing about life here. I'll call the home, *Hogar Jasmina*, Jasmina's Home."

Evelyn's announcement astonished Anne. Her cousin never ceased astonishing her. "Evie, what a wonderful idea!" she exclaimed. "But the money? Where will you get the money?"

"I've already received $4,000 in donations from my delegations, enough to begin the search for a building. My first choice is the Cuban hospital in Matagalpa where Tomás had his eye clinic. The hospital closed after the election when Cuban medical personnel were not as welcome in Nicaragua."

Ah, thought Anne, *Dr. Tomás Ruiz, the man who was in Evelyn's Jeep with Jasmina when it hit the landmine.* What a tribute to the Cuban ophthalmologist who had founded a small eye hospital in Matagalpa if the hospital one day housed abused and neglected children. Anne had no idea how her cousin would accomplish such an ambitious project, but knowing Evelyn, it would be done.

They left the Mercado Oriental with a rake, a shovel, a wheelbarrow, a toaster oven, glassware, pots and pans, dishes, lamps and linens, two bureaus and a rocker. Immediately upon arriving at the Casa Sánchez, Anne dashed from the truck into the house and vomited. As she spit and coughed she glanced at Hairy feeling almost grateful that it was witness to her misery. When she finally emerged from the bathroom, Anita handed her a glass of milk and papaya juice.

"*Bueno para el estómago,*" she said patting her own belly.

Healing drink in hand, Anne settled into a newly purchased rocker while Evelyn organized the other purchases. "You'll be accustomed to Nicaragua bacteria in a few days. Milk and papaya is the best remedy for settling the stomach," she said encouragingly.

Anne nodded and took a sip. "Doesn't living here depress you at times?" she asked.

"Are you having second thoughts?"

Anne pondered the question. "Seeing those kids at the market was depressing. They're like the ones I saw in the airport at Guatemala." Anne's voice broke as involuntary tears nudged her eyes.

Evelyn immediately abandoned her task to sit down in the rocker next to Anne's. "What's bothering you, Annie?" she asked.

Anne blurted out the incident with the pretzel boy, lamenting that she had kicked him away as though he were an attacking dog. "I feel so guilty. Maybe I don't belong here. I couldn't even manage working in a Boston slum without falling apart. That's what sent me into the arms of Keith and pregnancy. How do you manage, Evie? After all you've been through and all the terrible things you've seen, how do you manage?"

Evelyn reached for her cousin's hand and held it lovingly like a mother would hold the hand of her child. "I go on," she whispered. "That's it. Nothing more. I just go on."

"You're an inspiration, Evie. I came here to learn from you."

"Annie, I'm not all that special. Anyone who refuses to be broken by tragedy can be inspiring. I mourned and mourned after Jasmina's death. I screamed. Why? Why? Why? I hated the Contras. I hated America for sending the landmines. I still feel that hatred from time to time, but I push it away. One day Doug said, "enough," and urged me to focus all that mournful energy into founding a children's home. It was his idea, not mine."

In her mind, Anne imaged Padre Doug, his large physically imposing body stuffed into an always rumpled black shirt and jeans on the edge of raggedness. His manner was as casual as his clothing, rough, yet funny and kind. "I wish I had a Padre Doug," she said plaintively.

Evelyn looked directly into Anne's eyes. "Annie, what you did at the airport was try to survive. And you will. You may not have Doug, but you have Danny and Lynn. Be grateful for them, release the guilt and go on."

CHAPTER FIVE

Before she left for the day, the Butlers' maid put a casserole of *arroz con pollo* in the refrigerator and a loaf of home baked bread on the sideboard. Dr. David Butler, the first to arrive home, slid the rice and chicken casserole and the bread into the oven to warm. He was selecting wine when his wife Pat brushed in, plopped a kiss on his cheek, and flung herself into setting the table while delivering a running commentary on the day's events at Managua University.

"Ramón predicts a major showdown with the government over the six percent allocation to universities in the national budget," she declared animatedly. "The government refuses to agree to the allocation."

David shook his head. "Confrontation will create enemies," he warned in a barely audible voice.

Pat poised a thin arm in midair, fork in hand. "Then what can we do, David? The Chamorro government is faced with the requirements of the International Monetary Fund. They need IMF loans to keep the country afloat and the IMF says cut spending and privatize everything you can. They'll continue cutting aid to education no matter what it says in the Constitution."

"Ramón needs to keep talking," David insisted. He knew IMF priorities focused on international debt reduction, not benefits for ordinary people. He knew Nicaragua's economy was in shambles and the country needed the IMF. He even sensed talking would be like tilting at windmills. Yet, he had to hope. Hope and faith had sustained him through the bloody rebellion against the dictator Anastasio Somoza. It had sustained him through the blood of the Contra War. Hope and faith were his companions during the euphoric days of the Revolution's social programs when the country had dared to reach toward social transformation, and they would now once again see him through this era of cutbacks and depression. Unlike the parade of people begging at his front door, he had a way out. Go home to Iowa. But most of the Nicaraguan population had no way out, and he would have to hope for them. He had to believe economic fairness would one day reign in Nicaragua. Equality of opportunity and social justice were what God wanted for humanity, not that a few would reap the rich fruits of the country and others would be denied.

Pat fell silent. Practical minded and realistic, her task in the marriage was to deal with things as they were and do her best to cushion David from daily disappointments. She had no reservoir of hope for a brighter future, although she was careful not to admit it to him. She found little solace in his unswerving belief that the Kingdom of God existed in the here and now and all we had to do was manifest it. Manifestation was next to impossible in Nicaragua demoralized from generations of dictatorship followed by a bloody revolution followed by another bloody civil war, a US economic embargo, and now, the dismantling of the small, but hopeful gains made toward uplifting the country's poor. As always, however, she allowed her emotionally closed husband to retreat into his brilliant mind, enriched with scholarship and mired in impracticality, and turned her own attention to the task at hand. She laid the fork by a plate and arranged the cloth napkins into their wooden rings.

They were awaiting the arrival of Evita and her cousin, Anne, whom Pat had not seen since last year when she accompanied Evita to Stoneham, Massachusetts after the death of Jasmina. Evita was like a daughter. She and David had taken her into their house when she first arrived in Nicaragua in 1980, naïve and broke. Years later when Evita joined La Esperanza as a delegation leader and purchased a house of her own, emptiness dwelled in the Butler home, interrupted only by visits from Evita, Rudy, and then the precious Jasmina. Now two of the three people who had brought them joy were gone.

The doorbell rang, and Pat prayed that it was their guests, not another plea for food or money. She opened the door to Evita and they hugged effusively. Then she turned her attention to Anne, offering a quick hug.

Anne was disturbed by how the Butlers had aged. She remembered Pat as an angular self-contained woman whose face masked distress, but now tiny wrinkles at her mouth and deeper frown lines between her brown eyes gave her a worn out appearance. A ghost pale David greeted her, his lower lip quivering as he shook her hand. Aware that Dr. David Butler allowed more demonstrative expressions only when deep bonds of friendship had formed, Anne extended her hand. He had recently been diagnosed with Parkinson's Disease, and she sensed infirmity within the limpness of his handshake.

The aroma of the warming bread drew the group into the kitchen.

"Are your twins still angry with you for coming to Nicaragua?" Pat asked Anne in her usual direct way as she removed the bread from the oven.

"Yes," sighed Anne. "Danny is distantly polite, but Lynn explodes frequently. Danny graduated early from the university in December and his father found him a job in finance at the World Trade Center in New York City. Lynn left university in December to join my mother and her husband Jake in California. She has one semester to complete for her degree. I hope she returns soon."

"It must be difficult for you," Pat said.

Anne nodded. "I had no idea the kids would react so negatively to my decision to spend my sabbatical year in Nicaragua."

"You are their security. They're afraid of losing you."

"I considered that in Guatemala, but sometimes I think they don't like me."

"Then you don't really know them," said Pat turning her attention toward arranging a plate of cheese and crackers. "We think we know our kids, but I guess we never know anyone well, including ourselves. One day your children will admire you for taking the risk to come here."

"I hope you're right."

"Pat is always right," commented Evelyn. "People in distress seek her counsel, and she always delivers the support and sage advice needed." A warm affection floated between Evelyn and Pat uplifting Anne into near optimism over her quandary with the twins. *I'll have to have a serious talk with Pat,* she thought as she set her gaze upon David pouring wine into glasses arranged on a tray. Looking up, he cracked a thin smile. Wine glasses filled, he moved past her lethargically, his salt and pepper hair straggling around his sallow face.

Dr. David Butler, a Christians United Churches missionary assigned to the Nicaragua Christian Theological Institute as theology professor, had always displayed the pallor of someone chained to his desk, but so profound was his enthusiasm for scholarship that when engaged in conversation about his work, his face shone like a man who had found the Holy Grail. But that was the David of the past. Anne concluded that the David of that moment seemed as fragile as the wine glasses he carried.

The women ambled after David into the dining room. Anne had been inside the Butler house twice and was especially impressed with its style. The floors throughout the house were polished white tile and the furniture was elegantly hand-crafted from Nicaraguan hard woods. A baby grand piano that had been in David's family for generations dominated the *sala*. The cost of shipping it to Nicaragua had sent the Butlers into financial crisis, but David had to have his music played on his piano, no matter where he lived. On the piano, Pat had arranged photos of their three children and grandchildren and a photo of Evelyn and Rudolfo with Jasmina, her sweet baby face captured forever. The portrait Pat had painted of Jasmina that had once graced the wall to the right side of the piano was missing, leaving a light patch behind. Anne knew Pat had removed it to spare Evelyn from the pain of encountering a larger-than-life Jasmina in all her bright childish innocence every time she walked into the room.

David settled into his easy chair and dozed off, his chin resting on his chest, his wire frame eyeglasses tilting tentatively on his nose. Anne could hear his soft snore as she sat down opposite him on the soft cushions of the bamboo sofa.

"Is he not feeling well?" she whispered to Pat.

Before Pat could answer, David roused himself to defense. "I'm fine. A little tired is all." He wearily rubbed the back of his neck and sat up straight.

"Tired or not feeling well?" asked Evelyn, with easy familiarity, daring to demand a truthful answer.

David waved her question away. He did not want to talk about his health, preferring his own inner world, secure as the churches of old. There he dwelled with God. God had given him a good life, allowing him to do the work he loved in the place he loved, and if God chose to end that life, he would accept that decision without complaint.

Evelyn changed the subject. "How many courses will you be teaching when classes at the Institute begin next month?" she asked.

"Two – one on the history of the Protestant Church in Nicaragua and one on liberation theology. Only a few have matriculated into the latter one. Because liberation theology declares that only through solidarity with the poor do we know God, it is eschewed by those eager to take Nicaragua into the New World Order of unbridled capitalism. They have lost the imperative to embrace the Kingdom of God here and now by fighting for social justice here and now. Instead, they are returning to a theology that proclaims a pie-in-the-sky Kingdom of God where the poor receive justice in paradise after death." David, as always, spoke as though he was giving a lecture, and his voice betrayed an uncharacteristic bitterness.

"But you are teaching theology students," Anne protested.

"And many of them are poor," added Evelyn. Turning a frank gaze upon David she exhorted, "Come on, David. What's really happening?"

Pat answered. "Some on the Board of Directors of the Institute are unhappy with David's course on liberation theology," she explained.

"*Radical*, they call it," David burst out. "A faith perspective that proclaims Jesus as liberator and calls upon us to liberate the poor from their poverty is radical!" His hand chopped the air in emphasis. The emotional outburst drained him and he retreated into his mind for a moment. When he emerged, he spoke in a tone edged with disappointment.

"The theology of liberation is fading along with the revolutionary social project. Free public medical care is giving way to private pay clinics, and some in the Ministry of Education are calling for privatization of the public school system. Measles, eliminated by the vaccination campaigns, has returned and illiteracy lowered by the literacy campaigns is increasing. No one cares about the poor anymore."

"You do," said Pat.

Ignoring her comment David continued. "By refusing to drop my course, I am making things difficult for Elías."

"Rev. Elías Jimez is the Rector of the Nicaragua Christian Theological Institute and a dear friend," Pat explained to Anne. "He supports David on this."

"This must be hard on both of you," Anne said.

"Yes, it is," responded Pat, as she stood up and disappeared into the kitchen. Evelyn suspected Pat had departed abruptly to hide her emotions, so she deliberately changed the subject.

"Annie, I call David, Elías Jimez, and Ramón Morales, 'the three disciples.' They've been working together since 1972 after the earthquake that destroyed much of Managua. Ramón was a graduate student at Managua University when he approached David and Elías with the idea for the Medsalud health clinics. The earthquake razed six-hundred city blocks and crumbled ninety percent of Managua's buildings. Three hundred thousand were homeless. Somoza's National Guard looted what little remained following the earthquake. With Managua in ruins, Ramón recognized a fortuitous opportunity to raise funds from sympathetic sources for continuous medical care for earthquake victims. Together they developed a plan and solicited financial help from medical schools outside the country and within the business community in Nicaragua. Even Managua's elite were disgruntled over the situation. The father of Elías was a respected businessman on the Board of Managua University. He convinced the department head of MU's medical school to support the idea as a practicum lab for training doctors, nurses, and medical technicians. By the time of the Triumph in 1979, Managua University was operating five Medsalud clinics in Managua's poorest neighborhoods and three in the countryside. When the Sandinistas took over and began their vaccination campaign, Medsalud cooperated with them."

David observed Evelyn with loving eyes, his countenance softening as she spoke. Leaning forward he laid his hands palms down on his knees and said, "Medsalud manifests God's Kingdom."

The group gathered around the dining table where David said grace, then drifted into a glassy-eyed reverie as he ate. Small talk bored him. When the doorbell rang, he excused himself and shuffled to the door. Pat's expression darkened.

"The doorbell rings constantly," she commented irritatingly.

The home of the Butlers was located in an affluent neighborhood, abutting a poor barrio, and a flow of humanity from the barrio arrived daily at the Butler door. Other houses on the street had erected gates and walls, but the Butlers had decided not to insulate themselves from the beleaguered around them. Years of ringing doorbells and interrupted meals and conversations had made Pat regret that decision. From the corner of her eye, Anne could see David handing crackers to three little children.

"It never stops," Pat complained as David shuffled back to the table. "We never have peace. Without my art and David's music, we would have lost our minds years ago." David looked at his wife and a pained expression passed across his face. Regretting her lapse into self-pity, Pat immediately asked Anne about Guatemala. Anne told them about Gregory Garner and the imminent arrival of the Marines.

"The so-called 'advisors' are already here," said Pat.

David sprung to attention. "Everyone is jockeying for power," he declared. "By sending advisors, the US sends a message to rivals and dissidents: America favors the policies of the Chamorro administration; don't interfere."

"Anne, tell us more about this man Garner," Pat continued attempting to lighten the conversation.

"I have to admit, he's handsome."

Pat smiled as though she had been informed of a secret romance and they kept the conversation upbeat through dinner. Later, David played the piano. Anne had never heard Chopin played with the passion expressed in David's hands. Relaxing into the Preludes, she imagined herself stretched out on a blanket at the Charles River Esplanade in Boston on a warm summer's night.

"David is extraordinarily talented," she said to Evelyn as they drove home after dark.

"Pat wants to take him back to Iowa where he can get better medical care. He will miss Nicaragua and so will Pat even though she is eager to leave." Evelyn recalled Pat's soulful portraits of poor Nicaraguan children. Her rendition of their faces expressed her love for the very people she sometimes resented.

"If we could only live with clear, clean lines, always know how to act for the betterment of others while protecting ourselves from hurt," she reflected.

When they turned onto the *Carretera Sur*, the South Highway two policemen gestured with flashlights for them to pull over.

"A routine check. They're searching for guns left over from the war," Evelyn assured Anne as she stopped at the side of the road and opened the glove compartment for the registration. The policemen approached the car. One went directly to the trunk and opened it, the other asked for her registration papers.

"Oh, Renaldo damn!" Evelyn exclaimed to Anne. "I took the registration papers out when Renaldo was cleaning the truck for your arrival and I forgot to return them."

She explained this to one of the policemen who was not impressed. He wrote a ticket, seized her driver's license, and he and his companion climbed into the back seat of the truck demanding to be driven to the police station on the other side of Managua.

Anne's body tightened. Unlike Antigua, the Managua police did not carry automatic weapons, but they were young and twitching with nervous macho energy.

When Evelyn turned the ignition, nothing happened. "The battery is dead. We need a jump," she announced.

"This truck is new, Señora," barked the ticket-writing policemen, intimating that she was making excuses.

"Still it happens sometimes," Evelyn said. She suspected an inferior battery had been substituted for the original in the Managua car dealership and the original sold on the black market, but she knew the police would not be interested in her suspicions. "Can you find us a jump?" she asked.

Without further comment, the policeman shoved a ticket into Evelyn's hand and along with with her driver's license, he and his companion leaped out. In seconds, they had pulled over another car and climbed into its back seat.

"Shit! They were just looking for a ride back to the police station. There aren't enough police vehicles, so they find any small infraction for a ride," declared Evelyn.

"But they have your driver's license!" exclaimed Anne.

"And I'll probably have to make several trips to police headquarters to get it back, even after I pay the fine. They'll file it away in a shoe box and no one will be able to find it."

"In a shoe box?" asked Anne incredulously.

"Not a real shoe box, but it looks like a shoe box. There are stacks of them on the desks."

"How frustrating."

"Living in Nicaragua takes patience and flexibility, especially for spoiled North Americans, like you, my cousin," teased Evelyn.

"But how are you going to drive without a license?"

"With yours. They'll honor it if we get pulled over again."

"But what if I'm not with you."

"Then I will either offer a bribe or cry, sometimes both. Once in a while a chocolate bar works. But our first concern is to start this truck. We need help."

Evelyn slid out into the dark. Pressing her back against the truck she circled a flashlight toward the haze-edged headlights of oncoming vehicles, which at that time of night, were sparse. Thirty minutes later a battered pick-up stopped and in the dim light the young man that hopped out looked to Anne like the kind of juvenile gang members she had seen on the evening news in the US. A hot bolt of fear ran through her and she scanned the inside of the truck for a makeshift weapon. Spying the books David had lent them, she dumped the contents of her purse and shoved a heavy book inside. With her homemade weapon at the ready, she exited the truck and stealthily moved toward Evelyn and the man she had identified in her mind as a hoodlum. But her cousin and the hoodlum were laughing.

"Zorro will give us a jump," Evelyn explained as Anne approached.

The man, his face in shadow, bowed ostentatiously. "Zorro here to rescue *las señoras*," he declared in a burlesque parody of the legendary Zorro. He set to work and connected the jumper cables, but when he turned over his ignition, nothing happened. "Your battery is no good," he announced.

Within minutes he had removed the battery from his truck and installed it in Evelyn's, placing her disabled battery in her truck bed.

"You stay in Zorro's truck, Annie. I'm going with Zorro to try to save this battery or buy a new one."

All Anne's inner warning systems went off at once. "You don't know this man. He could take your truck and leave you stranded or worse. Just look at him. Look at his junky vehicle," she pointed out.

Evelyn grasped Anne's hands in hers and said softly, "Zorro belongs to a Christian Base Community. CBCs are where the liberation theology movement flourishes. He was on his way to a CBC in Costa Rica to pick up supplies for the community here in Managua, yet he is willing to stop and help us."

Anne still wasn't convinced. Although they had spoken in English, Zorro sensed Anne's concern.

"Do not worry, Señora," he said. "My uncle manages the Shell garage in Barrio Pasa Robles. The garage is closed, but he will help."

Anne watched them drive off into the abyss of darkness, a cold chill zigzagging through her body. She climbed into the front seat of Zorro's vehicle, rancid with male pheromones, acrid cigarette smoke, and diesel fuel. Sliding over the rips in the seat she scrunched down whenever cars approached, fearing her blondness would spotlight her for robbery or attack. An eternity passed. When Evelyn and Zorro returned, she stifled a yelp of relief. Zorro installed the batteries in their vehicles refusing Evelyn's offer of money for his efforts.

"Much pleasure," he said bowing again. After planting sloppy kisses on both of them he took off waving.

"It was kind of him to help," Anne finally managed to say.

"Acts of kindness are common here," Evelyn said looking at her cousin with a sense of foreboding. Could she find the energy in her tired, stretched-tight soul to hold Anne's hand through her months in Nicaragua?

***

At a welcoming luncheon for Anne in the Managua University Board Room, she was seated between Dr. Elías Jimez, Rector of the Nicaragua Christian Theological Institute, and her new boss Dr. Ramón Morales, Rector of Managua University. The two rectors and David spoke animatedly as though they were holding a meeting to which she had not been invited. Her Spanish was not accomplished enough to join them in their fast flowing conversation, but she hoped she would be able to say something intelligent before the luncheon was over. When Morales asked her to speak to the larger gathering of professors who would be her colleagues, she said something about looking forward to working with them and offered to help them with English if they were interested.

Judging her words insipid, she sat down chagrined, yet Morales was gracious. "I am sure you will have us all speaking English before you go," he joked eliciting a murmur of subdued laughter.

Following the luncheon, Pat introduced Dino Fuentes, the English-speaking Cuban who taught English and also worked with Pat escorting potential donors around campus. A cheerful young man with olive skin and dark brown hair, he spoke in clear, but stilted English enunciating every word with precision. "I offer my services to you at any moment, Professor Harrison," he said. "We will take a tour of the university tomorrow, if this is pleasing to you."

"Yes, of course, thank you," Anne said amused by his English phraseology, realizing she probably sounded as stilted in Spanish.

As they exited the university dining hall, Pat satisfied Anne's curiosity over the intense conversation she had witnessed, but not understood during the luncheon.

"The news is bad," she explained. "Three Medsalud clinics are closing due to lack of funding. I knew it was coming. Not only are the medical programs underfunded, but so is the university. And our students are angry. They know the Constitution dedicates six percent of the government's annual budget to higher education. Many of them are ex-soldiers. They fought for their Constitution and they will demand the six percent."

The following day Dino took Anne to the classroom where she would teach and oriented her to the meager supply of English books available. Anne was relieved that she had filled one suitcase with instructional material expecting supplies in Nicaragua to be inadequate, so she approached her classes with her usual confidence.

Fifty students had enrolled in the beginner class and twenty in the intermediate class. Anne was delighted with the turnout, but soon she was confronted with frequent student absences complicating continuity in classroom work.

"The students carry many burdens. Some work two or three jobs. Some have no job and are hungry," explained Dino when she complained.

Feeling ashamed of her complaints, Anne developed an individualized curriculum for each student who did not attend regularly. There were days this gargantuan task overwhelmed her, but she was determined not to disappoint Dr. Morales. As Evelyn had predicted, he worked her hard, and she would not let him down.

CHAPTER SIX

"**G**od has chosen you to spread the Word in Nicaragua. And that Word is *Salvation*. Jesus died for our sins. Salvation is paramount," proclaimed Pastor Theodore Hicks pounding the lectern as if chopping wood. The Director of the Saving Waters Christian Mission, wagging arms that seemed as boneless as tentacles, his face blazing with holy fire, sent bolts of electricity through his twelve disciples-in-training.

"It is our task to bring the Truth to the Nicaraguan people. For too long they have been befuddled by communists and Marxists who dare to call themselves Christian. They have given their souls to Satan. Jesus has set our task before us, and He will lead us forward until every Nicaraguan that enters our church drinks the elixir of Christ."

"Hallelujah!" someone shouted.

"Hallelujah!" responded Pastor Hicks from pencil-thin lips.

A day ago Tim Haverford felt proud and grateful, brimming with the manic eagerness of a chosen one. Many in Young Adults for Christ had applied for assignment to Nicaragua, a country in great need of redemption, and the church that had nurtured him since infancy had chosen him. At that moment, however, Tim was disconsolate, squirming and shuffling his body to find a position that didn't irritate his sunburned back. His blistered hands cracked painfully as he held the Bible, yet the physical pain did not match the humiliation of being sidelined. No more work on church construction until the disabling second-degree sunburn had healed. The specter of infection threatened Tim, who had thought that two weeks of working under a scorching sun had exposed him enough to forsake sunscreen, but he should have known better with his fair skin. The stupidity of it embarrassed him, and the unsympathetic comments of Pastor Hicks about his self-inflicted plight shamed him further. He struggled with anger at himself and resentment of his pastor and prayed for forgiveness.

Tim wanted this one-year mission assignment to test his mettle. Not everyone who proclaimed himself called to the pastorate was blessed with that calling, and he wanted to be sure. The young Texan had overflowed with enthusiasm at the task set out before him by the Lord; now with one setback, that enthusiasm was waning. When everyone stood up to sing *Onward Christian soldiers, marching as to war, with the cross of Jesus, going on before,* Tim caught his mind wandering. Painfully he hiked himself upright and joined in.

Following the hymn, Pastor Hicks exhorted, "The task before us is not easy, but in the Lord, all things are possible. We shall build this church and we shall fill this church! Praise the Lord!" The words reverberated within the small chapel of simple wooden benches, where a table covered with a white sheet served as pulpit. The sheet shrouded the bottom half of Hicks except when he jutted around it, twisting like an acrobat with an emotional exuberance that elevated his young charges to new heights of fervor where they would remain until rejuvenated by evening vespers. His daily dramas were performed before a print of an auburn-haired, blue-eyed Jesus on the wall behind him. Another print of a brown-eyed Jesus with darker hair at the Last Supper decorated a side wall.

"Praise the Lord!" the pastor's disciples shouted, and with a final benediction the Sunday morning service was over.

For the remainder of the day, Tim secluded himself on the top of a bunk bed in the men's dorm, reading his Bible but not seeing words. He fiercely concentrated his thoughts on how to demonstrate to Pastor Hicks his own aptitude for Christian service. Obvious enthusiasm to do the Lord's work was not enough. He needed to be bold.

After dinner, Tim sat in the dark on the front steps of the Saving Waters Christian Mission listening to the evening vespers. They were making a joyful noise unto the Lord, clapping and singing and stomping, but he couldn't participate because the pain would have been excruciating. As he sat alone feeling sorry for himself, an idea germinated. He would prove to Pastor Hicks that he wasn't a bumbler by bringing the wayward self-proclaimed Christian Anne Harrison to Christ. When he had plunged into the punishing work of excavating for the new church, his belief that Anne needed to be saved had faded. Maybe God had stricken him with this sunburn so he would once again turn his attention to Anne. The next morning, Tim related his idea to Pastor Hicks explaining that the Christian United Churches denomination had sent Anne Harrison, an unsaved woman, to Nicaragua to rebuild a church in an agricultural community some distance from Managua. He explained that the Nicaraguan church was a mission focus of Anne's church.

Pastor Hicks was interested. "I am familiar with Christians United. The Nicaragua Christian Theological Institute employs an American professor from that denomination, name of Butler. A proponent of liberation theology," commented Hicks with disdain ringing in his voice.

"What is liberation theology?"

"Crap, Tim. Believers are Marxists who claim to be Christians," said Hicks. "They believe that God sent Jesus not for our Salvation from sin, but to liberate the poor from their poverty. They use the church to promote a socialist agenda."

Astonished, Tim exclaimed, "Marxist Christians!"

Pastor Hicks expanded on his previous comments, seldom missing an opportunity to impart the insights that fifty-two years of good Christian living had taught him. "These liberation theology people call themselves Christian, but some of their Catholic priests were in the Sandinista government. Marxists priests gathered a few disgruntled Catholics together and declared themselves to be the Popular Church. The Nicaraguan Archbishop Miguel Obando y Bravo and other traditional Catholics had little use for them or the Sandinistas. Even Pope John Paul II publically admonished the Sandinista government's Minister of Culture Father Ernesto Cardenal when he visited Nicaragua in 1983 for not resigning from the government."

Tim listened, grateful for the personal attention Pastor Hicks was giving him.

"The evangelical churches of the Nicaragua Christian Theological Institute did not throw out pastors that supported the Sandinistas. As far as I know the Christians United Churches denomination financially supports the Nicaragua Christian Theological Institute, at least in part. They could have insisted NCTI fire the communists who dare to call themselves Christians. Anne Harrison could be a communist, or at the very least, a socialist, and she is almost certainly apostate," he declared dogmatically.

"It's hard to believe Anne is a communist. She's a nice lady," Tim protested, remembering Anne's kindness to Eduardo and his family.

Pastor Hicks studied his young charge. The youth's tall body was slender but not weak. Boyish freckles speckled above his eyebrows below his light brown receding hair. He had the bright look of eagerness to serve the Lord, but Hicks had seen too many young people like him whose faith was not grounded in Truth. They had disintegrated at the first sting of a reality incompatible with untested beliefs. Hicks felt a special responsibility to nurture the promise in these young people through hard work, prayer, and consistent reading of the Scriptures. Tim would need more of his guidance than most.

"Tim, she may be nice, but she's misguided," he said in a fatherly voice. "You will meet many nice people in Nicaragua. Some do not even know they are communists. Many are humanitarian aid workers and some even call themselves missionaries. But Satan has confiscated their souls. Our task is to save them." He paused rubbing a smooth chin. "It would be interesting to know how the Nicaraguan church of this woman reconciles its calling to Christ with a sympathy for communists."

The pastor's serious face produced a barely perceptible smile. "Call her and visit the church," he ordered, "but keep your mind focused on Jesus. Satan may be in that church. I want a full report. Perhaps we at Saving Waters can bring the woman and, if need be, the church to Christ."

Pastor Hicks lifted bushy gray-brown eyebrows revealing filmy pale blue eyes seldom seen clearly except when he flashed them from the pulpit. They briefly met Tim's causing an exultation to fill Tim's chest. Pastor Hicks had given him a special assignment! He immediately called Anne.

"How did you find me?" she inquired in a polite but frosty tone.

"You said you would be teaching at Managua University, so I called and they gave me your home phone," declared Tim unfazed. He recalled her muted response when he had triumphantly announced the recovery of Juancito as vindication that the Lord had saved the son of Eduardo, a believer, by sending Anne and him into their lives. He assumed Anne remembered this as well and felt uncomfortable hearing from him because she was not ready to acknowledge her fragile faith.

Annoyed, Anne realized she had neglected to ask the office secretary to withhold her phone number. She had been thinking of Gregory Garner at the time, but if Tim had located her so easily, Garner would find her too if that was his intention. Her feelings about this were mixed, hoping Garner would make the effort but unsure she wanted him to do so.

"I want to see you and your church," Tim said. He heard the audible catching of Anne's breath.

"Well, my cousin and I are going to Los Ríos to visit the Betel Christian Church next Sunday," Anne said hesitantly.

"Can I come?" asked Tim.

"I guess so," Anne responded, irritated at herself for agreeing to see him again.

A week later, Evelyn drove to the Saving Waters Christian Mission in Colonia Cielo passing by the United States Embassy, a massive compound surrounded by a high concrete wall enclosed by a spiked gate and crowned with razor wire. Settlements of forlorn shanties and dirt streets framed the compound on each side.

"The contrast is obscene," Anne noted as they drove on.

Tim was waiting outside the chain link fence of the Mission House. Behind the fence, a large grayish-white block building abutted a construction site cluttered with dirt, lumber, and concrete blocks. Anne waved to Tim who bounded into the truck, guitar in hand, looking as if he had been dipped into a barrel of flour. The skin on his hands and arms was a patchwork of pink and brown.

"What a sunburn that must have been!" Anne exclaimed.

"No, just messy," he declared. Embarrassed by dead skin falling like snowflakes onto the back seat, he quickly brushed the offending flakes onto the floor.

"Let me introduce my cousin, Evelyn Gutiérrez," Anne said.

"Cousin? You look Nicaraguan," Tim declared, startled by her Latina appearance.

"My maternal grandmother was Mexican, but thank you for the compliment," she responded; then added, "The journey to Los Ríos will take almost two hours. You'll see some beautiful countryside today."

Tim welcomed a break from sweltering Managua and the unrelenting demands of life at Saving Waters. They drove out of the city taking *la Carretera al Sur,* the South Highway, up the hill to the town of El Crucero where they shut off the air conditioning and rolled down the windows to breathe the fresh cold wind of the town situated atop the Managua Sierra. From there they turned right into the countryside, entering a virgin land of wide skies and radiant light. They climbed hills and descended valleys of brush and foliage rich trees. Evelyn identified a stately ceibo, with its thirty-foot straight trunk, and a canopied guanacaste, saucer-like seedpods hanging from its branches.

"They are survivors of the old growth forests that once blanketed Nicaragua," she explained. "Deforestation has taken most of them."

Between villages they traversed stretches of land peppered with a few small shanties. Then they climbed a hill skirting the edge of a cliff from which, over a stunning expanse of rolling hills, the blue-green haze of the ocean shone. Evelyn narrated their journey in a soft, musical voice. Enchanted, Tim watched the silky blackness of her hair float to and fro and then chastised himself for his sensual thoughts.

"Ahead on the top of that huge hill to the right is a small village. One of the projects of the Revolution was to bring electricity into the countryside, but this village is too remote for electrification. Padre Douglas Michaels, a missionary priest from Canada and Rector of the Saint John the Baptist Primary School in Managua, chugs his Jeep up the hill every week to bring beans, flour and rice to the people," she said.

Tim cranked his neck. "It's like a roller coaster. What a cool ride that must be!"

"It looks a bit chancy to me," commented Anne dryly.

"I agree, but taking risks is as normal for Doug as drinking and eating, especially when he is on a mission," Evelyn remarked, a tinge of pride for her dear friend in her voice.

She veered toward a less intimidating hill on their left, and they climbed and then descended into the next valley where shanties appeared next to open fields of peanuts, cotton, and tobacco. Within thirty minutes they had reached the small town of Monte Horeb, where they rumbled over deteriorating paving stones until they arrived at a dirt road that would take them to Los Ríos.

"I've never been to a *campesino* village or a *campesino* church," Tim declared like an excited boy anticipating Disneyland.

"You'll love the people in the Betel Christian Church. And they will love you, especially if you sing them a song," said Anne, swiveling her head around to look at him. In the weeks he had lived in the same house with her, he had never viewed her as an attractive woman, but this morning he saw her differently noticing that her blue-green eyes sparkled from a pretty face. These older women were seducing him. Pastor Hicks had warned him to beware of Satan's power. Tim understood he must be strong.

"I know a praise song in Spanish," he proffered, lowering his head toward the floor.

"Good idea," Anne said turning forward much to his relief.

The truck heaved as though it were out of breath and Tim had to admire Evelyn's ability to control it as it ploughed over ruts, rocks and tree roots, raising billows of dust that coated the windshield. Sturdy rural men and women hefting hemp sacks on their strong shoulders walking along the road shouted for rides as the truck neared. Evelyn stopped and they quickly jammed into the truck bed with bodies and loads squashing a suitcase filled with sewing supplies, Anne's gift from the women of her church for the Betel Sewing Collective. The truck sank with its newly acquired cargo, and Tim worried the weight would rip away the undercarriage.

They crossed bridges spanning deep ravines.

Their structures appeared fragile but were secure enough to bear the limestone loads of huge trucks bound for a nearby cement factory.

"Limestone is quarried from these surface mines," explained Evelyn. She pointed to yawning valleys of exposed earth barren as a moonscape. "The limestone is used to make cement. When an area is mined out, the excavators move deeper into the countryside, edging closer to the agricultural cooperative of Los Ríos."

"Like an encroaching army," Anne added.

"Unfortunately, yes," agreed Evelyn. "But work at the cement factory provides employment for some of the locals."

As they approached the last bridge, they met Lucía Ríos, rumored to be the most affluent woman in Los Ríos since she owned a house near where the two rivers of Los Ríos joined. It was constructed with the more expensive cement blocks made in a factory, not homemade earthen blocks or boards and thatch like other village houses. A tall woman with a narrow face, Lucía moved proudly in her simple cotton dress covered by the frilled apron of Nicaraguan working women. Her muscled legs swung easily over the uneven road, her long black hair bound in a neat braid encircled her head, and she balanced a small hemp sack on her shoulder. When she saw the truck approaching she waved, and Evelyn stopped.

"*Hermana Evita*! Sister Evita!" Lucía shouted as she climbed into the back seat of the truck next to Tim after dumping her hemp sack onto the lap of one of the hitchhikers in the truck bed. Evelyn introduced Tim to Lucía who moved close nudging his thigh. Tim shrank away from her. To him she smelled like rotten eggs.

Lucía and Evelyn chatted in Spanish so rapidly, Tim and Anne could not understand what they were saying. At the entrance to Los Ríos, Evelyn stopped the truck and the truck bed passengers scurried in all directions. Then she pointed to a cultivated plot of land.

"Pastor Rafael Cortez is the leader of this village farm. It is called the 19th of July Agricultural Cooperative in honor of the Day of Triumph of the Revolution."

"It's brown like Texas in summer," observed Tim.

"Poor farmers can't afford irrigation," said Evelyn. She restarted the truck and turned onto a rocky dirt road in worse condition than the one they left.

"Welcome to Los Ríos, Tim," declared Anne cheerfully.

As they rattled slowly through the narrow main street, children loped alongside the truck, giggling and calling *"Hermana Evita!"* Evelyn waved and shouted, *"Hola! Hola! Luisa, José, Carlos, Antonio, Yessemina."* They all looked the same to Anne, little brown bodies with wide bright smiles. To Tim they were no different from the waifs of Managua in their dirty oversized clothes from bundles of second-hand shirts, pants, and dresses shipped into Nicaragua from North America and distributed through charity. Like in Managua's filthy neighborhoods, the littlest boys wore oversized T-shirts and went shoeless.

They drove slowly, passing shanties made of cornstalks and scraps of wood with thatch or pieces of metal for roofs.

"It's so poor," observed Tim.

"It is poor," agreed Evelyn. "Most villagers are subsistence farmers, some are members of the agricultural cooperative, and a lucky few have jobs at the cement factory. You'll see houses made of pressed earth blocks, adobe. They mold the blocks here. The house of the pastor of the Betel Christian Church was built with these blocks."

"Do they have latrines?" asked Tim aware of his own bladder.

"A few do, but most use the *aire libre* for bathrooms. One of my delegations is sponsoring a latrine project. It should start soon."

"Aire libre?" Tim asked.

"They go anywhere," explained Evelyn.

Tim stared wide-eyed as goats, pigs, and chickens meandered next to the truck intermingling with the gleeful children. He expressed surprise to see the goats.

"Agronomists from Managua University's Graduate School are working in rural communities with goats. They're better providers of milk and meat than cows, and they don't take as much space or eat as much of the grasslands," Evelyn declared.

Tim noticed some small shops interspersed with the houses.

"What can they sell?" he asked, thinking no one could afford to buy anything.

"Bread and soda in plastic bags and a sour milk treat called *leche agria,*" answered Evelyn. "One store sells notebooks and pencils for kids fortunate enough to go to school."

"Life is a struggle in Los Ríos, Tim," said Anne.

"Yeah," agreed Tim acknowledging a sympathetic tug from within. There was no main center in the village, no gas station. No one owned a vehicle that used gas. Transportation was by foot, horseback, or oxcart. They continued down through the main village street with its many alleys that ran to the rivers where women washed clothes and those without wells fetched household water.

A burly man on horseback trotted up to the truck and shouted, "The gully is bad, Hermana Evita!"

"What did he say?" asked Tim.

"The gully," Evelyn explained. She pointed to a cavernous ditch lined with tree trunks and exposed roots. After years of crossing it, she held a healthy respect for the gully.

"Is there a way around it?" asked Tim nervously.

"The gully stands between us and the Betel Christian Church. We could park here and walk to the church, but I like the challenge of the gully."

Anne preferred to forgo the challenge; nonetheless, she braced herself. Tim's heart quickened, not knowing what lay ahead.

Even though one wrong maneuver would disable the truck leading to a long horseback ride into Monte Horeb to find a vehicle to extricate them, Evelyn challenged the gully once again as Anne held her breath. The truck eased down the jaws of the large ditch, pitching like a boat riding a huge wave. Lucía Ríos fell into Tim sending a wave of revulsion through him. A gathering of village people stood enthusiastically watching the spectacle they had seen many times. With each twist and turn they sighed and when the truck landed upright on the other side they whooped and cheered.

"Jesus!" exclaimed Tim. "Why don't they fill it in?" Realizing he had uttered the Lord's name inappropriately, Tim silently castigated himself and blamed Evelyn for rolling the truck into the gully in the first place. After all, they could have walked.

"The gully washes out during the rainy season so they don't bother to fill it in. No vehicles use this road except mine," Evelyn responded.

They continued on a narrowing road, inching through the crush of waving, cheering people until a small wooden structure came into view. As they neared, Tim saw a three-sided church with long wooden supports along the absent side. The three existing sides were bare wood, a few flecks of brown paint clinging desperately to rotten boards.

"I can see why you want to build a new church," he commented.

Evelyn pulled the truck to a stop and Tim's eyes followed her as she stepped out into a sea of welcoming people, her white cotton dress floating like dandelion dust in a warm Texas breeze. Tim launched himself toward her, desperate to be away from Lucía Ríos, and collided with a craggy-faced man who uttered a hearty greeting while grasping his hand in a bone-crushing shake.

"Welcome, my son. I am Pastor Rafael Cortez of the Betel Christian Church." Rugged as a dry hide, the pastor's earnest black eyes, shaggy ash-gray hair, calloused hands, and massive shoulders reminded Tim of his rancher grandfather. The pastor's wife Sonia standing next to him, like Tim's grandmother, was sturdy and hard, looking years older than her husband in the work-worn way of country women. Both welcomed him with more interest and animation than he had received from anyone in Nicaragua, including his colleagues at the Saving Waters Christian Mission House.

Anne joined them, wisps of hair forming blond wet commas on her neck. She hugged Pastor Rafael and then Sonia. A motherly woman shriveled as a raisin leaned on Sonia for support. Soon Evelyn was beside her cousin kissing the wrinkled, blue-veined hand of the old woman.

"Hermana Leticia," she declared.

"The *señora* is the sister of Hermana Sonia," she explained to Tim. Then, encircling her arms around a young woman standing nearby cradling a baby she said. "And this is Marlene Cruz, the youngest daughter of Hermana Leticia, her baby is Estrellita, and the little guy hugging her leg is Lucas. He's four." The child, face pressed against his mother's leg, peered up at Tim, and Tim smiled.

"Hermana Ana, I have much pleasure to see you," Leticia was saying in a raspy voice, her deep-set black eyes poking through a web of wrinkles. Looking at Tim, she said, "*Joven*, you are friend to Hermana Ana and Hermana Evita, *verdad?*"

"*Sí,*" said Tim. "And you are the mother of Hermana Marlene?" The woman looked old enough to be the young woman's grandmother.

"*Sí,*" Leticia said. "Marlene is my eleventh child. All the others are gone away, some to God, but not my Marlene. And I have my grandchildren."

"You are a fortunate woman, Hermana Leticia," said Anne, rescuing Tim from having to respond.

Marlene plopped her pink-clad baby into Evelyn's arms. Remembering Jasmina, Anne sadly watched her cousin draw the baby close. The hearty voice of Pastor Rafael broke Anne's brief retreat into melancholy.

"We receive the gift of your church with gratitude, Hermana Ana. We will take the old building away; then we begin construction on the new."

"*Gracias a Dios,*" added Sonia.

"Yes, thanks be to God," agreed Anne. "And Hermana Sonia, the women of my church have sent some material and thread for the sewing collective."

"*Gracias a Dios,*" repeated Sonia. "We will make school uniforms."

Pastor Rafael crooked a finger toward Tim.

"Come, Hermano Timoteo. You must meet my sons. My son Rafael Jr. works at the cement factory. When I was a *joven* like you, only *Somozistas* could have this work, but now my son is there," he declared proudly as he led Tim away from the women toward two men looking as burly and broad as their father.

Rafael Jr. had a hard jaw, tendoned neck, and deep chest, and he pumped Tim's hand with the familial force of his father. Roberto, the youngest son, his muscular arms wedged into a T-shirt proclaiming *Nicaragua libre,* jutted his hand forward, but Tim, wary of subjecting a sore hand to further abuse, brushed through a handshake.

"He is a policeman in Managua," said Pastor Rafael. "My third son lives in Costa Rica with his family. We have two daughters in the mountains near Matagalpa. Sonia and I lost one son in the uprising against Somoza."

Tim said, "You have a big family."

"The Lord says to be fruitful and multiply," said Pastor Rafael with a half-smile and a wink.

Aware he could no longer ignore the need to find a latrine, Tim asked and was directed to the back of the church where a shack emanated the odor of human waste. He held his nose not allowing himself to breathe until he had finished. When he rejoined the gathering, Pastor Rafael was grouping people into loose lines.

"Together we visit the graves of our fallen brothers," he explained to Tim somberly as he raised his arm for silence. Only the whimpers of babies and the giggles of children interrupted the quiet as the group reverently followed Pastor Rafael through scrubby brush and around low trees until they reached a horseshoe clearing ringed by luxuriant purple orchid bushes embracing four graves with simple wooden crosses. Heads bowed when Pastor Rafael murmured a prayer. After he had finished, Evelyn and three other women moved with fawnlike grace to the graves and knelt before them on the dusty earth.

"Whose graves are they?" Tim whispered to Anne.

"Evelyn's husband Rudy and three others who were killed in a Contra raid on the village three years ago," she responded quietly. "Rudy's body was beheaded."

"Jesus Christ!" exclaimed a shocked Tim. A swish of heads whipped toward him, and he clapped his hand against his mouth mortified over another defamation of the Lord's name. He shuddered as he observed the kneeling women in the fading afternoon sun. Anne reached for his hand and laced her fine-boned fingers into his as Pastor Rafael began to pray.

"God, we are a humble and poor people who praise you for your love for us and for our fallen pastor Rudolfo Gutiérrez and his companions buried here. We will never forget they sacrificed their lives to save us, just as your Son, Jesus Christ, sacrificed his life to save us. Give us strength to live on knowing they will always be among us. In the name of Jesus, we say Amen."

The gathering repeated "Amen," including Tim who spoke the word with a vague sense of unreality as he struggled to impose order on his thoughts. Startled he jumped when Pastor Rafael called, *"Pastor Rudolfo, presente!"*

The people responded, *"Pastor Rudolfo, presente!"*

Pastor Rafael proceeded to name the other fallen men eliciting the same response.

"Was Evelyn's husband a pastor?" he asked Anne.

"Yes. He was the pastor of this church," she replied.

Observing the bewildered expression on his face, Anne gently squeezed his hand.

The women left the graves. Like a silent forest creature, Evelyn brushed by him, her face as unreadable as the antique china-skinned doll with coal-black hair that sat in queenly elegance in the glass cabinet of Tim's childhood home. On the surface, Evelyn appeared fragile, but to have lived through the beheading of her husband, Tim thought that she must be undergirded with steel-like strength. As she passed, he averted his eyes.

Anne looked at Tim like a loving family friend. For a few moments they stood in silence, joined only by the warmth of their hands.

CHAPTER SEVEN

People fanned away from the tiny cemetery into the hazy half-light of late afternoon, moving like tortoises. No one in Los Ríos was in a hurry. The congregation would return around seven *more or less* for the church service.

Pastor Rafael led his American guests to the family house where they gathered on the walled-in concrete patio of the oblong gray building that served as living area for the family and separated two bedrooms on the left from a dirt-floored kitchen on the right. Photos of the Cortez family, taken by various members of Evelyn's delegations, enlivened the surrounding dull-whitewashed walls. Three non-electric pedal sewing machines donated by English missionaries abutted shelves where Sonia stored her dishes. The family, thanks to monthly checks from their son in Costa Rica, had electricity and a refrigerator, always stored in a locked bedroom. The furniture in the patio living area was limited to two rockers and a scattering of straight-backed chairs. The old woman Leticia was swallowed by one of the rockers, the baby Estrellita snuggled into her tiny lap. A zinc roof protected the area from the fierce rains of the rainy season. Looking toward the backyard from the patio, one could see a pig, a rooster, chickens, and a goat foraging among overgrown vegetation.

Sonia cooked on a stove made from cinder blocks and a grate, using wood for fuel. Three pots simmered, wafting delicious odors. One pot contained the omnipresent beans, another the omnipresent rice, and the frying pan contained chicken poached in a tomato and cilantro sauce. Sonia had slaughtered the chicken herself for this occasion. Smoke was everywhere drifting upward through ventilation slits leaving an inferno of heat behind. Tim peeked into the kitchen where a wizened old bulldog of a man hunched over the fire, stirring something in a pot. "He cannot speak," Evelyn explained. "He showed up sick one day and never left. The hammock in the backyard is his bed. During the rainy season, it is strung up to the patio posts inside. He has food and a place to sleep thanks to Pastor Rafael and Sonia."

"Pastor Rafael is a good Christian," Tim said.

"And a good leader," Evelyn added. "He is respected in this community for his leadership of the agricultural cooperative. He is the Sandinista delegate from Los Ríos and has the organizational skills of a general."

Tim considered asking about this Sandinista affiliation but decided the question would be better left for another time.

"They are poor but they are rich in love," Evelyn added.

Tim agreed. "Those who know God's Salvation are never poor."

"Do *you* know God's Salvation?" asked Evelyn wryly catching Tim's eyes, surprising him with her question. Was she trying to trick him, to insinuate he was lacking in faith? He forced himself to tear away from her glance.

"Of course I do. I'm saved," he responded defensively. He turned away, but still felt her magnetic gaze charging through the back of his neck like electricity. Sonia rescued him when she seated him, along with Anne, Evelyn, Rafael Jr. and Marlene's shaggy husband Rolando around the table. The old woman Leticia watched everyone from her rocker as though viewing a movie. Roberto had departed earlier to catch a bus for Managua. Evelyn offered to drive him to the bus stop in Monte Horeb, a four-mile hike down the road, but he refused knowing she would not have had time to eat before the church service.

Anne asked Evelyn whether the mango juice was safe to drink. "It's made from well water. It may make us sick," she said, taking a large gulp. Anne followed suit and hoped for the best.

As was customary in the households of poor farmers, the women and children waited to eat until after the men were fed. Because they were Americans, Evelyn and Anne were treated as honorary men and were seated at the table. Anne understood she had entered a society where sexism still flourished in spite of the equal rights amendment in the 1986 Nicaragua Constitution. Even heroic female revolutionaries like Dora María Téllez, who during the Insurrection had led a raid on Somoza's National Palace and negotiated the release of rebel political prisoners, had probably not surmounted the obstacles of machismo within Nicaraguan politics, although being a heroine would convey privileges not accorded poor peasant women, like eating alongside and not after the men were finished.

Rudy, much to the dismay of his congregation, had insisted on men and women eating together. When they were in his presence, the men agreed grudgingly, eyebrows raised in incomprehensible triangles as women pulled up chairs at the table. Rudy had been born in Los Ríos and everyone loved the bright curious little boy who made them proud by graduating from the Nicaragua Christian Theological Institute. Usually when the village people were fortunate enough to become well-educated, they did not return, but not only did Rudy return, he returned with an American wife. Even though Rudy's successor was intelligent and kind, Pastor Rafael believed God had assigned certain roles to each sex, and it was the natural order that women should defer to the men who protected them. Thus, Sonia and her niece Marlene served food after Pastor Rafael said the grace and they ate what remained after the others were finished.

When darkness fell at six, as it always does in Nicaragua, moonlight painted silver shadows over trees, and the hammock serving as the homeless man's bed cast a spectral air. Gazing into the yard, Anne sensed the presence of the ghosts of the slaughtered ones of Los Ríos, and goose bumps rose on her arms.

After eating, Pastor Rafael announced it was time for church and the small group dutifully followed him toward the three-sided building leaving Sonia behind to wash dishes and put her older sister Leticia to bed. Upon entering the church building, the Americans were seated in the front row.

The service began with a long chorus or *coro* accompanied by the clapping of hands and the shaking of a tambourine by an elfin-like young man standing behind Pastor Rafael. People drifted in dressed in their Sunday best, the children in their blue and white school uniforms. A chubby little girl flashed a broad grin at Tim, who sat between Anne and Evelyn, and he drew his lips into a tight smile. Anne remembered the electric energy of a *campesino* service as exhausting and exhilarating, yet she expected this *culto* to be bittersweet without Rudy.

Following the singing, the entire congregation rose for the reading of scripture. More families straggled in. Night completed its sweep of the village, leaving illumination to the mercy of a few light bulbs hanging like limp balloons from old church rafters. The punishing humidity increased as the numbers of bodies increased. Anne's face glistened with moisture, and she twisted a perspiration-soaked handkerchief in her lap. From past visits, she knew she would be asked to speak and went over and over again in her mind what she would say.

The singing and Bible reading pattern was repeated three more times before Pastor Rafael finally called upon her. Despite her limited Spanish, she prayed she could convey the fond sentiments of her church for the congregation of Betel. Pulling a sticky skirt from her legs, she rose and approached the pulpit.

"We at the Christian Community Church value your friendship and we ask God's blessing upon each and every one of you," she said, adding a few phrases about the friendship between the two churches that she hoped made sense. Pastor Rafael motioned and the congregation shouted, "Amen!"

Anne looked to Evelyn for affirmation and Evelyn nodded positively. After another two rounds of singing and Bible reading Pastor Rafael called upon Evelyn to speak. The cheers began immediately. *"Viva Evita! Rudolfo, presente! Jasmina, presente!"*

"Jasmina? Who is Jasmina?" Tim asked Anne as he watched Evelyn walk slowly forward her white dress swaying across her hips.

"Evelyn's daughter. She was killed by a landmine last year," Anne said.

Color drained from Tim's face and he gulped as though punched in the stomach. Anne immediately regretted assaulting him with such a terse comment about Jasmina's horrific death. At the gravesite of Rudy and his companions, she had observed the naïve certitude of the young man falter. Perhaps she should have not agreed to bring him to Los Ríos. He was young, inexperienced and had probably led a sheltered life. As much as he irritated her, she did not want to be the one to shatter his worldview or his faith.

Tim shifted forward, fixing a drained face white as ash on Evelyn. Anne placed a comforting hand on his arm, but nothing in his demeanor indicated he was aware of her concern. When the last *viva* had been uttered, Evelyn gestured toward the missing wall and spoke.

"I see many from this community who are not part of the Betel congregation. My husband Rudy used to say 'God's kingdom is everywhere, sometimes in the church, but always in the lives of everyday people.' You have endured an Insurrection followed by the Contra War. And you have lost over 50,000 people in the violence of these wars. Thousands of you have been hurt, yet you have survived and with the spirit of love, you go on. Like Rudy, I celebrate you. God's kingdom is alive right here in Los Ríos. *Viva, Los Ríos! Viva, Nicaragua!"*

Pastor Rafael shouted, "Praise God." Exhortations exploded from the crowd, and they continued as Evelyn returned to her seat at Tim's side. The anguish painted on his face puzzled Evelyn, and her eyes met Anne's querulously. Pastor Rafael invited Tim to come forward. He stood up reluctantly and moved with glacial slowness, guitar in hand.

Standing awkwardly at the pulpit, he recalled the child who had jumped from the Sassafras Bridge into Sassafras Creek and sank ponderously into cool deep water. For a terrifying moment, the boy Tim was drowning. With a strength fueled by panic, he pushed himself to the surface like a deer fleeing a crocodile. The same panic engulfed him at that moment, but this fear had no name.

"Uh, I don't know what to say, so I'll sing," he choked and began to strum and sing, his barely audible voice strangled with emotion. As though the congregation understood he was in trouble they boomed the familiar *coro* with him.

> *Somos uno en Cristo,*
> *un solo Dios, un solo Señor, una sola fe,*
> *sólo un amor, un solo bautismo,*
> *un solo Espíritu.*
> *Él es el Consolador.*

As they sang, Tim regained composure, and several choruses later he was singing as spiritedly as were they. Voices rose up from the crowd gathering in volume from the open side of the church. Verses were repeated over and over, accompanied by clapping and tambourine shaking. Finally Pastor Rafael approached the pulpit and Tim ended the *coro.*

"We thank our brother Timoteo for singing his deep praise to the Lord," declared Pastor Rafael. "Hermano Timoteo, you are welcome in our humble church anytime."

An elated Tim returned to his seat where the affirmative smiles of Anne and Evelyn filled him with pride, but after another sixty minutes of congregational Bible reading and preaching by Pastor Rafael in the sauna-like three-sided building, the euphoria had dissipated and Tim's mind returned to wrestling with what he had learned in Los Ríos.

An avalanche of conflicting emotions assailed him. He had never suffered the death of a close relative. His parents required that he do his best in whatever he undertook and behave like a gentleman. He had never questioned them or rebelled against these requirements. In fact, he had rewarded them with achievement at school and as a youth leader in church, and he basked in the light of their praise. It never occurred to him what suffering they would experience if he died. He knew for those who had accepted the Lord as their

Christ and Savior a future life in paradise awaited, yet the presence of so many in Betel that had lost loved ones wasn't right even if they did follow the communists. Throughout the remainder of the service, Tim struggled to banish thoughts of death from his mind by focusing on scripture he had memorized. When the last *coro* was finally sung, he and the women were inundated with kisses, handshakes, and hugs from the congregation. With so much affection showered so generously, Tim felt loved.

Later when Pastor Rafael laid a fatherly hand on his shoulder, Tim remembered why Pastor Hicks had sent him to Los Ríos. He desperately wanted to avoid asking this loving man what he knew Pastor Hicks would want to know, but he must. Pastor Hicks expected it. They walked outside where Tim swallowed and said haltingly, "Pastor Rafael."

"*Sí.*"

"Pastor Rafael," Tim began again.

"What?" asked the pastor, intuiting that Tim had something significant to say.

"You are a good Christian." Pastor Rafael smiled and waited. "But the Sandinistas are communists and you are a Sandinista. I do not understand. Communists are not Christian. They are apostate."

Pastor Rafael raised thick eyebrows in a mixture of curiosity and annoyance. Tim was saying the same things a preacher from America had said when he came to Los Ríos. Some had believed him and left Betel to start a new church. He began to walk, but Tim remained rooted in place until Paster Rafael stopped, turned around, and said, " Come. "

Tim caught up with him and the two walked away from the church. "It is your government that calls Sandinistas communists, Timoteo," the older man said in an even voice. "The Communist Party in Nicaragua is separate from the Sandinistas, but they, we, and others fought together to throw out Somoza. Your government sent money to the Somoza dictatorship for forty-five years to oppress the Nicaraguan people, yet it calls the Sandinistas oppressors. When we liberated Nicaragua, we, the Sandinistas, tried to make a new society. Three priests held ministries in our government. Many churches supported us, but your CIA paid the Contras to destroy us because we are socialists and friends with the Cubans and the Russians." Pastor Rafael stopped walking and faced Tim, his expression serious but not angry.

"I do not understand," said Tim perplexed. Pastor Rafael gave him a quick, friendly pat on the arm.

"What you must understand, Hermano Timoteo, is what we both believe as Christians is more important than our politics. We believe in God and in Jesus Christ, His Son, and in the Holy Spirit, *verdad?*"

"True."

"We believe in Salvation, *verdad?*"

"True," said Tim again.

"And we believe in liberation. We believe that all people should be free, *verdad?*"

"*Sí.*"

"*Bueno,*" said Pastor Rafael, and the subject was closed. As the two men walked and talked like recent friends sharing their stories, Anne and Marlene sat under moonlight on benches in front of the church listening to the musical purrs of insects between outbreaks of conversation.

"My husband Rolando has no work," Marlene lamented to Anne. "Sometimes I work at the public school when a teacher is sick. And Rolando grows food in the village cooperative, but it is difficult. *Que nos ayudará, verdad?* Will you help us?" As she spoke she played nervously with the top button of her white blouse, grayish from too many river washings. A soft sag of flesh beneath her chin pulled her tired face down toward her chest. The baby Estrellita slept in contentment nestled into her mother's body.

Anne welcomed the opportunity to reconnect with the young woman. Five years ago during Anne's first visit to Nicaragua in 1986 for Evelyn's wedding to Rudy, Marlene was a lively teenager bursting with intelligent energy. For five years she had walked four miles to a bus stop, taken the bus to secondary school, and returned the same way until she had acquired her high school diploma, a rare achievement for poor country women. She was rewarded after graduation with a job as an assistant preschool teacher in the public school. Now an aura of weariness had settled over her. Like David Butler, she was disheartened by the continuing collapse of the social programs of the Revolution, culminating in the loss of her job when the new government cut back money for the schools. Unlike David, she was desperately poor, and her poverty presented Anne with a dilemma.

Anne ran her fingers through her hair as though to command her brain to produce the words she must say to Marlene. She must tell Marlene that taking on the support of one family in Los Ríos would encourage others to ask and that, in spite of what was believed about rich Americans, she could not support an entire village. Her brain, and her Spanish, failed to produce the words she needed.

"What can I do?" Anne asked defeated.

Marlene's dark eyes brightened and Anne braced herself.

"Give us a school," Marlene declared directly.

"What?"

"We need a school in Los Ríos. Many children no longer go to school because they are too many and the public school is too small. The new government says that the two new classrooms we were promised will not be built. Fifty children wait for school. They must wait until someone drops out. The government says we can have a legal school if we have a place to hold classes and have teachers and have no cost to the government. Isabel Martine, a member of our church, went to normal school in Managua and taught there for two years before she came home to care for her sick mother. Isabel has no work in Los Ríos, so she can teach in the school and I can help Isabel. We will need a building for our school and paper and pencils and books."

Anne sighed as she considered the complexity and cost of establishing a school and employing at least two teachers, probably more. She was tired and hot, and her stomach was in rebellion from the mango juice served at dinner.

"You are teacher, and you will make this school for us, *verdad*?"

Anne looked at Marlene speechless.

"This I know," Marlene said with surety.

Anne wrote to her church the Christian Community Church in Quincy. Given their past generosity, she hesitated to ask them to subsidize at least two teachers in Los Ríos. That implied a long-term commitment, and she doubted they would send the estimated $5,000 to construct another building so soon after they had donated a similar amount for the Betel Christian Church's renovation project. On a long shot, she mailed another letter to the denominational headquarters of Christian United Churches, framing the proposal for the school in the most mission-oriented language she could think of. Then she wrote to her mother and expressed her doubts about raising any more money from either organization.

Her church replied immediately assuring her that they would discuss the request, but budgetary cutbacks were in the offing as donations had fallen. The denomination's reply was short and to the point: That kind of mission project was a local church responsibility. Anne scoured her personal budget for a surplus, but there was none. She and Keith were still paying on college loans for their children and were stretched financially.

A month flew by during which she attempted without success to squelch all thoughts of Marlene's plea. "I have failed Marlene," she admonished herself. Tentacles of guilt squeezed her shoulders, adding to the aching tension from the demands of a crowded teaching schedule. Beggars at the door of the Casa Sánchez were constant and distressing. Neighbors pleaded for intervention with the American Embassy for visas and she had to explain why she could not help them. She felt angry, sad, and guilty all at the same time when she saw their disappointment. Daily bouts of stomach pain, a losing battle to keep cool in the unrelenting heat and humidity, power outages, water stoppages, annoying bugs crawling up her legs, and fearful trips over Managua's damaged streets all contributed to her toxic store of tension. She was rife with tumors of doubt. Even Evelyn's assurances that inner coping strategies and strengths would surely emerge could not dispel her thoughts of admitting defeat and going home.

CHAPTER EIGHT

"The government says it has no money to pay teachers," Padre Douglas Michaels declared to Evelyn as she maneuvered her pick-up through Managua's streets choked with 5,000 angry teachers. She was driving him home after a program-planning meeting they had attended to arrange speakers for the weekly lectures at Solidarity House, a community center established by North Americans living and working in Nicaragua for political and economic education and as a place to socialize. Waves of strikers with placards protesting low pay surrounded the truck. Padre Doug signed V for victory, eliciting enthusiastic whoops from the strikers.

"I know," sighed Evelyn sadly. "And, as usual, kids whose parents can't afford private school tuition will suffer. Anne was asked to start a private primary school in Los Ríos."

"She'll need to negotiate the bureaucracy for certification. I know who has to be persuaded to move things along."

"I expected you to offer, my dear friend, but before you do anything, Anne has to find funding for the project." As she spoke Evelyn patted his knee lovingly.

Richly eccentric and given to rum, cigarettes, and profanity, the old priest filled the role of Evelyn's surrogate father, but not in a religious sense, for she held a skeptical disdain for religion. After the death of Jasmina, she saw God as impotent and had vocalized her private torments to the priest aloud. Unlike David Butler, Padre Doug was as warm and cuddly as the stuffed animals that had brought her so much comfort when she was a child, and his passion was neither intellectual nor theologically-driven like David's, but centered on what he called "the potential" in economically marginalized children. That passion, melded with drive and shrewdness, led him to found the tuition-free Escuela Primaria de San Juan el Bautista and fill it with four hundred problematic kids.

Blessed with a sense of humor as integral as his heart and lungs, Padre Doug refused to take life too seriously and he also refused to despair over the cruel conditions his pupils faced. "Despair will not improve anyone's life," he would say. He had not allowed Evelyn to remain despondent when Jasmina was lost, thus delivering the "kick in the ass," as he put it, that resulted in the plan to start a children's home in the dead child's memory.

"Your help with the Nicaraguan educational bureaucracy will relieve Anne of one of her burdens," Evelyn went on, her voice quavering. She tried to disguise the churning uneasiness she felt whenever she thought of Anne. But she was biting her lower lip sending Padre Doug a signal of her emotional distress.

"Anne has other burdens?" Padre Doug asked as he tapped the ash from his cigarette into the ashtray. Smoke wafted between them. She had never chided him for smoking in her presence. Indeed, there was a silent compact between them that any relief – God, booze, cigarettes, food, sex – from the unspeakable tragedies that often touched their lives was acceptable.

"She's searching for a new direction in her life," Evelyn said with a nervous laugh.

Padre Doug smiled knowingly. "How many searchers from the wealthy North have come down here to find themselves in our rubble?" he asked rhetorically, remembering that thirty years ago he had been one of them. That was long before the promise of the Nicaraguan Revolution drew thousands to Nicaragua from North America and Europe when groups of educational delegations were squired around the country by organizations like the one Evelyn worked for to see the Revolution's social and economic initiatives – schools, water projects, agricultural collectives and agricultural cooperatives, medical clinics serving the poor. Other groups came to construct schools, set up temporary medical clinics or teach skills needed for the new Nicaragua. Some remained long after their one or two-week commitment, however most returned to their home countries bursting with satisfaction for the experience, bordering on joy, in some cases.

When Padre Doug had first met Evelyn at Solidarity House in 1980, twelve months after the Triumph, he recognized a deeply spiritual woman of twenty-seven possessing extraordinary wit and intelligence. She interviewed him about the San Juan el Bautista Primary School for a magazine article in *The Latin America Review of Progressive Thought,* and he suggested that she contact Padre Fernando Cardenal, Minister of Education in the Sandinista government, for an article on The National Crusade for Literacy.

"It was launched five months ago," he explained. "Young people are dispersing into all parts of Nicaragua to promote and teach literacy." She thanked him and obtained the interview. Like him, she believed the literacy campaign and the health campaign and the ongoing economic restructuring would ultimately create a just society in Nicaragua. Later, they would look back and declare this their "euphoric period."

Within a year after her arrival in Nicaragua, Evelyn left her poorly paid job as correspondent for *The Latin America Review of Progressive Thought* and joined La Esperanza as a delegation leader. By this time Padre Doug had learned that prior to arriving in Nicaragua, she had wandered around the United States for years supporting herself as a stringer, selling just enough stories to survive. Always in search of new experiences, she had lived in Mexico with the family of her maternal grandmother. It was there she was hired by *The Latin America Review of Progressive Thought* to write articles on political and social issues within Mexican society from an American perspective.

On July 19, 1979, the Somoza dictatorship fell to the Sandinista led rebels and the magazine sent Evelyn to Nicaragua to report on the formation of the new government. Like so many others from America, she soon fell in love with the physical beauty of Nicaragua and the warm hospitality of its people. When she left the magazine to join La Esperanza, she found herself introducing curious and somewhat adventurous Americans to the Revolution at a time when the newly elected president of the United States, Ronald Reagan, vowed to liberate Nicaragua from what he characterized as the "communist" Sandinistas in control of the Nicaraguan government.

The Contras, funded by the CIA, drew soldiers from members of Somoza's National Guard and others within and without Nicaragua opposed to the socialist Sandinista approach toward economic and social development. The soldiers trained in bases in Honduras on Nicaragua's northern border and infiltrated into northern Nicaragua. People began to worry about a US military invasion when the Contras started attacking agricultural collectives and cooperative farms, the core of the Nicaraguan economy. When she wasn't squiring people around Nicaragua for La Esperanza, Evelyn enthusiastically continued to write articles about the horror of war within Nicaragua's borders. For the articles she often traveled into war-torn areas putting her life at risk.

"Things are getting too dangerous," Padre Doug told her, advising her to return to America, but she insisted that the Revolution would soon triumph over a few disgruntled soldiers backed by American dollars, but on October 2, 1983, the CIA boldly entered Nicaragua's ports and blew up five fuel tanks causing the evacuation of the port city of Corinto. Padre Doug again urged Evelyn to go home and she continued to refuse. The next year against international law, the Reagan Administration approved the mining of Nicaragua's harbors.

"International opinion will turn against American interference. They will be forced to abandon funding the Contra War and to remove the mines," Evelyn declared hopefully.

Padre Doug admired Evelyn's optimism, although he believed it to be wishful thinking. Yet when Nicaragua took its case to the International Tribunal at The Hague, the mines were removed. The war continued, however, and US spy planes caused sonic booms over Nicaragua, magnifying the people's fear of an invasion.

The more aggressive America's pursuit of the war, the more delegations from the United States arrived in Nicaragua. Young and old, clergy and the non-religious came to see the government's social programs, and this invasion of curious civilians lessened the chances of a military one. Evelyn enthusiastically led the uninitiated to places that would change their perceptions forever, and they returned home with stories of life in Nicaragua which was much at odds with the version they were told in their own country. She reveled in her work and Padre Doug reveled in her happiness. He knew that whatever awaited them in the future, they would always be grateful to have lived through this extraordinary period. By 1984, Nicaragua had endured three years of war without buckling, and the Contras had not captured one city. A year later, the US economic embargo began and the resulting shortages forced Evelyn's delegation visitors to carry in their own toilet paper along with a myriad of supplies for the Nicaraguan people.

During that year, Evelyn tumbled into love. Young men had always fluttered around her like moths around a flame, and her enigmatic reserve only increased their resolve. To Padre Doug she had declared, "Men will distract me." Admiring her determination not to be subsumed into a relationship with one of Nicaragua's many handsome but macho young men, he encouraged Evelyn's independence. Thus, he was disappointed when she announced she would marry a Nicaraguan theology student she had met through Dr. David Butler. Padre Doug respected Dr. Butler for his scholarship on liberation theology, although they were not close friends at the time.

Even though he had his doubts, the padre found the young Rudolfo Gutiérrez progressive, intelligent and courageous, but he fretted over their union. When he graduated from the Nicaragua Christian Theological Institute, Rudolfo was assigned as pastor to his home church in Los Ríos, an area where the Contras were active, and he traveled to Managua by bus on a dangerous road each week to be with his beloved.

Evelyn Harrison and Rudolfo Gutiérrez were married in 1986, and Jasmina Gutiérrez Harrison arrived soon after in 1987. David and Pat Butler became honorary grandparents and Padre Doug and Rudolfo's best friend, the Cuban doctor Tomás Ruiz, were honorary uncles. They loved the pudgy little girl with the cinnamon skin of her father and the dark violet eyes of her mother. She was born into a Nicaragua where shortages persisted, but the bloodiest days were behind them. Wrapped in the fabric of their little family, Evelyn and Rudolfo felt safe, even though there was still a war going on.

As the American public opposition to the war grew, rays of hope poked through the dark cloud of relentless violence. Listening to increasing public protests against the war, the Congress of the United States refused to vote more war funding. Nevertheless, the war went on. Then a Contra supply plane was shot down, and its pilot Eugene Hasenfus was captured along with documents disclosing the illegal sale of arms to Iran to continue funding the Contras. The Iran-Contra scandal rocked Washington, and peace talks began. All was quiet except for a few marauders who refused to acknowledge the march toward peace.

The raid that killed Rudolfo arrived shockingly in 1988 while the peace talks were being held. Evelyn immediately fled Nicaragua with Jasmina into the bosom of her family in Massachusetts. Padre Doug hoped for their sakes she would remain there, but she returned, and within a year-and-a half, Jasmina and Tomás Ruiz were two more casualties of war.

The child's death sent Padre Doug into a hellish black pit, but he had to be strong for Evelyn, even though his own soul was seared. He prayed for guidance and when that didn't work, he guzzled rum. Disguising his own pain in her presence, he pushed and prodded her until he found the idea that would sustain her - a children's home in memory of Jasmina.

What irony life is, he thought. He shared more emotional intimacy with Evelyn than with anyone in his family or his church. Through the tragedies they had bonded, and nothing would separate them. As he contemplated these things, he watched her with compassionate eyes.

"Anne's classes at Managua University are challenging," she was saying. "Adjusting to life in Nicaragua is stressful. We're still dealing with the lingering effects of war."

"It's good for her."

"I hope you're right," Evelyn said, drawing her lips into a tight smile. He could feel the heaviness in her heart. Her feelings always seeped through her skin and into his.

"Trust me. I'm always right, Evita," he said lightly.

"Most of the time you are. You and Pat are the most right people I know, and I love you for it."

They emerged from the crowd of striking teachers and Evelyn sped up until they had reached the peach colored *Iglesia San Juan el Bautista* the San Juan el Bautista Catholic Church in Barrio Hermosa where Padre Doug lived in a small apartment at the back. Behind the church building loomed the school, a testament to his dedication and persistence.

"Turn off the engine. We need to talk," Padre Doug said. He clasped her hand in both of his. "Evita, I detect anxiety in you about Anne. What is it that you are not telling me?"

Evelyn's eyes fell on her friend's crooked nose and the webbing beneath his eyes that chambered years of joys and sorrows. Behind black spectacles, the Irish sea blue eyes reflected a vivid and questioning mind. A pudgy round face bore a resolutely cheerful expression even when he was serious. The stout, but sturdy body was clad in dungarees and a black shirt. A clerical collar identified him as the foreign priest who liked drinking rum and saving street children with equal gusto.

She paused, lifting her face skyward as if hoping there was a God above to call upon for help. She wasn't sure about God anymore. Expelling a weary sigh, she lowered her head.

"I fear Anne hero-worships me, and I cannot deliver what she wants. I don't even know what she wants," she whispered.

"I see," said Padre Doug releasing her hand. "I respect your worry, but I find Anne to be an intelligent woman. She'll find her own way."

"I know that in my head," said Evelyn. She pressed the released palm to her forehead and leaned forward, her elbow resting on the rim of the steering wheel.

"But not in your heart?"

"Yes."

"Evita, Anne will find her own way even if she has to suffer for it. And I suspect, she will. Character can be formed from torment. We both know that, and we'll be there to cushion the blows. Right?" He gently laid a liver-spotted hand on her shoulder and she covered it with her own.

"Right," she whispered.

Padre Doug smiled, his tenderness sprinkling her like warm rain and she felt bathed in his certainty.

"Thank you," she whispered.

He gave her a kiss on the cheek. Then bounding from the truck, he patted his pocket and withdrew the pack of cigarettes that bulged there. Evelyn watched him frame the match with his hand against the gentle breezes from Lake Managua, light the cigarette, and take a drag. With a jaunty wave he scooted up the stairs of the church, taking two at a time.

**

When the check from Anne's mother arrived, everything changed.

"Evie!" she exclaimed waving the letter like a kite in the wind. "My mother has collected $5,000 from our family for the school project. And Lynn and Danny contributed!"

"Bless Aunt Lynn," Evelyn declared happily. "And how wonderful that Danny and Lynn are supporting you. They've accepted your decision to come here."

Anne wanted to believe her cousin, but she doubted Danny thought twice about it. Contentedly ensconced on the fourteenth floor of the World Trade Center, he manipulated computers to demonstrate his value as a market-analyst-in-training, a job his father had pulled strings to secure. He probably wrote his check automatically in response to his grandmother's request. As for Lynn, Mom reported that she was learning computer repair skills at a shop in Bishop, California, not far from where she lived in her grandmother's house, abandoning plans to return to college to complete her senior year. Lynn had chosen her grandmother as a refuge and she could not refuse the request that she contribute. Anne had not heard from either of her children since flying out of Boston over two months earlier. She had been banished from their consciousness. Expressing none of her thoughts to Evelyn, Anne turned her mind toward the school.

"God, Evie, starting a school! How will I do it?"

"Doug will guide you. The school may be your most significant contribution to Nicaragua."

"The money is enough to construct a building, but how will we pay the teachers?" Anne asked.

Evelyn smiled. "The money will be found."

"Yes, it will," agreed Anne, half-believing her words. "We'll start a school and name it after Rudy."

"Yes, we'll name it after Rudy," Evelyn repeated happily.

To celebrate the future establishment of the Rudolfo Gutiérrez Primary School and Anne's forty-second birthday, Evelyn took her cousin on a weekend holiday to San Juan del Sur, a quiet fishing village of white sand beaches near the border of Costa Rica.

There they located a guesthouse owned by an expatriate Spanish fisherman who in a burst of idealism had arrived in Nicaragua shortly after the Triumph to work for the Revolution. He bought a boat, joined a Sandinista fishing cooperative, and married a Nicaraguan woman. Together they purchased a sprawling house overlooking the ocean, the former vacation home of relatives of the deposed dictator Anastasio Somoza.

Early morning light fell on the genteel wooden structure badly in need of paint. The lady of the house, her comely face fixed to a scarecrow body, prepared them a breakfast of the Nicaraguan national dish *gallo pinto*, rice mixed with beans, along with fried eggs, and tortillas. After eating, Evelyn and Anne stepped into a sun-radiant morning and glided over uneven paving stones, their bodies light with temporary freedom from Managua. They ambled past unopened shops and adobe restaurants with thatched roofs, toward the village beach cradled by a horseshoe bay. Painted peach, turquoise, and violet, the small village buildings reminded Anne of a watercolor painting on a note card. The women drifted onto the beach, as low tide lapped at the shoreline and melted into the sand. Anne removed her sandals and burrowed her feet into warm fine grains. A wide-brimmed straw hat perched gracefully on her head, she raised her face to the bright sun as she surveyed the imposing cliffs arranged unevenly around the bay.

The two cousins swam languidly in a becalmed blue-green sea. They greeted a Nicaraguan couple strolling hand-in-hand taking an early morning walk. A few cows and pigs zigzagged around the humans preferring their own company. Two thin dogs, but not emaciated like those roaming Managua's streets, romped in the surf, reminding Anne of the frisky dog sprinting past her and Gregory Garner in the Parque Central of Antigua, and eliciting a surprising pang of longing to see the man again. Several moored sailboats swayed lazily in the distance, but fishing boats had already departed for a day at sea.

"Paradise found," said Anne as she spread her long legs over a bright orange towel. Evelyn sat next to her on the sand resting her chin on bent knees and hugging her legs. "Remember the vacations at Cape Cod when we were children? We loved running into waves, daring them to knock us over," Anne said dreamily.

"And we dug in the mudflats for clams."

"And we buried our dads under mounds of sand."

"Nothing bad could happen to us as long as we stayed together. It feels like that again when I am with you."

Her comment roused Evelyn enough to swivel her head toward Anne. "Yes, it was fun, but we're not children anymore, Annie," she said softly, then turned her face toward the sea and remained silent, leaving Anne with an unspoken unease.

After lunch, the women explored the shops. The glaring poverty of Los Ríos with its stick and cornstalk shanties was not present in San Juan del Sur.

"Village people make their living fishing. Affluent Nicaraguans vacation here and serving them provides jobs too," explained Evelyn. "It's in the rural areas outside of the village where the poverty is abominable."

They lunched at a small family beachside restaurant, where they felt like houseguests, not patrons. A little boy dressed in his blue pants and a white shirt school uniform brought them glasses of water. An older sister similarly dressed but in a blue skirt brought them tortillas and a jar of hot pepper slivers to spread on whatever was to follow. The mother, a plump-faced woman, took the order for shrimp, rice, and salad. Her oldest son, a teenager, brought Anne a rum and cola and Evelyn a beer. Anne leaned back, sipped her drink, and studied the beach. A group of children were kicking a semi-deflated ball. The dogs, which had loped past Anne and Evelyn earlier, now weaved around the children, tails wagging, as frigate birds soared above in a bright blue sky.

Anne's drink tasted better than any rum drink she had ever tasted. She tried a sip of Evelyn's beer and concluded that Nicaraguan beer was excellent, even though she didn't like beer. At that moment everything satisfied her beyond her most extravagant expectations.

A shadow approached their table arriving in the form of a tall man familiar to Anne; her heart somersaulted.

"Shit! Gregory Garner!" she exclaimed.

"You remember me. That's a good sign," he declared cheerfully.

"Of course, I remember you," Anne sputtered.

"You're the man my cousin met in Guatemala," said Evelyn rescuing Anne from further embarrassment.

"She spoke of me. Another good sign," said Garner, smoothly extending one hand toward Evelyn and the other toward Anne. The women grasped his hands and shook them. Garner winked at Anne mischievously as he and Evelyn exchanged introductions.

"It's a shock to see you here," Anne said blushing.

"Obviously, given your welcoming expletive. May I join you?" he asked. The cousins exchanged quick glances. "I hope I'm not intruding," he added.

"No, of course not," responded Anne recovering her composure and motioning to a seat. Gregory snatched the chair and sat down. He wore a jersey crew neck and cotton twill pants. A shock of his thick gray-streaked sandy hair escaped from the wide-brimmed Tilley hat that he promptly removed. Anne remembered the appealing silver-gray eyes, which now glittered greenish in the sunlight.

"Anne thinks I am a spy," he said teasingly to Evelyn.

"Are you in the Central Intelligence Agency?" she responded. The question, even if it were in jest, alerted his antennae.

"I'm an officer in the United States Marines. Specialty is cultural affairs," he responded studying Evelyn. She had an appealing exotic quality he had seen before in women of mixed ancestry. He wondered if she was part Nicaraguan.

"Why are American Marines in Nicaragua?" Evelyn probed.

"The Nicas requested advisors. And to answer your unspoken question, Señora Gutiérrez, we are only advisors, not combatants. We are not poised to invade in spite of the current instability in this country."

"That's novel, but then, I suppose, after past interventions, you may be tired of Nicaragua. Same people, same language, same poverty, same dirt. Time to try another country," Evelyn responded, her voice dripping with sarcasm.

A flicker of annoyance brushed over Garner's face as his probing eyes remained fixed on the woman who had suddenly declared herself his antagonist. It was his job to know another's unspoken message and to prepare an appropriate counterpoint. With the practice of a man whose life had depended upon quick and correct observations, he intuited he had nothing to gain and everything to lose in pursuing the conversation.

"*Touché,* Evelyn," he chuckled, assuming a familiarity by using her first name. He waited for a response and she did not disappoint.

"How are you advising the Nicaraguan government? Have you updated your training manual specifying ways to intimidate the Nicaraguan population into submitting to America's plans for Nicaragua?" Evelyn grilled, refusing to be sidetracked. Her calm and mellifluous voice contrasted with the dark conclusions she had drawn about his work.

She is politically astute, thought Garner. He assumed Evelyn was a member of the leftist naïve do-gooder North Americans who associated with the Solidarity House in Managua. She was apparently aware of the CIA's training manual on low-intensity warfare used during the Contra War that outlined strategies for undermining the Sandinista government by sending Contras into Nicaragua to attack agricultural cooperatives, medical clinics, schools, and villages and, thus, to demoralize Nicaraguans in the countryside. He was certain she was referring to this manual, but he could not reveal that he even knew of its existence. Assuming an expression of amused confusion he said, "As a cultural affairs officer, my job is to train our personnel in cultural sensitivity and Nicaraguan history. We try to reign in attitudes of, for example, unctuousness that may be found in some of our personnel."

"An acceptable description of American attitudes," commented Evelyn. "I hope you're good at your work."

"I'm good. And I'm harmless," he said spreading his arms in a gesture of openness and telegraphing an end to the sparring. By her silence she acquiesced and the subject was closed. Turning to Anne he asked, "Have you ordered?"

"The shrimp."

"Good choice. The fried fish is also good. I had it yesterday. It's caught right out there daily." He gestured toward the sea, and then ordered another round of drinks and fried fish for himself.

Over lunch, Garner's eyes fastened on Anne. She had a sophisticated, yet approachable look, very American, unlike her cousin. "I'm here alone," he remarked. "Yesterday, I discovered a remote beach, through a patch of jungle not far from here. May I show it to both of you this afternoon?"

Although sure of himself and his attraction to women, he realized that Evelyn's antipathy toward him would be a challenge. He watched Anne hesitate, her eyes searching her cousin for approval. "We'll have to drive through a rugged jungle path about twenty minutes until we reach the shore. What do you say, Señora Gutiérrez?" he asked Evelyn directly.

She whispered, "Yes."

He had won that round.

Within an hour the cousins were bouncing along a barely navigable jungle road in Gregory Garner's rented jeep, swimsuits under their cotton dresses. He had invited Anne to sit next to him, but she declined and climbed into the back next to Evelyn. Heat gathered in his crotch as he envisioned both women naked. With these pleasant thoughts, he pushed the recalcitrant Jeep through the underbrush while howler tree monkeys frolicked above them. The sun framed out behind the trees casting tiny shards of sunlight on the animals. When they crossed a stream, a crocodile slithered at its edge. Blue herons on toothpick legs waddled in the winding salt-water river that they followed toward the beach.

"It's a different world," Anne declared.

"I haven't seen much of this Nicaragua. I've been too busy," Evelyn noted ruefully.

They entered a clearing that led onto pristine white sand flowing into an expansive bay of sparkling water spreading out toward the horizon under proud floating masses of wandering clouds interrupted by a deep blue sky.

"It's beautiful!" Anne exclaimed. Gregory beamed as though he himself had created the natural beauty. He was surprised at what pleasure he took from her happiness. She had been in his mind ever since he first spotted her on a park bench in Guatemala, rose-cheeked, healthy, and tempting.

"Down the beach you'll see a shack. An old woman lives there. I spoke with her yesterday," he announced.

"How does she survive out here?" Anne wondered aloud.

"Let's find out," suggested Gregory, parking the Jeep and turning off the ignition. "Pass me that bag next to you, please. It's groceries."

They walked toward the shack where an old woman, shriveled as a dried apple, stood in the doorway. A soiled yellow shift hung loosely on her emaciated body. Pencil sketch legs, loose and blue-veined, jutted crookedly toward the ground. She greeted them through a toothless mouth as Garner handed her the bag.

"Gracias, Señor, mucho gracias, muy amable."

"I gave her my picnic lunch yesterday. She's the kind of sturdy soul living on next-to-nothing that I admire in third world people."

The old hag spoke, peering at Anne from the pouches of her eyes. When she asked her a question, Anne looked helplessly at Gregory. "I don't understand her idiomatic Spanish," she whispered.

"She wants to know if you are from the cold country," Gregory explained. "She told me yesterday that a tall blond woman visited her once to ask her questions. She must have been Norwegian. A city in Norway holds a sister city relationship with San Juan del Sur. I told her that you are from a cold country, but not from the same country as her previous visitor."

Anne chuckled. Since arriving in Nicaragua, she had received more stares and comments on her blond hair than anything else, even than her height.

"Soy Americana," said Anne.

"America. My nephew goes to America, but they send him back. He has no papers," croaked the old woman.

"That happens often," commented Garner.

"Claro," she agreed. "He tries again soon." She gazed past them up the beach. *"Mi familia."*

Two oxen were lumbering toward them with several adults and children perched in the attached cart. When the family arrived, a small boy jumped off and ran to the old woman, throwing his arms around her thin waist. The woman told her family of the gringo's generosity. A thin semi-toothless younger man pumped Garner's hand and after a brief conversation, Garner, Anne, and Evelyn bid them all *adios.*

"That's how she survives. Her family brings her food," he said.

"But she's alone. Anything could happen. She could fall. She could die. Her family must worry," remarked Anne.

"I don't think they worry at all," said Evelyn. "When her time comes, they will be content that she died where she wanted to be. Nicaraguans see death and illness as part of life."

"They're closer to death than Americans," added Gregory. He paused then added, "Except for those in our urban jungles."

After a refreshing swim, the three explored the hot sand, searching for unusual stones and shells. The air shimmered with a blanket of humidity. Anne was compelled by a force beyond her control to look at Gregory, and each time he caught her gaze, he smiled revealing the dimple on his right cheek, sending electricity coursing through her veins. She chastised herself for her fascination with him.

Gregory understands the old woman's Spanish perfectly, she thought. *Why was he in language school in Guatemala? Or was he in language school at all?*

CHAPTER NINE

The afternoon passed quickly. The sea grew choppy with an incoming tide that smashed against jutted rocks, flinging ever-expanding fingers of water over glistening sand. The indentations of their feet on the wet sand filled in quickly with pools of water. At 5:45 when the sunlight began to slant, they watched in reverent silence as a brilliant blood red sun began its slow slide into the sea, shooting across the horizon a bow of pink and orange tinged at the edges by a hint of blue-green. It was time to go before blackness blanketed the jungle road.

Garner drove the women to their bed and breakfast, but before they parted they accepted his invitation to dine at El León y La Serpiente, a restaurant perched on a hill overlooking the Bay of San Juan del Sur.

Preparing for dinner, Evelyn noticed that Anne preened carefully applying makeup, sweeping up her long blond hair and fastening it with a colorful Mayan barrette she had purchased in Guatemala. Then she tucked and smoothed her turquoise skirt billowing it out to capture a satisfying fall of material.

"You're attracted to him," Evelyn noted.

"I'm afraid I am," Anne responded honestly. "After I left Keith I swore off men, but my hormones are starved."

Evelyn laughed. "Of course they are. You're only forty-one, excuse me, forty-two. But be careful. You don't know who he is."

Garner was waiting at a table on the restaurant patio. He rose to greet them, whispers of blond chest hair peeking from the neckline of his crisp white shirt. He kissed them on both cheeks, first Evelyn, then Anne. The whisper of breath on her neck heightened Anne's senses.

The beefy owner welcomed them to his restaurant in English laced with a thick German accent. He and his wife had immigrated to Nicaragua from East Germany five years earlier and opened the restaurant. Below the patio, a small reflecting pool shimmered at the feet of a stone lion sprouting water from its mouth. The thatched roof of the restaurant was supported by tree poles carved into snakes, representing its name, The Lion and The Snake. Jasmine vines were energetically climbing up the carved snakes emitting a soft sweet fragrance that reminded Anne of the abundant jasmine in the Parque Central of Antigua.

The owner turned them over to a shallow-cheeked young man. Formally dressed with a red cummerbund separating black pants from a white shirt, he looked like a bridegroom as he served them tropical punch spiked with rum.

"Such elegance for this simple village," Anne observed, keeping her voice light.

"This simple village is on the verge of a tourist explosion. These Germans are astute enough to understand this. If I were planning to live in Nicaragua, I'd buy property right here in San Juan del Sur," stated Garner.

"But you're not planning to stay," Evelyn prodded. He thought he heard a note of hope in the statement that was really a question.

"Our assignments usually last a couple of years."

They ordered lobster tails and roasted potatoes. The waiter brought them cerviche, appetizers of chopped raw red snapper marinated in limejuice, served in cocktail goblets over lettuce.

"How long have you been in the Marines, Gregory?" Anne asked filling a short silence that had fallen among them.

"Almost twenty-two years since I graduated from Emory University in Atlanta. I can retire in three years with a good pension. I think I might like to teach."

Anne brightened. "I teach English at a community college in Massachusetts," she said, initiating a conversation that filled most of the evening.

Relegated to observer status, Evelyn watched their process of discovery unfold as Anne and Gregory related their life stories to one another. She divorced. He divorced. She mother of two adult children, who resented her for divorcing their father. He father of two adult children, who blamed him for the divorce. The intimacy of their revelations astonished Evelyn, not acquainted with the changes in American culture during her years of absence. She had not experienced the human potential movement with its emphasis on open expression about private matters. She had missed the touch-feel seminars where strangers formed instant, intimate friendships with each other over a weekend. She feared this kind of instant intimacy. With suddenness, life had snatched away those she loved and she wanted to protect Anne from the heartache of a similar loss in spite of Padre Doug's advice to let Anne find her own way. Wary of Garner, Evelyn suspected his outward charm masked a private man harboring loathsome secrets. With his cultivated inscrutable expression, he seemed disingenuous. In the background, the sound of waves crashing against the shore was carried upward by the wind, a drone that continued endlessly, as did the conversation of the would-be lovers. When she could endure no more, she interrupted them.

"Yesterday was Anne's forty-second birthday," she announced.

"A toast!" exclaimed Garner, gesturing toward the waiter to bring them champagne. He raised his glass.

"To emerald eyes discovered. They can only grow more beautiful with each passing year. Happy birthday." They clicked glasses.

When they returned to the Spaniard's guest house, Evelyn said good night and thanked Garner for picking up the tab. She entered the foyer, but not surprisingly her cousin remained behind.

"When will I see you again?" Garner asked Anne.

"I'm not sure," Anne said. She cracked the entrance door and placed one foot on the stoop. A haze of defused light beckoned a myriad of tiny moths. Anne quickly closed the door and leaned her back against it facing Garner, who pressed his lips to hers. It was a light, tentative kiss, the sensation filling Anne with a warm tingle. When his hands spanned her waist to draw her to him, she pulled away, flustered by the contact she knew was coming but feared as much as she desired. This mysterious man offered seduction and she yearned for connection, but she brushed her hand quickly over her eyes as though to force them to see the folly of becoming involved with an unknown American Marine officer, possibly a spy. He brushed the backs of his fingers tenderly across her face.

"Another time?" he murmured huskily.

"We live in Managua in Lower San Linda. Casa Sánchez," she said quietly and went inside.

Anne had retreated from him a second time, yet Gregory lit a cigarette and lingered in the darkness watching the closed door knowing she would be his before long.

The next morning a Nicaraguan teenager arrived with a letter for Anne from the *gringo con el pelo rubio*. She glanced at Evelyn and then slowly tore open the envelope. She could feel Evelyn's eyes on her as she read the note aloud.

Dear Anne,
I am anticipating the most pleasurable feelings –
the opportunity to explore with you your thoughts,
your hopes, your dreams, your fears, and your frustrations
to whatever limits are comfortable to you.
I have been called back to Managua a day early
Then I must go to the Atlantic Coast for a week.
I will contact you when I return.
Fondly,
Greg

"I can't get involved with this man. I simply can't," Anne sighed as she slipped the note back into the envelope.

Evelyn shifted her eyes toward the endless sea and murmured, "That's what I said about Rudy."

***

"El Americano come. Look!" announced an excited Anita when her *señoras* arrived home from work ten days later. She extracted two chocolate bars from the pockets of her apron. "For me!" she exclaimed. "And this is for you, Señora Evita." Anita handed Evelyn a large box of Swiss chocolates, then continued to speak, her voice elevated in revealing these delightful surprises. "And for Señora Ana, look on the table."

A huge basket wrapped in rose-tinted cellophane awaited Anne who tore at the wrapper. "Apples!" she exclaimed. She picked up a bright red apple and examined the sticker. "From New Zealand."

"New Zealand apples are quite a treat here. Expensive. Did you tell Garner you liked apples?"

"You think they're from him?"

Evelyn smiled knowingly as Anne tore open an envelope tucked in with the apples.

Dear Anne,
I have tried to get myself thinking about work, but there is only one
thing on my mind - you. I am filled with gratitude for having met
you. Inside this envelope are two tickets for you and Evelyn for
a Mozart concert at the Rubén Darío Theater performed by the

Nicaragua Symphony on Friday evening. It would be my pleasure to accompany you. Please call me at home or at my office. My card is also in the envelope. I eagerly await your call.
Fondly, Greg

"Gregory has invited us to a concert at the Rubén Darío on Friday."

Evelyn bit into a luscious apple she had snatched from the basket. "Did you tell him you liked apples?" she asked again.

Anne smiled dreamily. "Yes," she admitted.

An I-told-you-so expression graced Evelyn's face as she handed her apple to Anita who took a bite.

"We'll both go to the concert," Anne said.

Evelyn shook her head. "Not me."

On Friday a shiny black Lincoln with a US Embassy insignia purred up the dirt road of Lower San Linda and stopped at the gate of Casa Sánchez. A tall, urbane gentleman in a white suit stepped from the vehicle into the shadowy darkness of seven p.m. to open the gate. A small curious crowd had gathered across the road in the hazy twilight, and the driver looked at them suspiciously until, recognizing Anita, he waved, returned to the vehicle, and drove up to the house.

Never had an embassy car been seen in Lower San Linda. One traveled three miles through the woods to Upper San Linda where professionals, business executives, and government leaders lived to see luxury vehicles. Many did just that for their jobs of cleaning the homes and tending the gardens of its affluent residents. The arrival of such a car in Lower San Linda summoned the curious inhabitants of poor and working class villagers.

Approaching the patio, Garner smiled broadly revealing the dimple that set Anne's heart hammering when she opened the door. "Stunning," he declared looking her up and down through the screen while waving away iridescent moths flinging their bodies toward the light.

Anne wore a long, black sleeveless dress with white pearls at her throat. A white shawl, which she had crocheted when the twins were babies, draped lazily over one arm.

"You look like a pair of Nordic gods," commented Evelyn as he entered and kissed her first on the cheek, then Anne.

"Greg, this is too much," Anne declared peering over his shoulder toward the limo that would whisk them into Managua for an evening of symphonic music. She had not come to Nicaragua to socialize with affluent theater patrons. Gregory ignored her comment and turned his attention to Evelyn noting her informal clothes.

"You're not going?" From the tone of his voice he was neither surprised, nor disappointed.

"Have fun," she said shooting him a glance that he returned with a wide smile. With a proprietary gesture, he took Anne's arm and walked her to the car. Their showy appearances and the embassy vehicle within the humble village raised Anne's doubts, and when she caught Anita's expression of wide-eyed wonderment, she realized the outing was a lapse in judgment.

"Excuse me," she said and gathering her skirt she scurried back into the house leaving Garner holding open the passenger door. He slammed it shut and breathed an exasperated sigh. The woman was like a green-eyed cat, mercurial, unpredictable, wanting him, fearing him.

"This is wrong," Anne sputtered to Evelyn as she swept into the house.

"You go and have a good time," urged Evelyn looking out the door at an obviously annoyed Garner. Evelyn could not help feeling a tinge of satisfaction. Anne wouldn't be an easy catch, and her infatuation wouldn't last long. Even as she offered herself these assurances, however, she knew she was worried.

"It's wrong, Evie," Anne repeated. "Look at the homes in this community and then look at that car."

"How will justice come by staying home?" Evelyn asked grasping her cousin's arm firmly and leading her to the door.

"I'm not being rational, am I?" asked Anne.

Evelyn shook her head no. "If you want my approval, you have it, Annie. I don't think any less of you for going, but be careful of that charming man waiting for you."

Anne hesitated, then turned on her heels and left, sauntering like an elegant giantess over the dirt. She took Garner's extended hand and slid into the passenger seat. He turned toward Evelyn and waved, receiving a half-wave in response. The Lincoln with its well-tuned engine purred once again on the dirt path leading to the main road. Gregory beeped the horn, which played a few bars of "Mack, the Knife," and two teenagers shook their hips to the music.

"My boss let me borrow his car," Gregory explained to Anne. "Isn't that some horn?"

"Yes," Anne said. "I can't imagine what my neighbors are thinking."

"They're not surprised. After all, you are *Americanas.*"

They drove under the iron arch announcing San Linda toward Managua chased by a few young men who watched the red glow of taillights fade into a pale blur in the darkness.

Gregory said, "Let me put on my cultural affairs hat and teach you about the Rubén Darío Theater. As you know, it was named after Nicaragua's most famous poet. The last Somoza had it built in 1969 as a present to his wife. And it was so well built that it withstood the 1972 earthquake that leveled most of Managua. We'll be seated on red plush seats. I can't promise great music, but the theater is worth the concert."

Anne shivered. "Ostentatious extravagance in an impoverished city."

"Condemning the theater won't change anything, Anne," Gregory chided.

"Evie said something similar."

"Your cousin is a wise woman. You should listen to her."

It took forty minutes to reach the theater parking lot. A man in a blue guard's uniform directed them into a spot while younger men in black pants and white shirts stood nearby. Gregory exited the car, and then opened the door for Anne. As they started to walk toward the theater, he motioned to one of the young men and dropped coins into his hand, promising more upon return.

"He'll guard the car," he explained.

"Have a good evening," the young man said pleasantly.

"He's polished," observed Anne dryly.

"They select their guards carefully."

They walked arm-in-arm along with other formally dressed concert goers toward the massive glass doors of the theater. Gregory looked at Anne with proud eyes. "People are staring at us," he commented.

"Our blond hair. As Evie said, we look like Nordic gods."

They entered the theater and Anne's eyes swept the lobby drinking in its opulence. Men in suits and tuxes nodded and smiled. Women in long dresses and sparkling jewelry watched her warily subtly nudging their staring men. Heads bobbed and nodded vigorously in conversation.

"I had no idea there was so much money in Nicaragua," Anne commented.

"Meet Nicaraguan high society," said Gregory. "Some foreign embassy people are here as well."

"Are these rich Nicaraguans returnees from Miami?"

"Some are from Miami and other cities in the US. Some are former Somoza supporters and people of wealth, some are from Nicaragua's elite business families, some are in the current government, and some are Sandinista muck-a-mucks. The Sandinistas gained a few plums from their years in government, as do all that enter so-called 'public service,'" Gregory commented sarcastically. "I've heard that 1200 people will attend tonight. Terumi Ueno, the Japanese pianist for *Concert for Piano and Orchestra, No. 21 in D Major* is world renowned."

He took her elbow as they climbed the stairs to their balcony seats. A young woman dressed in a frilly white blouse and black skirt, her hair pulled into a bun from which sprouted a blood red rose handed Gregory a program. Anne opened the program printed in raised black lettering on white linen paper and read the selections.

"This is going to be wonderful," she said to Gregory and it was. Applause rose in great waves as people leaped to their feet.

"Impressive," Gregory said.

"Enchanting," Anne added, heady with the music.

"This is a special time for us," Gregory whispered in her ear as they made their way into a sensuous Managua night. Anne removed the shawl she had snuggled under in the air-conditioned theater. As the crowd dispersed toward the parking lot, ragged children tugged at skirts and trousers begging for córdobas.

"Looks like our polished guards were asleep on the job or the kids were too smart for them," noted Gregory.

A few theatergoers reached into their pockets, but most ignored or admonished the children for bothering them. "These people are so callous," Anne remarked.

"They may not think of the poor as human as themselves, Anne. That's not an excuse, just a possibility. The same kind of thinking prevailed with our Founding Fathers when they declared all men equal, but kept slaves."

"How do you know they weren't bothered by the contradiction?" asked Anne.

"They didn't free their slaves, did they?"

As he spoke, Gregory dropped coins into the hands of a dirty-faced little girl in a torn dress. He took Anne's arm and guided her away from the crowd of beggars heading for the parking area. "Let's look at the lake," he suggested.

They stood silently before water as still as a millpond on an unusually breezeless night. The lake was pitch black except for the reflection of the moon, vaguely outlining the Chontales Mountains that hovered at its edges. Gregory intertwined his fingers with Anne's. His fine hands felt like silk, a gentleman's hands.

"To me every hour of light and dark is a miracle. Every cubic inch of space is a miracle," he uttered.

"You're quoting Walt Whitman," said Anne recognizing the poet's verse. "You're a puzzle, Greg. Your notes are poetic and you are familiar with at least two poets – Rubén Darío and Walt Whitman. Strange behavior for a military officer."

"You, my young lady, are stereotyping the United States Marines."

They spoke softly, as though in a church, respecting the sanctity of the beauty of that moment. When Gregory pulled her to him, she did not resist. She had denied herself the pleasure of male affection for so long, she encircled his neck with her arms, and her eager mouth hungrily met his in a long euphoric kiss. She felt the force of his desire, and when they parted there was a fire burning in his eyes that made her tremble, wanting to touch him, to know him.

He sighed, wiping his wet forehead with the sleeve of his immaculate suit, and whispered. "We have something to look forward to."

Suddenly Anne felt powerful. It had been years since she had felt the impact of her womanliness on a man. Keith had been too preoccupied with work to pay attention to her needs, or maybe he was just tired of her. Their marriage had grown stale long before their parting.

She reached for Gregory's hand, and he led her toward the statue of Rubén Darío, proudly standing by the theater that bore his name.

"Born in 1867, died forty-nine years later, my age," Gregory noted. "He's Nicaragua's greatest poet and a leading poet in the Spanish-speaking world. Nicaraguans are a nation of poets and artists. I have two primitive paintings in the Solentiname style hanging in my study in Atlanta. Bought them during my first visit here."

"When?"

"Around '77 or '78."

"During the time of Somoza."

"Yes."

"Did you meet him?"

"Who?"

"Somoza."

"Of course, I didn't," Gregory declared good-naturedly.

Anne pondered if she should question Gregory more or surrender to his charm for this one evening. Didn't she deserve an evening of romance after years of struggle with an emotionally distant husband? When they returned to the Casa Sánchez, they could slip into her bedroom without awakening Evelyn. Desire rose within as she considered the idea, but her inner voice nagged her to continue with her questions. "Why were you in language school in Guatemala?"

"In-service training, but more of a vacation than training for me."

"In-service training at the José Rodríguez Language School known for training CIA operatives?"

"*Hell!* Are you still suspicious?" Gregory gave her a loving poke on the tip of her nose and attempted to draw her close again, but she resisted.

"That's not a good enough answer."

He shrugged. "It's all I can give."

Anne sighed and changed the subject. "There is so much beauty in the theater, with the music, with the lake, and then, there is so much ugliness."

"It's difficult to leave an affluent society and enter third world culture," said Gregory. "You want to find someone or something to blame for the unending poverty. Unlike in the United States, you cannot escape it. You cannot sequester yourself in the suburbs. The poor are too numerous here, they surround you, and you see their misery. Even those who live behind walls will see the misery if they allow themselves to see it. You think if you find the reason for such misery you can somehow change things. But you can't. Did you know that about 10,000 homeless children lived on the streets of New York City in the mid-1800's, just like the kids we saw tonight? Unlike these kids, they were cold as well as hungry. The authorities rounded them up and shipped them to families in the Midwest. The trains were called orphan trains. Some of the kids found themselves with brutal families who used them as unpaid servants or abused them. Every country has this history."

"Why are you speaking to me in this way?" demanded Anne, not bothering to disguise her irritation. "I don't like being patronized."

He lowered his face to hers. "I'm sorry. I didn't mean to offend you."

Anne accepted his apology in silence hesitating before she asked directly, "Are you with the Central Intelligence Agency?"

Gregory took her hand, raised it to his lips and kissed it while fastening his penetrating gray eyes on her questioning face. "Anne, I make no excuses for who I am. The people I work for have not always made the right decisions, but we have saved many a country from their own cruel bastards."

"The people you work for? I don't know who you are."

"And I don't know who you are either," said Gregory.

Anne's body tightened. A chasm had opened between them. The fantasy evening faded along with her sudden desire, and her mind demanded flight. She slipped her hand from his.

"Whatever happened to you, I'm sorry, Anne," Gregory said. Anne did not respond, unwilling to share Evelyn's tragedies with him. *He probably knows anyway,* she thought. They drove home in a silence punctured only by occasional uncontroversial remarks about the heat, the darkness, animals on the road. When they reached Lower San Linda, he drove through a gate left open at the Casa Sánchez in anticipation of their arrival. He walked her to the door, and she let him kiss her goodnight on the cheek, silently vowing never to see Gregory Garner again, a promise she would keep for all of two weeks before agreeing to meet him for lunch.

CHAPTER TEN

Gregory Garner, Ernesto Flores, and Renaldo Aguilar, shovels in hand, hovered over a cesspool of feces, urine, and mud looking like question marks. They shoveled the stench in the heat of the sun for two hours, finally extracting tree roots that had clogged the piping of the septic system and caused the toilet to back up.

The day had not unfolded according to Garner's plans. He had arrived at the Casa Sánchez that afternoon, with another basket of New Zealand apples and a determination to bed Anne no matter how much patience was required. For the last week they had shared lunches and their life stories and perspectives, on each occasion stripping away more layers of reserve revealing two lonely people who delighted in each other's company. He would wait no longer to share the ultimate intimacy with Anne Harrison.

As he neared the house that afternoon, he spotted Anne, Evelyn, and two men clustered in the side yard. Evelyn greeted him unenthusiastically, but Anne smiled shyly, took the apples with a subdued "thank you," and handed them to the perky Anita, who flashed him a broad smile. He silently chided himself for not bringing the maid more chocolate, assessing her usefulness as an ally in his quest.

"Anne told me you had eaten all the apples," he said to Evelyn. The blank look on her face informed him that Anne had not revealed their shared lunches to her cousin. Convincing Evelyn to overcome her suspicions of him would be a challenge, but he was confident of victory. His plan for the day had been to deliver the apples and openly take Anne out for the afternoon and evening. If he had asked her outright, she would have protested claiming she needed more time before dating him again. So he would take the risk, show up, offering in hand, and insist.

But instead of a pleasurable afternoon and a tantalizing evening with Anne, he found himself standing in her yard, surveying the foul-smelling ground. Concluding Anne would not leave Evelyn to deal with the mess alone, he offered to help.

"After fifteen years in the tropics, I have a healthy respect for the damage tree roots inflict on a septic system, and I have acquired some practical knowledge on how to repair the damage," he said.

So he's lived in the tropics for fifteen years? I wonder where? thought Evelyn.

"Do you have any old clothes laying around?" Garner asked.

Anita produced tattered jeans and a stained shirt of Renaldo's, a scarecrow of a man that Garner soon learned was her husband. The clothes, from boxes of used clothing that arrived in Nicaragua from American charities, included a black T-shirt with a skull and crossbones design and the name of a forgotten rock band.

"Not exactly my style," Garner commented, reading the lettering on the T-shirt, but he put it on along with the pants. The cuffs reached his shins.

"You look like a cross between a rock star and Little Abner," Anne laughed.

"With a couple of braids you could pass for Daisy Mae. I'd love to see you in her short shorts."

"I bet you would," Anne returned the flirt. To Evelyn, she whispered, "He's a horny American." It was the way she wanted to think of Greg, not as an agent mired in intrigue to subvert the social progress by governments out of favor with the United States. He was horny, and he found her attractive. He was harmless. She had misjudged him in Guatemala, and her interactions with him after the concert were colored by misguided preconceptions. Greg was a military career officer, plain and simple. Anne's uncle and grandfather had served in the military, and they were good people. So was Greg. The lunches they had shared revealed an intelligent, sensitive man with a subtle sense of humor. She would put her suspicions aside and continue to get to know him better, but cautiously, as Evelyn had advised.

They worked all afternoon. Gregory felt good to accomplish something physical again, even a job as disgusting as cleaning a septic system. And he liked Ernesto Flores, the handyman of Francisco Sánchez, owner of the Casa Sánchez. Flores was a friendly young man with useful ideas on how to proceed and the strength to do the bulk of the shoveling. When Anne brought Gregory glasses of cold juice, their eyes met telegraphing that Anne would be his before the evening was over.

Anita also made periodic juice runs, offering the refreshing drinks first to Gregory, second to Ernesto, at whom she smiled coquettishly, and finally to her husband Renaldo. Gregory sensed the start of a romance other than the one he had in mind for Anne and him.

By dark a new drainage pipe had been installed and the ditch had been covered with earth. At Evelyn's insistence, Ernesto showered in the bathroom before he returned to Managua on the bus. Anita pounded the dirt from his clothes laying them over the clothesline and assaulting them with a broom while Renaldo went home to wash off with the hose in the shower hut behind their house. His sister Olga, who lived on the other side of Lower San Linda, would soon be returning the two boys, seven-year-old Hernández and five-year-old Camilo.

"Evelyn thinks we may have a problem with Anita's interest in Ernesto," Anne whispered to Gregory in English. Ernesto sat in a rocker opposite them wrapped in a towel.

"If she follows through on what I saw this afternoon, I'd say so. But her situation is unlike ours," he said.

"What do you mean?"

"There are no obstacles between us like unwanted spouses." *Only cousins,* he said to himself.

"You're assuming a lot about us," she countered coyly.

Gregory's eyes moved toward the front door. "Look, here comes the soon-to-be aggrieved husband."

Renaldo peered into the house and glared at Ernesto. "Where is Anita?" he asked.

"At the clothes line," called Evelyn from the kitchen.

"Anita," he called. "Olga brings Hernández and Camilo. Come."

"*Momentito,*" said Anita.

"Now," demanded Renaldo.

Anita inflicted a few additional blows to Ernesto's clothing with the broom, scooped up pants, shirt, and underwear in her arms, and upon entering the *sala,* she handed the pile to Ernesto.

"*Muchas gracias, Señora,*" Ernesto said as Anita's eyes fastened on the towel wrapped around him.

"Anita!" barked Renaldo from behind the screen at the front door.

"Anita, you may go. Señora Ana and I will finish cleaning up," said Evelyn with an eye on Renaldo.

Anita looked toward Evelyn, hesitated briefly, and then left. After Ernesto had also departed, Evelyn invited Gregory to dinner. "We're having pork and rice, squash with cream, and fried plantains."

Gregory ran his tongue over his lips. "Sounds delicious!" Not his original plans; still not a bad substitute.

When they had taken their last sip of coffee and done the dishes, Evelyn brought out her guitar at Gregory's insistence and they sang songs made popular by Peter, Paul and Mary – *"Blowing in the Wind," "This Land is Your Land," "Puff the Magic Dragon,"* and others. Peter, Paul, and Mary were Evelyn's favorite musical group aside from the music of the Godoy family in Nicaragua. Anne and Gregory held the melody while Evelyn's clear sweet voice created a harmonic accompaniment. Stomachs were full, the house reverberated with music, and Evelyn's unicorns smiled down on them with their good-luck magic.

After an hour of singing, Gregory suggested a walk. "I need to exercise the aches out of my muscles."

"I'm too tired," said Evelyn. "I want to go to bed with a good book." Even though she expected to face Gregory across the breakfast table in the morning, she added, "I'll probably be asleep when you return from your walk, so thank you again, Greg, for all your help."

He gave her a kiss on the cheek, lingering close as he whispered into her ear, "And I thank you for the time alone with Anne."

Anne and Gregory strolled out the door into a floral-scented blanket of tropical air. Hand-in-hand, the pair followed the road toward the woods and climbed up a hill overlooking the lights of Managua. There he halted to light a cigarette, his first of the day. He was trying to quit and prided himself on not smoking during the theater evening with Anne, but now he was desperate for a relaxing smoke. He caught a frown on Anne's face.

"You don't like smokers, I know," he said with a sigh.

"I fear for their health."

Gregory took one long drag luxuriating in the soothing smoke tickling his lungs, and then dropped the cigarette, smothering it with his foot.

"You're a challenge," he teased. A barely discernable smile edged across her lips. Was it a power smile or a caring smile? He couldn't read it, but he knew she cared for him and his skin tingled.

They stepped over ferns and eased by dragon trees and philodendrons, their senses absorbing the sounds of rodents, lizards, and insects. A lizard scooted up a malinche tree whose spreading branches provided a canopy over its path, crickets serenaded them. They walked stealthily, silently replete in the presence of each other.

"This wood leads to a wealthy development in Upper San Linda," Anne informed him. "There is talk of clearing the woods for expansion."

"Not good," said Gregory.

"Not good," agreed Anne squeezing his hand. *He loves nature like I do.*

When they returned to the house, Evelyn's bedroom door was shut. Hand in hand they slipped into Anne's room and closed the door. Gregory removed her plaid sundress, feeling the curves of her slender body as he slipped it down and eagerly drew her to him.

The next morning, Anne lazily stretched into wakefulness hearing the songs of toucans and macaws and the chirping of the lizard on the bedroom wall. She reached a lazy arm toward her lover, but he was gone. Disappointment stung until she saw the note. Hesitating before opening it, she feared the worst.

> *My dear Anne,*
> *Life has suddenly become a valued thing to me.*
> *I am filled with anticipation and excitement and warmth.*
> *Sleep well, my dear Anne. I will contact you soon.*

"Evie, I feel like a teenager in love. It's wonderful," Anne said happily at breakfast.

"You're lucky," Evelyn responded.

"You're not going to tell me to find out who he is, to be careful until I do?"

"You know that already."

Anne poked at an unappetizing poached egg. "The saints speak of ecstasy for God. Do you think it is all that different from ecstasy for another person?" she asked.

"I don't know. Passion is passion."

The following Friday, Anne met Gregory for dinner at Los Antojitos located across from the Intercontinental Hotel on the Avenido Bolívar. The restaurant served authentic Nicaraguan food amid black and white murals of an impressive Managua replete with tall buildings prior to the 1972 earthquake. Caged parrots and macaws in multicolored brilliance welcomed patrons with guttural squawks.

After dining on artfully prepared native cuisine, they drove to the barrio of Batahola Norte for the weekly dress rehearsal of the Batahola Norte Children's Choir of Voice and Recorders. Anne hoped Gregory would be as emotionally affected by the music as she had been the two times she had heard it. She also hoped he would be as moved by the story of Batahola as was she. If he was a cultural affairs officer, he might know it already, but if he was not a cultural affairs officer, perhaps the poignant story would resonate within his heart. She related the story as they inched their way through Managua traffic.

"In 1983, Father Ángel Torellas, a Dominican priest from Spain, and Sister Marguarita Navarro, a sister of St. Joseph's from Ohio, came to Batahola, one of the poorest barrios in Managua, and built a chapel," she began. "Father Torellas is a trained musician and created a program of voice and recorders for the children there. Later they founded a cultural center where children were taught to sing and play the *Misa Campesina Nicaragüense*. Did you know there is a Christian Base Community at Batahola Norte and that the they use the *Misa Campesina* throughout their liturgy?"

"Yes, I know a CBC exists there. It's one of eleven or so left in Managua from the liberation theology movement," said Gregory. "And I know of this peasant mass, the *Misa Campesina*. It draws upon liberation theology and integrates it into Nicaraguan folk music. Folk musician Carlos Mejia Godoy wrote it and, I think, the poet Padre Ernesto Cardenal also made a contribution. Padre Cardenal founded the artistic community of Solentiname in Lake Nicaragua before he became the Sandinista Minister of Culture."

"Ah! I'm impressed. You know about this music and its history," said Anne.

"It's my job. Cultural Affairs, you know."

"Ah, yes."

"You still don't believe me, do you?" asked Gregory. "You still think I'm a spy."

"I'm not sure."

"Okay, I'll accept that for now."

"Evie calls the Batahola Cultural Center the most spiritual place in Managua," remarked Anne.

They entered the Barrio of Batahola Norte and quickly found the parking area for the Cultural Center where they left their vehicle under the watchful eye of a guard. As they walked over rough dirt toward the open-air auditorium, they passed the mural of Heroes and Martyrs dedicated to two hundred young people that Somoza's National Guard had slaughtered during the death throes of his regime in June of 1979.

Much to Anne's disappointment, Gregory made no comment about the mural. They walked in silence toward the open air auditorium with posts that supported its raised roof. Three-fourths of the seating was already occupied.

"The choir has performed outside Nicaragua. They tour in Europe and in Canada," remarked Anne. "Are you aware the choir applied at the US Embassy in 1988 during the war to tour in America?"

"No."

"They weren't allowed into the country. The embassy claimed they were too busy to process their applications. Evelyn wrote me to bring this to the attention of my district representative and the two Massachusetts senators."

"Did you?"

"Of course."

"And did it change anything?"

"No," said Anne. "Given your line of work, don't you find it significant that they were denied entry into the States during the Contra War?"

"My job is not to determine our government's policy. My job is to orient American military personnel living in Nicaragua to understand the country's culture and history," declared Gregory, a hint of impatience in his voice.

In an attempt to defuse his irritation, Anne placed her hand over his and gave it a squeeze. "Did you notice the mural of Heroes and Martyrs?" she asked.

"It's an impressive piece of art, but nothing like what is in front of us. Look at that mural, Anne. Isn't it extraordinary?"

The front of the auditorium was dominated by a mural thirty feet wide and eighteen feet high depicting a dark-skinned baby Jesus surrounded by mothers and children of Nicaragua. To its side stood the young people who had been murdered by Somoza's National Guard. Surrounding the baby Jesus were Carlos Fonseca, the intellectual founder of the Sandinistas; Augusto Cesar Sandino, the popular leader of the fight against American Marines in Nicaragua in the 1930's; Che Guevara, Latin American revolutionary allied with the Cuban Revolution; and Archbishop Oscar Romero of El Salvador, champion of the poor, who was gunned down in 1980 as he was saying mass in San Salvador. They stood together – rebels, soldiers, and religious who had died for the common people. Those for whom they had sacrificed their lives were depicted reaching toward the baby Jesus and blessed by brown female angels and the sunrays of God.

"I've seen pictures of this mural, but none expressed its power to connect emotionally," whispered Gregory.

Anne cradled her lover's hand in hers. She understood parts of him - his physical sensuality, his poetic sensitivity, his command of historical knowledge, his intellect, but there was so much more to understand and she yearned to surmount her barriers of doubt about him.

Sister Marguerita appeared in front of the mural and introduced Padre Ángel, a slight man, a great deal older than Anne remembered from the last time she saw him. The priest director of the choir gave a few words of introduction. "Music is important in the lives of these children. Some work in the streets of Managua selling and begging. Others are fortunate enough to attend school. Music gives them all hope." As he spoke, the sun's rays on the mural splayed around him as though God was blessing him and the children of Batahola.

Anne was surprised to see Gregory's gray eyes water when the choir sang *Canto de Entrada* from the *Misa Campesina*, celebrating God as one of the working people. Following that came the *Kyrie,* in which Christ is bid to be in solidarity with the oppressed. Throughout the performance they held hands, unified and transfixed by the music. At the end of the performance, the audience was invited to sing the anthem of the Revolution, *Nicaragua, Nicaraguita*, and the air reverberated with hearty voices declaring Nicaragua a beautiful flower watered with the blood of Diriangen, an indigenous leader who had fought the conquistadors. With the Triumph of the Revolution, Nicaragua was proclaimed in the song as a country free from dictatorship and foreign domination.

The spiritual power of the music had claimed the lovers who returned to the car in silence knowing and fearing that their diversionary love affair had become something more significant.

CHAPTER ELEVEN

A nita Guadeloupe de Aguilar patted her stomach feeling the churning of new life. She imagined the baby as Ernesto's even though that was not possible; they had not yet made love, not for want of desire, but for want of opportunity and place.

Long ago Anita had lost all feeling for Renaldo. They lived in stony silence, separated by the walls of his drinking and womanizing. Life equaled ongoing frustration, punctured by turbulence whenever his mistress, the *Negra* Patricia from the Atlantic Coast, came to them for money. Then an agitated Anita lashed out at Renaldo so loudly that neighbors commented, "The *costeana* is at the Aguilar house."

At such times Renaldo would sweep Patricia and her child toward the shower hut where they waited until Anita had calmed enough for Renaldo to bring them food and put them on a bus for Managua. He would join them later at the shack in the Mercado Oriental from which he occasionally sold charcoal.

Anita hated that woman who claimed the little girl Raquel with the tiny round face crowned by the tight curls of Africa was Renaldo's child. The child was almost four, a year younger than Camilo. She had been conceived after Camilo's birth when Anita had refused to satisfy Renaldo's voracious sexual appetite. She wanted no more children with a man she did not love or respect.

She supposed Renaldo had met Patricia during one of his drunken binges when he would disappear for days, then reappear, stumbling over the roads of San Linda, shirtless and shoeless, and vomiting into bushes. Anita especially despised him during those times. Once she went to see a witch from the Miskito tribe who sold herbs that made a drunk violently ill, enough to stop drinking immediately. The witch frightened her with her bulging black eyes and scratchy parrot voice. Even so Anita bought the herbs, chopped them into a fine powder, and put them into Renaldo's rum bottle. After drinking from it, he groaned and moaned, curling himself into a fetal position, clutching his stomach. When he coughed up blood Anita began to worry, but if he died, she would not care, except for the damnation to hell that would befall her for murdering him. She didn't want to go to hell, just to be rid of Renaldo. He recovered, and the memory of that terrible sickness kept him away from the bottle for over a year.

The unfortunate child of Patricia clung to her mother's skirt, looking up at Anita with dark plaintive eyes, while her mother, who always reeked of rum, demanded money to feed Renaldo's daughter. Anita knew that any money that woman managed to beg or steal went for rum even when the child was hungry. She would give Raquel a hunk of bread, and the poor girl devoured it like a hungry animal, but Patricia never extracted a *centavo* from Anita.

Once Renaldo suggested they take Raquel into their home. Anita knew women who were raising the children of their husband's mistresses, but she refused to raise another woman's child because of her man's stupidity. Still the sad little girl remained in her mind, a loathsome weight of guilt.

One night when Renaldo was especially nice and Anita was especially needy she broke her vow to never sleep with him again. Now, here she was at twenty-three, pregnant and stuck with Renaldo. But not for long. She would leave him, and when she did, she hoped he would go to Patricia and care for their little girl. As lazy and stupid as he was, he would never allow a child of his to starve or be without a place to lay her head at night. That part of her plan alleviated guilt over separating the boys Hernández and Camilo from their father.

Her plan for the leaving took shape slowly. The new life she fantasized for herself made every day bearable. The arrival of the American women made the plan possible, and the promise of Ernesto Flores made it worth the risk. The minute she laid eyes on him, Anita knew with pulse-pounding certainty that he would be her man.

At the Casa Sánchez, Ernesto had immediately recognized Anita as the pudgy, spirited, and cheerful young girl he remembered from the dangerous days of the Insurrection. He often saw her alone, then whipping around Managua in a faded yellow dress with big pockets, filled he knew, with communiqués for revolutionary militants hidden in obscure places around the city. He too had been a messenger for the rebels, but unlike Anita, he had carried a gun. Boys were always more suspect than girls and were more likely to be stopped by Somoza's National Guard. Later after the Triumph Ernesto was surprised to learn she had married Renaldo Aguilar, well known among the militants as a slacker.

Ernesto knew of the family of Anita Guadeloupe. They owned a small store selling bread, pastries, and *leche agria*, the popular sour milk snack, along with combs, soap, school notebooks, and whatever they could get to sell after 1985 when America imposed a trade embargo. At the back of their long block building, the family lived in a three-room apartment with running water and an indoor toilet. Even though they were located at the edge of one of Managua's poorest neighborhoods, Barrio Hermosa, they were not poor; not like the beggars that hounded Anita's mother with their daily incursions into the shop. Ernesto's mother, Rosita, told him that Señora Lillian Palacios de Guadeloupe, although often a disagreeable woman, generously passed out tortillas to the bothersome beggars before she chased them away.

During the rebellion, Anita's father Iván fought side by side with Ernesto's father Mario in the north of the country near the city of Estelí. When the rebels captured Estelí on their way to Managua, Somoza sent planes of death to bomb them out of existence. The outgunned rebels shot back with simple rifles or pistols, and although in the end they were not driven away, death came to Iván when he led terrified civilians to safety within the stone walls of a local church as the bombs fell. Ernesto's father had informed Iván's widow Lillian of her husband's heroism while shedding unashamed tears.

Eleven-year-old Anita delivered her communiqués, her dress always dirty from hiding in bushes or between buildings when she was on the move. The ever-present National Guard paid little attention to the grimy girl undistinguishable from other poor children in Managua. The communiqués were given to Anita by Renaldo, a pseudo-customer at the Guadeloupe store. Anita's mother Lillian did not like or trust Renaldo who claimed to be a Sandinista militant, but never seemed to see any action, but to an eleven-year-old, he was a brave soldier fighting for the freedom of his people.

Those were dangerous, exhilarating days. Lillian forbade Anita to leave the house after June 10, when the Sandinistas called for a general strike against the Somoza government, but she did anyway, mingling with people on the streets, chanting *Viva Nicaragua! Viva el Frente Sandinista!* The entire city rose up against Somoza and people streamed into the streets like ants. Gunfire crackled everywhere. Anita kept low to the ground, sometimes crawling, but not wanting to miss history in the making. Renaldo, her protector, remained with her all day, taking her home when night fell.

"It won't be long now before we kill the bastards!" he exclaimed, and she knew he was right when she heard that US citizens were being evacuated. After a few days, Managua quieted down, but the revolutionaries soon surrounded the city. On July 19, 1979 - the day of the Triumph - the revolutionaries took over what had been the Somoza government.

Following the Triumph, Anita joined the Sandinista Youth and completed secondary school, Renaldo returned to his wife and children in San Linda, and a relieved Lillian set about running the store alone. When Anita was sixteen, the Sandinistas recognized her quick intelligence and offered to send her abroad to be trained as a medical technician in East Germany. Lillian was thrilled. Her daughter's future was filled with promise.

Then Anita met Renaldo again at the Mercado Oriental where he was selling charcoal. The euphoria of their shared militancy during the Insurrection surged through her. When he claimed that his wife had fled to Costa Rica with the children because he had been wounded in the leg during the last days of the Insurrection she believed him.

"She does not want to live with a cripple," he said ruefully. Pity filled Anita. What a terrible blow for a man who had suffered so much for the Revolution.

Her mother forbade her to see Renaldo. "He is too old for you, and everyone knows he is lazy."

"He was wounded during the fighting and deserted by his family. He has suffered, *Mamá*. We are friends, nothing more."

Lillian snorted. "Friends? That man wants a mistress not a friend. I forbid you to see him."

Anita's rebellious spirit prompted her to slip away to be with Renaldo, trusting him as she had as a child in the chaos of those terrible yet wonderful days when Managua fell. Soon she became pregnant. A furious Lillian confined her to the store and sent her two older brothers to confront Renaldo.

"You have ruined your future!" her mother screamed. "They will never send you to study with a child."

Anita slipped out to warn Renaldo before her brothers could find him, and together they went to the house of his sister Olga in San Linda. Soon the truth in her mother's warning overtook and demoralized Anita. Renaldo lived from one disaster to another, mostly due to his inability to keep his pants zipped and his lips sealed from the rum. He wasn't even a good Sandinista, skipping party meetings and taking his responsibilities lightly. Even his leg wound was not a war injury. She learned at a party meeting that he had been hit by a bus during a drinking spree. No wonder that Renaldo's wife had deserted him.

Renaldo's sister Olga resented their presence in her small house and the obligation of supporting them. Renaldo brought home a few córdobas occasionally from selling charcoal at the Mercado Oriental, but not enough for their support. When he was drinking, days would pass before he returned to San Linda, broke and filthy. It fell on Anita to change their circumstances, and with one child to care for and another on the way, she felt trapped in a web of her own weaving. Only a lively imagination of what life might become kept her going.

One day she saw Francisco Sánchez as she was buying vegetables at a small store across the street from the Casa Sánchez, a house he owned and rented to foreigners, and she remembered that he had been a friend to her father. Screwing up courage, she asked him for a job.

"Anita Guadeloupe, you were one of our best child messengers," he declared. "And I remember your father, a hero in Estelí. You will never be without work as long as I am alive."

Sánchez hired Renaldo and her to work at the Casa Sánchez, which was the nicest house in the village. Her greatest fear was that Señor Sánchez would one day sell the house to Nicaraguans. Americans and Canadians always paid better than Europeans who occupied the house, and they all paid better than some Nicaraguans who expected hard work for little recompense. Within a year, Anita bought a three-room shanty with the money she and Renaldo had earned across the dirt road from the Casa Sánchez, but out of sight deep in the woods. Anita knew how to save, a trait taught to her by her merchant parents, and she never allowed Renaldo to get his hands on their money. She hired Olga to care for the boys allowing her sister-in-law to reduce her trips into Managua for work cleaning the houses of affluent Nicaraguans and foreigners.

Every day Anita said her Rosary, giving thanks to Mother Mary for sending the American *señoras* to the Casa Sánchez. The house was easy to clean; she especially liked the large *pila*, spacious enough to store laundry on one side and with grooves so deep for scrubbing that washing clothes hardly seemed like work. She could scrub an entire week's clothing in one morning. Señora Evita complemented her on the speed with which she did the laundry and Señora Ana raved over the bread and pastries she made for them. Although Anita was disappointed that they did not want her to cook all their meals, she felt valued by the women, especially Señora Evita who loved her two boys like a doting aunt and took Camilo to the Baptist Hospital to see the asthma doctors. And even though Señora Evita was aware of Renaldo's thirst for rum, she had never mentioned it. Anita prayed to the Virgin that the *señoras* would never see him drunk.

As her twenty-fourth birthday neared, Anita decided to have a birthday party and invite her employers for supper to taste her specialty of *chicharrón,* fried pork skin with chopped potatoes, rice, and tomato in a tortilla. They would be impressed, and she would inform them of her plan to break free of Renaldo and ask for their help.

The Saturday before her birthday, Anita boarded the bus into Managua leaving Renaldo at home with the boys and a lie that she had been urgently summoned by her mother who was not well. Unlike most workers, including maids, her workweek was five days instead of the customary six, as the generous *señoras* insisted she spend the entire weekend with her family. The doors of the bus heaved open and she boarded feeling nervous tremors in her legs. This would be a momentous trip. Today she would meet Ernesto's parents.

The bus dropped her at the entrance to Barrio Monsignor Lezcano where Ernesto lived with his parents and younger sisters near his father's bicycle repair shop. Ernesto, named after Ernesto Che Guevara, his father's hero, worked for Señor Sánchez only when he was not working at the shop. He had prepared his parents for Anita's arrival with some trepidation, especially his father, still he knew *Papá* would accept her eventually because she was the daughter of Iván Guadeloupe. Nonetheless, Ernesto would have to assure his father he would continue working in the bicycle repair shop, and he would never be taken away as had his older brother during the Insurrection. Most of all, he would have to assure his father that Renaldo would not harm him. Men were killed for liaisons with the women of other men, but Renaldo was skinny and weak and Ernesto did not fear him.

"I killed a *Somozista guardia* when I was eleven," he confided in Anita. "I wanted to kill anyone in the National Guard of Somoza so bad I dreamed of it, but when I saw the blood spurt from the hole in the guard's head and his body convulse, I vomited. I never wanted to do it again. Then they took away my older brother. My mother cried and cried and cried, and I wanted revenge. I joined the rebels to fight when I was thirteen. My mother begged me not to go. My father was fighting in the North and when my brother was taken away I was the only male left in the house."

"And you killed again?" asked Anita.

"*Sí,* I killed many. After a while, it was easy to kill - too easy."

"That is the bad thing about war. It is easy to kill and hate and hard to forget," Anita sighed.

"Yes, it is hard to forget. After the Triumph, we never found my brother, not even his body. My father fell into deep sadness. I took my brother's place in the bicycle repair shop. When the Sandinista Army drafted me to fight the Contras, I prayed for my life, not because I am a coward, but because I did not want my mother and father to lose me too."

"You are a good son. I will not take you away from your parents. I promise this," said Anita. She loved him because he shared himself in words - uncommon for a Nicaraguan man. She loved his muscular body, his thick black hair, the blazing brightness of his dark eyes, the way he looked at her longingly. Memories of the old days flooded them during their too brief meetings over coffee at the *cafetín* in the Mercado Roberto Huembes in Managua. They spoke of their hopefulness after the Triumph, their struggles during the Contra War, and the difficulty of the present.

"I will leave Renaldo," she told him, "but there is a child coming."

Doubt flashed across Ernesto's face, and her insides twisted in panic. After an interminable few moments, he said bravely, "I will accept this child as mine."

It was then, she realized she needed to meet his parents and assure them they had nothing to fear with her in his life. She wanted to tell them how much she loved Ernesto. She wanted to tell them she would cherish him forever.

Anita entered the bicycle repair shop pausing at the doorway nervously biting the nail of her thumb. Ernesto spied her and jogged over to place his arm around her waist. An older man, a little heavier than Ernesto with the same full black head of hair and broad face, scowled in her direction. He held a wrench in one hand and grasped the handlebars of a bicycle with the other. A graying wisp of a woman hovered behind him.

Anita's eyes swept over the clutter in the shop. Bicycle parts littered the concrete floor and intact bikes lay carelessly against a dingy cement wall. She raised her head confidently as side-by-side she and Ernesto approached his parents.

"My son tells me who you are. How is your mother?" Mario Flores asked sternly.

"She is fine, as are my brothers. The family does well with the store in Barrio Hermosa."

"*Bueno.* Iván can rest in peace."

"I am going to visit the store after I leave here, Señor Flores. I want Ernesto to meet my mother." Anita's eyes darted to the *señora* of the house. The woman cracked a thin smile from a mournful face and Anita acknowledged it with a nod.

"What will your mother say when you bring Ernesto and not your husband?" asked Flores ignoring Anita's gesture toward his wife. His voice was scratchy from a wound he had received in the neck during the Insurrection.

Anita smiled. "She will be happy. She has never liked Renaldo and has never allowed him in her house or store."

The older man shook his head with displeasure. "Did you defy your family for him?"

Anita lowered her eyes. "*Sí.*"

"The foolishness of youth," Flores spat. He moved closer to Anita probing her with suspicious cold eyes. "So now you want my son to leave his family and take care of your children." The tone was edgy, the body rigid, and he had balled his fists as though to fight. Ernesto grasped her hand protectively and his father shot him a glance of steel.

"Never," Anita declared.

"Then what?" he asked.

"I want to open a *pulpería* in San Linda like the one my mother has in Barrio Hermosa.

The older man nodded. "Go on."

Anita knew Mario Flores was threatened by her relationship with his remaining son. He had given his other son to the Revolution. She had given her father. They had suffered grievous loss, as had the silent woman inching forward, her small hand raised to gently touch her husband's arm. Anita chose her words carefully. "I will ask the American women who live in the

Casa Sánchez to ask Señor Sánchez for the use of the shack he owns near the village school. The Americans are my employers and I know they will help me. The shack was used for secret Sandinista meetings during the days of Somoza, and later for a store that sold vegetables. No one uses it now."

Mario Flores studied her intensely. She was fearless, a quality he had admired in the women who fought by his side during the Insurrection. But the use for such women was over. He and his family were safe now in the world behind the walls of their bicycle repair shop.

Anita continued, "I will also ask the American women I work for to loan me money to buy a refrigerator, and my mother will help me to find things to sell. The Canadian priest from the San Juan el Bautista Primary School comes to her store and has known me since I was a little girl. He helps people. He pays for many children in Barrio Hermosa to go to school. He gives them pencils and notebooks. He gives loans to their parents to buy things to sell on the street. Maybe he will help me buy snacks and school supplies for my store. With a refrigerator, I can sell soda and juice and ice cream and cheese and *leche agria*."

Mario crossed his arms and shifted on his feet, spreading them apart. He stood before her like the cement walls of his shop and demanded again, "So what do you want of my Ernesto?"

Anita put her hands on her hips and leaned toward him. Ernesto shot her a look of caution, his body taut. Like him, this woman had been honed by war and would not be intimidated. "I want him to help me prepare the shack for the *pulpería*. I will run it alone. Ernesto must stay here with you and keep his job with Señor Sánchez. I would never ask him to leave. I promise you, Señor Flores." Anita paused and looked at Ernesto's mother adding in a more gentle tone, "I promise you too, Señora Rosita. I love Ernesto and I would never make him choose between you and me."

"I believe you," said the woman Rosita, speaking for the first time.

Flores grunted. Anita could have inherited the business acumen of her mother. She had a certainty and confidence usually found in men. But there was the problem of the husband and children. "You have two sons, Ernesto tells me."

"*Sí*. Two sons, seven and five," Anita said. "And another child in my belly."

Mario looked surprised. "Another in your belly?" he repeated.

Anita looked at Ernesto and lowered her head, hoping he would surmise Ernesto was the father. She knew this was wrong and so did Ernesto, yet he did not contradict her. Rosita Flores slapped her palm over her mouth to squelch what, from the starburst in her previously lifeless eyes, would have been a cry of joy had she dared to utter it. Mario looked as though a bullet had hit him. Those days of terror in Estelí were locked inside him, and terrible melodramas about the liaison of his son and this cherub-faced woman played in his head: Ernesto could be taken from him forever, killed by a jealous husband. His jaw clenched and his cheek muscles bulged with the fierceness of these thoughts. Fascinated, Anita watched the arteries throbbing in his neck. He audibly gulped like a drowning man before he spoke again.

"And what will your husband do to you, the mother of his children, who is carrying another man's child in her womb? What will he do to my son?" he asked, his voice quavering slightly.

"My husband is a coward, Señor Flores," Anita responded softly. "When I leave he will threaten me, but then he will get drunk and send for his woman from the Atlantic Coast. They have a girl child. Renaldo's sister Olga lives in Lower San Linda. I will ask my employers to hire Olga to take my place in Casa Sánchez, so she will allow Renaldo and his woman to live with her. I give Olga a little money to take care of my sons when I am working for the Americans, but she has always wanted to work at Casa Sánchez. I will find another woman to care for my sons when I am working."

Flores squeezed his temples, reluctantly admiring Anita for the thoroughness of her plans. *She is a smart one,* he thought. But in spite of the assurances of her husband's cowardice, he remained apprehensive about Renaldo whom he knew had been a Sandinista militant during the Insurrection. He lowered his hand to glare at her again. "I warn you, if any harm comes to Ernesto from your husband, I will kill him and you," he threatened between clenched teeth.

"Papá!" Ernesto objected swiveling his body between his father and the woman he loved. Anita reached forward and placed her hand on Ernesto's arm to draw him away. He stepped back allowing her to meet the conflicted eyes of the older man, more frightened than hostile. There was no fear in her eyes, and Flores blinked and turned away. The child messenger had grown into a strong woman, the true daughter of Lillian Palacios and Iván Guadeloupe.

"Señor Flores, I will not fail you," Anita promised.

The shoulders of Mario Flores relaxed, and a tremor of relief passed across Ernesto's face. With a rush of tenderness he reached for Anita's hand, and the couple left the bicycle repair shop to catch a bus to the store of Lillian Palacios de Guadeloupe at the edge of Barrio Hermosa. As they watched them walk away, Mario and Rosita noted Anita's strong body, the firmness of step, concluding that the woman would produce many fine grandsons.

"Your mother said little," Anita observed when they were out of earshot.

"She is happy. She wants grandchildren."

Anita smiled knowingly.

Ernesto hailed an American school bus lettered Bridgetown Central School District, one of many buses donated to Nicaragua during the Sandinista era. Its creaky doors heaved open and they climbed aboard, their faces radiant. Once seated, they pressed hip to hip, hands interlocked, while the bus rumbled up the Avenida Bolivar, passing the large black silhouette of Sandino commanding the Loma de Tiscapa. This hill was the site of Somoza's palace and prison where revolutionaries were said to be tortured and killed. A priest in the Sandinista government had placed the steel statue there to remind Nicaraguans of the country's proud history of defying oppressors.

Anita and Ernesto were aware of the horrific events that had occurred at the site. Some who died there were not revolutionaries at all, but just unfortunate, like Ernesto's brother, singled out because he looked old enough to fight. Perhaps the remains of young Mario rested in that place among the bones of so many others that had disappeared.

A wave of emotion swept over the couple. They had been through so much. They had endured the blood of the Insurrection, and following the Triumph, seen their dreams of a better life fall victim to the Contra War. Finally there was peace, but at a terrible cost.

"*Sandino, presente,*" uttered Ernesto quietly.

"*Sandino, presente,*" repeated Anita. They squeezed their hands together until their fingers turned white.

When they arrived at the store, Lillian was hooting like a hyena at a joke Padre Doug had just finished telling. He always sent Lillian into spasms of laughter with his crude jokes. He spoke with a gringo accent in a tobacco-roughened voice, running his words together, and demanding full attention if he was to be understood.

Because the San Juan el Bautista Primary School was only a few blocks away, there were always customers at Lillian's store. In addition much to her delight, the priest drew visitors from Canada and America like flies to honey. These visitors bought the sweets she baked every morning and yogurt to soothe stomachs unaccustomed to Nicaragua's bacteria.

Lillian had never known a priest with so many contradictions: a jolly old man with a love for drink and tobacco and curse words, yet legendary for his generosity. Had he been younger she would have attempted to seduce him. At forty-seven, she was still bursting with life and she had enjoyed the juices of a few men, including priests, since Iván's death.

Financially well off for a working woman, Lillian was the respected, honored, and sometimes feared *Mamá* of the neighborhood and scoffed in derision at Nicaraguan women who groveled at the feet of their men. Even upper class women were not immune to such groveling. With the exception of Iván, the love of her life, she dismissed Nicaraguan men, her own sons included as users of women, and she refused to allow any man to use her. She knew Padre Doug admired her. He often complemented her on her good humor and her quick, perceptive mind. She was a survivor, and more importantly, she was unafraid to be unique. He told her she dressed like an extravagant shop window in Toronto. That afternoon she was wearing a brassy red shift sprinkled with white triangles, and a gaudy collection of pseudo silver rings covered her fingers.

When the young couple entered the shop, Lillian's mouth fell open. "Anita!" she exclaimed.

Padre Doug rotated toward the couple as Lillian trilled again, "*Anita, mi hija!*" lunging at her daughter and swooping her into hefty arms. Her body was not unlike Anita's, only larger, and they shared the same curly black hair that sat wig-like upon their heads.

"*Mucho gusto*," Padre Doug said kissing Anita's cheeks once her mother had released her.

Anita gently nudged Ernesto toward them. He smiled shyly, an expression of uncertainty on his face. "This is Ernesto Flores, *Mamá,* the son of Mario Flores who fought with *Papá* in Estelí," Anita announced.

Lillian covered her cheeks with her hands.

"*Dios mío!* Mario! He told me how your *Papá* died. *Bienvenido*, Ernesto." She flung herself at Ernesto, and he stood rooted in place, looking bewildered by her ferocious embrace.

Realizing he was intruding, Padre Doug said *adiós* and started to leave, but not before asking Anita to deliver his greetings to the *señoras*. She loved his evening visits to Casa Sánchez when he and they talked and laughed and sang *la musica de protesta*.

"*Por supuesto*," promised Anita.

Lillian shouted for the family to greet Anita and her new friend. The couple were quickly surrounded, hugged, and kissed until Lillian shooed away the assortment of relatives and led the pair into a back room where she kept her records, some supplies, and a small cot. Settling her bulk into a chair, she motioned to Ernesto and Anita to sit on the cot where she studied them, surmising they were in love.

Ah, this is good. The son of Mario Flores. But it is good only if Anita has dumped that fool. Thinking of Renaldo raised a swirl of angry emotion within her. She exhaled a little gasp. "How are my grandsons, Anita?" she asked, keeping the conversation neutral until Anita told her what was going on.

"They are well. Camilo coughs with the asthma, but Señora Evita gets medicine for him, *Mamá,* and he is better."

"*Gracias a Dios.* You have a birthday soon. Will you visit us on your birthday?"

"No. I cannot on that day. On my birthday, I will invite the *Americanas* to my house for a fiesta. I will cook *chicharrón* the way you do, *Mamá.*"

"*Bueno*," said Lillian. It was time to mention Ernesto.

"Why do you bring this young man to visit us?" she asked, struggling to control her excitement.

"I have a plan, and I come to ask for your help. Ernesto will help me, and I am sure the *Americanas* will help too."

Anita explained her plan and when she had finished, Lillian's heart gyrated.

"A very good plan, my daughter," she declared clasping hands together as though in prayer at church. In spite of Lillian's many sins, Mother Mary had answered her prayers. Renaldo was to be dispatched, and Ernesto, the son of Mario Flores, would soon be in Anita's bed. The son of Mario Flores. *Caramba!* She could never have foreseen such a turn of events. She would get the money for the store supplies her daughter had requested, even if she had to ask Padre Doug for it. He would certainly assist Anita, but she would not ask him unless she had to. First, she would review her inventory and give Anita what she could.

"Such a good plan, *mi hija*, such a good plan!" she exclaimed over and over, unable to hide her glee.

Anita had not expected her mother to react so positively, except to Renaldo's departure. For her mother to overflow with optimism over a business plan that required the cooperation of Señor Sánchez, her employers, and, perhaps the old priest was a blessing.

"And, *Mamá,* I have more to tell you. You will soon be a grandmother again," she announced. An inner chill warned her not to associate Renaldo with the child.

Lillian thought she would burst. *"Gracias a Dios!"* she cried as she threw herself at them hugging first one, than the other, while chortling a stream of joyful phrases.

Neither Anita nor Ernesto told Lillian the child was Renaldo's, even though they knew she assumed it was Ernesto's.

CHAPTER TWELVE

Evelyn was fond of Anita and her precious children, especially shy, sickly, and precocious Camilo, the more vulnerable of the two. The boys were well behaved and loving, a tribute to Anita, the backbone of the family. For her birthday, Evelyn purchased a cotton twill sundress in burnished gold at an upscale shop recently opened by returnees from Miami. But Anita's exuberance over chocolate called for more.

Leaving behind Managua, Evelyn drove toward a store specializing in imported goods for diplomats and others who could pay in dollars. It had been established in 1985 after the economic embargo by the United States and its presence during that era had made easier the lives of foreigners living in Nicaragua who had access to dollars and for Nicaraguans fortunate enough to acquire them by whatever means. As it was in the same direction as San Linda, Evelyn was relieved that Garner would pick up Anne that day, thus saving her another trip into the center of Managua. A creeping uneasiness still lay heavily on her heart when she thought of Anne's lover. As Padre Doug had said, Garner's presence would eventually present Anne with a painful and perhaps life-altering choice, one she had not expected to face in Nicaragua.

At the gated compound to the store, a uniformed guard checked Evelyn's residency card and license although he knew her from many years of patronage. The concrete building, unimaginative and ugly was smeared with a patina of mud splashed up by the recent hard-driving rains. It was May and the rainy season was upon them; the dust of the dry season had given way to the expected torrents of rainfall bringing mud, heavier humidity, and more insects. Inside the store, a hot, wet haze stifled the air. Looking around, Evelyn sighted only four customers. Not long ago, the place had swarmed with diplomats and other foreigners. Now the store was an anachronism in a Nicaragua that had opened its economy to foreign corporate businesses and investment and flooded its markets with imported goods from America. Foreign diplomats and others, along with Managuans with money now shopped at the air-conditioned American style supermarkets, sprouting in Managua like bananas on banana palms.

Evelyn snatched a tin of cookies from Holland, a box of Swiss chocolates, and five chocolate candy bars from Belgium before proceeding to La Torta Sabrosa, the best bakery in Managua. An admitted chocolate addict, Evelyn salivated at the sight of the waves of silky dark icing on the chocolate layer cake as she carried it to her truck and eased it into a carton to cushion it on the deteriorating highway to Lower San Linda. All the way home she hugged the shoulder of the road as the truck droned up into the golden hills of the Managua Sierra greening more and more with each deluge of rain, her ears sensitive to any shifting of Anita's birthday cake cushioned in the carton. The cake must survive without so much as an infinitesimal smudge to its perfectly frosted chocolate glory.

Thirty minutes later she eased off the highway onto Lower San Linda's unpaved road. Suddenly the clamor of an engine hurtled toward her. Her blood pressure rose like a spouting geyser as the blur of a motorcycle rocketed by lightly scraping the side-view mirror. She slammed on the brakes and a screeching reverberated through the air. Earth shivered under the tires as the truck shimmered to a stop centimeters from the still moving motorcycle in front of her.

"You fool!" she screamed, her heart thumping in her ribcage. The blurred figure on the bike sputtered to a stop, swung off his rotund body, and approached the truck. Evelyn glowered at the burly man, shirtless, barrel chested, his hair a tangle of wooly brown-gray spattered with mud. He was trouble, and she took a deep calming breath before she spoke. *"Está bien, Señor? Está herido?"* she asked, disciplining her voice to maintain control.

He stretched out thick-fingered hands palms up and placed them flat on the door of the truck as he spoke to her through the open window in English. "I'm not a believer, but something up there saved me." He jerked his head upward toward the sky and Evelyn saw that his gray sweatpants had slipped down revealing dark crotch hair.

"You took a chance passing me like that. You could have flipped your bike," she stated with controlled fury.

He stared at her through squinty blood-shot eyes set in a drinker's veined face filmed in sweat. "Nah, not my time," he said, projecting a sour breath in her direction. She winced and turned her head away.

Shooting a beefy hand through the window, he introduced himself, "Harry Albert." She brushed the hand with her fingertips.

"Evita Gutiérrez," she replied withdrawing from the aborted handshake. He wiped the hand on his sweatpants as though he could sense her revulsion.

"You live around here, Evita?"

"Yes."

He picked at some mud splatter in his hair. "I just moved into the Casa López on the hill near the woods on this side of San Linda. Where're you from?" She identified his drawl as American South.

"I live here."

"No, I mean in the States. You're not Nicaraguan. You have a Spanish name and you look a little Latina, but I know Nicaraguans, and lady, you're not Nicaraguan. You from Canada?"

"No. Massachusetts."

"I'm from South Carolina but haven't lived there since I got back from Nam. I lived in Jamaica for twelve years. I was the only white face in a sea of black faces. I liked the life but got sick of being robbed all the time, so I left and came to Nicaragua. In the States, life's too restrictive. Did you know that America, Germany, Japan, and Sweden consider themselves successes? But what is success? Germany has the highest teenage suicide rate in the world, America is second. Sweden has the highest adult suicide rate in the world, Japan is second. Not success at all. Not at all." He spoke like a machine gun, gesturing wildly. Was he hallucinating?

"Are you sure you're okay?"

"Nothing wrong with me that a cold beer and some good conversation wouldn't fix." He raised thick eyebrows in mock suggestiveness.

Another crazy foreigner seeking escape in a poor country. "We should move our vehicles," Evelyn suggested.

Harry Albert looked up the road. "No cars, no hurry," he declared. "Are you a missionary?"

"No."

"Good. Religion. Bunch of shit." He spat on the ground.

"If you will kindly move your motorcycle, Mr. Albert, I need to get home," Evelyn insisted in a forceful tone.

He grunted. "You call me Harry, hear?" he commanded, shooting a forefinger in her direction. With a push against the truck that rocked it like a canoe on soft waves, he rotated on his flip-flops, and lumbered back to the motorcycle. Mounting, he tossed an enigmatic smile at Evelyn, and took off with a vroom.

As he roared up the road, two of Anita's chickens wandered into his path. Evelyn heard a pitiful squawk, and Albert whooped, raising his right hand in a V.

Children playing nearby immediately summoned Anita and she had bounded onto the road when Evelyn reached her and maneuvered her truck around two bloodied chicken carcasses. Anita snatched the smashed chickens by their claws, splattering their blood on her apron.

"A crazy American. He has moved into Casa López," Evelyn explained as she opened her gate.

Anita shrugged her shoulders in a, "that's life" gesture. "I boil the chickens for soup."

"*Claro*. When Anne and Gregory arrive, we will come over. I will bring lemonade and the cake."

"*Gracias, Señora Evita*. You will like my *chicharrón*. It is the best in all Nicaragua, except for the *chicharrón* of my *mamá*." Blood from the dangling chickens continued dribbling down the apron and Anita wiped it away with the back of her hand. "I have something special to tell you tonight," she added breathlessly and hurried off.

Evelyn drove through the gate and parked. Then she snatched a rag from the trunk and wiped the hand smudges of Harry Albert off the door. When she looked at the cake, one side was flattened but she thought she could repair the damage. Carefully she carried the wounded cake into the house and settled it on the dining table after which she snatched a cold beer from the fridge and flung herself into a rocker where she tried to dispel her anger.

Later when Anne and Gregory arrived, the three American guests strolled across the road, Gregory carefully carrying the precious cake, which had been restored to the best of Evelyn's ability, and Anne tugging a shopping bag of lemonade and gifts. Evelyn led the way, her guitar slung over her shoulder and vase of freshly picked poinsettias in her hand. Gingerly they pushed through bushes and swiped at low-hanging fronds negotiating roots, rocks and ruts, until they reached the trampled path leading to the small dilapidated three-room plank house of Anita Guadeloupe and Renaldo Aguilar nestled among tall palms.

Hernández bounded like a jackrabbit toward them with Camilo skipping after him coughing. Evelyn handed the vase of flowers to Anne and swept Camilo into her arms. As he snuggled against her chest, an unexpected bounty of tears brimmed in her eyes. She wiped them away before climbing the uneven steps of the creaky porch fronting the tiny Aguilar home.

"Do you need more medicine for Camilo?" Evelyn asked Anita.

"*Sí.*"

"When you are low, you must let me know so that I can get it at the Baptist Hospital. It is scarce sometimes."

Anita nodded. "We go to Medsalud in Managua once a week for his shots," she said defensively.

"But did not the doctor say he needed the liquid medicine too?"

"*Sí,*" said Anita.

"Then you must let me get it for you before you run out."

"*Claro,* "said Anita lowering her head like a chastised child.

"Anything I can do to help?" Evelyn asked regretting the sharpness in her voice.

Anita brightened. "I do everything," she answered proudly.

Gregory maneuvered around animal droppings as Anne and he approached the house, his eyes fastening on a pig waddling near the latrine in one corner of the yard. The rancid stench of pig and chicken droppings unearthed unpleasant memories of his boyhood on the farm in Georgia, and he wrinkled his nose and scowled. When he caught Hernández staring, he attempted a thin, albeit unconvincing smile, and the usually outgoing Hernández looked at him warily. The boy snatched Anne's arm pulling her away from him and toward the house.

"I think he's jealous of you, Greg," Anne laughed.

Chickens followed the guests into the house, clucking and fluttering their wings from time to time as though to chase the human occupants away. Anita hugged and kissed her guests. Anne placed the bottle of lemonade on the table, stored the gifts behind the front door, and directed Gregory to take the cake into the kitchen. A rough wooden table and four chairs filled a narrow space opposite the front door. The chairs looked unsteady, one tilting crookedly. Anita invited them to sit down.

"I made the chairs and the table," announced Renaldo proudly.

"Good work," Gregory lied.

A clean bed sheet, yellow with age, served as tablecloth. On it was the vase of poinsettias that Evelyn had picked.

Anita seated Anne near a back partition that separated sleeping quarters from the living area. The humid heat mixed with a pungent odor of human bodies and food agitated Anne's stomach. Feeling trapped in the insufferably close room with her back against the wall, she shrilled in a high-pitched voice, "Anita makes delicious bread and brings it to us for breakfast, Greg. Would you like to see the oven where she bakes it?"

The strangeness of her comment and its tonal elevation startled Gregory. Noting the red blotches on her cheeks, he reached over the table and laid a calming hand on her arm. Anita, oblivious to Anne's distress, beamed at the compliment.

"Come, I show you," she said to her guests and they followed her into the kitchen, a step down from the living area. Unlike the uneven concrete floors in the rest of the house, the kitchen floor was dirt. Smoke from a cooking fire curled around them like enveloping fog, and Anne could hear Camilo coughing behind her. Gregory's eyes fell on the slow burning wood glowing in the fire pit next to a tall potbellied clay oven. Behind the pit and oven was half a wall open to the yard. The fire pit was a typical Nicaraguan stove constructed of large rocks topped by a grate. One simmering pot on the grate contained the recently killed chickens and another, rice for their *chicharrón*.

Anita opened the ponderous oven door and pointed inside. "I build a wood fire," she explained. "I shape dough into loaves and I place them on metal sheets." She pointed to two large metal trays resting against the oven. "When the oven is hot I put out the fire and scrape out the ashes. Then I put the bread into the oven to bake."

"You must use a lot of wood," Gregory said, aware of Nicaragua's disappearing forests.

"We have no money for gas," said Anita defensively. Then, she added with pride, "But my mother has a propane stove and many nice things." She looked up to a grouping of shelves over the pitted wooden worktable where Gregory had placed the cake carton. "I have some nice things too. Those are my things," she said.

Gifts from former residents of the Casa Sánchez occupied one shelf where an electric socket had been installed with a thick black electric wire slithering up the wall through a window like a snake until it reached the post delivering electricity to the house. The gifts included an electric blender, a hand mixer, and a cassette radio. Another shelf held plastic dishes, cups, and a few utensils. Anita owned three pots, plus a large frying pan. To the side of the shelves was the *pila*, its water hose meandering through a crack in the wood wall to the water spigot outside.

Following the kitchen tour, Anita led the group back into the living area and around the wall that had sent Anne into near panic. A double bed sided one wall and three shelves laden with family clothing sided the other. A small television was perched on one shelf. Evelyn surmised it was acquired from a dumpster in Managua, where people left their discards for the poor to pick over. An extension of the main bedroom, separated by a curtain, held twin beds for the boys.

The Aguilar family was poor working class. Malnutrition did not haunt their doorstep. With the hose, they had indoor water and they had electricity. They also slept in beds, not on the floor or in hammocks. Anita felt lucky to live in the open spaces of Lower San Linda, unlike her mother's house in Managua, which, although nicer, was hot and crowded.

When the group reseated themselves, Gregory assumed the back seat crunching his long legs under the table allowing Anne to take his seat in front of the door. Renaldo carried in two stools for the boys, and he and Anita stood.

The feast began. Anne detested the taste of the popular Nicaraguan dish *chicharrón*. The sight of fried pork skin turned her stomach, and she hoped Anita had washed the vegetables thoroughly. She swallowed the food and the bile rising in her throat simultaneously with a lemonade wash. Evelyn and Gregory appeared to thoroughly enjoy Anita's creation, and comments of *sabrosa* filled the room.

Evening fell and the living area darkened until its occupants looked like cartoon sketches. When the line between day and night disappeared and black swooped over the village, Anita whooshed the door shut to minimize the influx of insects. She turned on the one lamp in the living area, a bare bulb attached to a primitively carved tree branch. Gregory surmised that Renaldo had made that too.

Before the cake could be served, a sudden deluge pounded them with torrential fury, and not unexpectedly, the electricity succumbed to the storm's wrath. Unperturbed, Anita placed white fat utility candles on the table, and Gregory scrambled to light them with his cigarette lighter.

"Better for fingers than matches," he noted, referring to Nicaragua's short, thin wooden matches that burned fingers almost immediately upon striking. Rain sprinkling through a leaky roof extinguished the candles almost as fast as they were lit, giving Gregory an ongoing task. Water dribbled on them too but they welcomed its wetness.

"I want cake," proclaimed Camilo.

"*Por supuesto*, cake," declared Evelyn. "A little rain will not keep us from the cake." She snatched her flashlight and motioned to Anne to follow her into the dark kitchen where they lit birthday candles. Using the lid to one of Anita's pots to protect the cake from the rain, Evelyn carried it to the table.

"Anita, happy birthday!" everyone exclaimed, then burst into song.

Anne whipped out a camera to photograph Anita blowing out the candles. They feasted on the massive cake chatting like old friends. Evelyn shined her flashlight over the chocolate-smeared faces of Camilo and Hernández, and everyone laughed including the boys. When the last cake crumb had disappeared, the deluge stopped, and Evelyn brought out her guitar.

De Colores is a song of the beautiful colors around us in trees and flowers and birds and rainbows, she said to Anne and Gregory inviting all to sing along. Hernández squealed and clapped his sticky hands together as he bellowed the familiar song. He was accompanied by squeaky noises from Camilo. Anita laughed when Anne and Gregory tried to follow along. Renaldo made no effort to sing, but grinned at the others.

Following *De Colores,* Evelyn sang Nicaraguan folk songs, and Anne and Gregory joined in when they knew the words. Her sweet voice and the candle lulled the group into contentment. Anita hooked her feet around the rungs of the stool and drew little Camilo into her lap, closing her eyes and swaying her body to the music. Gregory and Anne pulled chairs away from the table and sat side by side where she slipped her hand through his arm and squeezed him to her. Renaldo leaned his emaciated body against a wall observing the subdued guests. As she sang, Evelyn studied him; at one time, sparks of idealism and bravery must have glowed within him. He had joined the Sandinista cause at a dangerous time and risked his life; yet whatever had once motivated him had long departed, replaced with jaded sullenness. He spoke in monosyllables, resisting Evelyn's attempts to know him better, and tonight was the first time she had seen him smile. What was going through his mind at that moment?

When electricity returned, Evelyn piled the gifts on the table.

"*Mucho*," Anita cried, bursting into tears as she tore at the wrapping of the dress box.

"*Muy, muy linda,* very pretty,*"* she choked, holding it lengthwise against her body and stroking it lovingly as though it were a child. Next she grasped the cookie tin, opening the lid to sniff the cookies inside and slamming it down before anyone asked for one. She wanted to savor them one by one over many weeks. She did not open the box of chocolates but sniffed it, and she counted the five candy bars.

"I want candy, I want candy," shouted Hernández. Anita broke off two pieces for Hernández and Camilo; then she offered them to her guests hoping they would decline, and they did, much to her delight.

"A beautiful dress and so many good things to eat," she stammered.

"Are you enjoying your party, Anita?" asked Evelyn.

"Sí, Señora, muchas gracias; muchisimas gracias!"

Gregory could not recall experiencing such happiness. Among this community of disparate people he felt strangely at home.

When it was time to leave, Anita insisted on walking with Evelyn, Anne, and Gregory to the Casa Sánchez. With hugs and kisses to the boys, the four left Renaldo behind, but he was not annoyed, believing she who had denied him so many times would welcome him tonight. He would settle the boys into their beds and wait with anticipation for her return. Life had been hard for Anita and him. She was a difficult woman, one who tried to boss him. Unlike other wives, she had no understanding of his need for other women. Her family claimed she was better than he was, and she probably thought so too. But tonight was different. Tonight would be good.

Anita and her guests smelled fresh-fallen rain that tickled their noses as they ploughed through the brush in the blackness parting sodden palm fronds and sopping bushes until they reached the muddy road. Earth softened from the downpour oozed like unbaked dough under their feet. Anne wanted to pull off her shoes fearing they would be ruined, but did not, more fearful of what lay in the mud. On the concrete walkway leading to the Casa Sánchez, they removed their shoes and toweled off mud-spattered legs as Anita scurried to make ice tea. Not until they were comfortably ensconced in rockers with glasses of ice tea, did Evelyn ask, "What have you to tell us, Anita, that Renaldo cannot hear?"

"I have to say *gracias* for all your kindness."

"Our pleasure. Now, tell us what is on your mind."

Anita stood before them, a nervous fluttering pricking her chest. She studied her feet reviewing the words she wanted to say, and when she felt confident, she said. "I have a plan and I ask for help." She outlined her plan for the business, prudently leaving out the part about Ernesto, Renaldo, and his sister Olga. Her audience was markedly still when she had finished, and she assumed the worst: they did not like it.

Gregory studied the young woman with frizzy hair and a face as round as a pie plate. Behind the innocent, friendly demeanor lay a shrewd, goal-oriented mind and the political acumen to achieve her goals. She had spotted an opportunity when Anne and Evelyn arrived at the Casa Sánchez and she was taking advantage of it. Extracting $300 American dollars from his wallet, he stood up, approached her, and shoved it into her hand. "This is my birthday present, Anita. Buy yourself a refrigerator. This country would fall apart without women like you."

Anita's mouth fell open, words failing her, a situation she seldom experienced. "*Gracias, Señor Gregorio,*" she sputtered, wiping away a tear with her apron. She had never expected such generosity and respect from the lover of Señora Ana.

"It is a thorough business plan, one that would make a professor of marketing at my college proud," added Anne.

Evelyn spoke next. "The store is a wonderful idea. I will speak to Señor Sánchez. I am sure he will charge you a small rent."

"*Bueno,*" said Anita.

"Now, explain about Ernesto," declared Evelyn. "What are you not telling us?"

Anita hesitated. They waited. "I will leave Renaldo," she lowered her voice as though Renaldo could hear from across the road. "I will ask him to go to the house of his sister Olga. Renaldo has another woman and a little girl. They are from the Costa Atlántica."

San Linda gossip had informed Evelyn about Patricia and her child, and the break-up was no surprise. "Does Renaldo know about this, Anita?"

"No."

Gregory whispered to Anne, "All evening Renaldo looked like a happy rooster awaiting his hen." She jabbed him good-humouredly.

Evelyn stood up to face Anita. "You are full of surprises, but I know you well enough to expect the best. We will miss you here, and we will help you financially." She wrapped her arms around her employee in an affectionate hug.

Anita swallowed the lump in her throat. She would remember this momentous day all of her life. She would remember every detail: the birthday party, the friendly chat in the dark, the enthusiasm with which they embraced her plan, and most of all, Señora Evita's respect for her abilities. She would not disappoint them.

"Thank you, Señora Evita," she whispered.

Before she left Anita made one last request of her benefactors. "Please keep Renaldo as your employee. If you ask Renaldo's sister, Olga, to work here she will say yes. She has always wanted to work at Casa Sánchez. And she works very hard."

Evelyn and Anne exchanged glances before Evelyn spoke. "We will interview her. We cannot promise to hire her, but we will keep Renaldo."

Anita hugged and kissed both women and Gregory. "*Estoy agradecido. I have good fortune.*"

As she made her way to the door Gregory declared in English, "That woman could run the government."

Later Anne and Gregory lay in each other's arms under mosquito netting, a necessity with the proliferation of insects during the rainy season. "Evelyn once told me the rainy season is the time when children die because the swarms of mosquitoes brought by the rains carry dengue fever and malaria," Anne said.

"Their immunities are compromised by this country's endemic poverty. Nicaragua is dangerous to anyone's health," commented Gregory.

"Especially now that health care for the poor is being abandoned."

Gregory placed a finger over her lips. "Let's leave politics alone for tonight," he whispered. He drew her toward him, but she wiggled away in spite of her desire.

"I want to talk."

"You are a tough woman," he sighed, falling back and covering his eyes with his arm.

She propped herself up on her elbow to look at him. "We have all night for sex."

"Sex? Is that all it is between us?" he asked. "The giving and taking of pleasure?"

The question hung in the air challenging her to think of something she was not ready to consider. She rubbed four fingers through her eyebrows. "I want to talk about Anita's plans."

"Fine," he responded, irritation in his voice. "She developed the plans thoroughly and a bit mercilessly. Renaldo will be angry, possibly dangerous." He paused. "How did you tell your husband you wanted to leave him?"

The question was disturbing. Her confrontation with Keith played like a film in her mind. After the twins had left for college there seemed to be nothing to talk about. One night when Keith had retreated to his study, she had knocked quietly on the door.

"It wasn't a surprise," Anne began. "We were both relieved to speak openly about what had been hidden for so long. I wanted to move on to another life. I think he did too although he never admitted it. A few months after our separation, he left his job with a local bank and accepted a job in New York City with an investment-banking firm. I think he's happier living in an apartment in New York. He never liked the responsibilities of suburban home ownership and neither did I. I always felt guilty that my house wasn't all that important to me, as if I couldn't live up to the American Dream."

Gregory laughed. "How unique you are," he said drawing her close. His eyes burned with wanting and her heart reacted, but she would not be deterred from her need for conversation.

"How did your marriage end? Another woman?" Gregory responded with such a boisterous laugh that Anne placed her hand over his mouth.

"My cousin is just across the hall."

"Your cousin hears every groan of pleasure that falls from our lips," he said.

She pointed her forefinger into his bare chest. "I asked you a question. Was it another woman?"

Gregory grew serious. "No. I made a promise to Kate when I married her, and loyalty is important to me, so I didn't play around," he said softly. "After we separated, I ate up women like a starving man, but not when I was living with Kate."

Gregory didn't want talk about it. The old life was gone, the present life bearable, and a possible future life with Anne held promise. Was it too soon to think of that? Was it possible she was his last hope for redemption? He sighed loudly and laid back looking up at the ceiling.

"According to her, I was a bad guy. In her opinion, I didn't care about her feelings. I always took the last piece of meat on the platter, the last piece of cake without asking others first if they wanted it. I worked long hours. In general, I was a failure in almost every aspect of our marriage."

"What caused the final split?"

"Exhaustion. I was exhausted from the sham we called a marriage. We were stationed in Panama. The kids were twelve and fourteen. We were going to fly home to Atlanta for Christmas, but I couldn't force myself to get on the plane. That was it. My son blames me for the break-up, and like his mother, uses guilt to get what he wants. He started college, got a girl pregnant, and is now the father of a six-month old I've never seen. Kate wants me to make his child support payments because it's my fault, she claims, that he's a mess. My daughter keeps in touch – lots of letters. She'll be a senior in college this year."

Gregory fastened his eyes on frustrated insects flinging themselves into the mosquito netting. "I feel like one of those bugs smashing myself against life, hurting people."

"We can't live without hurting people sometimes. We're not perfect."

He turned to face her. "I love you, Anne." His need for her - more compelling than sexual fulfillment - was solace. She filled his cup, and it terrified him.

From across the hall, Evelyn heard the groans of their love-making. Oh, how she missed Rudy!

CHAPTER THIRTEEN

"The vote insults the dignity of all Nicaraguans," Evelyn lamented. "When I drove home yesterday I stopped for a light and a little boy, barely able to reach the windshield, wiped my window with a rag. I dropped coins into his hand as I have done countless times, but yesterday I could not keep from crying. A child so thin his bones protruded. How that seventeen billion could have helped him." She was huddled over the breakfast table, fingers gripping a mug, staring into the coffee, like a fortuneteller searching a crystal ball.

Anne sat quietly across from her absorbing her cousin's despondency. On June 5, 1991 the Nicaraguan National Assembly had voted to repeal Law 92 that would result in dropping the seventeen billion dollar judgment against the United States by the International Court of Justice for the illegal mining of Nicaragua's harbors by the US and for their support of the Contras.

"It's been a hard week," Evelyn continued. "My delegation is a woman's organization that works with families suffering from the effects of war. I have shown them an example of the depression, child abuse, and wife beating so prevalent in Nicaragua now. One mother who fled from her abusive husband locked her two preschool children in their shack all day and put out bowls of food and water for them on the floor while she went into the streets to sell grapefruit. When the women saw the children and the shack, they broke into tears, but I struggled not to show my emotions. They depend on me."

Anne felt a millstone of sadness in her chest. She had revered Evelyn for years, marveled at her bravery and strength of purpose, but at that moment her cousin appeared to be emotionally exhausted, at loose ends.

"Evie, you need rejuvenation time," Anne said softly. "Let someone else take tomorrow's delegation to the Atlantic Coast."

Evelyn slowly slid her brimming eyes upward to meet Anne's. "I'm the only one available. The North American and European summer is our busiest time," she whispered hoarsely. "I'll be fine."

Outside a car door slammed. "Let your man in. I'll finish my packing." Evelyn rose to her feet and disappeared into her bedroom.

"You look worried," were Gregory's first words. They would be driving with Padre Doug to Los Ríos where the priest would train Marlene to use the new school textbooks he had just obtained from the Ministry of Education. Marlene's dream of a primary school was about to be fulfilled thanks to Anne's family and, more recently, her church. To her surprise, they had agreed to an ongoing gift of two-hundred dollars a month for teachers and supplies, plus an extra two thousand for the school building. Anne's tentative promise to Marlene had evolved into a long-term commitment, and she was simultaneously proud and nervous about what lie ahead. When Gregory tried to kiss her on the lips, she turned her cheek to him signaling her worry.

"It's Evie," she said knitting her brows. "She's upset over the vote on the seventeen billion."

"I thought the news would rattle her," said Gregory. "They would have never paid the judgment anyway."

"Yes, I know." She moved away from him and sank into a rocker, glancing upwards through the window where she saw Sweetie Pie's long tail resting on the roof overhang. The iguana was there every morning reminding her that life that had existed since the days of the dinosaur would go on forever, long after humans had annihilated themselves. She found that somewhat comforting.

"She's depressed that the Nicaraguan government has capitulated," Anne explained. "After the Revolution, Nicaragua worked hard to be independent of the United States. Now, the country is right back where it started, panting after American loans and aid."

Gregory bent down and lightly pressed his lips to hers. Soap and masculinity; she loved his smell, drawing it into her whenever they were intimate.

"You can't help Evelyn by becoming depressed," he whispered.

His concern for Evelyn was mixed. The woman had put her trust in a political movement and, like all political movements, it had disappointed her. The Revolutionary Sandinista government had mishandled its relationship with the United States bringing the wrath of its powerful northern neighbor down upon it. A mouse doesn't spit in the eye of a lion. The Sandinistas had botched their attempt at a new society when they embraced too many socialistic policies, and in addition, they were inept leaders. Evelyn had to know this and she also had to know that she lost her husband and daughter because of their ineptness. Gregory admired Evelyn - she was courageous and spunky - but her idealistic naiveté had led to her undoing. He poured himself a cup of coffee, and when he spoke again, he did so with forced cheerfulness.

"So tell me," he began. "Tell me about this mysterious priest who's driving us to Los Ríos. Evelyn seems to think he's close to being the Second Coming."

Anne's face brightened, a welcome reaction. "You'll understand when you meet him. He's seventy years old and has lived in Nicaragua for thirty years. He rescues poor kids, some abandoned by their families. If they are selling things in the streets, he finds out how much they make and pays their parents for them to attend school. If they are abandoned, he finds homes for them or takes them home with him. About fifteen kids live at the school although it's not an orphanage. He's an extraordinary man."

"I'm sure he is. All of your friends are extraordinary. David Butler, for instance. I could spend hours listening to him talk about theology even though I think Christianity is just another way to manipulate people into all sorts of mayhem in the name of God. And, my God, can that man tickle the ivories. Then there's that professor at the Solidarity House who hates America."

"Peter Hartwick?"

"Yeah, Hartwick. He has an enviable grasp of history. I respect that. My quarrel with him is his unfounded antagonism to my country, and to yours too, I might add." Gregory gestured toward Anne with the coffee mug. He observed a flicker of annoyance on her face and congratulated himself for diverting her attention from Evelyn, even if the diversion was negative.

"And, last but not least, the Cuban guy who teaches with you and never misses an opportunity to rave about the glories of the Cuban Revolution."

Anne's face reddened. "His name is Dino Fuentes, and I've never heard him rave about the glories of the Cuban Revolution to you or anyone else, Greg. He sends a part of his paycheck back to his family in Cuba because they are struggling financially. Are you mocking these people?" Anne glared at Gregory, her bright green eyes telegraphing their displeasure over his words.

"I'm not mocking them. I respect them, but I am wary of them," Gregory said, realizing he had pushed too far.

"Oh, Greg, that's ridiculous!"

"Are you sure the Good Padre isn't the Second Coming?" he teased keeping his tone light, ignoring an inner warning to drop the subject.

Angrily Anne stomped toward the sink and proceeded to wash breakfast dishes. "Judge for yourself when you meet him," she snapped slapping plates in the dish drainer.

"I've upset you."

She waved her wet hands in the air, swirled around, crossed her arms, and leaned back against the sink to face him. "Because of Padre Doug, Marlene was able to get government approvals to start the school mid-year in July, so maybe he is the Second Coming."

He lowered his head to meet her angry eyes. "I'm sorry. I spoke out of turn," he apologized. He placed the coffee mug in the sink and took her rigid body into his arms. "I'm sorry," he whispered again. "I was trying to distract you from your worry over Evelyn." He felt her body relax. She wrapped her arms around his neck and gave him a quick kiss.

"I accept your apology and I'm delighted you finally agreed to visit Los Ríos. You may learn something important," she said, her voice softening.

"You're right. I may learn something," he agreed. He didn't want to go to Los Ríos. Evelyn's husband was buried there, and he would be reminded of how Rudolfo Gutiérrez had been killed. He would also be reminded of how Evelyn's daughter had been blown to pieces by a land mine manufactured in America and given to the Contras.

When Padre Doug arrived a few minutes later, he was wearing denim jeans that bagged at the seat into which a short-sleeved black shirt was sloppily tucked. The only nod to his vocation was a white clerical collar. The overall image was of a man who didn't give a damn. Gregory immediately liked him. The priest entered the house and kissed Anne. "Where's Evita?" he asked.

She quickly emerged from her bedroom and embraced him. "I'm not going. Have a delegation this week." Padre Doug looked disappointed. Directing her comments to Anne and Gregory, Evelyn said, "You are in for an interesting traveling experience with this man."

Padre Doug burst into a broad smile and bumped her affectionately on the arm. The three travelers went outside where Gregory immediately spotted the Jeep. He had seen vehicles on Nicaragua's roads that looked as though they were held together with bailing wire and duct tape, some missing doors, others missing fenders and the priest's Jeep was right up there with them.

"I can drive my car," he offered.

"Don't worry, young man," Padre Doug boomed. "Angela is good to go. She's been a good girl to me." He patted the hood of the rusty vehicle affectionately. "I buy discarded Jeeps so I can fix them. It's my salvation – besides God, of course. I'm still trying to get the kinks out of this one, so I'll need you two to give it a push to get us started." Noting Gregory's stern expression, he gestured toward the black sedan with the US Embassy insignia on both front doors and added, "We might get shot or kidnapped with that bull's eye." Slapping Gregory on the back with such force that the younger man wobbled, he added, "Have faith."

"I put my faith in me," Gregory responded sharply.

Padre Doug guffawed. "With all due respect, young man, we'll try God today."

Gregory raised and lowered his arms in surrender.

"Be careful," called Evelyn from the front door. She smiled as Anne and Gregory pushed the Jeep until it started and then jumped into the back onto cracked black leather seats. When the Jeep spit and sputtered its way out of San Linda, she waved goodbye.

"We're on our way!" whooped Padre Doug and lit a cigarette giving permission to Gregory to do the same. Anne frowned, but Gregory was not bothered by her disapproval with the admirable Padre Doug puffing away. He wondered whether the priest with his boisterous enthusiasm had a bottle of rum stashed somewhere. A few quick swallows might get him through what was surely going to be an auspicious day.

The vehicle clunked and clamored out of Managua, periodically coughing as though it were about to die. At the last second, however, an infusion of fuel would let it hang on a little longer.

"Are you sure we're safe?" Anne asked.

"I always drive Jeeps on the edge of disaster," chortled Padre Doug ignoring the question of safety.

Gregory smiled. He had imagined the admired priest as an austere do-gooder; instead, here was jolly old Saint Nick maneuvering Rudolf and crew through the sky. They were players in a fantasy comedy or tragic drama, depending on how the day ended.

"Why do you drive Jeeps on the edge of disaster?" Greg shouted over the cough of the Jeep's engine and the rattle of its frame.

"A psychologist friend says I have a death wish. He believes that I want to self-destruct and that is why I do what I do in Nicaragua."

"Nonsense," protested Anne. "You do it because you love Nicaragua's children and they love you."

"True, Anne. Very true," Padre Doug replied reflectively. He loved Nicaragua's children and he trusted God to keep him safe even as he tested fate in unsafe vehicles. Neither he nor his passengers would find themselves at the bottom of a ravine because God was not finished with him yet. Another project lay ahead, one blessed by God as much as his own San Juan el Bautista Primary School. The Catholic hierarchy in Nicaragua might have some problems with him helping an evangelical church begin a school, but hell, he had already been written off by them as friend to the priests of the liberation theology movement and the Christian Base Communities. There was nothing they could do to him other than convince the Chamorro Administration to expel him from the country, and the politicos would not do such a thing. He provided a service. With his school, there were fewer vagrant kids to clog Managua's streets or crowd its public schools; besides the San Juan el Bautista Primary School could not continue without an influx of cash from his diocese in Canada, and his presence assured that cash.

Thirty years ago after praying to find God's purpose for his life, he had asked the diocese for an assignment to an undeveloped country. Serving a middle-class parish in a suburb of Toronto did not satisfy him. He could have requested reassignment to Toronto's poor neighborhoods, but he yearned to flee from the adulation of his Irish-Catholic family. The oldest of six, he had been the one chosen for the priesthood. Too often he was summoned to settle family squabbles and provide family absolution, a role he abhorred.

When his bishop announced the overseas assignment to Nicaragua, young Father Douglas Joseph Michaels researched his future home and concluded the impoverished country in the grasp of a corrupt and oppressive dictatorship and inclined toward periodic rebellions would suit him just fine. From what he read the Nicaraguan people were spirited and good-humored in the face of whatever assailed them, his kind of people.

Even under Somoza, Padre Doug thrived. He first began the San Juan el Bautista Primary School by gathering waifs together in the courtyard of the church for lessons. After years of cajoling the diocese for money, he built a small school that continued to add rooms until they could educate four hundred. His school was even shown to visiting diplomats by the Somoza regime as an example of its humanitarian compassion. He acquiesced in this charade in exchange for being allowed to operate without government interference.

"When I was at Los Ríos last week, they were almost ready to paint the school building," Padre Doug said. "Your school is well-timed, Ana. The Minister of Education wants to charge parents fees to attend public school, one dollar a month for primary school children and two dollars a month for secondary. It's too much for large families making thirty dollars a month or less so they have to choose which children will go to school. Of course, they always choose the boys."

The priest's comments disturbed Gregory. "Padre, you imply the government is Machiavellian, but they are struggling economically to meet the demands of the International Monetary Fund. They need IMF loans and aid after the economic mess they inherited from the Sandinistas. They can't afford the kind of educational system we'd all like to see. The Sandinistas couldn't afford it either."

"True, young man, true," agreed Padre Doug. "Chamorro has to deal with the IMF, and the Sandinistas had to deal with the Contra War - financed by your government, I might add. They diverted funds from education and other social projects into the military, and that was the beginning of the end to what they called their social project." The Jeep suddenly jolted toward the edge of a cliff, shooting adrenaline into Gregory, who threw his arms around Anne.

"Fear not. Angela will not fail us," Padre Doug assured Gregory, who noted his thin self-satisfied smile in the rear view mirror.

He swerved deliberately. He's testing me.

"Look, you can see the far end of Lake Managua," Padre Doug continued, as if nothing dangerous had just occurred. A sliver of silver fronting the silhouettes of purple mountains was barely visible over the jagged hills.

"Such a beautiful country," Anne murmured.

It took them twenty minutes to reach the fork in the road where the two hills diverged. Padre Doug motioned to the steep one that had so awed Tim Haverford. "The community at the top of that hill is as poor as any I have seen in all my years in Nicaragua," he said. "No electricity. No potable water."

"Padre Doug brings them supplies," said Anne.

"The hill looks insurmountable," commented Gregory.

"Old Angela takes me up," responded Padre Doug patting the scarred dashboard.

They bore to the left, climbed, and then descended the lesser hill. Before them lay a valley verdant with the rains. Padre Doug wondered whether the recent downpours had turned the unpaved road leading into Los Ríos into a river of mud.

"You implied in San Linda that you are not a person of faith," Padre Doug said to Gregory.

"I have faith in many things, but I think religion is destructive."

The priest gave a grunt, cleared his throat, and spoke rapidly in a commanding voice, as though presenting a Sunday morning homily. "When religion is used as a means of power and control over others, it can be destructive. Antagonism between Protestants and Catholics in this country is less destructive than it once was, but, unfortunately, antagonism remains. Destructive antagonism also exists between Christians who believe in other-worldly religion and Christians who are socially conscious."

"Why are you a priest?" asked Gregory.

Padre Doug emitted a gusty sigh. "At times I don't know why I'm a priest. I question my vocation when church leadership seeks to limit the church to spiritual matters in a world of injustice. But then along comes a leader like Archbishop Oscar Romero in El Salvador, who advocated for the poor and was martyred for it, and nuns and priests in Nicaragua, like those at Batahola Norte who give the poor hope. These people of faith inspire me, and I say, yes, my life is fulfilled in the priesthood. I believe, like my good friend David Butler, that human beings can manifest God's Kingdom on earth. I believe in small projects of manifestation, like this school about to open in Los Ríos."

Gregory fell silent. Interactions with Anne and Evelyn's friends at the Solidarity House had introduced him to people, who, although they would not speak in theological terms as had Padre Doug, were, nonetheless, fulfilled by their own projects of manifestation. He had ridiculed them earlier in the kitchen of the Casa Sánchez, but he envied their inner fulfillment. He wanted to experience that kind of fulfillment, at least once during his lifetime.

The Jeep ploughed on through the soft but not impassable road that led to Los Ríos. A woman with firewood balanced on her head gracefully danced forward in long purposeful strides, her bare feet sinking into spongy earth.

It was Lucía Ríos. Her appearance brought Tim into Anne's mind, and she smiled remembering his discomfort in her presence. Anne waved at Lucía and she waved back.

When they reached the ominously encroaching limestone quarries Padre Doug said, "Within a year the mines will reach the village agricultural cooperative and take the land."

"Will the cooperative let it go?" asked Gregory.

"They'll be forced to. If they choose to fight in the courts, they'll lose. They may not have clear title to the land anyway. As you know, the Sandinistas were careless about registering titles for the thousands of acres they expropriated, and if the cooperative doesn't have one, they've already lost."

The Jeep groaned over wooden bridges straddling deep ravines, passing the agricultural cooperative, now green with the rainy season. Turning into the village, they swayed in the muddy road like a ship in a squall. Children materialized swarming around the Jeep like bees around a beehive to retrieve the hard candy Padre Doug shot out the window. Anne called out *hola* to the familiar faces, although she couldn't remember their names.

Gregory recalled identical villages in Panama, Guatemala, and Africa, all filled with hovels and outdoor kitchens and industrious women energetically brushing dirt away from entrances with brooms. He understood this was new to Anne and she believed that she was making a difference. But experience had taught him very little would change in Los Ríos because of Anne's school project. Women would continue to sweep dirt with brooms, people would sit in their hovels, and hunger would reside on their doorsteps.

"Oh, no, we're coming to the gully!" Anne shouted a warning.

Before she could explain any more Padre Doug had gunned the Jeep. "Hang on!" he shouted as they went airborne. Fearing ejection Gregory protectively covered Anne's body with his. The Jeep landed on the other side of the gully with an ominous thud, shivered like gelatin, sputtered, and was silent.

"We made it," Anne sighed.

Gregory winced. A projectile of pain rocketed through his right shoulder.

"Are you all right?" asked Anne.

"Fine, fine," he lied, biting his lip against the pain. They climbed out of the Jeep, and stood at the lip of the ditch; Gregory was astonished they had cleared it. A crowd of hefty strong men converged to push the vehicle the few remaining yards to the church. The three visitors followed the men, Gregory walking stiffly next to Anne and Padre Doug, a knife of pain searing his shoulder. He grimaced and grasped his shoulder with the opposite hand.

"Greg, what's wrong?" Anne asked.

"I wrenched my shoulder during our airplane ride over the gully," he answered through gritted teeth.

"It's probably dislocated," declared Padre Doug. He probed with his fingers until one spot elicited a yelp that Gregory could not contain. "I can fix it."

Padre Doug secured the offending shoulder between his two vice-like hands and rotated it with such strength, Gregory feared he might pass out with the pain. When the priest released his grip, the shoulder pain had melted into soreness.

"Thank you," Gregory said.

"Here we learn how to be our own doctors," said Padre Doug nonchalantly. "You'll be sore for a few days. Avoid physical strain."

Anne, her face shimmering with sweat, turned to Gregory and apologized, "I'm so sorry. I just wanted you to see the school."

He curved his good arm around her waist and drew her close to his side. "I wanted to see it too," he lied.

"How will we get out of here?" he asked Padre Doug. He was convinced that the heap of junk they had traveled in to Los Ríos was finished.

"No problem. Our friends will push Angela up the road until she starts. Then we'll turn her around, fly over the gully, and they will push us again until we start."

"You're crazy!" declared Gregory.

Padre Doug arched his eyebrows and smiled. "Faith, young man," he said. "Faith."

Near the church, Anne saw the school, and sunshine flooded her face. "My God, look how quickly it's gone up!" she exclaimed as she swept her eyes over the long oblong building painted a bright turquoise. *"La Escuela Primaria Rudolfo Gutiérrez.* How wonderful! I can't believe it!"

Padre Doug leaned toward her touching her arm. "Ana, this school is your gift of love to Evita," he said softly.

Gregory's mouth went dry. One day Anne would be faced with a choice between him and Evelyn, and he knew he would lose.

"Anne!" someone called. Over the shoulder of Padre Doug, Anne saw a grinning young man with a freckled high forehead smeared with white paint wearing a yellow T-shirt with *Saving Waters Christian Mission* stenciled across his chest.

"Tim!" Anne exclaimed. Months had passed since she had seen him, and he looked tan and confident as he stood ramrod straight, arms dangling by his side, embarrassment on his face when Anne hugged him enthusiastically. "What are you doing here?" she asked.

"We're painting a church," Tim announced proudly.

Work on the Betel Church building had stopped since the most urgent task was readying the school for mid-year classes in July. With the Rudolfo Gutiérrez Primary School completed, construction had resumed with urgency and now the church was ready for the final task of painting.

"Come meet Pastor Hicks," Tim said, gesturing toward a balding man with a long angular face wearing the same message T-shirt as Tim. Rivulets of dirty perspiration trickled down the older man's face as Anne's smooth hand met his rough palm.

"Tim speaks of you and your mission here often," he said to Anne in a nasal voice betraying a slight rasp in his chest, leading Anne to wonder if he had a respiratory illness.

Watching Pastor Hicks speaking to Anne, Tim's heart quickened with happiness. God once again had answered his prayers by sending her to Los Ríos at this auspicious moment.

"We have several people down with dengue fever, so I closed our construction site temporarily," Pastor Hicks was explaining. "We arrived yesterday not realizing at the time that God had a church project for us to work on here as well as in Managua."

"They worked here yesterday and today. We are grateful for the friendship of our American Christians," Pastor Rafael added as he joined the group.

Anne quickly introduced Padre Doug and Gregory to Pastor Hicks and Tim. The pastor stared at Padre Doug, but did not offer his hand.

"It is good of you to help," Gregory said and shook the hands of first Pastor Hicks and then Tim.

"We evangelical Christians are a minority in this country. We need to help one another," Pastor Hicks said with a furtive side glance at Padre Doug.

Pastor Rafael observed the interchange sensing antagonism in Pastor Hicks toward the priest. "Much pleasure in seeing you again, Padre Doug," he said shaking his hand. "My niece Marlene is waiting for you." Then turning his gaze toward Gregory, he asked, "You are a friend to Anne?"

"I am sorry, I forgot you do not know each other," Anne apologized answering for Gregory. "Greg is a friend to me and to Evelyn. He was raised on a farm in America."

Pastor Rafael brightened. "*Mucho gusto, Señor.* I am happy to show you our cultivated fields." He offered his hand and Gregory shook it. "Come with me," Pastor Rafael urged.

Gregory did not want to be anywhere near vegetables growing under a hot sun, but the alternatives of hanging around the site with Pastor Hicks or shadowing Anne while she and the others were holding a meeting were even less appealing. His arm hurt too much to even consider joining the work crew in painting so he found himself trudging alongside Pastor Rafael past the gully and up the dirt road leading to the village's entrance, and across the road where they plunged into the fields of the 19th of July Agricultural Cooperative.

"Do you work the land in America?" asked Pastor Rafael.

"No," Gregory said quickly. "I was raised on a farm, but I am not a farmer. How are your crops doing?"

"Our biggest problems with the corn are too many pests and a lack of rain, but the rains have finally come, and the corn is growing now," explained Pastor Rafael as he and Gregory skirted the cornfields, each step sending tiny jabs of pain through Gregory's sore shoulder. "We pray we can sell the corn we do not eat ourselves. Our government used to buy our produce at a fixed price and lend us money for planting. Now we have to compete with Costa Rica and their farmers have better equipment and seeds. Some of our farmers thought we would do better without fixed prices under the new government. That has not happened and most of us cannot get loans to plant at the private banks because we have no collateral, except our land. It was that way under Somoza, and many lost their land when their harvests failed."

The fields abutted lush green pastureland where the cumbersome bodies of oxen moved in slow motion. Cows meandered nearby and Gregory could hear their snorts and smell their musky odor. Several *campesinos* bent over weeding looked up briefly as the two men passed, grunted a greeting, and returned to their tasks.

"Anne, she is your woman?" asked Pastor Rafael.

"Yes," Gregory mumbled.

"*Claro*," said Pastor Rafael. "You come to Nicaragua to visit her," he concluded.

"No, I work here. I am in the military. US Marines."

Pastor Rafael stopped suddenly. "Marines?" he asked in a suspicious tone.

"I seem to get that reaction whenever I am among Anne's friends," Gregory commented laconically.

Pastor Rafael resumed walking. "At times, your country has not been kind to Nicaragua."

"I know," Gregory agreed.

They walked mostly in silence for thirty-minutes, past fields and into a semi-forested grove where they sloughed through elongated yucca leaves and stepped over the buttressed roots of trees. The throb in Gregory's shoulder grew so familiar he ignored it, preoccupied as he was with flicking away clouds of insects descending and hovering around their faces. The older man stealthily led the way, like a bush guide moving through the jungle until they reached one of the two rivers of Los Ríos where they splashed the gritty perspiration off their faces and necks.

Women were scrubbing clothes, rhythmically pounding them with rocks in the murmuring river and spreading them over higher rocks to dry. Pleased, Gregory recalled the happiest moments of his childhood when his stern father finally gave him permission to leave the fields and he jumped into a stream cleansing himself of sweaty grime. Afterwards, he darted home into his mother's kitchen inhaling the aroma of supper cooking. His mother, always humming, made Gregory feel like he was the most important person in the world. When he was twelve, however, his mother died of cancer. His heart turned to stone with her loss. His father soon remarried and started another family leaving Gregory feeling abandoned by him also. He left home the day after he received his high school diploma, fleeing from his losses.

"Is your cooperative safe from confiscation?" Gregory asked Pastor Rafael.

"The mayor in Monte Horeb tells us we are not legal. He says, the former owner is returning to Nicaragua to reclaim the land soon."

"Do you have a paper with a legal title?" asked Gregory.

"No."

"That is not good," Gregory observed.

"Not good," Pastor Rafael repeated. Organizing the cooperative had fulfilled a life-long dream. For the first time in memory, the families of Betel Christian Church received a daily allotment of food that met their needs. He shuddered at the thought of their community losing the cooperative. A question stuck in his throat. Could he trust this American Marine? He must be a good man or Hermana Ana would not have taken him as her man.

"Señor Gregorio, can you help us save our land?" he asked.

While Pastor Rafael and Gregory trotted around the outskirts of the village, Pastor Rafael's niece Marlene Cruz was preparing supper with her Aunt Sonia. She flipped tortillas on the iron skillet, baby Estrellita gurgling happily on her back in a sling. Rolandcito played a quiet game with stones on the patio between the living area and the kitchen. When Padre Doug and Anne approached, the boy scrambled to meet them and Padre Doug ruffled the child's hair affectionately.

"Hermana Sonia, you look well," he greeted planting a kiss on her puffy cheek. "How is your family?"

"My sister Leticia is not well. She sleeps now," replied Sonia.

"What is wrong?"

"Her fever comes and goes, but she is better today, *gracias a Dios*."

Sonia's answer concerned Padre Doug, who was worried about cholera that was on the rise, especially in poor rural communities like Los Ríos lacking dependable, uncontaminated potable water. Near the border with Honduras, cholera was approaching epidemic levels. Former Contras, their bodies often weakened from HIV or full-blown AIDS acquired from the Americans at their training bases in Honduras during the war easily succumbed to cholera and carried the disease into their villages.

"You must be wary of cholera," advised the priest.

"We are, Padre Doug. Whenever we have a sickness, we go to the Medsalud clinic near the public school. The student doctor comes two days a week. There are few medicines, but she will tell us if we need to go to Managua for help."

"I have brought acetaminophen, rehydration fluid, and antiseptic for the medical clinic."

"*Gracias.* You are a good man," said Sonia.

Marlene removed Estrellita from her pouch and handed her to Anne as though giving her a most precious gift. The young mother wore an apron over her Sunday-go-to-church dress. Dark straggles of her long black hair, wet with humidity, graced her brow. With her baby safely in Anne's arms, she removed her apron and she and Padre Doug sat at the table on the patio.

As she cradled the placid baby, a flood of maternal instinct swept through Anne releasing memories of her daughter Lynn. Anne had wanted to protect her emotionally fragile daughter from the assaults of life, to nurture her and guide her into a confident young woman. She had wanted Lynn to sail into adulthood without a burdensome ballast of bad decisions. In this, she believed she had failed her daughter, and in spite of his smug self-assurance, she had failed her son Danny as well.

"Isabel Martine is in Managua visiting her grandmother who is ill. She is disappointed to miss this meeting," Marlene explained the absence of the certified teacher who would help her with the school.

"I will remember her grandmother in Mass and her mother too," said Padre Doug. He pulled the textbooks from his backpack recently obtained from the Ministry of Education and laid them on the table.

"She will be pleased. She is Catholic," said Marlene as she flipped back the cover of one of the books and exclaimed. "Look, a hard cover, thick paper, and many pictures in color."

"The Americans financed seven million new textbooks designed to teach family values and rules of law, provide civic education, and, most important, according to the administrator at the Ministry of Education, depoliticize the curriculum," explained Padre Doug with sarcasm in his voice.

"What does all that mean?" asked Anne.

Padre Doug leafed through a book as he spoke. "In my opinion, the texts reflect the new government's political and religious perspective. As someone in your political history said, 'to the victors belong the spoils.'" From deep in his throat Padre Doug made a sound of infinite frustration.

"Our teachers were not asked what they wanted to see in the new texts," Marlene said plaintively.

"For your school to be recognized by the government, you are required to use these texts, but at San Juan el Bautista, we add to them," Padre Doug explained. "We teach our students the story of Augusto Sandino and his efforts in the 1930s to rid Nicaragua of the occupying US Marines; we teach about the social projects of the Revolution and we look at the Contra War and its aftermath. We have a wonderful artist that creates little books with cartoon characters. The children love the drawings of Sandino in an oversized sombrero. I will bring this material and show you and Isabel Martine how to use it."

Padre Doug and Marlene planned all morning, peppering their conversation with interruptions of laughter. Anne lamented that she could not understand the humor. By now she accepted that she would never be fluent enough to grasp the nuances of Nicaraguan idiomatic Spanish, yet she was grateful that she could communicate well enough to participate in everyday interchanges of life.

When they had finished, Marlene produced a wide and genuine smile for Padre Doug, her slightly protruding coffee-brown eyes reflecting the depth of her feelings.

"We are grateful. *Dios le bendiga.* God bless you." She kissed the priest and quickly disappeared into the kitchen to help her aunt.

Padre Doug joined Anne and gazed with fatherly interest at the sweet-smelling Estrellita sleeping in her arms. He stroked the baby's tender skin gently with a thick forefinger. She twitched and dreamily whimpered before resuming her soft baby snore. Anne wondered if he missed having a family of his own.

"Thank you for everything you have done for Marlene and for me," she said.

"*Mucho gusto, Ana,*" he responded. "Thank you for starting this school."

Later in the afternoon, Sonia and Marlene seated five men and Anne around the table and served them beans, rice, plantain, and tortillas. Anne's eyes fell to the hands of Pastor Hicks, the rough-hewn hands of a man accustomed to hard work. She admired leadership that worked alongside underlings, and just as hard.

Pastor Rafael related the visit of Gregory and him to the 19th of July Agricultural Cooperative and Pastor Hicks said, "Anne mentioned you were a farmer before you joined the military."

"I was raised on a farm in Georgia, but I never farmed."

"I was raised on a farm in Tennessee. A good, clean life," said Pastor Hicks.

"Not always so clean," commented Gregory dryly bringing a half-smile to the lips of Hicks.

164

"I should have said… morally clean. It's a comfort to know our military are here in Nicaragua," he continued as he raised his glass of juice toward Gregory in salute. "All the blabber about land titles and the violence when landowners robbed of their land try to reclaim it. The presence of the US military will soon put a stop to that."

"We are here to train, not to interfere in Nicaragua's political squabbles," said Gregory.

"But we know what you can do covertly," Hicks remarked, slyly winking at him as though they shared an important secret.

"The United States military has had a checkered history in Nicaragua," Padre Doug interjected.

Hicks cocked a thin suspicious eyebrow at him and proclaimed through a mouth curled somewhere between a smile and a sneer, "We are all safer with our military here. This land-title issue is polarizing the country. The Sandinistas expropriated homes for their politicians. Shameful."

Padre Doug shoved a forkful of beans into his mouth and munched thoughtfully before he commented, looking first at Pastor Rafael before he spoke. "Homes for a few Sandinistas are not important. What is important are the thousands of properties given to *campesinos* for small and medium-sized farms. The agrarian reform program provided these people with a way to feed themselves and earn a living. It made a stab at correcting the terrible economic imbalances in this country."

The narrow eyes of the shallow-cheeked Hicks fastened on Padre Doug. Anne's neck stiffened with unease. She felt for Gregory's hand and entwined her fingers with his, but he pulled away and leaned forward on the table, folding his hands in front of him.

"The land of the agricultural cooperative of Los Ríos is threatened with the return to Nicaragua of its former owner," he announced.

Tim squirmed in his seat at Garner's comment, his eyes mutating from anticipatory interest to concern.

"We must not lose our cooperative," added Pastor Rafael grimly. "The Chamorro Administration says they want a compromise to allow some farmers to keep their land. I pray we are among them."

Pastor Hicks pondered the comment, then declared, "We must remember the rain falls on the righteous as well the sinner. Unfortunately, Pastor Rafael, people like you will suffer for the sins of the past ten years." As he spoke

Hicks considered that the loss of the agricultural cooperative might be the catalyst to turn the Los Ríos pastor toward a true understanding of Biblical scripture. Perhaps he, the Reverend Theodore Hicks, had been chosen to lead this sincere, but hoodwinked man into new life.

"Fear not, my friend," he declared, "for the more the suffering, the greater the paradise for those who are born again when they leave this difficult, but temporary life on Earth to be with God and his Son Jesus Christ."

Absently Tim bit his fingernails, a stricken expression on his face signaling that he had comprehended the insensitivity of Pastor Hicks toward Pastor Rafael's dilemma. His previous visit to Los Ríos had left him shaken and wishing he had never met Anne or her cousin Evelyn, a woman who disturbed him even more than did Anne. Over the following weeks uncertainty had plagued him. He could not accept Anne as an apostate. And Evelyn had lived through unspeakable tragedy. Ennui and a vague uneasiness were his daily companions. He questioned his commitment to the Saving Waters Christian Mission and had considered returning to Texas. Screwing up his courage, he had shared his doubts with Pastor Hicks.

"Tim, I want you to arrange a visit for us to the Betel Christian Church. God is calling us to save this church and its pastor, and we will do so," Pastor Hicks had said.

Tim brightened. The presence of Pastor Hicks in Los Ríos would help him understand what had happened to him. He fervently prayed the certitude in his faith would be restored. Unfortunately, with the challenges of building a church and expanding the mission at the Saving Waters Christian Mission, months had passed before they could find the time for a visit.

Pastor Rafael pointed to the empty juice pitcher and motioned to Sonia. All eyes watched Sonia refill the pitcher as though she was performing an extraordinary act. Then Pastor Rafael spoke and they darted toward him.

"Pastor Hicks, the indignity of poverty is like war. God does not want us to go hungry. These are the things of man. God does not want us to be exploited. These are the things of man. Spiritual hunger and physical hunger are mixed. You cannot feed the one without feeding the other."

"Salvation is the most important food," declared Pastor Hicks. "Jesus said the poor will always be with us. Always, Pastor Rafael. Always."

Throughout the tense interchange, Tim kept his head bowed as he dug at his fingers tearing at hangnails and other loose bits of nail until they bled. An hour ago he had rejoiced over Anne's arrival in Los Ríos. If Anne could be brought to Christ, Pastor Hicks, the most solid Christian Tim had ever met, was the one to make it happen. But now Pastor Hicks seemed rude. Perhaps he was tired.

When he raised his head, Anne took note of the bewildered expression on Tim's face and yearned to tell him that he was a better person than his leader.

"Pastor Hicks, we count you as one of our good North American friends," Pastor Rafael continued kindly. "We appreciate how you and Timoteo helped us yesterday and today. You must return to preach in our church someday. It would be our honor."

Pastor Hicks looked at Pastor Rafael trying to read his face and his body language for signs of his sincerity and concluded that the Betel Christian Church pastor seriously recognized the value in the message he had tried to convey. As for Padre Doug, the gates of hell would welcome him. By the looks of him, that would not be a long time in coming.

"I accept your invitation, Pastor Rafael."

Pastor Rafael smiled. *"Bueno."* He paused briefly as his eyes swept the guests at his table, then announced, "Now, my niece Marlene will tell us of the plans for the Escuela Primaria Rudolfo Gutiérrez."

He motioned to Marlene who pulled up a seat next to him. "We want to open on July 4," she began.

"Independence Day," muttered Gregory, but nobody heard him except Anne.

CHAPTER FOURTEEN

*A*nne *in an unfamiliar place frantically searching for Gregory, surrounded by strangers, fearing she would be crushed, clawing her way through the crowd, shouting Greg! Greg! Greg!*

She shot upright in bed, a silent scream caught in her throat. Droplets of perspiration dribbled down her neck as she reached for the tissue box to wipe her face. The iridescent clock on the bed table proclaimed three; quiet hung in the air suspended like a watchful sentry. Her heart pounded an ominous drumbeat urging escape and she sighed deeply searching the darkness - for what she did not know. When she spotted the curved rope near the bedroom door illuminated by the glow of a sliver of moonlight, she reached for a flashlight and slowly angled the light toward the rope. A hot fear burned through her: a deadly coral snake was slithering under her bedroom door into the hall. Grabbing the omnipresent tire iron on the bedside table, she gingerly reached toward the floor and slowly picked up her slippers shaking them thoroughly. Satisfied they were snake-free, she slid into the slippers and shuffled toward the door circling the flashlight around until she reached the light switch and snapped it on. The snake was nowhere to be seen. Except for the hissing sounds of cicadas, it was quiet. Mouth dry, she continued to shuffle, swirling the beam of the flashlight into the kitchen, every nerve on edge like stretched elastic until she reached the kitchen light switch and threw it.

The coral's bright colors were slithering toward the front door. There it languidly angled through the crack where the black rod iron security door did not meet the threshold and disappeared from view.

Anne listened to her loud breathing, feeling her lungs pump and deflate as she waited perfectly still, tire iron in hand, before cautiously tiptoeing toward the door, praying the snake had slid under the wooden and screen doors too. She gingerly threw the bolt on the security door, then opened the front door. No snake. Opening the screen door, she rotated the flashlight from side to side over the patio. Nothing. She had always known a snake might enter the house one day, although it was rare. Renaldo had once dangled a beheaded coral in front of them claiming to have found it in his boot and that he had quickly dispatched it with his machete, but scorpions were more likely to be found in boots and shoes and slippers. Snakes usually remained in their natural habitat, and Evelyn even suggested that Renaldo had probably found the snake dead and created the story for attention. A dark premonition filled Anne with dread. Was the snake following on the heels of the terrifying dream an omen? Gregory had taken Evelyn and her to *El León y La Serpiente* Restaurant when they met in San Juan del Sur. The Lion and The Snake. Was she being warned?

Snatching a towel from a kitchen drawer, she stuffed it at the bottom of the screen door, and then after closing and locking the front door and the security door, she went to the kitchen sink to rinse the sweat off her face. But no water came out. "Pumps must be out again in Managua," she said aloud to no one.

Lower San Linda depended on water pumped up the hills from Managua. The pumps were old, and the electricity that powered them was erratic, so every house that could afford one had a storage water tank for daily use. Anne made her way down the hall toward the laundry carefully, her eyes riveted on the floor for signs of snakes. When she reached the back door, she switched off the hall light to avoid attracting a myriad of insects. She gingerly stepped onto the dirt floor of the gated fenced-in laundry room and black soup of night, flashlight in hand. She unlocked the laundry room gate and stepped out into the yard surveying the ground with the flashlight as she went. All clear. She turned on the valve of the water tank, quickly reentered the laundry and locked the gate feeling quite proud of herself for not bothering Evelyn.

The next day Evelyn and Anne sifted methodically through rice removing small stones with the potential to crack a tooth. They had breakfasted and shopped for groceries at the dismal market near Siete Sur. Because it was a locally owned market, it could not compete with the two US style supermarkets in Managua recently opened by Nicaraguans who had fled at the onset of the Revolution only to return when the Sandinista government fell, sensing economic opportunity. Even Nicaragua's small middle class consumers would add an additional twenty minutes to their commute in order to shop in an air conditioned supermarket stocked with imported goods from the United States. Although rice was grown in Nicaragua, the consumers preferred bagged, cleaned, and ready to cook rice to rock-speckled rice sold from bulk bins.

From the refrigerator Evelyn removed the chicken they had purchased at the failing market and set to work plucking remaining feathers from its scrawny body.

"The Nicaraguan chicken industry doesn't have a prayer. How can it compete with corporate farmed chickens from America, fattened by technology," said Anne.

"No trade between unequals is fair, and it's going to get worse for our farmers," Evelyn said as she washed the plucked chicken, seasoned it, and plopped it into the toaster oven to bake. After eating dinner, they dove into large bowls of Eskimo ice cream. They purchased it by the gallon from the Eskimo factory in Managua, and although Anne could foresee a fatter woman returning to Massachusetts, she hoped Eskimo would not also fall victim to an import.

The remainder of the evening passed peacefully with satisfying reading punctuated by bursts of conversation, none of which included Anne's terrifying dream. Knowing how Evelyn felt about Gregory, she had decided not to speak of anything relating to him to her cousin. And in spite of the dream and the frightening events of the previous evening, she had to admit her life in Nicaragua was unfolding well. She had finally gained control of her classes at Managua University; the school in Los Ríos had opened with grades kindergarten through third; her lover continued to lift her to a passion she had never experienced, even in the early euphoric days with Keith; and Evelyn seemed to have overcome her detour into depression brought on by the government's dismissal of the World Court judgment against America, in part, Anne believed, because of emotional support from her. Yet an unfocused unease remained with Anne throughout the day, a sense that something unresolved lay dormant at the ready to create havoc in her life.

After they went to bed, she awoke once again in the middle of the night to shouting and pounding. "Not another horrible dream," she muttered as she floated into consciousness and groggily checked her watch. Two a.m. She quickly identified the noise as a pounding on the front door and a sudden rush of a too familiar dread whirled inside her as she whipped out of bed and slapped her bare feet on the floor, neglecting to check for poisonous snakes. Clutching the ever-present tire iron, she stepped warily into the small hall leading to the *sala* where she met Evelyn equally alert to the ominous pounding.

"Quién es?" called Evelyn.

"Señora Evita, help me," cried a strangled male voice.

Evelyn switched on the light, unlocked the rod iron security door, and cautiously eased the front door open to an ashen-faced Renaldo. "Anita vomits and bleeds and cries, she is dying," he gasped, his hands fluttering like the wings of panicked bats.

"Dear God!" Anne cried, noticing a flicker of fear shadowing Evelyn's face, quickly replaced by a forced controlled calm.

"We will go to the doctor that lives in Upper San Linda," said Evelyn, well trained to take charge in emergencies. "Renaldo, get Anita and the boys outside your house. We will meet you there," she ordered. Renaldo darted across the road.

Evelyn shouted to Anne as they threw on clothes and bolted outside. "Bring the tire iron. This is going to be a difficult ride."

Evelyn jerked the truck into the road, barely missing the gate left swinging by their frantic gardener. She parked outside the gate and plunged across the street and into a void of velvet black separating them from the Aguilar's house. Anne followed, and with flashlights ablaze, they pushed through brush, ruts, and roots until they arrived at the path where they met Renaldo, carrying Anita and swaying precariously. The two little boys yawning and rubbing their eyes, trudged behind him wearing only their underwear. Anita, wrapped in a blood-soaked bed sheet reddening more by the second, was moaning arms flopping loosely like a marionette.

Fearing he would fall, Anne threw her arms around Renaldo's back supporting him as he stumbled his way forward. Evelyn scooped up the confused and frightened Camilo and re-entered the thick and hazardous opaque blackness. Hernández stumbled after her, while Renaldo and Anne plodded behind them. Drawing upon an adrenaline-fueled strength, Anne kept Renaldo upright supporting his body as best she could, giving encouragement to the frightened man in the calmest voice she could summon. "You are doing well. Stop and get your balance. Straighten."

When they reached the road, they laid Anita onto the back seat where she fell into low moaning. Renaldo hopped into the truck bed with the boys, and Anne slid into the passenger seat. Evelyn started the ignition and eased the truck into the murky black soup of woods leading to Upper San Linda. The truck rattled, crunched, and groaned along a woody path, booby-trapped with fallen branches and protruding boulders. Aiming her flashlight at the road, Anne's eyes vigilantly searched for hidden hazards, her jaw clinching so tightly that her muscles ached. Evelyn hunched forward over the steering wheel, straining to keep the truck on the path. Low branches and saplings slapped at the vehicle like angry hands. After what seemed like an eternity, they saw a pale blur ahead.

"Thank you, God," Anne sighed.

Emerging from the inky blackness, they bumped up onto the paved road of Upper San Linda, expelling an audible tension-relieving sigh in unison. Evelyn continued to drive slowly while Anne studied the names posted on the stone walls of elegant houses until they finally reached the residence and private office of Dr. Danilo Membreño. A forest of green plants snaked up a stone wall surrounding the expansive house. Evelyn parked and darted to a black steel gate, tire iron in hand. She clanged against the gate until a security guard appeared. They exchanged a few words and he left to summon Dr. Membreño. Anne mopped Anita's fevered and perspiring forehead with the corner of the sheet, muttering words of assurance in English because she was too distressed to think in Spanish. She heard the boys crying in the truck bed behind her and Renaldo's inaudible mumbling.

Evelyn returned to the truck and accompanied Renaldo who carried his bloodied wife into the house. Anne climbed into the truck bed with the boys drawing them to her. Their saucer eyes reflected terror, and she held them tight, fear knotting her stomach. *Anita could die.*

They waited in a sitting area, the husband and his employer, while Dr. Membreño worked on Anita in the examining room. Renaldo stared ahead vacantly. Evelyn's eyes roamed over the room's cornucopia of Nicaragua's exquisitely crafted ceramics proudly displayed on cedar shelving. The décor expressed wealth, as befitted a physician whose practice was limited to those who could pay for his services. Evelyn knew her presence had opened his door to Anita and suspected that his care of her would be minimal at best.

If Anita dies, the boys have no future with Renaldo. Anita, you have to live, you have to live, she pleaded silently.

The doctor, a middle-aged light-skinned man, taller than the average Nicaraguan reappeared, his white medical coat stained with blood, an irritated expression on his face. "The woman is your servant?" he asked as he removed black plastic-framed glasses and cleaned the blood spatter from them with a tissue extracted from a pocket.

"Yes," Evelyn answered.

"She has miscarried and hemorrhaged," he announced flatly. Evelyn looked at Renaldo for reaction, but his eyes were milky and uncomprehending, and he remained seated. "She will need dilation and curettage surgery to clean out the remaining cells and the infection. She may also need blood. Go to the public hospital near Siete Sur. It is the closest and time is crucial. Her blood pressure is dangerously low and she could go into shock. I have given her oral antibiotics, but she needs intravenous antibiotics for her infection."

Suddenly Renaldo's mind exploded with awareness. "Miscarried?" he gasped, bolting to his feet. The doctor ignored him and walked over to a wall cabinet where he removed a large container. "Intravenous antibiotics," he declared handing the container to Evelyn. "They may not have enough at the public hospital."

"The bill is two hundred córdobas for the examination and four hundred for the antibiotic," he said. "You can pay me in dollars if you wish. I would prefer dollars."

"Miscarried!" Renaldo gasped again, his face reflecting an ominous melding of rage and fear. He glared at Dr. Membreño, provoking the startled doctor to back away toward the door to the examination room.

"Renaldo, take Anita to the truck. She has to go to the hospital," Evelyn said in a calm, steady voice. Renaldo assumed a wildcat crouch as though prepared to spring at the doctor, but he did not move. The doctor shifted nervously.

"Renaldo, go get Anita," Evelyn said again. Renaldo lunged forward toward the doctor who flung himself away from the door as the distraught man barged past him into the examination room where Anita was prone on a stretcher. Renaldo gently scooped his unconscious wife into his arms and walked slowly toward the exit trailing the drip of Anita's blood behind him. The previously alarmed expression of Dr. Membreño screwed into disgust as his immaculate white tiled floors spotted with dark red.

"It cannot be helped," said Evelyn in a disparaging tone handing him six hundred córdobas. She knew the doctor had overcharged her, and she was angry. He had observed the "servant," as he phrased it, was poor and the foreign employer would pay. Without another word, she exited the house leaving him shaking his head over what had happened.

The truck clamored out of the other end of Upper San Linda onto a newly constructed paved road that circled back toward the ragged main highway. Driving with a fury born of anger and fear, Evelyn sped toward the hospital. Anita was stretched out in the back seat, her head on Anne's lap moaning like a mewing cat. When they arrived at the hospital, two men in white coats gingerly lifted her from the truck onto a hospital stretcher and gratefully accepted the intravenous antibiotic from Evelyn.

"It will save her life," said one. They rushed her through the Emergency Room doors leaving Renaldo and the others to make their way into the hospital to wait for word of her condition.

The little group settled on a cracked bench in a narrow corridor of the depressing hospital. Anne gathered the trembling bodies of Hernández and Camilo, pressing them next to her and praying silently. Evelyn's face was stoic. Renaldo looked bewildered and bloodless as if life itself was pouring out of him instead of his wife. His head fell forward into his hands, his elbows spiked out from his body.

"Anita is strong. She will be fine," Evelyn assured him, sounding so confident Anne wondered if she truly believed it. They fell into a doze listening to the distant murmur of voices. An hour later, a doctor materialized still in his surgical scrubs. He was a small young man with the ramrod posture of a soldier and the compassionate demeanor of a humanitarian. *He has served in the army,* thought Evelyn.

The doctor addressed Renaldo, who looked up at him with bleary eyes, "We cleaned her out. She has lost blood but she will not need a transfusion; she will be fine."

The audible expulsions of relief hovered in the spaces among them as the doctor, smiling kindly, looked down at the two sleeping children wrapped in Anne's arms. "These are your boys?" he asked Renaldo.

Renaldo nodded, his mouth pursed as though he would burst out crying at any moment.

"They are handsome boys. They need their mother." Renaldo gulped.

Evelyn shook the doctor's hand. "Thank you," she said gratefully, her voice quavering. The doctor addressed Renaldo again. "Your wife is anemic. She will need vitamins, particularly iron. We have none to give her here. You can purchase them at a pharmacy in Managua."

Evelyn laid a hand on the depleted man and said assuredly, "We will buy the vitamins, Renaldo."

"*Bueno, Señora Evita,*" he choked.

They left Renaldo to attend to his wife, necessary in a hospital with few nurses. The women went home where they fed the boys cheese, bread, fruit, and milk, and then tucked them into Evelyn's bed.

Anita, paler and thinner, came home two days later.

"You will not work until you are better. We will continue to pay you," said Evelyn sitting next to her bed in one of Renaldo's rickety chairs, a tissue box in her lap.

"*Gracias. Gracias, Señora Evita.* God bless you," Anita whispered weakly. She grasped the hand of her benefactor and kissed it. "Thank you for not telling Renaldo about my plan," she added.

"You need to do that, Anita, and soon. I have spoken to Señor Sánchez and he will let you use the building without charge. He says you are a good Sandinista and should be rewarded."

"*Gracias a Dios,*" choked Anita. Saliva gathered at the corners of her mouth and Evelyn handed her a tissue.

"It is sad to lose a child of God, but it is not good to have another baby with Renaldo," Anita whispered hoarsely. She flew into a fit of coughing that was eventually calmed with a glass of water. Evelyn gently wiped her chin of water dribbling toward her neck.

"Then the baby was not Ernesto's?" asked Evelyn.

"I wanted everyone to think it was. I am a bad woman. God has punished me by taking away my child." Tears spilled from Anita's eyes. More tissues flew out of the box.

"Anita, God has not punished you. Your body is undernourished and before you have any more children, you must nourish it."

When Evita prepared to leave, Anita called after her in a near whisper. "You and Señora Ana are angels. I say Rosary for you every day."

Two weeks later on July 11, 1991, Anita, rosary beads in hand, joined her employers on the patio of the Casa Sánchez to witness the awesome power of a total solar eclipse. At two p.m., the brightness of day faded into a blanket of darkness, and the world stood still in silent reverence welcoming a dark peaceful serenity. Then, in slow motion darkness flowed into light and the day returned.

"Then God said, 'Let there be light! Genesis, Chapter One, Verse Three." Anne declared. "Light to darkness to light again."

"Is not that what life is?" added Evelyn.

"*Gracias a Dios,*" said Anita.

***

Anne was the first to observe a skinny man, shirtless and shoeless, staggering in the road when she and Gregory approached the gate to the Casa Sánchez. They were returning from a daylong sojourn through the White Towns south of Managua. When she saw the drunk, her heart sank and she prayed he was not the eyeless beggar, a drunken old man who periodically staggered to the doorstep of the Casa Sánchez, with one eye dead in a blank stare, the misshapen victim of a knife wound. Evelyn always checked the grotesque hole for sign of infection, bathed the cuts on his feet with antiseptic, and gave him food. Off he would stagger until he faced the desperation that would send him back to the generous *señora*.

Anne could not bring herself to approach the repulsive man who reminded her of the misshapen beggars in the Park of the Wretched in Antigua. Even her guilt over her rejection of this lost soul did not motivate her to go anywhere near him. However, she would cleanse the wounds of children who brought their hunger and need for medical attention to their doorstep, making amends with each act of compassion for her panicked reaction to the pretzel boy in Guatemala.

They neared the staggering figure and a chill of recognition coursed through Anne. "Oh, no. It's Renaldo!"

"Anita must have told him of her plans," commented Gregory, maneuvering the car alongside the inebriated gardener.

The disheveled appearance of Renaldo cast a dark shadow on what had been a perfect day for the lovers initiated by Gregory when an artist meticulously feathering a vase, his brush delicately poised, appeared on the screen during an orientation on Nicaraguan art at the embassy. The artist lived in the folk art community of San Juan del Oriente. Gregory had visualized Anne so graphically behind the painter that he had to blink away the image. At that moment, he decided he would take her to San Juan del Oriente.

"We will celebrate us," he declared decisively to Anne, knowing he was being reckless in continuing to see her following a warning by his supervisor that he and Anne were being watched. He should drive her from his heart; yet whenever he glimpsed the joy in her face as she spoke of the school in Los Ríos, he could not part from her. She and her cousin Evelyn were hope givers, and he had too often destroyed hope. He sensed Evelyn must certainly be aware of what he had done. She seemed able to read hearts and understand what wonders or darkness they held.

As he and Anne passed through the White Towns south of Managua with their unique whitewashed houses and lively street bustle, Gregory stamped the experience into the indelible ink of his memory. He wanted to remember these moments of shared delight, recalling them at will in the days ahead when she would be gone from him. They went to Diriamba, where the legendary Caique Indian Diriangen fought the Spaniard Gilberto Gonzáles in 1522, the battle immortalized in *"Nicaragua, Nicaragüita."* They visited Niquinohomo, the birthplace of Sandino, to see a bronze statue of this most famous warrior standing proud in his wide-brimmed sombrero, a bandolier of bullets flowing to his waist. They drove through the sleepy village of Masatepe, a center of handcrafted hardwood furniture, then on to San Marcos the birthplace of the infamous Anastasio Somoza García, the first of the three Somoza dictators. After San Marcos they explored Jinotepe, the capital of the district, where they drank *cacao con leche* under a forest of shade trees within its central park. Later, they ate lunch in Catarina at *El Mirador,* a cliff overlooking the Laguna de Apoyo, Nicaragua's largest volcanic lake. Anne marveled at the panorama of pristine water sparkling with diamond ripples reflecting the sun and she recalled the sparkling waves of San Juan del Sur. After lunch, they drove to San Juan del Oriente, where they sauntered over narrow winding adobe-bricked roads filled with the distinct fragrance of wild orchids.

"To think what my date for the senior prom had to pay for an orchid corsage, and here they are everywhere," Anne declared with girlish enthusiasm, prompting Gregory to brush his lips against the side of her face.

Lumbering oxen pulled carts packed with pottery, and the back yards of simple houses held kilns and long tables of recently painted pots and ceramics. Primitive oil paintings in the Solentiname style of primitivist art depicting lush flora and exotic birds - white egrets, blue herons - hung on lines to dry, dancing with each puff of wind.

They continued sauntering into yards to review finished art for sale and they perused pottery of the familiar black and red pre-Columbian style as well as contemporary designs. Anne's eyes rested on a bowl with a nativity scene sketched in black on a rust background.

"It's beautiful," she pronounced. Gregory immediately purchased it for her, and by doing so he associated himself in her memory with the rich hours of that day.

They meandered back to the black sedan with the US Embassy insignia, Anne supremely happy as she looked at the boyish tangle of sandy hair falling across her lover's forehead. She reached over to brush it away, but oddly, at that moment, unease crept into the bottom of her heart. Was she in love as she believed, or simply enchanted? She had fallen in love with Nicaragua, its generous and friendly people, its warm and sultry climate, its breathtaking natural beauty, and the exhilaration of possible danger in this exotic place still reeling from the legacy of war and its violence. Was her love for Gregory real, or was it part of her enchantment with Nicaragua? They drove back to San Linda in silence, the question unanswered. Then she spied Renaldo.

"Hola, hola amigos," her gardener slurred, a foolish grin on his dirty unshaven face, waving a limp hand in greeting.

"Go home and sober up, Renaldo," Anne demanded sharply.

"Sí, sí, Señora," he agreed, as he turned and staggered toward the Casa Sánchez flopping against its gate like a Raggedy Anne doll.

"Not here. Go home!" Anne shouted out the front window of the sedan pointing in the direction of his house. Renaldo bobbed his rum-soaked head up and down.

"Sí, sí, Señora," he agreed again, staggering off in the opposite direction, away from the house he shared with Anita. Anne wondered if she should pursue him, but she could not force him to go home and she did not want him with her either.

"Leave him be, Anne," Gregory said as he drove onto the grounds of the Casa Sánchez and parked.

"Anita, you must tell Renaldo to go home," Anne declared at the threshold of the house. Anita peered at her wobbling husband.

"He is going home, Señora Ana, to the house of his sister Olga."

Anne glowered at her. Anita's decisions had created this situation, and while she admired the woman's spirit, she chafed over its consequences.

"You are angry, *verdad?"* Anita observed.

"I wish you well, Anita, but breaking up a family is difficult on everyone. Camilo and Hernández should not see their father like that." As soon as the words left her mouth, pangs of guilt assaulted Anne as she remembered Lynn screaming the same words at her when she left Keith. "You broke up our family!" She could not sit in judgment of Anita with her own bricks of guilt weighting her down.

"It is not good," Anita agreed, looking crushed. Anne considered asking for the woman's forgiveness, but remained silent feeling her words would be inadequate and maybe a little inauthentic.

"Señora Evita asks you to call this number," Anita said nervously.

"That is strange," murmured Anne. "Evie is with a delegation in Ocotal. Why would she call me from Ocotal?"

"She is not in Ocotal. She is in Managua," Anita declared.

Puzzled, Anne went to the phone and dialed.

"Hospital Bautista," intoned a woman's voice.

"Hospital Bautista?" Anne repeated loudly, capturing Gregory's attention.

"I am seeking Evita Gutiérrez. She is an American," Anne said into the receiver.

"Yes, she is here. She says to come," responded the disembodied voice.

"Why? What has happened to her?" Anne demanded.

"What's wrong?" Gregory asked.

"I can't understand the Spanish," she sputtered handing the phone to him. He spoke for several moments knitting his eyebrows while Anne remained suspended in anxiety until he hung up.

"Anne, Evelyn's fine," Gregory said. "But there's been an accident."

When he explained, Anne cried, "Oh, my dear God!"

"Qué pasó, Señora," asked Anita.

"Señora Evita is fine, but we must go now."

Gregory and Anne dashed to the car leaving Anita open-mouthed at the front door.

They entered the Baptist Hospital, an oblong building with several wings connected by long corridors, and rushed down a corridor into a stark white room containing two patients. Evelyn was sitting by the bed of one of them, a sleeping Tim Haverford flat on his back strapped tightly to a board.

"He broke his back," explained Evelyn. "I've been on the phone at the Saving Waters Christian Mission House for most of the day arranging a medical evacuation for Tim and for the coffin of Theodore Hicks to be flown back to Texas."

"How awful," Anne sighed. "How did it happen?"

"They were driving to Los Ríos; Hicks was going to preach at the church," related Evelyn.

"Yes, Pastor Rafael invited him," said Anne.

"The accident occurred at the top of the tall hill in El Crucero where the wind blows constantly. A gust apparently caught the Jeep Hicks was driving and as it left the road, Hicks hit an abutment crushing him and throwing Tim out of the vehicle. Two young people from the mission who were in the back seat were also ejected. One required stitches and another broke his arm. They called the house looking for you. Anita didn't know where you were. They were not able to express in Spanish why they were so frantic, but Anita concluded it was serious enough to call me to see if I knew where you were. The young people of the Saving Waters Christian Mission have no idea how to negotiate through Nicaraguan bureaucracy. They do not even have a good command of Spanish. Apparently Hicks took care of everything. The Saving Waters Cristian Church in Dallas is flying someone in late tonight to pick up the body and take Tim back to Texas."

Anne sank against Gregory, her eyes filling with tears as she gazed at Tim. He looked so innocent. She thought of Danny, who shared the same confidence of youth as Tim. What if it had been Danny? She shuddered, and Gregory drew her close.

"Does Tim know about Hicks?"

Evelyn nodded. "We spoke briefly before they sedated him again. He cried."

"He's so young to have to deal with this," choked Anne. "Is he paralyzed?" she asked, dreading the answer.

"No, but they need to keep him immobilized until they get him into a hospital in Texas. That's the reason for the board."

"Life is so unfair," lamented Anne.

"Yes, it is, *mi prima*," sighed Evelyn. Life could be grim and life could be transient. Evelyn hoped the Young Adults in Christ would return to America valuing every precious moment accorded them. She hoped, but she did not expect it.

The next day, Pastor Jim Bob Mullen of the Saving Waters Christian Church, a balding man with a wide girth and a bushy gray mustache, held a brief funeral service in Tim's hospital room for "Pastor Ted." Looking like a man who had not had enough sleep, Pastor Jim Bob was quick to inform all present that the Saving Waters Christian Church was not affiliated with the American Baptists who had founded the hospital. "But we are grateful for the medical skill of these fine Christians who saved our Tim," he added. Pastor Jim Bob thanked the doctor and two nurses present for their ministrations and then began the funeral service.

"Pastor Ted lived a life dedicated to God," he declared to the medical personnel present, the grieving young people from the Saving Waters Christian Mission House, Anne, Evelyn, Padre Doug, and Pastor Rafael. Early that morning, Padre Doug had driven to Los Ríos to get Pastor Rafael and drive him to the hospital.

"Pastor Ted always lived with the threat of death in Central America, but he felt called by God to help the people," continued Pastor Jim Bob. Evelyn translated.

"Pastor Ted left his mission in Honduras to come here after the Sandinistas were defeated," Jim Bob Mullen continued. "He felt called to bring Christ to a people that had suffered under communism for so many years. Now this valiant soldier of the cross has left us to be with Jesus. The mission on Earth of Pastor Ted is done."

Tears flowed from the Nicaraguan nurses taking their cue from the men and women of Young Adults in Christ who sniffled and blew noses. Pastor Jim Bob retreated momentarily into himself pressing a balled fist to his mustache as he struggled not to cry, then he suddenly burst out in song, his hearty tenor proclaiming:

> *Some day we'll leave this world of sin*
> *With all its dark despair,*
> *And, like Elijah, rise to meet Our Savior in the air.*
> *We'll be caught up in a chariot of clouds!*
> *Like Elijah of old, to the mansions of gold,*
> *We'll be caught up in a chariot of clouds*

When the singing ceased, Pastor Rafael whose eyebrows had raised perceptibly when the American pastor had referred to the Sandinistas as communists chanted, *"Teodoro Hicks, presente!"*

The doctor, two nurses, Anne, Evelyn, and Padre Doug repeated, *"Teodoro Hicks, presente!"*

Evelyn explained the Nicaraguan custom to Pastor Jim Bob. "By calling him present, Pastor Hicks will always be present in our hearts," she said softly. "Pastor Hicks was on his way to preach at the church of Pastor Rafael when the accident occurred."

Pastor Jim Bob's eyes renewed their watering, and he wiped at them with a handkerchief pulled from the jacket pocket of his white seersucker suit. He approached Pastor Rafael and hugged him. "Thank you, my brother in Christ," he cried choking back his tears. Although Pastor Rafael did not understand the English, he understood the sentiment and patted the distraught man on his back.

At the airport, Anne kissed Tim goodbye. "I won't forget you," he whispered.

"I won't forget you either. You must keep searching, Tim. God will listen to your questions without judgment. I'll pray for you," she said softly.

Tim's pasty white face blushed pink. "Thank you," he wheezed.

Two porters carried him on a stretcher into the medical evacuation plane followed by Pastor Jim Bob Mullen and the other injured young people, bandaged and limping. When the plane disappeared from sight, Anne said quietly, "I've only known him for seven months, yet he feels like a son to me."

"You were good for him, Annie," said Evelyn. "You encouraged him to open his mind. You gave him a gift of incalculable worth."

"Maybe," whispered Anne. "Maybe."

CHAPTER FIFTEEN

Anita's refrigerator arrived at the shack refurbished by Ernesto. Mario, a bold and canny shop owner who knew how to negotiate a bargain, accompanied his son to purchase the refrigerator from a departing Italian family finishing up a tour of duty at the Italian Embassy. Mario's father, Mario Duci, had immigrated to Nicaragua from Italy, but soon departed for the brighter lights of the United States, leaving behind the seeds of Mario in his mother, Isabella Flores. When Mario related his Italian heritage, the sellers lowered their price substantially.

Ernesto and Mario tied the refrigerator securely to the cab of Evelyn's truck, important to the safety of the goods headed for the Pulpería Iván Guadeloupe. Anita's mother Lillian squeezed her ample body into the front seat next to Evelyn while Mario and Ernesto settled themselves between cartons of goods and the refrigerator in the truck bed. Evelyn drove gingerly along the highway as a sudden move or a collision could snap the ropes. She warned the men in the truck bed to keep an eye out for the crazy American motorcyclist who zoomed by their house day and night, indifferent to whatever humans or animals were on the road, but fortunately, Harry Albert did not make an appearance.

They eased through the arch onto the rutted road of Lower San Linda and crawled past the Casa Sánchez to their destination.

Anne, Anita, Hernández, and Camilo were waiting by the store, brightly shining in its coat of still sticky yellow paint. Lillian slowly pushed her bulk out of the truck and waddled like a Japanese sumo wrestler toward her grandsons whom she surrounded with her flabby arms.

"Dios mío! Each time I see you, Hernández, you grow," she declared. She kissed him and Camilo, and then she shoved the two boys toward Mario Flores. "My grandsons," she said proudly.

Mario studied the boys intently for signs of good health, an indicator of the grandsons that would follow with Ernesto. The older child with the bright dark eyes of his mother looked sturdy enough, but the younger one appeared fragile. When he coughed, Mario frowned.

"He has asthma," explained Lillian, hoping the child's ill health would not displease Mario. Mario gave no reaction to her explanation and greeted both boys who looked up at him in wide-eyed curiosity before he turned away from them to help Ernesto unload the refrigerator. They rolled it over the rough ground on a dolly owned by Lillian and pulled it into the store, placing it at a corner where they plugged it into the newly installed electric socket, hoping for the best. To avoid installation charges, Anita had convinced her cousin Jairo, an electrician with the Nicaragua Energy Institute, to run an electric line from his house which was near the store, an illegal but common practice among related families in different dwellings.

Mario reviewed the renovated store and pronounced, "Good work, Ernesto."

The fifteen-foot-square building had once been a storehouse for the Sánchez family. During the heyday of the Sandinistas, it had served as the community's political headquarters, and for a brief time as a store that sold vegetables. For years a faded painted portrait of Sandino had remained on the outside of the building interrupted by a hole that cut into half of Sandino's face. When the building was vacant, village inhabitants felt free to take boards from its sides, but the zinc roof remained intact, and the building's frame had not fallen prey to villagers in need of construction materials or firewood. Anita scrubbed the concrete floor and whitewashed the interior. Ernesto built shelves for merchandise and a table for the cash box. The last task was to paint the building covering the desecration of their hero's countenance. Lillian expelled a full soprano sigh when she saw the sign painted in bright red and black proclaiming the store as *Pulpería Iván Guadeloupe*. "Iván is happy to see this," she trilled as though Iván were still among them.

Pride surged through Ernesto who watched his father examine the building thoroughly inside and out. There was not a man on earth whose opinion he valued more, a man who had fought for everything he had, including his life. To receive a compliment from his father raised Ernesto's confidence to lion status.

When the refrigerator purred proclaiming the success of the electrical installation, the group unloaded bags of beans, rice, flour, sugar, and small bottles of cooking oil. A portable cooler appeared next, filled with yogurt, milk, *leche agria*, eggs, and cakes of butter; then out came notebooks, pencils, combs, and cases of Coke, Sprite, and Rojita, a popular red soda drink indigenous to Nicaragua. The soda would be placed in individual plastic bags tied at the top for sale to customers so that the precious, scarce bottles would never leave the premises.

Evelyn carried in boxes of taffy purchased by Padre Doug from a candy factory in the Barrio of Acahualinca, one of the micro-business projects of Enterprises for the Future, a non-profit organization managed by three of her friends at the Solidarity House. Lillian hefted bags of oranges and grapefruit on her shoulders. From her own inventory, she brought bars of soap, tubes of toothpaste, and toothbrushes.

Mario patted his son on the back. "Your woman does well," he said. Mario possessed shrewd intuitions and Ernesto believed his father saw the potential in Anita, although grudgingly. He had accepted the coupling of Ernesto and Anita without additional comment after the first day he met her, and he had even expressed how sorry he was when Anita lost the baby. Rosita had dissolved into tears. Ernesto assured her there would be more babies coming. He felt slightly guilty in allowing her to believe the baby was his, but not enough to reveal the truth.

When his son left the bicycle repair shop at the end of the working day, Mario uttered a few disgruntled grunts, but bid him goodnight before he boarded a bus to San Linda to work with lanterns to complete the renovations. After Anita put the boys to bed, Ernesto stayed on to relish his new love's full body, and then caught the early morning bus back to Managua. This grueling schedule would have been unmanageable even for a man as strong as Ernesto had not Señor Sánchez released him from his duties as handyman until the "Guadeloupe Project," as he called it, was finished. Ernesto ached for sleep, but love fed him the energy he needed.

Shelf stocking completed, they followed Anita into her little house where she served them yucca fritters and *bunuelos*, small, hard Nicaraguan cookies shaped like doughnuts, both of which Lillian declared *sabrosa*, flashing proud eyes at her daughter. Anita felt she would burst with joy at the presence of her mother in her house for the first time.

"Where is your husband?" Mario eventually asked.

Anita had a satisfactory answer for him. "He stays with his sister Olga on the other side of Lower San Linda, " she explained.

"Your plans went well," commented Mario.

"*Por supuesto,* of course," responded Anita, utterly confident.

Mario let out a loud guffaw. *God, what a woman! A lioness like her mother, Lillian,* he thought. He looked at Lillian, his eyes glinting with pure masculine interest. That plump body and sharp mind opened up a hunger in him. After his son moved in with Anita, he decided he would pay Lillian a visit.

Later when the others had gone leaving Anita alone with her boys in the store, she surveyed the shelves and hugged herself. "The Virgin is smiling on us," she said to Hernández and Camilo. "We must thank our Mother Mary." She removed her rosary from the pocket of her apron, looked up toward the sky and whispered, "Mother Mary, my first child with Ernesto will bear your name."

***

Anita's good fortune presented her sister-in-law Olga with a dilemma that brought her to the gate of the Casa Sánchez to await the return of the American *señoras*. She had come to plead for her problematic younger brother who over the years had been a heartache. His marriage to Anita had tempered his excesses in drinking, but now Anita had dumped Renaldo, and the burden was Olga's once again.

When she was fourteen, her parents fell ill while working at a foreign - owned chemical plant near Ciudad Sandino. Many workers at the plant died, others became sick, and pregnant women gave birth to deformed babies. The workers claimed they were being poisoned by chemicals, but their protests to management and to the Somoza government were ignored.

Olga had to leave school to care for her sick parents and her seven-year old brother Renaldo. Fortunately for the children, the parents died before money ran out. Their deaths freed her to find work, and she sought employment as a maid cleaning houses to support her brother and herself. Their parents left them the small house in Lower San Linda with enough land to grow food and raise chickens. It was a nice house made of blocks with a zinc roof and four large rooms.

When he entered adolescence, Renaldo grew more and more unruly. One day he disappeared, finally surfacing ten years later with a wife and four children. The loud unruly family was homeless, and Olga took them in. One day he announced that he had joined the outlawed Sandinistas and would no longer be working at the Mercado Oriental because he had been assigned tasks far more important for Nicaragua. Then he disappeared from their lives altogether.

Following his disappearance, his wife declared, "I go to Costa Rica to live with my brother. Life is better there for my children."

Olga was relieved. Because she owned a house, she found it unnecessary to take on a husband. She needed no men in her life to suck out what energy remained to her. But after the Triumph, Renaldo returned home in terrible shape, hobbling around on an ulcerated leg he attributed to a war wound. "I am a hero," he said proudly.

Olga gathered enough money to send him to the Baptist Hospital in Managua where doctors cleared the infection leaving him with a nasty scar and a limp. After he recovered, he spent his nights drinking and his days sleeping it off. When Olga insisted he find work, he pointed to the leg.

"Work or leave," she declared one day, the most difficult statement she had ever uttered. Resentfully, he went back to the Mercado Oriental to sell charcoal and there he met Anita, the daughter of a store owner in Managua. Olga encouraged the relationship, expecting Renaldo to be incorporated into that family, ridding her of his burden. Anita's family, however, refused to welcome Renaldo, and the couple moved into Olga's house. Eventually Anita's boldness found them a job at the Casa Sánchez, and Olga was grateful when Anita had saved enough to purchase a small house on the other side of Lower San Linda. Renaldo was near enough to keep an eye on, but was not Olga's responsibility anymore. That is, until now. Olga's only hope was that the *señoras* in the Casa Sánchez would not fire him from his job because he had taken to the streets, soaked in rum, shirtless, and stupid.

Olga had heard rumors of a witch from the Atlantic Coast who supplied Anita with a potion causing Renaldo such sickness it took away his desire for drink, at least, until he forgot how sick he had been and went on another binge. She asked Anita to give her the name of the witch, and Anita promised to do so. Anita also told her she had recommended Olga as her replacement at the Casa Sánchez. Perhaps it would not be so bad if Anita provided her with the potion to keep Renaldo from drinking and the American women allowed him to keep his job at their house. And would it not be wonderful if she too was hired by the *señoras?*

Foreigners intimidated Olga with their many possessions and easy confidence seeming to command the very air around them. Still, Olga knew she needed to intervene on Renaldo's behalf. When the women returned, she swung open the gate for the truck and they waved in greeting.

"I am Olga, the sister of Renaldo," she introduced herself. Tall for a Nicaraguan woman, her face was soft and unlined, the black hair lightly speckled with gray hinting at her forty-five years. Although thin, hers was not an angular body like Renaldo's, but full around the hips and straight backed in a dignified sort of way. She wore an apron over a simple cotton dress, both of which she had sewn by hand.

They invited her into the house, but she stood on the threshold hesitating until the smaller one with the black hair took her by the arm and led her in.

"Me llamo Evita Gutiérrez," she said. "Have you been waiting long?"

Olga shrugged her shoulders. "I wait all the time. *No es importante, Señora Gutiérrez.*"

The other woman with the golden hair piled on her head brought her a glass of papaya juice. Unlike other foreigners she had known, they welcomed her even though they did not know her.

"Are you here to apply for the job of housekeeper? Anita told us you were interested," said the smaller *señora.*

"It would please me very much, but I am here to beg you not to send my brother Renaldo away. I will make him sober again. I promise. He is so sad without Anita. He will not be sad forever." Olga felt a thickness in her throat as she spoke.

The American women exchanged glances. The tall blond one nodded and the short dark one smiled and addressed Olga. "If he stops drinking, his job is safe," she promised.

Olga cried in relief. *"Ah, gracias, muchas gracias.* He will be good soon."

"And what about you, Olga? Anita tells us that you are a housekeeper with experience. We need a housekeeper. Anita will no longer be working here as she has opened the store."

"I work in the big houses of Managua for many years. I work very, very hard," explained Olga.

"Do you have references?"

"Sí, I have a letter from my last house. They are English and went back to England in January. I do not work now, except Anita pays me a little to care for her sons, my nephews."

"We will look at your letter and check your references, but first you must help Renaldo sober up."

"*Sí, sí.* Anita knows a way to do this and I will speak to her today."

When Olga left the Casa Sánchez, her feet flew lightly as though she was walking on air. A job at the Casa Sánchez! Renaldo, the source of so much discontent had finally brought her good fortune.

Disappointingly, Anita would not give her the name of the witch with the potion to make Renaldo sick. The two women spoke like adversaries, instinctively on guard, animosity hanging in the air between them. Olga felt as though she had become the target for Anita's rage at Renaldo. She wondered if Anita wanted Renaldo to debase himself so completely he would die.

Frantic, Olga took her brother's rake and cleaned the yard of the American women. She climbed up the high hill behind the Casa Sánchez to gather fallen bananas and dump refuse in the garbage pit. The extra effort prevented the women from immediately seeking a replacement for Renaldo, and they hired her in spite of her brother's continued drinking.

One day when the anesthesia of cheap rum could no longer dull the pain of an abscessed tooth, Renaldo appeared at the door of Casa Sánchez. Studying the swollen bulge on his gum, Olga could see that even if she pulled the tooth, she would need money for antibiotics. She had known people who had died from bulges such as his.

Señora Ana had already left for work by taxi. Señora Evita and her latest delegation were traveling down the Río San Juan to dig wells in a poor community.

"The *señoras* will not help you unless you are sober," Olga told her brother who slouched in pain against the door. Silently she muttered a prayer to Mother Mary for Señora Ana to be as generous as Señora Evita when she asked for money to take Renaldo to a dentist. She had heard many stories of the generosity of Señora Evita through her cousins who attended *la Iglesia Católica de San Juan el Bautista.* The Canadian priest at the church was Señora Evita's friend and when he said the funeral mass for street orphans, Señora Evita attended and often paid for the burial space in *el Cementerio del Corazón Segrado.* In Olga's mind, she was more Nicaraguan than American. Would Señora Ana find a place in her heart to help Renaldo?

"Go home and sober up," she ordered her brother shutting the door against him. Through the front window, she watched him stagger off moving in slow motion as if underwater. Leaning her back against the door, she blew out her cheeks in a long, shuddering sigh as her mind raced with how to present the dilemma to Señora Ana.

When she went outside to sweep the patio and spied a black woman and a little girl walking in her direction, Olga who had never met Renaldo's mistress and her child, instantly knew who they were. Something inside whispered that life was about to sour again. The woman, petite, and curvaceous, walked fluidly with the sensual sway of a whore. She had a dark polished face upon which pouted a full sensuous mouth exuding a daring sexuality. Her breasts spilled out of the low neckline of the flowered print dress that clung to her body. This dangerous, amoral beauty was clearly capable of destroying lives.

"You are the sister of Renaldo Aguilar, *verdad?*" the woman asked, a barracuda smile creasing the edges of her mouth.

"I am his sister," said Olga frigidly, holding her broom like a defensive weapon.

"We must talk. I am Patricia Archibald." Edging closer to Olga and pulling the little girl with her, she added, "This is Raquel, my child, and the child of Renaldo."

Olga froze, fearing whatever was to come next.

"Where is Renaldo?" continued Patricia. "My father tells me he is no longer living with his wife. *Papá* and Anita are delegates to the Sandinista Congress that is meeting in Managua, and she told him this."

"He is not here. You must leave. I am working," Olga said.

"I will not leave before I see Renaldo," Patricia countered. Olga saw tiny red veins in her heavy-lidded black eyes. Then she looked down at the child clinging to her mother's skirt. The little girl's querulous expression traveled upward over Olga's long body, and Olga's heart fluttered when she saw the sad charcoal eyes. Patricia hefted her daughter in her arms and moved close enough for Olga to smell the rum on her breath.

"Raquel is your niece," Patricia declared. Olga's heart chilled.

"My father brought me here with him from Bluefields to find Renaldo."

Olga felt her knees weaken. "Renaldo is drunk," she said uneasily. Everything was going wrong. The woman was using the child to pull her into an abyss of undefined and unwanted responsibility. She whirled around and started toward the house.

Patricia scrambled after her, Raquel still in her arms. The little girl had not uttered a sound. "Does Renaldo live with you?" asked Patricia.

"He is drunk. He will not give you money. He has none," snapped Olga.

"You must let us stay with you. Raquel and I have no place to live," Patricia said. Olga stopped and turned to face this woman who personified the end of whatever happiness she had begun to welcome into her life. She had always borne the blows of life dutifully. She had been rubbed raw and now that happiness was within her reach, she was about to lose it.

"*Salga!* Go!" she shouted angrily at Patricia.

A small strangled cry like that of a kitten in pain escaped from the tiny mouth of Raquel. Her face twisted and dissolved into tears. Fingers of guilt squeezed Olga's heart, and the manipulative Patricia violently shoved Raquel into her arms.

Olga pressed the child to her. *"Todo está bien,"* she purred, comforting Raquel as she patted the silky skin. Raquel's tears melted into whimpering and sniffles. Olga pulled a piece of cloth from her apron pocket to gently wipe the tears. Patricia watched knowingly, a malicious smile creeping across her face.

"Let us stay with you until *Papá* comes for us after the Sandinista Congress. *Papá* sleeps in a dormitory with other men. We cannot stay there. Raquel has no place to sleep," she pleaded with a forced humility, realizing she had already won.

"How old is Raquel?" Olga asked in defeat.

"She has almost four years." Raquel snuggled into Olga grasping her shoulder as though she was holding onto the ledge of a cliff. Olga loosened the tiny hands murmuring tenderly again, *"Todo está bien. Todo está bien."*

"We will stay only for a visit," added Patricia, but Olga heard the victory in her tone. She knew what "visit" meant as she gave Patricia the key to her house and the directions.

"You will find Renaldo there. He is sick with a bad tooth," she said.

When Patricia entered Olga's house tugging Raquel behind her, a moaning Renaldo, head down on the table drew himself up to look at her, and his face twisted in shock.

Anne came home early from work that afternoon, but Olga decided against telling her about Patricia and Raquel until later. The important priority was Renaldo's need for dental care. "My brother has an abscess in his tooth. *Es muy grande."* Olga spread her hands in emphasis. "He is in much pain." She hesitated, "And he needs a dentist, Señora Ana."

"How soon?"

Olga hesitated. "He is in much pain," she repeated.

Anne sighed wearily. "If he is sober, I will take him to a dentist in Managua tomorrow," she promised Olga, whose perpetually sad dark eyes brightened.

Olga clapped her hands together. *"Gracias, Señora Ana. Las Americanas son buenas.* I am lucky."

"And so are we now that you are working for us," responded Anne truthfully. She liked Olga better than she liked Anita, who annoyed her with her intrusiveness and excess energy. Also, Anita loved gossip. Even when informed of Anne and Evelyn's lack of interest, Anita would prattle on about their neighbors, informing them of whom was sleeping with whom or who had been arrested for drunkenness or theft. As a Sandinista delegate from San Linda, Anita felt it her duty to keep informed about every detail in the lives of those she represented.

Her exuberance about almost everything bothered Anne the most. The unceasing energy reminded Anne that her own energy levels were lessoning. At forty-two, she could no longer push herself all day and still be active late in the evening without unpleasant fatigue. Olga was nearer to Anne's age. Her pace was slow but thorough, and she did her work quietly and efficiently. Renaldo was another matter. She would take him to the dentist for Olga's sake, but she had little expectation that Renaldo, a weak and passive man, accustomed to being rescued by the women in his life, would stop drinking for long.

A sudden roar of a motorcycle approaching the house captured the attention of the two women.

"Look, Señora Ana. El Americano comes," Olga announced uneasily pointing out the front window.

"Olga, get the tire iron in my bedroom," Anne ordered as she quickly pulled the security door forward and latched it. Positioning herself at the door, she observed Harry Albert sputter his motorcycle to a stop in front of the house. He swung a beefy leg over the cycle and stopped to drag on his cigarette as though sucking in oxygen before clumping his big, ruddy body toward Anne like a worker carrying a heavy load. His usually disheveled hair was fastened back with an elastic band and he wore a T-shirt announcing the name of an auto dealership in an unfamiliar American city.

"At least he is dressed," Anne muttered, recalling the blur of topless flesh that often flashed by. Albert greeted her with a large audacious grin motioning with his cigarette-fingered hand for Anne to let him enter. He flicked ashes and they spilled down his jeans.

"Do you have a beer to offer a fellow American?"

"We're busy now," Anne responded aware of Olga's presence beside her, tire iron in hand, and feeling somewhat safer because of it.

Albert dropped his cigarette to the ground and crushed it with a sneakered foot after which he scratched his belly and tugged on a silver buckled belt that held his baggy jeans under a bulging stomach. "I met the other American woman a while back. Been too busy to be neighborly," he said. He shoved both flaccid hands through the rod iron security door wrapping them around its bars. The action startled Anne and she backed away a hasty half step. Albert leaned forward, peering at her. Anne noticed his eyes were covered with a milky translucent film.

"Your friend Evita told me you're not missionaries," he said, as though they were having a friendly neighborhood chat.

"No, I'm an English teacher," said Anne immediately annoyed with herself for responding to this unkempt stranger by offering him personal information.

Albert threw back his head and laughed. "A teacher! Dear lady, what this country needs is lessons – lessons in anything, even in English. If you want to do anything the right way, come to Nicaragua, then do the opposite of how they do it. I've lived under three governments here. Somoza's was a dictatorship, but Somoza was a good administrator. He knew something about efficiency. He ran the country like his own private business. Did you know that he called Nicaragua his private farm? No one liked him because America bought him and he let his national guard get out of hand. The Revolution had to come eventually."

He fired words like a pistol, not in even shots like Padre Doug, but in erratic scatters like buckshot, and the more he spoke the more Anne realized he was unbalanced, perhaps not dangerous but definitely unbalanced, and she wanted him to leave.

"The Sandinistas didn't know how to make socialism work. The Cubans tried to teach them, but they couldn't get it right. They knew nothing about running a government. They weren't socialists and they weren't capitalists. They didn't know what they were. They did have some pretty good people from East Germany and Cuba in medicine here for a while. The Cubans treated my stomach wound better than they did in the States." With that, Albert withdrew his grip from the bars, unbuckled his belt, and jerked down his jeans to display a tangle of scar tissue slightly above his left hip. Olga gasped at the sight of the scar and turned her head away.

"Skittish servant, you got there," Albert noted, smiling as though he and Anne shared an important secret. "You see this?" He pinched the scar. "It used to be inflamed with pus. The Cuban doctors here in Nicaragua fixed it. Six years and no pus."

The vulgar act annoyed Anne. "I'm glad you were able to receive the medical treatment you needed, Mr. Albert."

"Call me Harry," he said. "What's your name?"

"Anne Harrison."

"See you around, Annie," he said offering a salute and turning to go. *"Hasta pronto,"* he called and lumbered toward the motorcycle.

When he drove off, Anne felt a tremor of relief surge through her body.

"Está loco," observed Olga.

"He has a problem," agreed Anne. "I hope he will not become a problem for us."

When Olga went home later that afternoon, she found Renaldo slumped over in a kitchen chair, head in hands, groaning from a combination of hangover and toothache; Raquel at his feet played with an empty rum bottle. Patricia stretched out in the hammock between two trees behind the house, lay sound asleep and snoring. Olga prepared food for Raquel and Renaldo, demanding that Renaldo eat. He choked down the unappetizing rice and beans, his stomach churning with every bite. Olga warned him not to vomit, and he swallowed hard to keep the food down.

After the meal Olga ordered her brother to shower and put on clean clothes. The cold water sent waves of searing pain through his head and mouth. When he was presentable, Olga combed his hair neatly and reviewed him with a critical eye before they walked over to the Casa Sánchez bringing Raquel with them as Patricia was still sleeping.

Anne observed immediately that Renaldo was in pain, but he appeared sober and pliable, willing to do anything to stop the throbbing. Anne soaked a cotton ball with medicine she had brought from Massachusetts that was supposed to numb an infected tooth and gave it to Renaldo to place on the abscess. "Take the bottle home with you. I'll call a dentist I know for an early appointment at Managua Dental," She said.

"Gracias, Señora Ana," Olga sighed in relief.

"Be here at seven tomorrow morning, Renaldo," ordered Anne, and Renaldo mumbled something inaudible through the cotton in his mouth.

Anne looked down at the little girl clinging to Olga. "What an adorable child. Is she a relative?" she asked.

"She is the daughter of Renaldo and his mistress."

Anne rolled her eyes. "I see."

They left, Olga carrying Raquel and Renaldo holding on to his jaw, moaning. Anne closed the door and laughed aloud about the ludicrous situation. Then she called Dr. Sharon McGinnis, a medical missionary from Ireland who worked for Managua Dental, and made an early morning appointment.

Anne accompanied Renaldo in a cab to the clinic the next day and waited until the tooth was extracted. Later she put Renaldo on a bus headed back up the hill to San Linda and prayed he would go straight home and not to the drinking hut on Siete Sur. After she arrived at Managua University, she called Olga who assured her that Renaldo had arrived with the container of antibiotic pills given him by the dentist and was outside the Casa Sánchez garden rake in hand. Anne was relieved. She had handled that little crisis well without her cousin, and Evelyn would be pleased when she returned home tomorrow.

BOOK TWO
EVELYN

CHAPTER SIXTEEN

O n the morning of July 19, Evelyn parked her truck at the entrance of Lower San Linda overlooking the road to Managua where she and Anne watched an unbroken line of vehicles pass. Trucks crowded with jubilant men and women waving a river of red and black flags chanted, "*Sandino vive! Siempre la victoria!* Sandino lives! Victory always!"

"A historic moment," declared Evelyn. "The First Congress of the Frente Sandinista Liberación Nacional is opening today."

"How many Sandinistas are in Nicaragua?" Anne asked.

"The FSLN claims over 100,000, but no one really knows. The population of the country is under four million and the FSLN is the largest political party."

"Impressive," Anne commented as she viewed the parade of cheering and waving flags that saluted the morning. It called to her mind the Independence Day parades near Lake Quannapowitt in Wakefield, Massachusetts, which her family and Evelyn's family never missed. She and her cousins had hollered until their throats were sore as the lively bands and jaunty majorettes marched by. After the parade, the families set their blankets on the beach where they gobbled hot dogs and ice cream sold by beach venders. Later they frolicked in the cool waters of the lake and waited in impatient anticipation for the brilliant display of fireworks when dusk fell. Anne shared these thoughts aloud.

"Remember those days?" she asked.

"Yes, I remember," Evelyn responded distractedly, indicating that her fondest memories were not created at Lake Quannapowitt in Massachusetts. In a voice tinged with melancholy, she added, "During the early years of the Revolution, we thought nothing could stop us. We were high on hope believing we were creating a new society of social justice and economic equality. We were putting things right. Then came the war. Trucks of soldiers flooded out of Managua into areas of Contra activity, some down this very road. Wives and children left behind were crying."

Anne listened, a creeping annoyance invading her like the onset of a migraine. Evelyn knew her mother had cancer, and although she was in remission, it might eventually kill her, yet she chose to make her home in Nicaragua. During her childhood, there were times Anne would pretend with an unspoken longing that Uncle Roy was her father, Aunt Jane was her mother, and Evelyn's brothers were her brothers. Yet, her cousin had placed thousands of miles between her and her family for a life without security, without safety.

"The euphoria is long gone, and the party needs to elect fresh blood into the National Directorate or they will lose influence among those who yearn for new ideas and change. They need to include women in higher leadership levels. Women fought and died during the Insurrection against Somoza, and they fought against the Contras. They deserve a place in the higher leadership of the party," Evelyn was saying.

"I see," said Anne, confusion swirling through the mix of admiration and resentment she felt for her cousin at that moment.

"This is a historic moment, Annie."

Who cares? Anne thought. She knew she was being petulant like a little girl with hurt feelings, but she didn't care.

Evelyn spotted a break in the parade of vehicles and jammed the truck into the line. With the Nicaraguan National Hymn ringing in their ears, conversation became impossible, much to Anne's relief.

They drove past the United States Embassy compound where a small group of Nicaraguans were standing before the steel gate holding signs demanding payment to Nicaragua of the seventeen billion in reparations stated by the World Court, or the International Court of Justice as it was officially known.

"At the demonstration this afternoon this road will overflow with protesters – Nicaraguans, North Americans, and others," she said signing a V for victory as they drove past the handful of protesters and continued on to the Butler house. Managua University was closed during the FSLN Congress because a large number of delegates would be housed in its classrooms, so Anne would remain with the Butlers until they all left for the demonstration.

"See you later, Annie," Evelyn said when they arrived at the Butler house. "Now I'm off to pick up Dino at MU. We're going to meet Doug and Peter and Nellie for lunch at Los Antojitos. There have been rumors of Recontra activity in the Jinotega area near where my delegation is scheduled to visit. Nellie Franklin drove down from there yesterday and will give me an update."

Anne climbed out of the truck, but stood by its open door. The uneasiness that had settled in her stomach since the night of her disturbing crowd dream returned as she thought of Evelyn's delegation tour to Jinotega. On the way, her cousin would pass the spot where her daughter had been killed. "Are you sure Jinotega is safe for you, Evie?" she asked cautiously.

"Nellie will tell me," Evelyn responded. But that was not what Anne wanted to hear.

"It's just that – ah – well, this will be your first delegation to that area since...." Anne could not bring herself to articulate the tragedy of Jasmina. She rephrased the sentence into a question. "Are you sure you are ready?"

She studied her cousin, waiting. When Evelyn gripped the steering wheel so tightly her knuckles whitened, Anne knew she had understood the meaning of the question.

"In all honesty, *mi prima,* I don't know," she whispered.

"I'll pray for you," Anne responded in a near whisper and leaned into the truck to kiss her cousin on her cheek.

Evelyn expected the trip to Matagalpa and Jinotega to be emotionally challenging. She had requested Dino as driver of the La Esperanza minibus when her usual driver contracted dengue fever. She wanted Dino because with his English fluency he could help her with translation. Anne agreed to cover Dino's English classes for the four days of his absence, and with the lack of English speaking visitors to MU at the time, Pat had no need of him either; therefore, Ramón Morales released him to go on the trip.

Dino was waiting for Evelyn at the gate of MU. He lived in a small room on campus. He had always wanted to visit Los Antojitos but every spare córdoba he earned was converted into dollars and sent to his family in Cuba. Evita would pay for this treat.

He followed her to a table where three Americans were already seated. The only person he recognized was Padre Doug, so Evita introduced Nellie Franklin and Peter Hartwick. After greetings, Dino excused himself to look at the black and white murals of an intact Managua prior to the 1972 earthquake.

"He seems a pleasant young man," Nellie Franklin commented.

"He's a great help to Pat and to my cousin Anne. He will drive for me when my delegation visits Matagalpa and Jinotega in two days. We won't be any further north than the Victor Hebera Agricultural Cooperative. Are the Recontras active in that area?"

Nellie shrugged her shoulders in a "who knows" gesture and said, "Bloody conflict will be with us for a long time." A nurse from England, she had established a medical clinic in 1984 north of Jinotega where the fiercest fighting between the Sandinistas and the Contras had taken place. She had not only survived the war years but flourished by offering medical care to everyone regardless of political or military affiliation and had once saved a Contra military commander, ensuring the safety of her medical clinic from attack by them.

Her comments convinced Evelyn that a trip to the cooperative might be too risky.

"Maybe we should remain in the city of Jinotega," she remarked thinking out loud.

Nellie shook her head in a furious no; her long brown braid sprinkled with silver, a concession to her fifty-five years, flowed down her back. She was dressed in a long skirt and brightly colored beads like an American throwback to the 1960s, an era that suited her personality. "The Recontras are creating quite a row," she declared. "Even so, you should not shield your delegation from the reality of what is happening. Some of the Recontras are hoodlums, like gang members expanding their turf, but for most it's economic survival. They kill and plunder to live."

Peter Hartwick, sitting to Nellie's left nodded in agreement. A middle-aged bulky man as tall as Padre Doug and broader, he looked at Nellie with such intensity, Evelyn could feel the power of his devotion to her. He and Nellie were lovers even though one lived in Managua and the other in Nicaragua's dangerous rural North.

"The Contras that reformed as Recontras have enough arms to keep the violence going for some time, but I would not let that stop me from taking a delegation to the cooperative," he added. "Be fearless. Don't let the violent ones win."

"And you will bring your delegation to the protest at the US Embassy this afternoon," Nellie added in a tone that implied an expectation.

"The delegation is attending the FSLN Congress. Probably some of them will be at the demonstration, but I'm not bringing them," said Evelyn. Nellie looked disappointed. She pressed her lips together in a sign of pique. An eccentric, tough, and courageous woman, she was not averse to speaking her mind, regardless of the consequences.

"You must be forthright with them about ongoing violence in this country. They jolly well better understand what the Contra War has done to Nicaragua," she chided.

Evelyn was not about to engage in verbal sparring with someone whom she held in such high regard. For years Nellie had labored within a cauldron of war wounded, and she had seen the lunacy of it all. Speaking in a neutral way, without inflections, Evelyn explained, "At La Esperanza, we create an experience that allows people from abroad to see the reality of Nicaragua. From that experience, we hope they will be motivated toward working for political and economic justice at home, and against war anywhere as a way to solve political problems. But we do not force them to participate in anything with which they may feel uncomfortable."

Nellie paused for a moment, as if hesitant about voicing her next thought. Her bright blue eyes narrowed, but she did not push Evelyn any further. Instead she asked, "How is your cousin Anne managing?"

Evelyn pondered an answer and decided against mentioning Anne's infatuation with Gregory Garner. "It has been a learning experience for her," she said vaguely. "Of course, she's elated over the success of the school project in Los Ríos. Did Peter tell you about it?"

"Yes. It is a good project for a sabbatical year, more practical than sorting out some research problem that no one cares about," said Nellie, a thin smile gracing her face.

"You know, Evelyn, a sabbatical year first brought me to Nicaragua," Peter stated. Like Nellie he was deflecting the conversation from that afternoon's protest in order to disperse the subtle tension that hung heavily between the two women. A former Latin America Affairs professor from Arizona, he had first arrived in Nicaragua in 1985 with his wife and son and stayed on after his family had departed. He lived frugally on the royalties from his scholarly textbooks, honorariums from the lectures he gave at the Solidarity House to educational groups from Nicaragua and abroad, and the occasional course he gave on American history at Managua University. His ramshackle house was within walking distance of the San Juan el Bautista Catholic Church in Barrio Hermosa where he often dropped by the apartment of Padre Doug for rum and conversation.

"I know, and thankfully, you never left," said Evelyn, smiling warmly. She admired Peter and was grateful for the political insights he brought, not only to the North American community living in Nicaragua, but also to the numerous visitors that found their way to the Solidarity House.

"Peter and I never left Nicaragua, even in the worst of it," Nellie declared proudly. "And Peter never misses the embassy protests. I come down when I can, but these days we can only count on two or three other demonstrators besides us. It cheeses me off." Nellie looked as though she had just been wounded.

Once a week for eight years, Peter, Padre Doug, Pat, David, Evelyn when she wasn't squiring a delegation, along with Nellie when she came down from Nicaragua's northern mountains, and Americans, Canadians and some Europeans living or visiting in Nicaragua had gathered to challenge the United States in front of its embassy to stop funding the Contra War. With the end of that war, their numbers had dwindled, falling to a handful. Now only a scattering of protesters appeared week after week to demand economic aid without the strings of privatization they believed would worsen the plight of the poor.

"The Contra War is over," Padre Doug declared. "The world is filled with ongoing wars. Nicaragua is yesterday's news."

Nellie bristled at his words. "Padre Doug, Nicaragua is still in a bloody awful war. The powerful are killing hope for a better life for the poor majority in this country. They are taking away their chance for an education and for medical care. And like in the past under Somoza, they are robbing them of their property and their dignity. For God's sake, it's a war on the poor!" she protested with an edge of irritation.

Padre Doug's expression was compassionate. He had accepted the present reality of diminishing interest in the protests better than had she.

"We need to continue the protests!" she exclaimed looking directly at him; then turning her attention to Evelyn, she wagged her finger like a teacher admonishing an uncooperative student. "That's why you, Evelyn, must bring your delegation this afternoon. We need you there and you must come!" Nellie slammed the palm of her hand on the table rattling flatware, sending a fork flying. A startled Dino returned, stooped to retrieve the fork from the floor, and without a word, slipped into his seat at the table.

"Isn't she a tiger," laughed Peter gleefully, his eyes blazing as he clapped his hands in applause before placing a kiss on his beloved's cheek.

Dino observed the animated North Americans and the agitated Englishwoman, unsure of what to say. His dark thoughtful eyes rested on Nellie who began to speak, fanning the air with her hands for emphasis.

"With all the money they spent on the war, the Americans owe us. Nicaragua needs that seventeen billion in reparations recommended by the World Court."

"They will never see a penny of that money, Nellie," Peter said. "Come on, love, calm down." He slid his arm behind Nellie and gave her a little squeeze.

Nellie sighed. "Yes, I know. I'm just nattering on," she said dejectedly.

Evelyn lowered her head into her palm. "I'm tired of it all."

Nellie reached across the table to cup Evelyn's free hand with her own and said understandingly. "So am I Evita, but I cannot give up and neither can you."

After lunch, Evelyn and Dino drove toward the retreat center near Lake Managua that housed attendees at the FSLN Congress. Pulling up to the gate, they waited for the guard to contact the delegation leader of twenty of the American attendees. Seven of them would remain following the congress for the La Esperanza tour. Evelyn pulled into the gated compound, parked the truck and waited. Within minutes a distinguished looking man approached them and introduced himself as Paul Reardon, a law professor from California.

"I wish I could go on your trip, but work does not permit it this time," he said apologetically kissing Evelyn's cheek Nicaraguan style. "Would you like to meet your tour participants?"

"That's why we are here. The director of La Esperanza has learned of Recontra activity near an agricultural cooperative we had planned to visit. I've come to talk to the delegation about it."

Reardon shook his head knowingly. "Once you open the floodgates of violence, they are impossible to close," he said gloomily. "You may wait in the dining area while I round up your travelers."

The dining area was under a thatched roof behind a concrete block building of dorms. Evelyn and Dino settled themselves at a bench and waited until a middle-aged man with a short gray beard covering his upturned chin moved toward them distractedly as if in deep thought. To his side was a woman with spiked salt and pepper hair and thick tortoiseshell glasses. Evelyn looked at the list of delegation participants and pegged them as the university professors from Boston, Dr. Raymond Beckett and his wife Dr. Muriel Kent. The older couple behind them, the man balding, the woman stout, had to be the Presbyterian minister, Reverend Thomas Shaw, and his teacher wife, Shirley, from Minnesota. A muscular man of medium build with wavy chestnut hair trimmed to barber shop perfection looked vaguely familiar. He must be Ian Cameron, the engineer from Albany, New York. The slender woman with translucent skin and auburn hair walking with him would be his wife, Rhoda, a public health nurse. Finally, the young man around Tim's age, walking with a jaunty saunter had to be the university student from California, Benjamin Conway.

Evelyn greeted everyone, calling each participant by first name except for the Presbyterian minister, whom she addressed as Reverend Shaw. She introduced Dino, and heads nodded, hands shook, and polite greetings were murmured.

"Are you Nicaraguan?" asked the university professor, Dr. Muriel Kent, a prim and forbidding expression dominating her granite face. She had intimidated generations of students with her severe demeanor, which she embraced as an asset.

"No. I'm American," Evelyn answered.

"From your name, I thought we would have a Nicaraguan guide," said the professor, disappointment in her voice. "Would not a Nicaraguan be able to present a more authentic view of the reality in this country? But then, you have the young man, do you not? I assume he is your assistant." Her eyes nearly invisible behind her thick glasses observed Dino with such intensity, he squirmed under her gaze.

"Dino Fuente will drive the bus and help with translation. He's Cuban," declared Evelyn tersely. Dr. Kent frowned and tossed her head derisively. Evelyn read the signs. After nine years of leading delegations, she could spot the problematic personalities immediately.

"Gutiérrez is my married name. I have lived in Nicaragua since 1980. I know Nicaragua. If you are unsatisfied because the leadership of this La Esperanza tour is not Nicaraguan, arrangements can be made to have your money returned. However, should you choose to remain, we welcome your participation." Evelyn spoke non-defensively and with authority. She stared directly into the professor's face until the woman lowered her eyes and conceded, "There is no other available time for me."

Benjamin Conway, the twenty-year-old university student oblivious to the unpleasantness of the exchange, asked with animation, "You lived here during the war?"

"Yes," Evelyn said.

"Is your husband a soldier?" Muriel Kent shot him a look of reproach.

"He was in a civil defense unit for his village, but he was not a soldier. He was an evangelical pastor," Evelyn answered patiently.

The Reverend Thomas Shaw's friendly round face lit up with that news. "I hope we get to meet him," he said brightly.

"I wish you could, Reverend Shaw, but he was killed three years ago in a Contra attack on his village." As she spoke Evelyn felt her throat tighten and hoped she had not betrayed the emotional vulnerability she felt whenever she spoke of Rudy. Above all, she must convey strength, confidence, and competence to these seven people who were literally putting their lives into her hands.

Shaw's expression morphed into one of compassion. "I am so sorry. God bless you, "he said. His pudgy wife Shirley added sympathetically, "Life can be difficult."

"Life in Nicaragua is difficult for many people," said Evelyn, "and that is why your presence among us is so important. It says to Nicaraguans, 'We care.'"

Uncomfortably aware that Ian Cameron was watching her, Evelyn's eyes moved toward his. He was a disturbingly attractive man with colbalt blue mischievous eyes. He was also perplexingly familiar. She rooted around in the distant corners of her mind for a memory of someone who looked like him. Then, with effort she slid her gaze away and said, "You have your schedules and I promise you this trip will be one you will remember. However, we may have to alter the itinerary."

As she spoke, Cameron's oddly familiar face drew her once again. Humor glinted behind the compelling blue eyes, and inexplicably, awakened a sweet feeling within her. She continued delivering information under his gaze. "We are scheduled to depart after the FSLN Congress on the twenty-first of July and return to Managua late on the night of the twenty-fifth in time for you to prepare yourself for your early morning flight the next day. The nine of us will be traveling in a twelve-passenger minibus so we will have plenty of space," she explained.

"We carried down a suitcase of medicines, hypodermic needles, and more," said Rhoda Cameron, standing at her husband's side and rocking nervously on her heels as she spoke.

"And we have a suitcase of notebooks, pencils, pens, and children's books in Spanish. My fifth grade class brought in the supplies and we ordered the books from a publisher in Los Angeles. The PTA paid for them," declared Shirley Shaw proudly.

"Your donations will be appreciated," said Evelyn with a collegial smile. "Shortages of basic medical supplies are a problem here as are educational materials. The American embargo has been lifted, but it takes time for supplies like these to filter into the country."

"You were saying about the schedule change," Muriel Kent abruptly reminded Evelyn.

"Yes, I was," said Evelyn pleasantly, even though she found the woman annoying. "We may have to eliminate the scheduled visit to the agricultural cooperative in rural Jinotega. Fighting is still going on in that area between Recontras and Recompas."

"Who are they?" asked the student Benjamin Conway interrupting her explanation.

"I was about to tell you," she said patiently. "The Recontras are remnants of the Contra Army and the Recompas are remnants of the Sandinista Army. They are both continuing the war, although the Recontras are the most numerous and active in their attacks. They have become a problem in the northern sections of Nicaragua."

Ian Cameron spoke for the first time other than during their greetings. His voice was soft, but the tone insistent. "Señora Gutiérrez, I am especially eager to visit the agricultural cooperative. It is my understanding that this cooperative is a model for projects in appropriate technology."

Evelyn returned her attention to him. He was dressed in khakis and a cotton short-sleeved button-down shirt, respectable but not ostentatious. "Please call me Evelyn," she said.

He smiled with warm spontaneity telegraphing a connection that felt uncomfortably intimate. "Yes, Evelyn."

"You're correct about the cooperative. They are innovative," she said.

"Will we be in danger, I mean, because of the fighting?" asked Conway interrupting again, his voice betraying youthful eagerness for such a possibility. Evelyn understood the implications of the question. She had dealt with affluent American youth before who had no visceral understanding of the horror of war. Conway would have to be watched. Any spontaneous risk-taking on the part of one delegation participant could endanger them all.

"That is what we'll have to assess," she explained.

"My reason for signing on for this trip is to observe this particular cooperative," Ian Cameron stated. "Would there be a way for me to go without exposing the rest of the group to danger?"

His wife Rhoda added, "As a public health nurse I'm eager to see the cooperative's approach to medical care in an isolated community." Wrinkling her nose, she turned to her husband and said, "But, if it's too dangerous, Ian, I don't think any of us should go."

"What about the rest of you?" asked Evelyn.

Thomas Shaw, his round bald head already sunburned, commented diplomatically, "We all signed up for different reasons."

His wife Shirley trilled, "Better to be safe than sorry."

Evelyn rested her eyes on the university professors. Muriel Kent pushed up the tortoiseshell glasses creeping down her nose before she spoke. "My specialty is life situations of women in developing countries. I am not going to miss the opportunity to interview women living on an agricultural cooperative in Central America within a country emerging from a war." She spoke crisply and with finality.

Evelyn nodded and looked at Raymond Beckett who stroked his beard pensively, then said without commitment, "I'll think about it." From the distracted look in his pale eyes, Evelyn concluded he thought about many things all the time.

"Well, I'll think about it too," she said. "La Esperanza is responsible for your safety so I must speak with our director. He will make the final decision."

As the seven walked away, Evelyn's eyes remained on Ian Cameron, who looked back over his shoulder and caught her gaze bringing a warm flush to her face. The man drew her in like quicksand. He was unlike Rudy in physique, demeanor, and speech, but he was touching something fearfully exciting inside her and she did not like it. Anne's morning reminder that in two days she would be traveling over the road where Jasmina was killed had rippled the forced equanimity on which Evelyn struggled to float. The interchange with Nellie during lunch was unsettling. Now she was confronted with inexplicable feelings for this stranger. Apparently she felt more ambiguous about this delegation than she had believed when she had decided to accept the assignment.

Evelyn and Dino made their way back to the truck, observing gray clouds marching across the sky like soldiers. A downpour was coming. The torrent burst as they drove along, water pounding the windshield, blurring the hulking earthquake ravaged buildings. She dropped Dino off at MU and proceeded on to the United States Embassy. By the time she arrived, the storm had ceased and the muted sun of late afternoon spilled over her.

She walked toward the crowd of spirited protesters. They were chanting, "Seventeen billion! Abide by the World Court! Abide by the World Court! Seventeen billion for Nicaragua!" Managua police had closed the road and stationed themselves in a line between the protesters and the gates to the US Embassy.

Evelyn surveyed the crowd for people she knew. Long timers from the Solidarity House were there, including Nellie, Peter, Doug and the newest Solidarity House member, Dr. Sharon McGinnis, the dentist who had treated Renaldo. She had made a valiant effort to save Renaldo's tooth, but it was too decayed and infected and had to be pulled.

Anne and Pat were present, but not David who was home in bed recovering from a bad cold. Evelyn spotted Rhoda Cameron, and her eyes roamed the crowd until she found Ian standing next to Benjamin Conway. Both were raising fists and shouting along with the more vocal protesters. At the sight of Ian, Evelyn's heart leaped in her chest. If she could only connect him with someone in her past, maybe some boy she once had a crush on, his mysterious effect could be understood and eliminated. Tearing her eyes away from him, she swept the crowd for Shirley and Thomas Shaw, but neither they nor Muriel Kent and Raymond Beckett were present.

The thought flitted through Evelyn's mind that Gregory Garner might be watching them from his office in the fortress like compound. For Anne's sake, she hoped it was unfounded speculation.

CHAPTER SEVENTEEN

On the afternoon of July 21, after the final speech of the FSLN Congress had been delivered and delegates had begun their trek home, a yellow minibus growled out of Managua. The city was dense with wetness, and the bus jostled over scarred streets, trailing a pall of exhaust. Seven sojourners filled with an eager expectation of adventure and in blissful ignorance of that day's dramatic event in the Department of Jinotega where they would arrive in two days, traveled the highway north to Matagalpa, a city one hour south of Jinotega. When they opened the mini-bus windows, rainy season mud splattered upward, settling on sticky arms like chocolate syrup on a sundae; yet that was better than the sauna like atmosphere when windows were closed.

Muriel Kent wet a handkerchief from her water bottle and swabbed at her face. "This water is hot enough to brew tea," she complained to her husband who had disappeared into his thoughts, oblivious to the rivulets of sweat dribbling toward his tailored short-sleeve shirt. She wacked him on the arm with the water bottle to rouse his attention and he nodded and mumbled an irritated acknowledgement.

When they exited Managua the discomfort lessened, encouraging the delegates to fall into muted conversation or to doze. Thomas Shaw snored softly as his wife Shirley rested her head on his shoulder. Never in all her days had she imagined she would be traveling in Nicaragua with her husband, savoring one more extraordinary experience in their forty years together. Theirs was a regenerative marriage, loving, and committed. Soon they would retire, and they planned to travel as extensively as their finances would allow. Gazing at him, the woman inside her started to come alive. Even after all these years and three grown children, she found him attractive in the privacy of her own heart.

As the minibus gobbled up miles through the countryside, Benjamin Conway slept, long legs sprawled across the two seats he occupied. Rhoda and Ian Cameron pointed to unfamiliar trees, scouring a handbook on the flora in Central America. The subdued rays of late afternoon sun seeped between treetops stirring with the whisper of a hot breeze. The countryside transitioned into a darker richer green as the minibus climbed high bluffs intersected by ravines, passing thick and lush pastureland dotted with brown cows. Faint puffs of vapor hung over cultivated fields of rice and stubby guinea banana palms. A feast of natural beauty created an atmosphere of peace within the bus, nudging the travelers to speak in whispers as though in a library or a church. Signs of village life appeared, framed by the higher purple silhouettes of mountains. Along the way the scorching heat of Managua had faded into a spring-like warmth.

Ian asked Evelyn about the heaps along the roadside that looked like they had been blackened by fire and were glistening wet in dark ugliness. "People burn their garbage and farm wastes," Evelyn explained.

"Such an unhealthy practice. I hope they compost some of their waste," commented Rhoda thinking of the high rates of asthma in undeveloped countries.

"Some do," responded Evelyn, "but not everything can be composted."

As the minibus neared Matagalpa, Alfonso Miranda, director of La Esperanza, learned that Recontra had just sacked the offices of the Central American Hydroelectric Plant in the Department of Jinotega, killing a guard and abducting two workers. The plant was located in a rural area some distance from the city of Jinotega, but not far from the Victor Hebera Agricultural Cooperative. Miranda cursed himself for agreeing to provide the gringos the trip they had been promised, including a visit to the cooperative. He should have known better than to trust assurances by army officials that Recontra activity had been contained in that region. "We chased them far into the mountains," the officer had assured him.

After learning of the attack, Miranda dialed the Hotel Milagro in Matagalpa where the delegation would lodge for two nights, and spoke to Señora Zenobia Ricardo who owned the small hotel. Word had not yet reached Matagalpa about the attack, but the *señora* was not surprised given rumors about the Recontra activity in the countryside. She assured Miranda that she would deliver a message for Señora Gutiérrez to return to Managua following the Matagalpa visit, but first to call him at La Esperanza.

In late afternoon, Dino rumbled into the city of Matagalpa bumping over gray brick roads, and shook to a stop in front of a small nondescript cinder block building with a dark wooden sign announcing *Hotel Milagro*. Before they exited the minibus, Evelyn stood before her delegation to provide a brief orientation.

"Matagalpa was founded by the Spanish in the mid 1500s. Nicaraguans call it the Pearl of the North. The City of Matagalpa is located within the Department of Matagalpa and the economy within the Department is based on coffee, cattle, and milk. We'll be visiting a medical clinic, a public school, and the grave of Benjamin Linder, the young American whose killing by the Contras contributed toward turning the tide in the US against the Contra War. There will also be plenty of free time to explore on your own. You won't want to miss La Catedral de San Pedro de Matagalpa, Nicaragua's third largest cathedral. It was built in baroque style with paintings, carved wood, and sculptures. You may also want to visit the childhood home of Carlos Fonseca, an important early leader and founder of the Sandinistas, and there are some interesting historical statues."

After she spoke, the travelers spilled like school children from a school bus into refreshing breezes floating in from the mountains. They trooped into the hotel lobby, dotted with traditional Nicaraguan rockers, where they were greeted by Pablo Ricardo, an older man with a protruding pot belly whose demeanor bore an incomprehensible nervous unease as he spoke to Evelyn, his hands fluttering like butterflies.

"*Lo siento, Señora Gutiérrez.* My wife knows where the rooms are, but she left suddenly to attend to her niece who is giving birth. I do not find the list," he apologized, projecting an image of someone constantly disorganized. Evelyn spoke to him calmly, and together they decided where the guests would sleep.

The bedrooms were small: two twin beds to a room, one bureau of ancient vintage, and a sink with one faucet. The bath was located down the hall where one toilet and one shower served all nine guests. The toilet lacked a toilet seat and toilet paper. One of Evelyn's pre-trip instructions had been to carry toilet paper at all times, so the travelers were prepared. The shower stall had one faucet that dispensed cold water and a plastic bucket for storing the precious liquid as water was often shut off in Matagalpa due to deteriorating piping and pumps that were erratic.

"You will find the rooms simple and clean. La Esperanza has taken delegations here many times," Evelyn assured her delegation before they migrated to their assigned rooms. They all agreed to gather together in the lobby at five-thirty and then proceed to a local restaurant for dinner. Evelyn asked Señor Ricardo for a phone to call the offices of La Esperanza to check on any up-to-date information about the Recontras.

"*Las líneas que no funcionan, Señora Gutiérrez.* The wind breaks them off and on all day," he declared. Evelyn was not pleased to hear of the downed lines. With two hours of unstructured time before dinner, she went to her room for a nap, but her mind raced with a jumble of unrelated thoughts, from Ian Cameron to Recontras. Misgivings about this tour gnawed at her. Before they left Managua, Alfonso said he had spoken directly to the government military commander following the July 17th attack on the rural town of Pantasma in the Department of Jinotega, an hour to the north of the city. Alfonso had been assured that the La Esperanza delegation would be safe; nevertheless, instinct told her to be wary.

The Shaws stayed in their room cuddling during the two-hour respite. Rhoda settled into a rocker in the lobby and pulled out her latest copy of *Capital Region Health.* Muriel Kent retreated into the dining area to write in her notebook, and her husband Raymond Beckett joined Ian Cameron and Benjamin Conway for a walk. The three tall men collected curious stares from the locals as they strode along Matagalpa's cobbled streets. Feeling conspicuous, they smiled and greeted everyone they met with, *"Buenas tardes."* Within minutes, they came upon La Catedral de San Pedro near the Parque Morazan. They entered the magnificent structure with its unusual ceiling of intricately carved patterns.

"The ceiling is unique to Nicaraguan churches. This opulent cathedral is the most important non-political monument in town," stated a young woman sitting quietly in a pew.

"You speak English," declared Benjamin, observing her ash blond ponytail.

The woman stood up. She was slender, freckled-face, and dressed in green medical scrubs. "I'm from Oklahoma. Dr. Eileen Leonard," she introduced. "You must be with the La Esperanza delegation. Evelyn said you were arriving today. My husband and I are in charge of the Koch Centro de Salud a few blocks from here. We don't have much time for relaxing, but I stop by the cathedral when I can to meditate. Your delegation is scheduled to visit our clinic after dinner. Please tell Evelyn I will offer dessert."

"Yes, we will," said Ian observing the woman who, although wholesomely attractive, betrayed her weariness by the drooping pouches under her eyes.

"She always visits when she's up this way, although that hasn't been for over a year since her daughter was killed," declared Dr. Leanord.

"Her daughter was killed?" asked a surprised Benjamin.

"She never mentioned it," commented Ian.

"That's Evelyn." Eileen Leonard shrugged her shoulders.

"What happened?" asked Benjamin.

"The Jeep in which her daughter was riding hit a landmine," she said.

"Holy shit!" exclaimed Benjamin.

Raymond Beckett shot him a disapproving glance. Noticing the disdain on his face Dr. Leonard assumed he was the disapproving father of the over-expressive young man and changed the subject. "If you're looking for other interesting places to see, the monument on the east side of the main square commemorating the deaths of those who fought to end the dictatorship of Somoza is sobering," she suggested.

"My personal interest is the Museo Casa Cuna Carlos Fonseca," said Raymond Beckett. "I'm a professor of history specializing in Latin America. Fonseca was one of the founders of the Sandinistas and I must see his museum."

Dr. Leonard nodded her approval. "For that you will need at least an hour, first to find it, then to appreciate it. The house is filled with memorabilia and descriptions of Fonseca's life. He lived there with his mother and four brothers and sisters throughout the early 1930s." As she spoke, she slid the strap of her purse onto her shoulder. "Must go. See you tonight." She sprinted off with an athletic step turning back briefly to wave. Benjamin's eyes followed her intently. "Pretty for an older woman, like our delegation leader," he declared. "Isn't that something about Evelyn's daughter being killed by a landmine?"

Ian looked thoughtful. "If I remember correctly, Evelyn said her husband was killed in a Contra raid on his village. She's courageous to stay in Nicaragua after the two tragedies."

Raymond Beckett looked at his watch. "It's getting late. Shall we visit the monument recommended by Dr. Leonard?" he asked impatiently.

Without comment, the three allowed Beckett to lead. "What brought you to Nicaragua, Benjamin?" the professor asked as they walked. He arched an eyebrow in the young man's direction, his face mirroring his suspicion of his motives. The expression was not lost on Benjamin.

"It's a long story," he replied, barely audible.

"You must share it with us sometime."

They found the monument: rebels dramatically frozen in stone poised for battle. Ian swept his eyes up the statue. "We immortalize those who kill, but do nothing to honor those who work to prevent war," he commented wistfully.

"Sometimes war is necessary," Beckett remarked as he touched the base of the statue. "Matagalpa was a center for fighting during the Insurrection. The rebels liberated it from Somoza's National Guard in July of 1979. This monument immortalizes that liberation. Without war no liberation would have been forthcoming."

Ian nodded. "You're right, Ray. Sometimes war is necessary, but too often war is the product of armchair warriors and war profiteers."

Beckett nodded his agreement, and they stood in silence, each lost in his own thoughts.

When they returned to the Hotel Milagro, they found the others waiting in the lobby. A visibly annoyed Muriel Kent declared in an angry voice emphasizing each word distinctly, "You are late. It is six."

"Don't be upset," said Ian. "We visited a cathedral and a monument immortalizing revolutionaries. Then we just walked around. We needed exercise after sitting in the bus for over two hours."

Muriel grunted but said nothing. Ian thought to himself that good ole Ray was probably going to hear from her when they were alone.

"We met an American woman doctor who said she would serve us dessert at the medical clinic tonight," stated Benjamin.

A smile graced Evelyn's lips. "That's nice of Eileen. She and her husband Frank run the Koch Centro de Salud. We'll visit the clinic after dinner, so let's go eat." Everyone rose and the others followed her.

"Today we will eat at the restaurant owned and operated by the Nicaragua Association of Mothers and Relatives of the Kidnapped and Disappeared. These are women who lost children during the Insurrection and the Contra War," Evelyn explained. "Since these children are no longer here to help support their parents in their old age, the restaurant provides an alternative form of support. I should tell you one of the mothers usually speaks to us about the work of the organization."

"That is perfectly acceptable to me," remarked Muriel Kent. "Interviewing women who lived through these wars is what I came to do."

"How's the food?" asked Benjamin thinking of hamburgers.

"Okay," Evelyn answered honestly.

"Not good, huh?" Benjamin asked, not attempting to disguise his disappointment.

"There are other choices in Matagalpa," suggested Evelyn.

"No. I want to meet these women," Muriel Kent insisted. The others murmured their agreement and they entered a wooden building that looked like a house, pushed three small plain wooden tables together, and sat down. Posters of four Revolutionary heroes hung on whitewashed walls and Evelyn gave a brief history of each: Thomas Borge, the old and revered Commandante of the Sandinistas; Daniel Ortega, the Sandinista Revolutionary President of ten years, voted out the previous February; Carlos Fonseca, the founder of the Sandinista party and inspiration behind the Revolution, whose museum Raymond Beckett wanted to visit; and Dora María Téllez, the respected Insurrection heroine, who had attempted to win a leadership position within the Sandinista party at the FSLN Congress, but had been defeated.

"They will regret their rejection of Téllez," Muriel Kent declared with disgust as she studied the poster. "Women activists at the congress were infuriated. Sexism is an evil that must be eradicated in Nicaragua."

"And worldwide," added Evelyn. "When Dora María Téllez led the attack that took Somoza's National Assembly hostage in 1978 and won not only the release of Sandinista political prisoners but a million dollars in ransom money, she inspired women to join the revolutionaries. I agree with you, Muriel. The Sandinistas will regret their rejection of her."

"*Buenas tardes,*" a wispy voice said turning their attention toward a small woman with a sagging face and thin lips turned down at the corners. She held a pencil and a torn piece of lined paper that she fanned nervously.

Evelyn spoke to the waitress, and then recommended *el plato típico.* "The dish is based on what everyday Nicaraguans eat." A murmuring of agreement followed; however, the waitress did not leave. She whispered to Evelyn who repeated her comments to the group. "Her name is Petronia Estrada and she asked for permission to speak to us."

Another murmuring of agreement followed over the rumble of hungry stomachs. Muriel Kent whipped out the notebook she carried wherever she went.

Petronia's voice was barely audible, yet Evelyn understood and translated. "Her youngest son was kidnapped by Contras in 1985. He was fourteen. Last year they found his body in a shallow grave in the hills. Two other sons were killed in the war. Her husband is also dead."

A visible sigh of distress emerged from the group of listeners. Muriel's eyes widened behind the tortoiseshell glasses. Petronia spoke in bland, unemotional language as though she were repeating food orders, not relating a monumental personal tragedy to foreign strangers.

"Usually we are presented with information about the history and importance of the association, not a personal history," Evelyn explained to the group. "Please continue, Señora," she said to Petronia.

The woman folded her hands, her head bowed. Raising her head slowly she spoke in the kind of low voice that is usually reserved for relating dreadful things. Her face looked spent as though all emotion had been rubbed away.

"I found my son, but other women do not find their children. A man from the government is here and he tells us, 'The war is over. Your relatives are dead. Let them remain where they fell.' This is not right. My friends need to find their children."

Her words and the pain they communicated touched the hearts of the nine people watching her. Even the harsh lines etched into Muriel Kent's stern expression softened like waves erasing footprints in the sand. Shirley Shaw dabbed at her eyes with a white handkerchief.

"Evelyn, would a contribution of money help?" asked Reverend Shaw.

"She will not refuse money, but I think she just wants to tell her story without being dismissed. She wants to be treated with dignity."

"Then, for heaven's sake, find out how we can help," said Muriel Kent impatiently.

Evelyn addressed Petronia in a gentle voice. "Señora, I am told that Witness for Peace is gathering lists of the disappeared. Do you know anyone in Matagalpa with Witness for Peace?" Petronia shook her head in the negative. "Then we will find you a contact. They will help your friends find their missing relatives." The faint beginnings of a smile, more like a wrinkle with teeth in it, creased Petronia's lips.

"Gracias, Señora. Dios le bendiga," she whispered and then disappeared into the kitchen.

"What did you tell her?" asked Muriel.

"I told her we would find someone to help her friends locate their missing relatives. Witness for Peace has documented hundreds of kidnappings. No one knows exactly how many are missing, but the numbers range up to 10,000. Communication is so difficult in rural Nicaragua that we may never know the exact number. What we do know is that Witness for Peace is actively working in the Department of Jinotega to find the missing. We will ask Tony Pizzano, the American we will be interviewing in Jinotega to locate the organization and have them contact Señora Estrada."

Raymond Beckett dramatically threw a substantial wad of córdobas on the table. Dino's eyes dilated at the sight of such a pile of money. "For Petronia," he announced. "Are not the rest of you going to contribute?" Everyone except Dino dug into pockets and pocketbooks like obedient followers.

"Such terrible goings on," sighed Shirley, clutching her husband's hand.

"What is Witness for Peace?" Benjamin asked hesitantly, clearing his throat. He was reluctant to show his ignorance, fearing they might discover he had come to Nicaragua without serious thought. Dr. Beckett was already suspicious of him.

"You don't know?" sneered Muriel Kent, who had regained both her composure and her abrasive manner of speaking. Benjamin shook his head.

"Do you know anything about Nicaragua?" her husband asked with equal antipathy.

Benjamin lowered his head. "I'm learning," he said sheepishly.

To prevent further caustic remarks, Evelyn answered the student's question. "Witness for Peace began in the United States in 1983 in response to the Contra War. Volunteers came to Nicaragua and put themselves in harm's way by going to civilian areas where the Contras attacked."

"The Presbyterian Church has had strong ties with Witness for Peace since its inception. And many of our young men and women volunteered," added Reverend Shaw proudly. "Only my church duties prevented me from signing up."

Evelyn laughed silently, amused by an image of the portly pastor living among energetic young WFP volunteers.

"During the war, Witness for Peace documentation provided the US Congress with severe human rights abuses," she continued. "And that documentation contributed toward pressuring Congress to stop war funding ."

Raymond Beckett added to her explanation. "When official funding stopped, operatives within the Reagan Administration resorted to selling arms to Iran illegally in order to secure continued funding for arms. You are all probably aware of the Iran-Contra scandal that followed." He paused and scowled at Ben. "You are aware of Iran-Contra, I assume, Benjamin," he said, his voice dripping with contempt. He had sized Benjamin up as a shallow young man, like the hundreds of shallow young people who passed through his classroom, desiring not to learn but to achieve good grades to get into a good business grad school and make the kind of money they did not deserve to make.

Benjamin lowered his head and murmured in a small voice, "Yes."

By now Evelyn knew she had correctly identified Muriel Kent as a disruptive influence, but she had not identified the negativity in Raymond Beckett. At first glance, he appeared simply introverted like David Butler, but his comments were as imperious and abrasive as those of his wife.

Fastening her eyes on him, Evelyn stated with quiet authority, "I am in charge of this delegation and I insist on courtesy and respect. Although it is highly unlikely that you will find yourself dependent on each other in a dangerous situation, it is important for the safety of all that we form a cohesive, supportive community during these four days."

A flash of astonishment played over Beckett's face; Muriel Kent turned white. Like an invisible mantle of chain mail, uncomfortable silence fell over the group. Evelyn could feel Ian Cameron's eyes bidding connection, but she refused the unspoken invitation. When the food arrived: rice, beans, a fried chicken leg, and fried plantain, served with a tomato and cabbage salad and tortillas, Evelyn said, "Please say grace for us, Reverend Shaw," and the pastor obliged, following which they quietly picked at the uninspiring food.

Raymond lifted his glass to the light, and seemingly satisfied it was clean, took a sip of the clear soda he had ordered. "When most Americans think of Latino food, they think of Tex Mex, but Tex Mex is not authentic Mexican food. What we are eating now is similar to what everyday Mexicans and Nicaraguans eat," he commented.

Evelyn accepted Beckett's effort at social conversation as a signal that he had decided to tone down his rhetoric and conform to her rules. "So, what brought you to Nicaragua, Ben?" he continued with friendly nonchalance as though nothing unpleasant had passed between him and the young student. He heaped a spoonful of beans on a tortilla and awaited an answer.

Benjamin hesitated, chewed, and considered carefully before responding. He could accept the overture or he could reject it. It was his decision. In the end he decided to explain honestly why he was really in Nicaragua, and dispatch the anxiety he felt over this secret.

"I came because of my girlfriend," he admitted keeping his eyes on the cola in his glass. "She signed up for the trip. Then her father had a heart attack and she had to go home, so I took her place. I've never been interested in Latinos or anything related to Latin America or to politics, but now I want to know more."

Evelyn smiled warmly. "It's good you are here, Ben. What a shame your girlfriend could not come. Did she sign up for the Matagalpa/Jinotega tour, or was that your idea?"

"It was my idea. I'm an anthropology major. I wanted to do more while I was here than listen to politicians." He made no mention of his desire for adventure, perhaps with enough danger to tell a good story at home.

"You made the right decision," Ian affirmed.

When the bill arrived they presented Petronia Estrada with $100.00. She burst into tears, sputtering *gracias* between sobs and wiping her eyes with her dirty apron. Shirley Shaw spontaneously hugged the weeping woman and the others applauded.

They walked back to the hotel, boarded the bus, and drove across town where Doctors Eileen and Frank Leonard emerged from a long narrow cement block building painted fire engine red with a medical white cross on its side proclaiming Koch Centro de Salud. After greetings, the couple led them into their living quarters at the end of the building: a bedroom, where they kept clinic files; a living area containing rockers, a short-wave radio, and a small TV; and a kitchen, where the clinic *pila* was located. They washed dishes, clothing, bed linen and towels in that small trough and on the four-burner kitchen stove, they sterilized the bandages that had to be reused. Four chairs and a square table were jammed into the kitchen along with a refrigerator where medicines were kept on separate shelves from the food items. Shirley Shaw, observing these crowded living conditions, was filled with admiration for the Leonards as she thought of the medical missionaries to whom her church denomination gave financial support. They probably lived with similar challenges as they did their healing work.

"This clinic opened seven years ago," explained Dr. Frank, as he was called by his patients. His wiry face bore too many worry lines for someone his age. "I don't know how long we'll stay open if we have to pay taxes on imported medical supplies as the new government is proposing. Our budget is so tight we would be forced to charge. The people we serve are poor and we believe medical care is their right." He led them into the examination room where medicine cabinets lined one wall, and an x-ray machine occupied a corner. From there they went into a larger room with four cots. "Our sick bay," he said.

"Where are the patients?" asked Benjamin.

"We are a clinic, not a hospital. When the Cuban hospital was open, we sent our serious cases there as they had adequate equipment and supplies; unfortunately, that hospital closed three months ago. Now we send our patients to the public hospital along with as many pharmaceuticals as we can spare."

Dr. Eileen asked the group to follow her husband out to the patio where she would bring them watermelon juice and cake.

"We serve about sixty-five thousand people," Dr. Frank continued as they meandered onto the patio and pulled up chairs. "Our work is chiefly concerned with tuberculosis, the number three killer in Nicaragua after diarrhea and malnutrition. We are named after Robert Koch, the German physician that discovered the TB bacterium."

"The consequences of not continuing medical vaccinations are disastrous," said Dr. Eileen carrying a tray of juice and cake. "The Revolution's vaccination campaign wiped out polio and put a huge dent in the TB caseload. Both diseases are making a comeback."

"It's so awful," lamented Shirley. "How can we help?"

"Take the message back that the war is not really over, only changed. People are dying again from illnesses that can be prevented."

"A shooting war is dramatic. Without the war people are losing interest in Nicaragua. Providing medical services to the poor is too esoteric a concept to interest people," commented Raymond Beckett with cynicism.

"But one must not give up hope," interjected Reverend Shaw. "God is present in all times and we must never allow hope to fade."

"God will need an army of helpers to address the medical, educational, social, and economic problems of Nicaragua," the professor responded, shooting a look of annoyance at Shaw. The naïve pastor had no real understanding of the cruelty and brutality perpetuated throughout history for power and wealth. Antipathy for those on the bottom is present in all societies; his so-called God had not intervened in the past and would not in the future.

"That army will be found," declared Reverend Shaw with a cheerful optimism that only increased Beckett's level of annoyance.

Ian's eyes flitted from professor to pastor, mirroring bemusement yet believing they had both spoken truth. "My wife and I are considering volunteering in Nicaragua for a year," he informed the doctors. "Rhoda is a public health nurse and I am an engineer. Where do you think we could be most useful?"

The faces of both doctors brightened like illuminated lights. "We would be glad to talk to you at length about it. Your skills are desperately needed here," responded Dr. Frank.

Reverend Shaw smiled broadly. "You see, there is hope," he declared.

Beckett grunted. The pious old man's vocabulary was irritatingly limited to the word hope. What a group he and Muriel would have to endure for the next three days – a vacuous college student and a naïve clergyman who had probably spent his entire life safe behind the walls of some culturally barren church along with his simple bleeding-heart schoolteacher wife. At least the engineer and his wife, and the Gutiérrez woman seemed worldly, especially Evelyn Gutiérrez, who was not only competent, but projected an inexplicable feminine appeal even when chastising him. He wished he could leave the others behind and be personally escorted by her. Impossible, of course, but a pleasant thought.

CHAPTER EIGHTEEN

The following day the minibus sputtered to a stop onto the gravel in front of a public primary school in the poor Barrio Hermano Pedro Narvas. The dingy building looked dejected below rising hills layered with shanties from which it drew its students. A scraggly wind-bent tree leaned toward the faded red zinc roof and clumps of trampled grass surrounded the building. Chickens scrambled over the grass on their way to nowhere.

A white-haired old man exited the dreary building and greeted them.

"Holden Willison, Rector," he introduced himself shaking the hand of each person with firmness. His fair complexion and light hazel eyes announced him as American, and they responded in English.

"Rector Willison only speaks a little English," Evelyn informed them.

"He's not American?" Ben asked.

"He is half-American, the son of one of the American Marines sent to Nicaragua in 1924 to fight Sandino and his rebels," Evelyn explained. Benjamin's hazel eyes, similar in color to that of Willison's, widened and he murmured, "Cool."

The visitors unloaded the notebooks and pencils and other materials that Shirley Shaw had collected and clumped over broken concrete leading to the entrance to the front door. Then they entered into a small room that served as a faculty lounge and registration area for students. The room painted a dispiriting yellowish green, displayed two large posters taped on one wall: Nicaragua's hefty Minister of Education Humberto Belli, dour and serious and President Violeta Chamorro, smart and tailored in her trademark white suit. Next to the president was a cork bulletin board haphazardly papered with notices.

After a few cursory comments, Holden Willison led them into the first classroom. Rows of children, some jammed into wooden desks, others sitting on small wooden chairs with notebooks in their laps, stared at them from curious faces. "The families of some students make their own desks and carry them to school every day. Other students use the chairs we provide," explained Willison in Spanish; Evelyn translated.

The walls were barren except for a few pictures drawn by the children. The blackboard was old and scratched with barely legible writing on its surface. A petite young teacher dressed neatly in a blue skirt and white blouse, the same colors as the uniforms of her students, smiled at the visitors, then motioned and the children all stood up. In unison they said *buenos días,* their sparkling dark eyes examining the foreign visitors.

"This is our first grade class," announced Willison. "The first grade meets in the morning; the fourth grade uses the classroom in the afternoon."

Shirley noticed that each child had a notebook and one pencil, but nothing else. "Where are the textbooks?" she asked.

"We keep them locked in a cabinet until we use them. We do not have enough for each child, so they share," Willison answered. His leprechaun demeanor seemed to amuse Shirley, who smiled broadly.

"I'll talk to teachers and librarians back home to find a way to raise money for books and posters for the walls. Children need to have visuals," she said. She wanted to promise to send Holden Willison a constant stream of educational supplies, but feared creating an expectation that could not be fulfilled.

"How old are your teachers, and what are their educational qualifications?" she asked.

"They are eighteen to forty and they need a secondary school education to teach," Willison stated in English.

"He speaks English very clearly," Benjamin noted. Willison's hand flew to his mouth as if to silence it.

Evelyn laughed, "Holden, you are a sly one. You speak English!"

"A little. *Poquito,"* he replied pinching his thumb and forefinger together.

"And I bet you understand everything we say," Evelyn laughed.

"Good thing I kept quiet about that pretty first grade teacher," Benjamin declared with a lopsided grin.

"That is a sexist remark," Muriel chastised eager to put Benjamin in his place. His straggly dark brown hair drooping over his forehead was not only too long for Nicaragua's heat and humidity but she felt an indication of indifference to a proper appearance. He wore a T-shirt with some sports insignia on it and his underarms emitted an odor she found disgusting. He was obviously an indulged child.

"I'm glad I came on this trip," Benjamin declared, ignoring her comment.

"I'm glad you did too, Ben," Ian said placing a friendly hand on his back. The action released a fragment of memory in Evelyn's mind. She had witnessed similar gestures of affectionate good will from her high school history teacher, Maurice Campbell. The memory tugged at her consciousness until she was able to image Mr. Campbell in her mind as a man with high cheekbones and a firm jaw looking enough like Ian to be related. She smiled knowingly to herself; the mystery of Ian Cameron was about to be solved.

"Ian, do you know anyone in Stoneham, Massachusetts?" she asked.

Ian smiled. "Stoneham was my childhood home," he declared. "Why do you ask?"

"Stoneham was my childhood home too," explained Evelyn.

Ian's face lit up and he stared at Evelyn with such intensity that heat coursed through her veins. "I'm trying to place you. When did you graduate from high school?" he asked.

"1970."

"I graduated in '67.

"Do you know my cousin Anne Harrison?" she asked. "She graduated in '67."

"Annie Harrison? I had a crush on her. I was in a play about unicorns once at her house. I think her cousin wrote it."

"I am that cousin, Ian. So your name is really Campbell, not Cameron, as it says on the list from La Esperanza."

"Yes, I am Ian Campbell. Your list is wrong."

"So it is," Evelyn agreed. "At times our Spanish-speaking staff confuse the foreign names. Campbell and Cameron are close. And Maurice Campbell must be your father. He built the set for my childhood play. How is he?"

Ian's hearty laugh welled up from deep inside. Evelyn had been in his life before. "Retired, but still woodworking," he declared.

"How extraordinary two childhood acquaintances should meet again in Nicaragua," said Reverend Shaw, delighted by the reunion of these two people whose lives had taken dramatically different paths. "It's a small world. And we must never forget how very small it is," he added.

The group remained at the school while Muriel interviewed the women teachers and Raymond and Rhoda interviewed Rector Willison, Rhoda asking questions about the health of the students and their families. Ian, Shirley and Reverend Shaw, and Benjamin intermingled with the children, Benjamin amusing the kids by drawing silly clown faces in their notebooks. Evelyn translated, when necessary, but the language of smiles and laughter flowed among children and adults more than words.

When they bid goodbye to Holden Willison, Shirley promised to bring the needs of his school to the attention of every educator she knew in Minnesota. They ate lunch at TipTop, a Nicaraguan fast food chain where, much to Benjamin's satisfaction, they feasted on fried chicken and French fries. While they ate, Evelyn related the story of another young man named Benjamin whose grave they would be visiting after lunch.

"Benjamin Linder was Jewish, yet he came to Catholic Nicaragua in 1983," she began. "He was a mechanical engineer, one of many internationalists who came here during the Contra War to help us. People said he wanted to make a difference in the lives of people. Contras shot him and two Nicaraguan co-workers as they measured water flow in a stream near El Cua where they were preparing to construct a hydroelectric installation. The project was to bring electricity to the people of the mountains."

The group fell into a reflective mood following her words and ate quickly with little conversation. After lunch they walked the five blocks to the National Cemetery, speaking in low, hushed tones as though participating in a funeral. Entering the old yet well-maintained graveyard, they passed ornate statues of revered saints watching over the dead and continued toward a dirt path meandering through grass, trimmed unevenly by machete, until they reached the final resting place of Benjamin Linder. He rested under an elongated flowerbed with a metal plaque pillow. Engraved on the plaque was a unicycle and a dove of peace. They listened quietly as Evelyn read the words from the plaque, her fingertips caressing the raised letters.

"*Benjamin Ernest Linder, Internacionalista, Nacido 7 Julio 1959, San Francisco, California, USA. Caido 28 Abril 1987, San José del Bocay, Jinotega, Nicaragua. La luz encendió brillara para siempre.* Benjamin Ernest Linder, Internationalist, Born 7 July 1959, San Francisco, California, USA. Fell 28 April 1987, San José del Bocay, Jinotega, Nicaragua. His light shines brightly always."

"Did you know him personally?" asked Ian sensitive to the solemnity with which she spoke.

"I met him once during a performance of the Nicaraguan National Circus in Barrio Monsignor Lezcano. He performed as a clown in full make-up and rode a unicycle. He often entertained children this way and they loved him. On his unicycle, he would lead them to the health center for their vaccinations."

"Lost to a needless war, like so many others," murmured Ian, mostly to himself.

"Nicaragua has suffered too many of these losses," Evelyn said with a deep sigh.

"Only one student like Linder would make teaching a worthwhile experience for me," murmured Beckett, inadvertently revealing his disappointment aloud in the profession he had so carefully crafted.

They remained in silent reverence at the Linder grave until Evelyn whispered. "Until next time, Ben." She led them back past the vigilant saints and towering crosses and out of the gates of the cemetery where she announced, "The rest of the afternoon is yours. This evening we will gather for dinner at the hotel."

Beckett immediately put distance between himself and his wife and departed to search out the Museo Casa Cuna Carlos Fonseca. Shirley and Thomas Shaw started toward the main street filled with shops. Ian and Rhoda Campbell strolled languidly through the Parque Morazan. Muriel Kent settled on a park bench to write in her notebook about the young teachers she had interviewed at the public school. Benjamin Conway reentered the cemetery to return to the gravesite of Benjamin Linder.

The story of a young man sharing his name and his Jewish heritage had awakened something in Ben. His own family was affluent, he was spoiled, and he knew it. Although his mother was Jewish and his father Catholic, his family eschewed religion, and he had little knowledge of the faith that may have influenced Linder to go to Nicaragua. His parents expected nothing less of him except to excel academically, get into an excellent university, move on to a top ranked graduate school, and become a financial success like them. He had grasped at the chance to go to Nicaragua thinking he might have some great adventure in a third world country. With his generous allowance, he had the money and his girlfriend Lisa had given him the opportunity, but he had not shared his decision with his parents knowing they would object fearing Nicaragua was too dangerous for their Ben.

How different he was from Benjamin Linder, who had risked his life and lost doing something grand at twenty-eight. Eight years from now when he reached twenty-eight, would he be consumed with such a fierce passion? Or would he play it safe becoming more cynical by the day?

***

Dino nosed the yellow mini-bus to an iron gate where a small dark-skinned guard in a gray uniform and the insignia of the Cuban flag on his cap approached, a surly expression on his face. Dino nodded to him and said, "My name is Dino Fuentes from Santiago, Cuba. My friend is Señora Evita Gutiérrez, friend to Dr. Tomás Ruiz."

The guard's stern expression morphed into a wide smile. *"Señora Gutiérrez!"*

"Emilio! Cómo estás, Emilio?" cried Evelyn, her eyes watering at the sight of the familiar face she had seen so many times during the happy days she and Jasmina had spent on the hospital grounds with Tomás.

"These are bad times," Emilio said depressingly. "Only three of us remain to guard."

"May we go inside?" asked Evelyn.

In reply Emilio swung open the gate. Dino parked directly in front of a stately white building. A sudden pang of grief besieged Evelyn as she stepped from the minibus into an aura of suffocating quiet. "What happened to the patients?" she asked in a strangled voice.

"Some went to the public hospital; others to their homes."

"All gone," she whispered.

"Sí, all gone," repeated Emilio, who stood closely by her side nervously observing her face drain of color.

"What is the Cuban government going to do with the building?" she asked.

"I do not know."

Evelyn walked slowly toward the entrance of the hospital, Dino and Emilio shadowing her every move. Emilio opened the door, allowing her to enter into a deathlike silence. Dino followed at a respectful distance as she moved through the building stopping briefly to look into each room. Everything was gone – beds, furniture, tables, lamps, but in the office of Tomás, the memory of him hung in the air like an omnipresent spirit. Nothing had been touched. His awkwardly constructed wooden desk sat forlorn and neglected awaiting his attention. His medical books were still crammed haphazardly onto dusty bookshelves. She picked one up and absently leafed through its indecipherable pages sending a cloud of dust into the air, and a tremulous smile flit across her face as memories of the play weekends with Jasmina and her "Uncle Tomás" floated through her mind. The child buzzed around him like a honeybee around a hive as he ploughed through paperwork grumbling about the necessary documentation he needed to submit to officials in Cuba. On his face, however, he wore the resolutely cheerful expression of one who loves his work even when he is complaining.

If only she had kept Jasmina with her on that fateful day. If only she had not acceded to the child's pleas to ride with Uncle Tomás. Usually she and Jasmina would join Tomás in Matagalpa, but that week he had returned to Managua by bus for a shipment of donated medical supplies and had crowded the supplies into Evelyn's Jeep. Without enough space to seat two people in the Jeep, Pat had offered Evelyn her sedan for the trip. Jasmina wanted to ride in the one remaining seat in Evelyn's Jeep because it would be driven by her Uncle Tomás. The remarkable unpredictability of life, one day simmering with heat and steam and the next day gone in a volcano of fire. Evelyn felt hollowed out.

"We gave everything to our patients, except this," said Emilio, gesturing toward the books and the office furniture. His gravelly voice jolted Evelyn back into the present.

They drifted through the building slowly and stealthily as if not to disturb the ghosts and eventually exited out onto the back steps. Evelyn sank onto the stoop where she gazed out at a backyard verdant with the season's rains, unaware of the tears streaming down her cheeks.

"This building is perfect for a children's home," she murmured.

Dino felt compelled to say anything, do anything to assuage her pain. He pressed clenched fists to his eyes willing the words that would comfort her and a thought materialized. "Evita, my uncle is a doctor in Havana. I will write to learn what he knows about this place. Perhaps they will sell it to you for the children's home."

She touched his arm unleashing streams of compassion within him. "Thank you, Dino. I will hope," she said. A barely perceptible smile graced her lips and Dino felt blessed.

***

Señor Ricardo and two maids pushed four small wooden tables together to form a banquet table in the foyer of the Hotel Milagro. Petronia Estrada with other women from the Association of Mothers of Heroes and Martyrs arrived bearing hearty bowls of chicken and rice that they placed on the white clad table along with baskets of freshly-baked bread. Evelyn had hired them to cook the dish, similar to Spanish paella. She had purchased choritzo, chicken, garlic, and onions, and instructed the women to use the ingredients liberally. "Americans like meat and salt," she said. Fruit juice, Nicaraguan beer, and wine from Chile that Evelyn had carried with her from Managua accompanied the food.

Three vase centerpieces of fresh cut flowers graced the table. When all were seated, Evelyn asked Reverend Shaw to say a prayer after which she raised a glass of wine in a toast. "Because of solidarity like yours, we in this little country are encouraged. *Salud!*" Wine glasses clicked together with a chorus of *salud.*

"Nicaraguans like Americans," Evelyn continued. "They even liked the individual Marines that occupied Nicaragua from time to time. After all, the Marines brought baseball to the country, and Denis Martínez, the Nicaraguan baseball star who played for the Baltimore Orioles is a national hero. The rest of Latin America is passionate about soccer."

"Except in Cuba," interjected Dino. "Cubans and Nicaraguans both love baseball."

"Oh, yes, how could I forget," Evelyn chided herself. "The Marines spent some time in Cuba too."

"Sports heroes, right up there with our war heroes," said Beckett, summoning a disgusted tone.

"Sports are a kind of war, aren't they? Especially American football," commented Rhoda.

The professor nodded. "Good metaphor, Rhoda," he complemented. "And war is a theme that repeats itself over and over again in American and Nicaraguan cultures. Did you know that at one point during the 1920's, there was one American soldier in this country for every one hundred Nicaraguans?"

"Yet they remain a hospitable people, Professor Beckett," commented Reverend Shaw.

"And courageous," added his wife Shirley.

"Yesterday I read Dr. Beckett's book about the CIA's strategy of low intensity warfare during the Contra War. The idea was to kill noncombatants like health care workers, farmers, and teachers so that morale was undermined and people would turn against the Sandinistas," declared Benjamin.

Beckett listened to Ben, with a faint smile born from the student's interest in what he had to offer. He had been surprised when Ben had asked him about Nicaragua's history and quite delighted to lend him the text that he himself had written.

"Nicaraguans were tired of war," Evelyn added. "And the Sandinistas made mistakes. They lost touch with their base, took them for granted. These things also contributed to their loss."

"Familiar story," commented Ian.

The conversation continued until stomachs were full and heads light with Chilean wine and Nicaraguan beer. Then Evelyn, guitar in hand, taught them her hand-clapping version of *Alabaré a mi Señor* giving a tambourine to Rhoda, another to Ian, and a tom-tom to Ben, who obliged her with a lively beat.

"This song is especially for you, Reverend Shaw," she announced. "I host delegations of church groups who come to Nicaragua to build churches and schools, and we always sing this song because it is simple to learn and quite lively. Listen and then repeat this chorus: *Alabaré, Alabaré, Alabaré, Alabaré, Alabaré a mi Señor.*"

The group moved away from the table, rearranged chairs, and quickly mastered the foot-stomping chorus of *Alabaré,* belting it out following each verse sung by their leader. The timbre of Evelyn's honeyed voice when she sang the verses vibrated within Ian as he shook the tambourine.

All but the professors joined in on the chorus of *Alabaré, Alabaré, Alabaré, Alabaré, Alabaré a mi Señor."* Noticing their lack of enthusiasm, Ian and Rhoda shoved the tambourines they were playing into professorial hands declaring, "Your turn." The startled duo tentatively began to shake the instruments.

"What is the translation?" shouted Muriel Kent above the singing.

"The chorus repeats I will praise the Lord," responded Evelyn.

"Praise God, *Alabaré!"* exclaimed Reverend Shaw. "That's spirit-lifting music," he declared, slapping his thigh for emphasis.

Benjamin's hands flew over the tom-tom elaborating on the beat, and the Shaws clapped and stomped their feet in syncopation as Evelyn sang three more verses.

"The final chorus. Everybody!" she declared and all voices except those of the professors shouted, "*Alabaré, Alabaré, Alabaré, Alabaré, Alabaré a mi Señor.*" Evelyn slammed into her guitar with a dramatic ending flourish, and Benjamin produced a drum roll while everyone clapped and Ian hooted.

Elevated by food, drink, and music, the group fell into enthusiastic chatter. "I am curious to know your church affiliation, Evelyn," said Reverend Shaw.

"I question religion," she responded tersely.

The pastor was surprised by her response. Had not she been married to a clergyman? Had he heard a note of bitterness in her voice? "I hope we can talk about your questions," he said, inviting her to his counsel. She smiled an acknowledgement of his invitation and brought them back to the music teaching them lyrics to simple Nicaraguan folk songs. After a while of singing together, the diverse group transformed into a community where the flower of trust between them began to blossom, so that even when they were spent with song and weighted with the need to sleep, they were reluctant to part. Voices softened as they shifted into sharing personal stories.

"What brought you to Nicaragua, Evelyn?" Ian asked.

She was cognizant of a flutter in her chest when he spoke. "I was assigned to Nicaragua by a magazine I was working for," she said briefly.

"You no longer work for the magazine, so you must have chosen to stay during the Contra War. Why?" he pursued, holding her with his eyes.

Rhoda took his arm. He extricated himself from her grip and sank back into his chair where he commenced to ruminate as though speaking to himself while cradling the back of his head in his hands and looking upwards at the ceiling. "You see, Evelyn, the generation we share had limited choices," he declared in a muted voice, commanding others to attention if they wanted to hear him. Everyone did. "We guys could fight and risk being killed in Vietnam, we could flee the country and be branded a traitor, or we could attend a university to escape the draft."

Slowly he raised himself upright and leaned forward; placing his elbows on his knees, he cupped his hands around his chin and looked directly at Evelyn. "As a woman, you did not have to go to war, yet you came here to war. Why?" The question hung in the air penetrating everyone with a sense of expectation. Except for the professors, they knew something was brewing between Ian and Evelyn. In the short time they had been together they seemed to share secret threads of communication.

Rhoda was aware of her husband's yearning to escape the burdensome memories of Vietnam. He had seen and done things in that beleaguered country that he was unwilling or unable to share. It was he who had insisted on going to Nicaragua, ostensibly to investigate his interest in appropriate technology, an interest he had developed in Vietnam, and, more disconcerting, to investigate the possibility of living in an undeveloped country for a few years. He said he wanted to give something back. Rhoda, who labored every day among the afflicted as a public health nurse, was not eager to expose herself to even more emotional turmoil. She understood Ian's need, however, and supported him, but that support was insufficient to infuse their marriage with the vitality she had expected. There existed a part of Ian forever distant, and his reluctance to have children seemed related to that part. Rhoda shuddered, feeling a kind of dread whirling inside her as she observed Ian's total attention focused on exotic, attractive Evelyn.

A library silence descended upon the room. Benjamin assumed the posture of Ian, leaning forward in his chair, elbows on his knees, head resting in his hands as though in deep thought. Thomas Shaw fixed compassionate eyes on Evelyn, and Shirley snuggled close to him, taking his hand in hers. Muriel Kent sat upright observing Evelyn with professional curiosity as if studying a cage filled with experimental mice. Raymond Beckett, legs stretched outward and crossed at the ankles, looked past Evelyn in a feigned display of disinterest.

Evelyn realized she had been maneuvered into talking about herself, something she was loath to do. She took great care with her delegations not to undermine her own authority, which she would need should danger arise. Choosing her words carefully, she responded to Ian in a quiet voice. "My worldview was always different, even as a child. After I graduated from high school, I wandered for nine years, three of which were spent in Mexico living with my maternal grandmother's family. Then Somoza was overthrown, and I came to Nicaragua. When I arrived here eliminating poverty, not perpetuating war, was the priority of the Revolution."

"But war arrived," Ian persisted.

"Yes," Evelyn responded.

"And as the saying goes, 'War is hell.'"

Evelyn became aware of a familiar anger, the anger she felt toward Doug when he probed and pushed until her inner bitterness lay exposed like a festering wound. Since Rudy's death, she had lived with emptiness beyond loneliness. Even her dear friend Pat Butler had no idea of the depth of her bitterness. Like gliding clouds, she still floated in and out of that darkness, until Doug forced her to step back into the daylight.

The recent visit to the desolate Cuban hospital had been wrenching. The ghost of Tomás haunted her and Ian's physical presence was jarring. She was losing control and she had to put a stop to it. Struggling to arrange her thoughts, she took a deep breath and spoke to the waiting silence of the room, her voice cracking as she voiced them.

"Many people have suffered and continue to suffer because of the wars in this country – first the Insurrection, then the Contra War. If you take anything back with you when you leave this place, you must take this: War does not end with a peace treaty. It stays with you forever."

No one said a word. They knew what the war had taken from her. The professors shifted their eyes downward not knowing how to react to a sudden sadness rising within them. Tears nudged the eyes of Tom and Shirley Shaw. Benjamin was reminded of his namesake in Matagalpa's cemetery. Rhoda's eyes pierced her husband like swords as he stared at Evelyn with a vulnerability she had never before seen in him. Reverend Shaw observed Rhoda's distressed expression and immediately realized its import. He had seen it all too often when he counseled couples.

Evelyn summoned the will to shoot to her feet and announced, "I think it's time to turn in. We will have a busy day tomorrow."

Like obedient children, they murmured muted good nights and went to their rooms.

The next morning, July 23, the delegation boarded the minibus for Jinotega. An hour after their departure, Pablo Ricardo picked up a folded piece of paper from the floor. *"Señora Evita Gutiérrez"* was printed on the outside of the note. Inside the message from Alfonso Miranda informed the *señora* of Recontra activity in the Department of Jinotega and ordered her to return to Managua. Of course, now he remembered. His wife had told him to deliver the message as she rushed out the door, but he had forgotten in all the commotion over the group's arrival. Once Ricardo read the note, he tore it into shreds. No one need know. If something happened, he would simply claim he had delivered the message to Señora Gutiérrez.

CHAPTER NINETEEN

The road to Jinotega had deteriorated even more since Evelyn's horrendous journey the year before. Early morning light magnified cavernous chasms rimmed by broken edges of asphalt creating giant potholes that became pond-like with the rains. Even though driving required the dexterity of a juggler, Dino guided the bus safely through the hazards, his hands frozen to the steering wheel. With Evelyn sitting behind him, he could hear her slow, shallow breathing, increasing his tension. Would she shatter like a dropped glass when they reached the place of the explosion? Would he need to take charge of the delegation and care for her simultaneously?

The bus shivered along under wide blue skies replete with proud white cumulous clouds. Although the rainy season was at its height, the skies in the mountains were clear. Windows rattled and gears ground, but Dino negotiated each obstacle with fierce determination. He was worried about landmines, even though there had been a thorough sweep of the area. During the last year hundreds, maybe thousands of vehicles had passed over the road safely. That Dr. Tomás Ruiz had probably hit the last remaining landmine on that road was an unjust twist of fate. Dino wanted to gun the minibus and fly over where Ruiz and Jasmina had died, but feared he would break an axle.

As they neared the fateful spot, Evelyn felt her jaw muscles tighten, her heart thump in her ears. Taking delegations to Matagalpa and Jinotega was her job; showing Americans the reality of her adopted country was her passion. The other delegation leaders at La Esperanza had willingly assumed the Matagalpa/Jinotega route, and Evelyn knew they would continue, forever if necessary. She also knew she had to face her tragic memories if she were to overcome them. Shutting her eyes tightly as the dreaded place approached, she cupped her mouth with her hands and sucked in her breath until her body constricted so fiercely it hurt. In a blink, they had passed the simple wooden cross that still remained planted at the side of the road in memory of the lives lost there.

A shudder of relief shook through Evelyn, who expelled air with such a deep sigh that she wobbled in her seat like a top about to fall. Dino felt his taut body release. It was over.

The city of Jinotega is set high in the mountains, surrounded by cattle ranches, vegetable farms, fruit orchards, and virgin forests. Dino drove to La Hacienda, a hotel similar to that of El Milagro, located in the center of the city. The proprietor, an elderly man with white hair and yellow teeth, flung Thomas Shaw's suitcase on his shoulder and jogged him and Shirley to their room.

"The people who survive into old age here are in better physical shape than our seniors," noted Rhoda who followed them.

After the group had unpacked and washed, Evelyn gathered them for a visit to a water pipe project supported by funds from a Swiss organization. The Swiss volunteer who directed the project spoke English. "One of our workers was almost killed two days ago when he came upon a Recontra ambush of a civilian truck in the countryside. He threw down his motorcycle and ran," he related.

"Was he hurt?" asked Evelyn.

"He suffered a few scratches, nothing worse, and he continues to use the same road to do our errands. We will not be intimidated by bandits."

The comments heightened Evelyn's concern. "Are the Recontra active near the Victor Hebera Agricultural Cooperative?" she asked.

"Two days ago the Central American Hydroelectric Plant was attacked. The agricultural cooperative is not far from there," he responded. Evelyn immediately realized the attack must have occurred as they were on the road to Matagalpa. With the telephone lines down, Alfonso had no way of warning her. She would call him for guidance when they returned to the hotel if the lines were working.

"Where is the military?" Ian asked the Swiss project manager noting Evelyn's worried expression and hoping he was misreading her intentions. He remained determined to visit the cooperative.

"The soldiers came. Yesterday they were here in the city and on the roads. This morning they left," the director replied, "but I think they are still in the area."

Ian realized convincing Evelyn to allow the visit to go forward would be difficult; he was not pleased.

At lunchtime they smelled the pizza as they approached the restaurant owned and operated by Tony Pizzano, the Italian-American, whose story they would soon hear. Pizzano, a muscular man with dark hair and walnut brown eyes, greeted them at the entrance. Dressed in a pullover of green and blue stripes, his hair pulled back in a ponytail, he looked like a nineteenth century sailor.

"Welcome," he said as the group entered the familiar environment of an American-style pizzeria. A mural of an Italian town overlooking the Mediterranean graced one whitewashed wall. "The home of my grandfather," Pizzano explained as he led them to their table. After they sat down, his wife Marina, a petite young Nicaraguan woman, joined them. Following greetings, Marina took orders of pizza, beer, and lemonade for the Shaws, and then departed with wishes of *buen provecho*.

Evelyn related to Tony Pizzano what had transpired in Matagalpa with Petronia Estrada.

"I'll get in touch with Witness for Peace," he offered. "The people who suffered in the war annoy both present and past governments. The Sandinistas do not want to be reminded of what was sacrificed for their Revolution, and the present government has little use for anyone at the bottom of the economic ladder."

"Thank you for following up," said Evelyn.

"Why would I do anything else?" Pizzano mused. With his fingers, he combed away a tangle of unruly hair that had escaped the elastic securing his ponytail.

"I assume you have a family at home in America," Reverend Shaw said to him while accepting his lemonade from Marina with a *gracias*. She nodded and disappeared again.

"This is my home," Pizzano corrected gently, "but I have a large family in Chicago. What Italian Catholic family isn't large?"

A murmur of subdued chuckles wafted through the group, followed by a grand chewing as they devoured pizza like recently rescued shipwreck survivors, stopping only to comment on the wonderful sauce.

"It's my grandmother's recipe," Pizzano noted proudly.

"Is your grandmother living?" asked Rhoda.

As he remembered his grandmother his face lit up with a smile. "Oh, yeah, she's the lively old matriarch of the family," he replied.

"How does your family feel about you remaining in Nicaragua?"

"My parents cannot understand it. 'You were almost killed in Nicaragua,' they say. Your grandparents left everything behind in Italy to come to America for a better life for their children. And they were so proud of you when you were the first in our family to graduate from college. Now you live away from us in that place.' I cannot explain what happened to me in a way that does not hurt them. My country could find enough money to arm Nicaraguans to kill each other, but not enough money can be found to rebuild what was destroyed. Recontras have developed an underground economy robbing for land or for money. The Contras were promised land if they disarmed, and some were given land, but too many of them have received nothing."

"Why don't they give them the land?" asked Benjamin.

"The International Monitory Fund and the United States have more to say where money is spent in Nicaragua than the Nicaraguan government," Raymond Beckett interjected.

Pizzano nodded his agreement with the comment and continued to speak. "How do I explain this to my grandparents and my parents?"

"You are faced with a dilemma," said Reverend Shaw empathetically. He searched for more profound words, but all that would come were the standard words of comfort he used when someone in his church had lost a loved one. Somehow they seemed inappropriate.

"Tony was kidnapped by the Contras in 1986 and has agreed to share his story with us," said Evelyn. The professors whipped out their notebooks, pushing aside their slices of pizza but not their beers.

Tony Pizzano took a bite of pizza and munched thoughtfully before he began. "I was kidnapped at a small village near San Filipe, not far from here. I was visiting a woman and her ten-year old son who had survived a Contra attack. At the time I was working for a Chicago newspaper, and a juicy story was what I was after. That was my reason for coming to Nicaragua – to be where the action was." He took a hefty gulp of beer before continuing. Benjamin leaned forward listening with an eagerness mixed with admiration as the story unfolded.

"The Contras shot the little boy in the leg, but they recognized me as an American and held their fire," Tony said. "After gathering the villagers together, they marched the older boys and men off in one direction and the older girls and women in another, leaving behind young children and old people. They raided the grain storehouse, took what they could carry, and set fire to the rest. I was taken with the men and boys. My captive companions were marched off in a different direction from me, and I was held alone with a group of about a dozen Contras for ten days.

I grew more and more exhausted by the day and thought death was just a matter of time. But to my surprise my captors grew tired of me. 'We are freedom fighters. We let you live because we love America,' they declared, and released me."

Benjamin exclaimed, "Surreal!"

Removing a cigarette pack from the pocket of his pants, Tony asked, "Mind?" gesturing with the hand holding the cigarette.

A murmur of permission followed. Even those that minded would not deny him after such a tale. He lit up, took a drag, and exhaled.

"Did you return to the village or find any of the people who were taken away?" Beckett asked.

Tony replied through a fog of cigarette smoke. "I returned to the village to search for the woman and her son. The boy was okay. His wound was superficial. The mother cried and hugged me for a long time."

"What happened to the younger women and the girls?" Muriel Kent asked in a hesitant voice as though fearing the answer.

"I don't know. I assume they were taken to service Contra men. Kidnapping women and girls was common practice. Some may have ended up in Honduras where staging bases were located," responded Tony.

Muriel's face reflected her distress. "I thought that might be the case," she said dispiritedly.

"God help them," muttered Shirley.

Ian stared down at what was left of his pizza, looking pained as an unbidden memory surfaced. "These things happen in war," he said quietly.

Tony stubbed out his cigarette in a heavy black ashtray and coughed behind his hand. "Yeah, these things happen in war," he repeated somberly. After a deep sigh, he continued, "I returned to Chicago, but within months I was back in Nicaragua. I met Marina and started this restaurant. We're expecting a baby."

Shirley Shaw brightened at the news. "Congratulations," she said happily.

After lunch, the group visited the Medsalud clinic in Jinotega where Dr. Tomás Ruiz had planned to deliver some of the medical supplies from the shipment he had acquired in Managua on that fateful day a little more than a year ago. He, Evelyn and Jasmina had planned to lunch in one of Jinotega's noted steak houses with Alexandra Silva, a Cuban nurse, and the woman in Tomás' life, after which they would deliver the supplies to Medsalud. They would then spend the night at Alexandra's apartment. In the morning Alexandra would drive Pat's sedan back to Matagalpa, following Evelyn and Jasmina in the Jeep, leave Tomás at the hospital, and travel on to Managua where she would participate in a medical seminar at Managua University. The plans were carefully laid, but unexpected tentacles of tragedy lay in wait to abort them. After the explosion, a heartbroken Alexandra Silva remained through the closing of the hospital before returning to Cuba.

Evelyn struggled to prevent the grief-filled memories from surfacing as she led her seven charges into the Medsalud clinic and eagerly turned the group over to the English speaking Managua University intern on staff. She listened absently as he described the prominent role Medsalud had played during the vaccination campaigns and in the training of health promoters for rural areas. Following the presentation, Rhoda was in her element peppering the intern with questions.

Relieved when the ordeal was over, Evelyn, as she had done in Matagalpa, released the group for a free afternoon in Jinotega. "We will meet back at La Hacienda at 5:30. For dinner we are going to one of Jinotega's steak houses. The Department of Jinotega is known for the quality of its beef; it's the best in all of Nicaragua," she announced, and promptly went back to the hotel to call Alfonso Miranda.

The delegation diners were in a jovial mood that evening, chatting amiably, sharing what they had learned, what they thought about what they had learned, and how they felt about what they had learned; they had become a community. Even the formal professors not only had something to say, but actually listened to the comments of others with some degree of attention. Once steaks had been consumed and desserts and coffee placed before them, Evelyn surprised the group with a summary of her telephone conversation with Alfonso Miranda.

"The director of La Esperanza has asked us to return to Managua early tomorrow, so we will not visit the Victor Hebera Agricultural Cooperative in the morning as we had previously planned."

Some faces expressed disappointment at the news; others relief. "Why?" Ian asked brusquely.

"You heard the director of the water project. Recontras are in the area," responded Evelyn.

Ian pulled back his shoulders and lifted his chin, "The Recontras will lay low for a while. The military is in the area. I, for one, am definitely going to the cooperative. I've waited for years since Vietnam to see appropriate technology applied again. I'm definitely going."

Rhoda added in a tone of defiance, "I'm definitely going too. I want to observe how they manage health care and medical emergencies in such an isolated community."

"Apparently both of you are willing to take the chance," Evelyn responded in an even voice.

"Me too," said Benjamin. The thought of entering an area where armed men might lie in wait heightened his thirst for adventure.

"I came all this way to document the lives of women on an agricultural cooperative facing danger. I intend to go too," remarked Muriel Kent.

"You're a feisty bunch," Evelyn noted dryly.

"Excuse me, but I don't think Tom and I should go," said Shirley. "My husband has a little heart problem."

Evelyn's eyes widened. "What? Reverend Shaw, you were cleared."

"It's not much of a problem. My digitalis keeps things under control," he said dismissively.

Sobered by the sudden awareness that someone in her delegation might possibly have a heart attack, Evelyn did not disguise the irritation in her voice when she confronted the pastor, "La Esperanza is responsible for your safety. You should have told us."

"We really wanted to make this trip," said Reverend Shaw contritely. "I apologize for not revealing my medical condition." He lowered his head and added, "I am truly sorry if I have caused you distress."

Evelyn wanted to react empathetically, but she alone understood the severity of a medical emergency on a delegation in a rural area. The reverend was unaware of the challenges of airlifting someone by helicopter. Throwing up her hands in a gesture of exasperation, she returned to the subject of the agricultural cooperative. "I'm sorry to disappoint all of you, but my boss has ordered us to return to Managua." The words were clipped, the tone determined.

"Can you talk him out of it?" asked Benjamin.

"I will not," Evelyn said with frustration.

"We will take responsibility for whatever happens, Evie," Ian said. Evelyn looked at him, her eyes betraying his noticeable affect on her. Addressing her by her childhood name implied an unnerving intimacy. A memory of the boy dressed as Papa Unicorn ruffled through her mind like wind on water.

"You may call me Evelyn or Evita," she said quickly. "Evie was my childhood name."

"Sorry," he stammered. "It just came to me, 'Evie', I mean, 'Evie' just came to me."

"Ian's point is that we are all adults responsible for our own decisions," Rhoda declared, coming to her husband's defense.

Crossing her arms over her chest, Evelyn observed her delegation with penetrating eyes. "This is not a democracy," she announced to the group as if daring them to challenge her. "As the representative of La Esperanza, I have been charged with responsibility for your safety."

Everyone stopped drinking their coffee and picking at their desserts. The atmosphere rustled with quiet unease until Shirley, who detested conflict of any kind, declared nervously, "Evelyn knows best."

Ian shrugged in a gesture of defeat. A moment later, his face brightened. "I have an idea," he declared. "We can ask Tony Pizzano to find someone to take us. Then La Esperanza is relieved of responsibility for our safety." He paused, waiting for a reaction.

"Cool!" exclaimed Benjamin.

"Possible," added Muriel, wrinkling her eyebrows in a we'll-see gesture.

"The Recontras are gone," declared Ian. "The attack on the Central American Hydroelectric Plant was two days ago. The director of the water project said that the area was swarming with government soldiers. The Recontras have retreated, at least temporarily. I'd bet my life on it."

"Your life and the lives of others," Evelyn noted coldly.

"I'm that sure," Ian countered.

Evelyn hesitated. "I don't know."

Dino intervened in spite of concern over Evelyn's reaction. "Señora Evita, I think Señor Campbell is right about the Recontras."

"This is a mutiny, Señora Gutiérrez," Ian said lightly.

Evelyn fell quiet and pondered their comments. "I'll talk to Señor Miranda again," she finally promised.

To her surprise, Miranda agreed with Ian and Dino that Recontras had retreated from that area. To protect La Esperanza, however, he required that those who chose to go to the Victor Hebera Agricultural Cooperative write a letter to his organization absolving it of responsibility for their safety. Also, the La Esperanza minibus could not be used for transport, and either Evelyn or Dino would remain in Jinotega with those who chose not to go, preferably Evelyn.

The next morning a bright red, double cabin, four-wheel drive pick-up truck rumbled out of the City of Jinotega into the countryside at 8 a.m. It carried three armed Nicaraguan guards, friends of Tony Pizzano, four American sojourners, and Evelyn. Dino, Thomas and Shirley Shaw, and Raymond Beckett remained behind in Jinotega. The Shaws settled themselves into rocking chairs on the front patio of La Hacienda, anxiously awaiting the return of their new friends. Beckett and Dino sought out the monument to German Pomares, a beloved Sandinista insurgent who had led his troops successfully against Somoza's National Guard.

For forty-five minutes the red pickup slugged through the forested countryside, swaying over rutted roads with a natural rhythm through light wind and tropical vegetation. Evelyn, Rhoda, and Muriel occupied the rear seat, sheltered from the hazards of low hanging tree-branches festooned with snakes. Two of the guards sat in the front seat, one driving, the other caressing a bandoleer of ammunition hanging over his shoulder like a deadly necklace. The third guard, also armed, sat in the truck bed with Ian and Benjamin. As the truck jostled onto ever-rougher roads, the three men tossed about under huge guanacaste, madroño, and chilamate trees that reached tentacle-like branches toward them. The ground was wet and the truck sank dangerously deep into rainy season mud.

Every several miles a small farm appeared with cattle grazing and children scampering about. For a time, oxen lumbering over the muddy narrow road slowed the truck to a crawl. The three men in the truck bed covered their faces with bandanas against mud splatter and held tight to the truck's sides as they shot over hummocks of wet earth and dived into water-filled valleys threatening to consume the truck.

In the back seat the women were quiet. Rhoda's thoughts whirred in pinwheel circles reliving the previous evening when in the privacy of their room Ian had spoken incessantly about Evelyn. Was it Evelyn's tragic past that captivated him? Was it related to whatever he had seen in Vietnam? Whatever it was, she feared losing him.

Ian was the first to sight a wooden sign brightly painted in red and black: *Cooperativa Agricultura Victor Hebera.* The truck pulled up to a rusted gate, and two guards in military fatigues approached them, assault weapons at the ready. Ian automatically flung his hands upward in surrender before realizing where he was and quickly lowering them.

"Hola compañeros," the Nicaraguan in the truck bed called. The cooperative guards recognized him and lowered their guns. He leaped out and sauntered toward the gate where the three men huddled for a few minutes; then one of the cooperative's guards motioned for the driver to move forward. They drove into the compound and with a jerk of his head, the guard indicated a parking place near a long concrete building.

Immediately a brown muscular man of about fifty dressed in baggy pants and a yellow guayabera shirt approached them. "I am called Sergio Córdoba," he said. "I am president of our cooperative. *Bienvenido."*

Córdoba walked, looked, and spoke like the hard laboring middle-aged farmer he was. They followed him into the concrete building, passing through four sections separated by thin sheet rock walls that did not reach the roof of corrugated steel. He described each of the sections as they went: the odiferous seed and fertilizer storage area; the food storage area where bags of rice, beans, and corn lined the walls; the medical clinic containing a cot and a small shelf of medicines; and finally a community meeting room that also served as a school.

When they reached the community room/school, Córdoba motioned to Ian and Ben to help him arrange some hand-hewn wooden chairs into a rough horseshoe after which the Nicaraguan began to relate the history of the Victor Hebera Agricultural Cooperative. He spoke from a face that seemed never to have known a smile.

"We began in 1980 with twenty-six members," he said. "Now we are seventy-eight. Many years before the Triumph, officers in Somoza's National Guard took this land. When the harvest was poor and we could not pay back our farm loans in full, they took our land - land that had been in our family for generations. They grew crops for export on our land while we went hungry. After the Triumph, people from the Sandinista Agrarian Reform came to us, and they said, 'This land belongs to all the people. You grow food for Nicaraguans first and for export second.'

At first the government took the land and we were a collective farm, but no one liked that, so we divided the land and became an agricultural production cooperative. The Sandinistas nationalized the banks so we got money to buy seeds and fertilizer, and when the harvest came, the government paid us a basic price for it. When the harvest was poor the banks did not take our land. Farmers like us fed the country and grew extra food for export," he explained.

Benjamin listened to Evelyn's translation of Córdoba's comments. The Nicaraguan was relating a history of which Benjamin was totally ignorant. He wondered how Córdoba and his family had survived under the Somoza regime and how they fared now under the Chamorro government.

"What was it like under Somoza?" he asked. Córdoba looked at him with his serious dark eyes.

"Under Somoza, so many farms were taken that large farms grew larger, but a poor farmer could not grow enough food for his family because his farm was too small. Many went to work on the farms of the large landowners. Others went to Managua to look for work. Others went into the forest and cleared land, but after one season the land no longer produced and the next season they had to clear more. People went hungry and they were desperate for change."

Benjamin admired this short man with a face lined in hardship. Córdoba looked at him and nodded, filling the student with pride for being acknowledged. He had never met men like Sergio Córdoba and Tony Pizzano.

"First, there were insurrections in the countryside, then there were strikes in the cities," Córdoba explained, "and finally, the business community turned against Somoza when he killed one of their own, Pedro Joaquín Chamorro, the husband of our widowed President Violeta Chamorro. We called the last Somoza Tachito. We have a saying: *No hay peor sordo que el que no quere escuchar.* There is no deaf person worse than he who does not want to listen. Tachito did not want to hear about the suffering of the Nicaraguan people. We are glad to be rid of him."

"How has the transition from the Sandinista government to the present one affected your cooperative?" asked Ian.

Córdoba raised his straight black eyebrows until they seemed to support his forehead. "The new private banks will lend to us only if we put up our land as collateral as we did under Somoza, and we will not do that. The government no longer pays a basic price for our harvest, but we can feed ourselves without loans, and we sell enough to buy the things we need. When I was a boy, we had no milk and sometimes no food. No child in this cooperative goes without milk or food."

"Are you in danger of attack? The guards at the gate were suspicious of us," Ian asked.

"We always prepare for the worst," Córdoba responded. "Two days ago, Recontras burned the hydroelectric plant and killed a guard. You may know this." He looked at Evelyn who nodded in the affirmative.

"But you are safe here. We have permanent vigilance. Every one of us, except the smallest of our children, can use a weapon. We do not want to fight. We are farmers not soldiers. The Contra burned us down once. My cousin Victor Hebera died trying to save the animals in our burning barn. Without our animals, we are nothing. Our cooperative bears his name because he is a hero."

"I saw your rope pump well when we came in," Ian commented.

"Yes, it is a good system," responded Córdoba. "We use rope pump wells, and we also have rainwater catchments on the buildings. We are modern now."

"Who provides your medical care?" asked Rhoda.

"We have two health promoters trained at Medsalud in Jinotega."

"May I speak with them? I am a nurse."

"*Sí. Entonces usted puede ayudar en la clínica por un rato,*" declared the cooperative's director as though it had already been decided.

Rhoda understood enough Spanish to conclude that she had been instructed to help in the medical clinic for a while.

"Are you concerned about clear land titles?" asked Ian.

Córdoba shook his head in the negative. "We have clear titles to these properties. They belonged to *Somozistas*, and *Somozistas* have no legal right to our land," he said forcefully.

"What is the role of women in this society?" asked Muriel.

A puzzled expression clouded Córdoba's somber face, and he asked Evelyn what the *señora* meant. Evelyn reiterated the question and he answered with a description of the tasks performed by women. "At four in the morning women start the cooking fires. They make the beans and rice and tortillas and coffee for breakfast. After breakfast they sweep their houses. Then they go to the land. All except the very young work the land."

Muriel scowled her disappointment in this response. "Are there no women soldiers or teachers or nurses on this cooperative?"

When Evelyn translated, Córdoba understood what the severe looking American woman wanted to know. "Our health promoters are women, our teachers are women, and women are in our militia. A woman teacher comes from Jinotega two days a week to teach children, and Zamora Martínez , who is a member of the cooperative, was a *brigadista* during the Literacy Crusade. She teaches adults who cannot read."

"I am a professor of women's studies. May I interview the teacher and the *brigadista?*" asked Muriel.

Evelyn translated, explaining what "women's studies" meant. Córdoba seemed surprised there was such a thing. *"Claro, profesora.* You may talk to Zamora, but the teacher is not here today."

Córdoba pushed to his feet. "I speak too long. Come with me and I show you our cooperative." Everyone rose in unison as though they had been given an order. The man's presence commanded obedience, and they trudged after him down a small path into an open field where the earth blossomed with healthy vegetables.

"People from a university in Mexico showed us how to conserve the soil to prevent erosion. We grow plants that will live during droughts, and we use chicken and cow manure for fertilizer." Eyes swept over an orderly patch of raised beds. "We raise goats for milk, pigs for meat and use their feces for methane," he continued. "We raise rabbits for meat and send the rabbit fur to Managua for sale."

They tramped through other fields shuffling through ruts and over rocks. Muriel stumbled, her feet chafing inside her sturdy leather shoes. Eventually they came upon a large wooden shed filled with crates of caged rabbits, and Rhoda poked a finger through a cage to caress the soft fur. Beyond the fields, they reached a residential compound sprinkled with small adobe houses. Muriel's sore feet were in full rebellion by now.

The sight of tall tube structures looking like funeral vessels from antiquity excited Ian. "Señor Córdoba, are those storage silos for grain?"

"Sí."

"May I examine them?"

Córdoba's response was to walk in the direction of the silos. "Such a sight," Ian said animatedly, as though viewing works of art. "They are perfect examples of appropriate technology. Were they constructed from cement and lightweight mesh fencing?"

"Sí," answered Córdoba. Legs spread, arms folded across his chest, he observed Ian with a gratified expression as the engineer expounded on the mysteries of silo construction and Evelyn translated.

Ian moved closer to the president of the cooperative. "Señor Córdoba, during my research on appropriate technology, I read about this farm. My priority in coming to Nicaragua was to visit here."

A hint of a smile raised at the edges of the Nicaraguan's mouth, his first expression of amiability since their arrival. "The university people from Mexico taught us this. They showed us dry latrines and better stoves too," he said.

"May I look at the dry latrines?" asked Ian.

Certain her feet were blistering, Muriel stifled a wince of pain. She desperately wanted to remove her shoes and soak her feet. Instead they trooped back toward the grouping of small houses, skirting them to where the outhouses stood. Ian knocked and then opened the door to one. He gestured at a large cement seat with two carefully positioned holes. "The toilet design separates urine and feces. Ash is thrown on the feces, and after about six months, the mixture of solid waste and ash produces compost safe enough for fertilizer. These types of latrines also last indefinitely, whereas an average pit latrine fills in five years. And the dry latrines do not pollute ground water. I saw a similar design in Vietnam."

"Do most rural Nicaraguans use them?" asked Benjamin.

"I doubt it because they cost more initially. My guess is only villages where the latrines are funded by an organization like the university from Mexico, would have them."

"Do you want to explain our better stove to your friends?" Córdoba asked Ian. Everyone chuckled when Evelyn translated.

"Absolutely," declared Ian.

"Come, we go to my house," said Córdoba.

The two men strode side by side, the Nicaraguan with his short, slightly bowed legs and the tall American purposefully slowing his gait.

The savory odors of cilantro and onions wafted toward them as they approached his house, an adobe dwelling of three rooms. "My wife, she cooks," Córdoba explained.

A stocky woman in a smudged apron stirred a pot on a stove made of a dozen pressed earth blocks arranged in a rectangle creating an oblong firebox. On top was a slab of hardened clay with holes shaped to fit two pots. The simmering pot was fit into one hole. A smaller third hole contained a round sheet steel stovepipe that led upwards through the roof. Evelyn was quick to note that unlike Anita's house, the kitchen was smokeless, the unpainted walls free of soot.

"I have only seen these stoves in illustrations," Ian said as he pointed to the chimney. "The stove pipe vents all the soot and smoke. Best of all, they use only half as much firewood as the grate wood fire."

Rhoda was aware of the correlation between inhaling smoke and asthma, a common disease among children in undeveloped countries and poor kids in inner city homes who lived with dust and flaking paint. "How many of your children suffer from asthma?" she asked.

He pondered the question. "We have little asthma here. Our health promoters will know how many are sick."

Córdoba muttered to his wife, and she left the pot to take Rhoda by the arm. "*Vamos a la clínica médica,*" the woman said through crooked teeth.

"She wants to take you to the medical clinic," Evelyn explained. "I'll join you later to translate after I take Muriel to interview the *brigadista.*"

"I think I can manage," called Rhoda as she and Córdoba's wife disappeared outside.

"Technology appropriate to the situation in which people live. Thank you for allowing us to come here, Evie," Ian declared forgetting his previous apology over using her childhood name, and he plopped a kiss of gratitude on her cheek.

CHAPTER TWENTY

Muriel Kent's temples were pounding with a headache born of fatigue and emotional exhaustion. Only her fierce dedication to interviewing women living on the cooperative moved her stiff legs and painful feet forward toward the community room that also served as a school. Zamora Martínez, the cooperative's literacy teacher, a brown middle-aged woman with lank black hair, greeted her and Evelyn with a warm smile. When they sat down at a small table, Muriel slipped her tortured feet out of her shoes and sighed with relief. Summoning the formality of her professional demeanor, she whipped out a notebook. "I want to know Zamora's story and what she does here," she said to Evelyn, whose eyes subtly fell toward the professor's bloodstained stockings. Zamora observed the American woman curiously, noting her perspiration streaked face.

"I will bring water for you, " she said and began to rise.

Muriel quickly responded. "No. I'm fine."

Zamora did not understand her words, but she did understand their meaning, and with an expression of concern she reseated herself. After Evelyn explained what Muriel wanted, the Nicaraguan woman began to speak. "We are four women – my two aunts, my sister, and I. We each have a little land. I joined my two acres to the land of the others and we farm. Because we live next to the cooperative, we asked to join for protection," related Zamora.

"So you did not marry? You chose to work your own farm?" asked Muriel, uplifted by the discovery of an independent Nicaraguan peasant woman.

"I was married," replied Zamora. "And my husband and I farmed our two acres. We grew enough to eat and a little to sell, but the Contras came to our house and took away my husband and my son. My daughter and I ran off with the baby and hid for many days in the outside. The baby was sick. She died."

Muriel's reaction to Zamora's words came in stages: first she shivered with bird-like choppiness; then she gasped; next her eyes exploded with water that trickled down her shallow cheeks; finally, she threw her notebook and pen on the table, snatched off her glasses, and covered her mouth with her palm. "I'm sorry. My head is raging," she whimpered. "And this tragedy is one too many."

"I have aspirin," offered Evelyn, plunging her hand into the carry bag she took everywhere. She handed Muriel a handkerchief, two pills, and a water bottle. After Muriel had swallowed the aspirin and wiped her face, she said hoarsely, "We may finish the interview now."

"If you wish," said Evelyn.

"Zamora, did you find your husband and your son?" Muriel asked.

"My son is in Managua. My husband is gone forever. My daughter lives with me."

Zamora motioned to Muriel's pen and notebook. Muriel handed them to her and she wrote: *Bienvenido, profesora. Estamos contentos de que ustedes han venido a visitarnos. Gracias por su visita."* She handed back the notebook and pen. Muriel could read enough Spanish to understand that Zamora Martínez had thanked her for visiting the cooperative.

"You see, I went to school," Zamora said proudly. "When I was a *brigadista* in the Literacy Crusade, I taught many how to read and write, and I taught them about our Constitution of 1986. We have laws to help women. We have a law that says women receive equal pay for equal work, but men ignore the laws, even good men like Sergio."

"It is the same in the United States," said Muriel.

"Do women sell their bodies in America?" asked Zamora.

"Yes."

Zamora pondered this information, puzzled why in a country rich as America women sold their bodies. "Nicaraguan men are macho," she continued. "Men want to use our bodies, and when we have too many children, they blame us. Then they run off and leave us to raise the children alone. My cousins in Managua tell me that women who sell their bodies are back on the streets. That is why I am happy to live here with my daughter and my aunts and my sister. I have two cows, chickens, a pig, and a horse."

"You are an extraordinary woman, Zamora," said Muriel, her voice breaking and her eyes misting again.

"Are you unhappy, Señora?" Zamora asked.

Muriel sniffled and wiped her eyes. "I suppose I am," she admitted, struggling to keep her tears from overwhelming her again. "But I am happy to know you."

Events like these sustained Evelyn in her chosen work. She had glimpsed the beginning of Muriel's transformation when the college professor was listening to Petronia Estrada describe the anguish of mothers whose children had disappeared during the Contra War. Muriel's steely eyes had moistened and lowered to her lap. When Tony Pizzano spoke of the women and girls kidnapped by Contras, Muriel's concern was palpable. It could no longer be contained when Zamora spoke of the loss of her baby. Evelyn wondered if Muriel had ever borne a child.

Leaving Muriel with Zamora, Evelyn walked to the medical clinic where she observed Rhoda, a stethoscope hanging from her neck, examining a child. A line of people awaited her attention. Spotting Evelyn, Rhoda called, "I won't need translation."

"Yes, you're doing fine," noted Evelyn admiringly.

An hour later it was nearing eleven and time to leave. Córdoba walked the group back to their truck gathering them together for a few parting words.

Muriel swiped the back of her blistered heel with a tissue. "It's bleeding; my heels are raw," she said to Evelyn standing next to her.

"I have some slippers in my bag," offered Evelyn.

"Thank you. It's been a difficult morning. Life here is as raw as my heel."

"The delegations are designed to present Nicaraguan reality," said Evelyn.

"You do your job well."

Before he bid them farewell, Córdoba scooped up a handful of wet dirt and held it out. "This soil is our life. It gives us food and freedom," he said moving his outstretched hand from person to person as he spoke. "You must tell people in America what you see here. All farmers love the earth. Farmers in your country must help us keep our lands. We have the title to our land, but many cooperatives and small farmers lose their land because their title is not clear. Tell your president to tell the Nicaraguan government that these farmers must not lose their land. The government listens to America."

The Americans murmured promises. None of them knew a farmer, but they did know politicians, and they would carry this stalwart man's concerns home. Emboldened by their promises, the director of the cooperative continued, "Tell your president to stop sending basic grains to Nicaragua. If America really wants to help Nicaragua, they will send things not already produced here."

"Nicaraguan farmers are being undercut by American imports?" Ian asked surprised.

Córdoba nodded in the affirmative.

"It's not just grain, but the chicken industry as well," explained Evelyn. "Small and medium-sized Nicaraguan farmers do not have the technology to compete with agribusiness from the more advanced economies."

The group, energized by the experience of the last two hours, climbed into the truck. They waved to Córdoba and his guards as they drove away, not at all worried over the possibility of an attack by Recontras.

Still in their rocking chairs, the Shaws welcomed the group back to the hotel elated that they were all safe. By one o'clock they were back on the road of crumbling asphalt under a sun winking fire behind threatening billows of grayish clouds. Dino resumed the practiced and precise maneuvers that would carry them to Matagalpa, and good will spread throughout the bus. Even Evelyn joined the lively conversations of the other sojourners chattering like long-time friends. Dino hoped she would remain preoccupied until they had passed the place where Jasmina had died.

About a half an hour out of the city, he spotted men in military fatigues silhouetted against the afternoon sun. They extended across the road like a police barricade, bandoleers of ammunition snaking down chests and automatic weapons pointed at the La Esperanza minibus. "*Mierda! Recontras!*" he cursed.

Evelyn's blood bubbled hot as she shot to her feet.

"Are you sure?" she asked. Then she saw them, and then turned to face her delegation. "We have a threatening situation," she announced with forced calmness.

"Holy shit!" exclaimed Ben when he saw the armed group. Raymond swiveled his head toward the window. "Blasted!" A rasping sound escaped from Shirley, and her husband prayed, "God help us." "What's happening?" asked Rhoda. "We're fucked!" Ian expelled between clenched teeth.

Dino slowly braked the minibus.

"Do exactly what they tell you," Evelyn said, wrestling her voice into evenness. "Do not protest. Bow your head and look at your feet. If you look at them directly, they'll feel threatened." She spoke as though she were laying out a travel itinerary. Ian was impressed by her coolness. She had obviously been well-trained to deal with crisis. Shirley began to wail in a high soprano.

Evelyn ordered Thomas Shaw to calm his wife. "We must all stay calm and alert."

"Rhoda, I'm going to help Evie," said Ian. "You stay with the Shaws. They're the most vulnerable." Ian threw himself to the front of the minibus, ordering. "Heads down," as he passed each seat.

By the time Dino had stopped the minibus, all its passengers were staring into their laps submissively, including Evelyn and Ian sitting side-by-side immediately behind Dino. Two Recontras approached, waving their automatic weapons. Dino opened the door, and a wisp of a man, nervously twitching like a flopping jack-in-the box, sprinted into the minibus followed by an older paunchy man with a black beard. Both carried assault rifles and pointed them directly at the passengers. The older Recontra scowled at them and growled in a sandpaper voice, "Who is in charge?"

Evelyn raised her hand.

"Out," he ordered, motioning toward the door with his gun. She pushed to her feet slowly, head bowed looking at her sandals. "You too," he addressed Ian and Dino. He and the twitchy Recontra followed them, only to be replaced by two other armed men. One moved up the aisle toward the back of the minibus. Muriel's downcast eyes watched the dirty, torn pant leg move past her, his foul smell causing her to suppress a cough.

Outside, they lined Evelyn, Dino, and Ian against the bus. Evelyn slowly raised her head to the nervous Recontra, a skinny boy she guessed to be no more than sixteen. In oversized fatigues, his dark eyes reflected bravado and fear as he ordered her to give him her carry bag. He rifled through itineraries and an envelope containing money and copies of everyone's passports, and then tossed them to the bearded man, whom Evelyn had by now identified as the leader.

"We want real passports," the man demanded.

"I don't have them," she answered, knowing they would take them from each person. Passports were valuable, especially American passports that were altered for entering the United States illegally. The Recontra grunted and removed the envelope of money, counting its contents with a grin of satisfaction. The younger man standing on tiptoes frisked Ian, removing his wallet and his passport.

Another Recontra took Dino by the arm and led him to the rear of the bus where he spread-eagled him. *"Cubano,"* he snorted contemptuously after examining his passport and slammed him against the fender. Dino's watch shattered, sounding like a pistol shot.

Benjamin, hearing the thump of Dino's body and the crack of his watch, assumed someone had been shot. In a thunderbolt of adrenaline-fueled fear, he leaped from his seat and tackled the Recontra nearest to him. The startled man fell sideways, discharging his weapon into the floor. Ben snatched the gun and plunged toward the Recontra at the front of the minibus. The bandit raised his weapon and pulled the trigger as Raymond Beckett thrust out his leg tripping the shooter and sending the bullet hissing past Shirley into the window next to her husband. It shattered, showering the reverend with broken glass. Pinpricks of blood spurted onto Shaw's shirt, dissolving what little control Shirley had gained over her terror. Her resultant scream chilled her husband to the marrow, jolting his heart into a thunderous pace.

Ben nearly made it to the front of the minibus before another Recontra charged in and shot him. He winced, grabbed his arm, and dropped the gun, tumbling over Beckett and a terrified Muriel, who had moved beyond fear into shock. As the student slid from their laps toward the floor, he left a trail of blood on both professors. Slowly blood soaked Ben's white T-shirt, and its hopeful message: "We shall turn swords into plowshares." Splayed on his back, Ben uttered strangled groans that were drowned out by Shirley's high-pitched shrieking. Meanwhile, the Recontras scrambled up and pulled Ben forward, slamming him into the driver's seat where he slumped over the steering wheel moaning.

"*Salga! Salga!* Out! Out!" the Recontras screamed at the other passengers.

Stumbling forward, Raymond and Muriel stepped through Ben's blood. Sobbing and gasping, Shirley wiped furiously at the blood on her husband's shirt as though she could somehow make it disappear. Shaw hunched forward, his head falling toward his lap.

"Get up," Rhoda ordered the hysterical woman and her dazed husband. Snatching the carry bag, which held medical supplies, she positioned herself behind Shaw and slid her arm around his waist, supporting his rotund body with a strength born of necessity. "Help me," she ordered Shirley, who took his arm and together they dragged him outside.

"His heart!" exclaimed Rhoda as they exited the bus, unsure of her instant diagnosis but certain that Shaw was in trouble.

"We must lay him down. He is a pastor of God," Evelyn pleaded with the Recontra leader, aware of the respect Nicaraguans held for priests and pastors.

"*Soy medico,*" Rhoda sputtered in Spanish. She realized she had identified herself as a doctor, but in her terror she had forgotten the word for nurse.

The leader waved his men away and allowed Rhoda and Shirley to lower the stricken man to the ground. His action signaled to Evelyn that their situation in the hands of this rag-tag band might not be lethal. She immediately fell to her knees and started CPR while Rhoda took his pulse. Shirley cried softly by her husband's side.

"Where's his digitalis, Shirley?" asked Rhoda.

"Pocket, pants," the frantic woman sputtered. Rhoda thrust her hand into a pocket and extracted a bottle of digitalis.

"Shirley," Shaw gasped as Rhoda placed a pill on his tongue.

"You'll be fine," his wife said softly, holding his hand and giving no indication that she had dissolved into hysteria a moment ago.

Rhoda tore away the bloody shirt and examined the reverend's arm and chest. To her relief, the cuts were superficial. Rummaging through the huge handbag for medical alcohol and antibiotics, she cleaned the wounds and slathered on ointment.

"El pastor es mejor?" asked the Recontra leader roughly. Rhoda nodded in the affirmative. She, Evelyn, and Shirley were pulled to their feet and lined up against the minibus while another Recontra knelt to search Shaw, extracting his passport, wallet, and wedding ring.

The others were relieved of their passports, purses, bags, money belts, and watches. The rings of Shirley, Rhoda, and Muriel were ripped from their fingers. Raymond voluntarily gave up his wedding ring. Ian wore none. The Recontra inside the minibus removed Benjamin's passport, wallet and bloodied sneakers. They demanded Ian's sneakers, but snubbed the scuffed worn shoes of Dino, the black pumps of Shirley, the sandals of Evelyn and Rhoda, and the slippers Evelyn had given Muriel. They also overlooked Thomas Shaw's black leather shoes.

They rifled through the luggage taking everything of value. Evelyn had instructed her group to carry only small sums of money in their wallets and to wrap the rest in plastic and stuff it into their underwear along with copies of their passports. Some bandits were aware of this trick, and Evelyn had heard stories of people being waylaid and stripped naked, some murdered, others left exposed under hot sun.

Ian studied the body language of the Recontra leader for clues as to his intentions. When he lifted his eyes to the hills, Ian's shifted upward too. Bandit lookouts lined a cliff overhanging the road. *From that distance they can see for miles,* Ian thought.

Rhoda desperately wanted to attend to Benjamin, fearing unless she applied pressure to stop his bleeding, he would bleed out. Evelyn asked the skinny boy who had taken her bag to tell his leader that the gringo who had been shot would die without help. She claimed Benjamin Conway was the son of an American diplomat, and if he died soldiers would hunt down his killers without mercy. The boy relayed this to the leader who glared at Evelyn and Rhoda before gesturing for Rhoda to reenter the minibus. At that moment, Evelyn was certain that they would not be killed.

Once inside the minibus, Rhoda heard shooting from a distance followed by a rumble. Through the windshield, she saw a flatbed truck hurtling in their direction. Her throat dry with panic, she turned to Benjamin who lay slumped over the steering wheel, whimpering like a newborn puppy. She could not change what was happening outside, but she could save a young man's life. Beckoning the strength that had been summoned to support Thomas Shaw, she gently lowered him to the floor and began to cut away clothing near the wound.

The Recontra bandits scrambled across the road as the flatbed approached, leaving their captives exposed to being crushed against the minibus. Ian quickly judged that clearance was adequate should the flatbed driver maintain control of his vehicle, but they were vulnerable if the Recontra opposite them on the hill shot at the rig as it passed.

"Crawl as far under the bus as you can," he ordered, knowing that should bullets penetrate the gas tank everyone would be incinerated.

Shirley made a gurgling sound as she and Evelyn gently maneuvered her husband under the bus. Muriel emerged from her daze and threw her head back in a guttural cry when Evelyn shoved her to the ground, yelling, "Crawl under!" Raymond, a few feet away, cranked his head up to see what was going on. "Crawl under!" Evelyn shouted, and from the corner of her eye she saw Dino scrambling underneath.

The eighteen-wheeler tandem flatbed was upon them. Evelyn and Ian lined their bodies perpendicular to the bus, shielding Shirley and Thomas Shaw, Muriel Kent and Raymond Beckett who had buried their faces into the dirt and covered their heads with their hands. The frightening pings of bullets slammed into the escaping flatbed as it hurtled on, damaged but not destroyed. Sizing up the situation, the Recontras scrambled into the hills, knowing that when the truck reached Jinotega, government soldiers would be dispatched to hunt them down. An eerie quiet hung in the air, like a curtain of suspense over the travelers, who lay as still as death.

Finally Ian whispered, "I'll check," and pushed to his feet, to search for signs of Recontras. "All clear," he announced, extending his hand to Evelyn, who once on her feet flowed into him, allowing his arms to comfort her until her shaking subsided.

"It's over, Evie," he said, his warm breath on her neck, his gentle hands stroking her hair. "It's over. It's over. It's over." She relaxed under his tender touch releasing the fear coiled taut within.

After a few moments, when her body had quieted and her head had cleared, she pulled away from him and whispered, "Go to Rhoda." He did not move. "Go to Rhoda," she repeated, and he stepped away.

Ian found Rhoda sitting on the floor, legs outstretched and cradling the unconscious Benjamin, whose head was in her lap. Careless wisps of reddish brown hair curled around her colorless face, and her clothes were crimson with blood.

"They're gone?" she asked quietly.

Ian knelt down beside her. "They're gone." He lifted her chin toward him. "Are you okay?"

"Yes."

"And Ben?"

"The bullet coursed through his arm." She breathed deeply to keep composed. "I stopped the bleeding, cleaned the wound as best I could, and gave him antibiotics, but he needs stitches."

"You're a trooper," Ian said releasing her chin.

"Not enough of a trooper for you," she said, lowering her head again.

He understood. "Rhoda," he said hoarsely.

"Now is not the time. See to the others. I'll be fine," she responded. She yearned to go home, to retreat to her comfortable apartment, good wine, or a satisfying dinner at Chez Francois. None of these distractions would be available in Nicaragua. Ian wanted to spend a year or more here, but Ian did not confront misery in his work, he did not frequent the poorest neighborhoods of Albany, New York, or comfort the relatives and friends of victims of neighborhood shootings in hospital emergency rooms. She was more prepared for life in Nicaragua than was he, but she didn't want it. That decision made, she knew it was just a matter of time before their marriage completely withered away.

Evelyn held the trembling Muriel until she had calmed. Raymond whispered ashamedly to Ian that he had wet himself, and Ian hid him behind the bus with his own body while Raymond changed. Thomas Shaw lay still breathing raggedly next to Shirley; he had entered a world where he and his wife snuggled together in their beds. She tenderly stroked his face and hair. They lay in a peaceful place free from violence and disorder. Dino sat stunned against the front wheel of the minibus. They had all survived.

When the soldiers arrived, Evelyn asked to be escorted to the Koch Centro de Salud in Matagalpa where the wounded would receive immediate attention. With Benjamin and the pastor cushioned by mounds of clothing, a soldier drove the minibus. When they passed the spot where Jasmina had been killed, Evelyn was too preoccupied to notice.

Dr. Frank Leonard connected Benjamin to intravenous antibiotics, praised Rhoda's dressing of his wound as excellent, and proceeded to stitch it. Dr. Eileen gave the reverend oxygen and made arrangements for a helicopter to whisk him and Benjamin to the Baptist Hospital in Managua where they knew he would receive the best follow-up care. Evelyn called Alfonso Miranda to arrange an appointment at the United States Embassy to get new passports and to rearrange for departure flights.

Muriel and Raymond retreated to the Leonards' tiny kitchen where they sipped coffee and spoke of the day's events. For a long time, Muriel had regarded her husband with little more than tolerance. Over the years, the tenuous link between them had grown thin. Remembering what had attracted him to her long ago, she studied his fine-planed face. He was her intellectual equal and together they enjoyed theater, symphonic music, and conversation with academic friends. Yet they talked past each other about personal matters. She studied the man she had once loved and maybe still did, if the terror she felt inside over the possibility of losing him was any indication. Muriel reached across the table and took her husband's hand in hers. He was startled over this sudden display of affection, but allowed his hand to be held, a tentative smile creasing his lips.

Evelyn entered the kitchen, glanced at the hand-holding couple, and poured herself a cup of coffee, careful not to indicate the delight she felt over their minute, but no doubt significant, gesture. Coffee in hand she joined Rhoda, Shirley, and Ian standing around Reverend Shaw's cot. Benjamin slept soundly under sedation nearby.

"Go rest, my dear," urged the pastor to Rhoda, lifting his oxygen mask as he spoke.

"Put that back on," Rhoda ordered.

"I feel fine," he protested weakly, but obeyed, keeping it down until Rhoda had left the room. Once again he lifted the mask. "Tell me your questions, Evelyn," he said in a weak voice.

Evelyn was confused. "Questions?"

"About God. You were ready to sacrifice your life for us. You are a spiritual person. But earlier when you spoke of faith, bitterness was in your voice." Observing the concerned expression on Evelyn's face as he spoke with mask upraised, he added lightly, "I only had an episode. I'm not going to die."

"You're an impossible man like my husband Rudy," Evelyn declared affectionately.

"Tell me about him, and I'll put my mask on," he promised.

Evelyn nodded agreement and the mask went down.

"Rudy was the pastor of a church in Los Ríos, a rural village over an hour from Managua, his home village. We lived in a four-room house with outdoor plumbing, but I spent most of my time in Managua or traveling for La Esperanza because we needed my income, especially after Jasmina was born. Rudy's parishioners paid him with vegetables and the use of the house."

Shirley took Evelyn's hand in hers. "Her name was Jasmina? What a lovely name. We know of the loss of your child. I am so sorry."

Shaw's eyes misted and he started to remove his mask again, but Evelyn mouthed no. "Rudy loved Jasmina," she continued quietly. "She looked like him with her curly black hair, but she had my eyes. It was 1988 and it should have been a good year for us. In Sapoa, the Nicaraguan government and Contra forces had signed a cease-fire accord. Rudy and I had so much hope for a normal life, but the Contra came to Los Ríos when I was in Managua with Jasmina. He tried to get people into the church; sometimes they won't be harmed if they are in a church. They said he died instantly, that he was already dead when they decapitated him."

"Oh, my God!" cried Shirley. Evelyn worried the woman would emotionally disintegrate again.

"It's okay, Shirley. I'm okay."

Ian's heart leaped in admiration for little Evie Harrison with her bright violet eyes and pale skin. He yearned to gather her in his arms and comfort her.

Breaking his promise, Reverend Shaw again lifted the oxygen mask. What he had to say was more important than a few gulps of air. "Your husband was one of God's chosen ones. I understand now why you are angry at God for taking him."

The comment disturbed Evelyn. "You think I'm angry at God?" she asked. His eyes answered her question, and Evelyn lowered her head. "You're right; I am," she whispered.

Reverend Shaw raised himself on his elbows motioning for Shirley to place pillows behind his back. "Give me a moment," he said. Weighing his words carefully before speaking, he said, "Unlike so many wishy-washy pastors like me who claim to be men of God, Rudy risked his life for others because of the fire of the Holy Spirit within him. I would have been honored to know him. And I am honored to know you, dear lady." With his voice faltering, Shaw placed the oxygen mask over his face again and inhaled deeply. He wanted to converse with Evelyn about God and faith. He knew she loved God, whether or not she acknowledged it, because despite two horrendous blows that took her family, she continued loving others and God and Love were the same. Her vision of providing a safe home for street children that she had shared throughout the trip, conveyed the depth of her Holy Love as did her willingness to shield them with her body. He wanted to hear more of her story; with God's help, he wanted to encourage her to release the anger and bitterness that remained within her, but fatigue was pursuing him and fatigue won.

"He's sleeping," Shirley said. "I'll sit with him." She looked lovingly at Evelyn and Ian as they turned to leave the room, walking out into the languid but cool Matagalpa afternoon. Dusk filled the hills around them with purple mist. A blurred blood red sun was drifting slowly behind the mountains where the light stopped when the darkness began.

"The rev is right, you know," Ian said softly.

Evelyn shivered imperceptibly.

"I know. I am angry about what happened to my family. And I am angry when I see poor kids crucified day in and day out by poverty. These people who attacked us, as awful as they are, might have been simple farmers or working men under different circumstances. Instead, they were manipulated to do the dirty work of war for the powerful. And they are as abandoned as the street kids of Managua. Of course, I'm angry."

Ambling slowly down the street, Evelyn greeted people sitting on wooden chairs and on steps in front of their simple houses.

Ian pulled her close. "I wish I could be with you," he whispered. Wrapping both arms around her, he crushed her to him, and she hovered in between disbelief and acceptance nestling against his ribs and aching to remain in his arms. But she didn't. Ian was a married man, and Rhoda was a brave woman, one she would willingly call friend.

Evelyn flinched and by force of will, rejected what she had just found. "Ian, I didn't mean to encourage you," she said pulling away.

"I'm sorry. I'm not being fair to you or to Rhoda, but...," he paused, then continued in a husky tone, "why couldn't I have met you a long time ago?"

The whir of a helicopter grew louder and they walked back to the clinic in silence. Eileen Leonard accompanied the two patients in the helicopter, and the others, drained and tired, resigned themselves to a two-hour trip to Managua. A soldier drove the minibus, as Dino was still too shaken to get behind the wheel, and a truckload of soldiers preceded them into the darkness.

CHAPTER TWENTY-ONE

When an agitated Señora Ana returned from Managua, her face flushed, Olga knew at once something bad had happened. "We almost lost her!" cried Anne. "Evie and her delegation were attacked by Recontra bandits on the road from Jinotega."

"*Dios mío...!*" exclaimed Olga. *"La señora --?"* Before she could finish, Anne interrupted her.

"She is fine, Olga, but a young man in the delegation was shot and an older man had a heart problem." Anne was shaking as she talked. Olga took her arm, led her to a rocker, and brought her a glass of rum mixed with papaya juice before presenting her with a bowl of chicken soup.

"You must eat, Señora Ana," she urged. "You must be strong for Señora Evita."

Anne allowed herself to be mothered. Since her conversation with Alfonso Miranda, anticipation and dread had whirled inside her: anticipation over what the incident had done to Evelyn's mental health and dread that she could have been killed. She called Gregory immediately, needing his support, but his secretary said he was on a field assignment so she left a message.

After Olga's soup, Anne made herself another drink and sank back into the rocker. Feeling the comforting liquid calm her beating heart, she drifted into a deep sleep. Gregory woke her when he arrived at eleven. Surprised that Olga was still there, Anne told her to go home to her family.

"I stay for when Señora Evita arrives," Olga protested.

"Gregory is here."

Olga shot Gregory an uneasy glance. She sensed Señora Evita didn't trust him and once more offered to stay, but when the second offer was refused, she left.

At midnight, Anne and Gregory, fully clothed, lay entwined on the bed in half-slumber when the gate opened. Anne sprinted to the door where she found an ashen-faced Evelyn who looked years older than she had four days ago. Wrapping her long arms around her cousin, Anne hugged her tenderly like a mother would a distraught child while Gregory hung back awkwardly. When Evelyn spied him, the anger on her face chilled Anne who feared her cousin was a time bomb and Gregory possibly the trigger. *Be careful of him* played in Anne's mind.

Concealing her unease, she asked Gregory to pour glasses of wine. At first Evelyn refused the wine, curling herself into a rocking chair as if withdrawing from the world. When Anne insisted she drink, she reluctantly agreed. They sipped their wine in silence, Anne and Gregory waiting for Evelyn to speak. Her cousin looked small and stricken curled in the rocker, both hands cradling her wine glass.

"The delegation gave me a $1,000 for the children's home project," Evelyn finally said in a near whisper.

"How wonderful, Evie," declared Anne.

Gregory sat on the edge of his seat in watchful hesitation. Tomorrow he would be traveling north to join the search for the Recontra leader, known as El León, who was behind many of the northern attacks. Evelyn could provide him with information that might be useful. Was this the right time to interview her about the attack? He was unsure but he needed any information she could give.

"How did the bandits stage the attack?" he asked directly, throwing caution to the wind.

Anne, puzzled by this sudden need to gather facts, placed a warning hand on his arm. "Greg, give Evie time to relax."

Her warning was too late. Evelyn leaped from the rocker sending the wineglass soaring spraying all three with droplets of wine before it shattered on the floor.

"If this is an official inquiry, I will tell you nothing!" she exploded, her hands chopping the air.

"Evie!" exclaimed Anne as Evelyn took a menacing step toward Gregory, spearing her rage through him, her mouth twisted in anger.

"We came close to being killed by Recontras who wouldn't exist without backing from people like you!"

Gregory raised his palms in conciliation, an action that slashed through Evelyn's fury leaving her shaken by the hostility she had violently discharged like the armaments she so hated. Throwing her palms against her cheeks, she cried plaintively, "I can't talk now," and fled into her bedroom slamming the door.

Astonished by her cousin's loss of control, a distressed Anne stared at the bedroom door praying silently she could find the words of comfort Evelyn needed to hear. Gregory pressed his body against hers. "I'm sorry," he whispered.

Anne heard herself state the obvious. "She's been through a lot."

"I shouldn't have probed for information. I'm sorry," Gregory repeated dispiritedly. He held Anne to him like a drowning man. Without her cousin's approval, they had no future. He had realized this weeks ago, yet a part of him remained hopeful. Now his hope lay in ruins; politics would always intrude.

"Are you staying the night?" Anne asked.

"I think not."

She watched him drive off aware of the sickening feeling in her stomach; their relationship had been profoundly altered. But before she could think of that, she needed to speak to Evelyn. Approaching the bedroom door she knocked lightly. "Please, may I come in?"

"No, we'll talk tomorrow," Evelyn murmured.

Anne returned to the living room and sank into a rocker. She believed she never could have sustained the life blows dealt Evelyn and go on so courageously. But still, she had much to give, and nothing could be given with wholeheartedness as long as Gregory Garner remained in her life. She had to let him go. Sinking her head into her hands, she wept.

The next morning Evelyn awoke before dawn, a time of semi-darkness before the sun rose bathing the world with light, beckoning dew-sodden leaves to life and flowers to blossom into daylight. At first not a whisper of human sound reached her ears, only the chirping and scrambling of small creatures; but with the sunlight, sounds proliferated: human voices, the braying and mooing of animals, the crowing of roosters, the hoof beats of horses, and the rumble of oxcarts heading into the forest.

As she observed the sunrise from the patio, coffee cup in hand, she noted the absence of Gregory's car and concluded she had driven him away, but she was not sorry, except for Anne. Gregory had not witnessed mothers mourn for their dead children during the war. He seemed unmoved by the heavy blanket of depressive passivity smothering war-weary Nicaraguans. He supported policies made in favor of what he thought were in American interests. He had to know that the American people would never have accepted CIA interventions in Nicaragua had they been informed of the cost in human suffering. Rudy was gone, Jasmina was gone, and Evelyn had almost lost seven people and her own life to bandits brandishing American made armaments.

She reentered the house and went to her unicorns, their proud wings raised in flight. Carefully touching them one by one, she felt their presence in her hands urging her to reclaim and fulfill her dreams of a hope-filled future. Kissing her father's wooden unicorn, she gently placed it back onto the shelf. Then pen in hand, she wrote a full report of the Recontra attack for Alfonso Miranda.

With Anne by her side, Evelyn drove into Managua that morning in silence. Other than the routine uttering of polite breakfast conversation, neither of them could bring themselves to speak of the previous evening. An emotionally distant conversation was welcomed by both women. When Anne offered to take a cab home after work, Evelyn gratefully accepted her offer.

***

Humberto Cartón, who had recovered from the fever that had sent him to bed during the time Señora Gutiérrez and her delegation were nearly killed, drove the minibus to the Baptist Hospital to pick up a young man named Benjamin Conway and an older couple named Thomas and Shirley Shaw. The two men were rolled out in wheelchairs, and Cartón with the help of Señora Shaw assisted her husband and the young man into seats in the minibus before proceeding to the office of La Esperanza where Señora Gutiérrez and the remainder of her delegation were waiting for them. He then squired the entire group to the United States Embassy and waited outside until their business was done.

Inside the embassy, a friendly officer in formal military dress served the group coffee and interviewed them about the attack while his assistant, the kind of bureaucrat who always fades into the background, scrutinized them from a face so expressionless it seemed to be carved from wood. Evelyn shared her belief that the Recontra bandits were a part of a new underground economy based on theft resulting from the deactivation of the Contras without adequate distribution of farmland or some other form of compensation for the now jobless fighters. The embassy officer listened without comment. When he had finished his business with them, he returned them to Humberto with new passports in hand, and Evelyn told her driver to take them to Los Antojitos.

Over lunch Thomas Shaw looked wan and serious, but Shirley seemed almost cheerful. Unassailable optimism had always been her strongest quality. On painkillers, Benjamin was smiling like the Cheshire cat, his bandaged arm inert on his lap. "I learned more this week than in my three years at university and maybe more than in my whole life," he declared through a thick tongue.

"Sometimes people are changed in unexpected ways, Ben," Evelyn said, smiling at the young man who grinned foolishly in return. Planting a spontaneous kiss on his forehead, she added, "You tried to save us. You're a hero." Everyone clapped.

An unusually sociable Raymond Beckett asked each person how they had felt during the ordeal and seemed genuinely interested in their responses. Muriel expressed enthusiasm about returning to Nicaragua with her students. A subdued Rhoda remained quiet when praise was heaped upon her for her quick actions in treating Reverend Shaw and Benjamin. Ian commented on how well everyone had handled themselves and everyone else praised him and Evelyn for the brave actions they believed had saved their lives. Evelyn quietly observed the others interact with one another feeling a kind of melancholy satisfaction. Clearly the profound experience had bonded them and they had changed in ways that could not yet be fully appreciated.

After lunch, Humberto took his passengers to the airport where Alfonso Miranda was waiting. "Tell people in your country what happened," he urged. "Supplying arms to the Recontras must stop, and we think the money is coming from their supporters in America."

"Rest assured we'll publicize our experiences," stated Muriel firmly. "I'll get a news interview in the *Boston Globe* and we'll move it through academic circles. We'll also get this story on the radio."

Beckett raised skeptical eyebrows. "We'll try," he added realistically.

When the loudspeaker blared boarding directions, Muriel thanked Evelyn profusely and hugged her briefly. "You will hear from me, Evelyn. I am coming back with my class," she declared in a tone of determination. Beckett gave Evelyn an awkward hug mumbling something inaudible. Shirley murmured her goodbye clinging to Evelyn as though her life depended upon it while Reverend Shaw seated in an airport wheelchair grasped Evelyn's hand pulling her down toward him and placed a kiss on her cheek. "One day you must come to Minnesota and we will talk about God," he said.

"Yes," she agreed.

"Is that a promise?" he asked. She assured him it was, and he released her.

Benjamin, also seated in an airport wheelchair, grasped Evelyn's hand and kissed it. "I'm coming back as soon as I can," he declared before he and the reverend were whisked across the tarmack toward the plane by airline attendants, with Shirley half-running behind them.

Both Ian and Rhoda Campbell shook Evelyn's hand. "You are a courageous woman," Evelyn said to Rhoda. Looking a little haunted, Rhoda responded dispiritedly, "This kind of life is not for everyone." She turned from Evelyn without further comment and walked away, leaving her husband behind.

Ian cupped both of Evelyn's hands in his. "Stay safe," he whispered. His words floated gently between them; the warmth flowing between their hands bid them to remain connected. Evelyn's heart ached for what could have been under other circumstances. With the hollow feeling of loss, she wrenched her hands from his and watched him jog across the tarmack and disappear into the plane.

When the plane soared purposefully into the sky, Evelyn whispered *adios* to seven people she would never forget.

Renaldo was in the yard, rake in hand when she pulled into the drive later that afternoon. He greeted her with a wave and a mumble and pointed to his cheek.

"No tooth," explained Olga opening the door. "Señora Ana took him to the Irish dentist. Renaldo drinks no more."

"Anne took you to see Dr. Sharon McGinnis at Managua Dental?" Evelyn asked Renaldo.

Renaldo tried to grin but grimaced instead and nodded. If the *señora* had been killed life would have become much worse for him. He was happy that she had survived, but did not know how to express his feelings.

"*Bueno,*" declared Evelyn. Renaldo nodded again and turned his attention to neglected looking yard brush in spite of Olga's efforts at containing it.

"How did you manage to stop Renaldo from drinking?" Evelyn asked.

Olga pointed to her mouth. "His bad tooth. Rum did not take away the pain."

"I am happy he is back," said Evelyn.

"It is good," Olga agreed, hesitating. Observing Olga's tight grip on her mop, Evelyn concluded something was wrong.

"Is there something you want to tell me?"

Olga opened her mouth to speak, but closed it.

"Tell me."

Olga sighed deeply. "I have troubles."

Evelyn motioned to a dining room chair. "Come, let us sit down," she said.

Olga sat down, folded her hands on the table, looked down at them, and spoke, "Renaldo's mistress Patricia came to me with her daughter Raquel. She will live with us now. Patricia drinks and I fear she will lead Renaldo back to the rum. I cannot let Raquel remain with such a mother as Patricia. She is my niece, my family."

Evelyn sank her chin into her hand, her fingers covering her mouth. After a moment, she lowered her hand and spoke. "Well, you do have a problem, Olga. We will do what we can to help."

"*Gracias, Señora Evita,*" Olga responded. "I have good luck to be your *empleada.*"

The following day when Evelyn and Anne returned home from work, a whippet thin black man with a shock of wiry soot-gray hair was waiting for them. "He says he wants to talk to the American *señoras*. He is the father of Patricia. He is so sad," Olga whispered in an apologetic tone, hoping they would not be upset.

Evelyn was exhausted. She had not recovered her emotional or physical strength. The ordeal had left her with bruises on her legs and a strained muscle in her back had assaulted her with painful spasms all day. She wanted nothing more than to retreat into the silence of her room. Instead, she asked Olga to set another plate for dinner. The unexpected guest rose from a rocker to greet the women. An elderly man, his dark chocolate face bearing a haggard expression, was visibly poor in his grayish white shirt, the cuffs frayed and too-short shiny dark pants that stopped at his ankles. Evelyn guessed the soles of his battered, yet polished, shoes were worn.

"I am Reverend William Archibald, pastor of Good Shepherd Christian Church in Bluefields. My former professor is Dr. David Butler who told me at the FSLN Congress that he is your friend," he said speaking in a Creole English reflecting his roots in the Southern Atlantic Coast region of Nicaragua.

Evelyn shook his hand. "You must join us for dinner," she offered graciously.

"Thank you, Señora Gutiérrez. A meal will be most welcome."

On the table, Olga placed a large bowl of rice, another of red beans, a plate of lettuce overflowing with slices of avocado, onions, tomatoes and jicama, and a plate of sliced roasted pork and tortillas. Archibald looked at the food, excited anticipation palpable in his dark eyes.

"With your permission, I shall give to God our thank you," he declared and lowered his head to pray. "Give us gratitude, Father, for all your blessings. Make us conscious of the needs and the rights of others. In the name of Christ, Our Lord and Savior, we ask this. Amen." Immediately he reached for the pork, filled half of his plate with meat, and launched into an account of his recent activities.

"I came for the Sandinista Congress and remained five days afterwards with other leaders from the Atlantic Coast. We discussed Autonomy. As you know, Señora Gutiérrez, the Sandinistas initiated the Autonomy Law in 1987, but it has not yet been codified, and codification, not empty promises, is what we want. Codification will legitimize our historic right to the national resources of our region on the Atlantic Coast. Next month we will have a conference in Managua about the Autonomy Law."

Archibald shoved food into his mouth like a starving man.

"I know little of the history of the Atlantic Coast. It's like another country, isn't it, Reverend Archibald?" Anne asked.

Archibald nodded as he chewed. "Yes, we are like another country. Our coast was settled by the English who brought with them the blacks from Jamaica. We are another country in all but name, and we have a sad history." He stopped to scrape what remained from the bowl of beans onto his plate, and then continued.

"In the 1920's the foreigners came with their timber companies and mineral companies. They used us as cheap labor; extracted our resources. When they departed after the Sandinistas nationalized their businesses, they left behind their contamination, but they took their equipment and technical knowledge with them. Now the foreign companies are returning, and we fight so we can make the rules, not the government in Managua. But it is not easy. Our independent mentality and our diversity are sometimes our biggest problems. We are African black and three different native Indian groups."

"I have read that the Atlantic Coast was not as much affected as was the Pacific Coast during the Contra War," Anne commented.

"The fighting was not as much, Señora Harrison," responded Archibald, "but we were affected. The Sandinista government was not popular on the Atlantic Coast. During the war they relocated entire villages of Miskito and Mayangna Indians. They claimed it was for their own safety and to prevent the infiltration of Contras, but these people were told to leave the homes of their fathers and grandfathers, causing great animosity, and many young people ran off to join the Contras."

Archibald piled food onto his plate again, even though Anne and Evelyn had finished, and he continued eating rapaciously. As he reached for the last tortilla, he cast a longing glance at the now empty bowls. In response to Olga's frantic gestures that the food was all gone, Evelyn helped Olga clear the table signaling the end of dinner. Reluctantly Archibald rested his fork on the edge of his plate.

"Shall we sit in the rockers?" Evelyn suggested. They moved into the living room and sat around the primitive coffee table Evelyn had constructed from packing crates a few days before Anne's arrival. Settling into the rocker, Archibald's emaciated body seemed to shrink physically. Evelyn studied the gaunt visage of the pastor wondering if he deprived himself of food in order to assure his family was fed. She observed him brighten when he saw the books in neat little rows occupying the bottom shelves of the divider between the kitchen and the living area.

"Books are important to me. Thanks to the generosity of our English friends and our friends in American churches who send us books or bring them to Managua on delegations, we have a small library in our church," he commented.

Olga brought mugs of coffee, and they sipped the hot, satisfying liquid and allowed a brief silence to pass until Archibald addressed the real purpose behind his visit.

"You may wonder why I am here," he stated.

Evelyn nodded in the affirmative.

"I will speak in Spanish now so Olga can understand," he said, and Evelyn swiveled her body toward the kitchen. "Olga, please join us for a few moments." Olga, dutifully washing the dishes, walked toward them wiping her wet hands on her apron. Archibald placed his mug on the table. Leaning forward, he clasped his hands together and spoke slowly and deliberately for the benefit of Anne, whom he had observed was tentative in her Spanish.

"Raquel, my precious granddaughter, is the reason I am here. Her mother Patricia is a heartache for my family. My wife cries every night over this lost child of ours. None of our other eight children are like Patricia."

Evelyn and Anne nodded sympathetically. Olga sat on the edge of her seat, an expectant expression on her face.

"I brought Patricia and Raquel with me to Managua. I hoped since Renaldo is no longer with his wife, he would take care of them. But now, Patricia is gone and she has left Raquel behind." Archibald gestured toward

Olga who began to speak. "This morning Patricia says to Renaldo, 'Do not try to find me.' She says to me, 'Olga, you are a better mother than I.' Renaldo took her arm, but she pushed him away, and she is gone."

"How awful for the little girl," Anne declared, recalling the beautiful child she had met earlier.

Archibald shook his head sadly. "My daughter must find her way in the world alone. It may lead to misery, but I cannot help her anymore. I have to help Raquel, who is three years old and without her mother," he lamented. Looking at Olga, he continued.

"Olga wants to take the child. In the house of Olga, Raquel will have her own room with a bed. In my home, eight of us live in three rooms. Life will be better here for Raquel, but I must ask a delicate question before I decide," said Archibald switching to English and lowering his voice even though Olga could not comprehend his comments.

"You see, I have to know if Renaldo and Olga will continue to have employment with you."

Compassion flooded through Anne for this man who loved his granddaughter. Evelyn thought of Jasmina and her eyes watered. "I wish we could give you a definitive answer, Reverend Archibald," she said kindly. "Historically people who live in the Casa Sánchez have offered employment to the Aguilar family, but we cannot guarantee it will always be so, and we will be leaving here at the end of December."

"I feared as much," he said sadly. "And forgive me if I insult your employee Renaldo, but he is not known to be responsible. Like my sad, tragic child Patricia, he has a thirst for the rum."

"You understand him well," remarked Evelyn, "but Olga is responsible and kind."

Archibald fell silent, placing his elbows on his knees and his chin in his hands. "What to do," he muttered. "What to do."

"Hello, friends!" a scratchy voice pierced the room startling them. Four pairs of eyes shot toward the large girth of Harry Albert pressed against the locked front door screen.

"Can I come in?" Albert asked, a strained grin on his face as Evelyn rose from her seat and approached him.

"Another time is better. We have a visitor," she said not bothering to hide her irritation over his unwelcome presence.

"But I must explain something important. And you must know it tonight," he persisted. "Please. It's urgent. It's a matter of life and death!"

Archibald joined Evelyn at the door. "May I be of help?" he asked. "My name is the Reverend William Archibald. Do you have trouble, my son?"

"It's urgent, rev. The women in this house must know the truth. They must not be afraid," the distressed man sputtered.

"We must all know the Truth," agreed Archibald.

"Please let me in. I need to tell you something," pleaded Albert. His wild blood-shot eyes signaled to Evelyn that whatever he wanted to say needed to be heard. Archibald saw it too and looked knowingly at Evelyn. She first unlocked the rod iron security gate, then the screen, and he entered.

"Do you have coffee?" he asked as he strode toward a rocker, sat down, and Olga brought him a mug of coffee that he sipped greedily. "I live up the road," he explained, his eyes roaming the room as he spoke. Arching his arm through the air he gestured at the surroundings. "Nice place you got here." He lifted the coffee cup in salute.

"You said you had something to tell us," said Archibald, raising his eyebrows expectantly. He sat down in the rocker opposite Albert studying him.

"Listen," Albert began. "The war wiped out a generation of young men in Nicaragua. During the fighting, the cities and towns only had young children and women left in them. No man was there to teach the children. Now there's a generation of undisciplined young people with no respect. They steal. There's no respect for anything. They don't know any other way of life but to steal and kill. Isn't this so, rev?" The words pounded through a clipped nasal voice in a monotone.

Archibald cleared his throat, hoping to phrase a cogent response to the man's disjointed rambling. "Nicaragua is faced with many difficult problems," he agreed. "But, Mr. Albert, what news do you have for us?"

"Harry. Call me Harry," said Albert.

"Yes. Harry, what is your news?" asked Archibald patiently.

Albert looked confused, launching into another ramble.

"The government should give the marauders the land they were promised. Those that want to continue to steal and murder should be wiped out. M-16's would do it. Ta! Ta! Ta! The real murders will never change. They love war too much." Albert stared blankly at the steaming liquid in his cup as he spoke.

Evelyn, Anne, and Archibald arrived simultaneously at the same conclusion. Albert was an extremely disturbed man.

"Thank you for stopping by, Harry," Evelyn said softly. "We must talk again another time." Everyone stood up to signal his dismissal, but Albert remained seated.

"Don't believe anything you read in the newspapers," he blurted out.

"What do you mean?" asked Evelyn.

"You will read tomorrow that the police are looking for me. They say I strangle women and cut them. It's not true."

Anne's hand rushed toward her chest and she took a deep breath. Archibald sat down again looking as though the wind had been punched out of him. Evelyn shivered, her head pounding painfully. Olga realized something terrible had been said.

"Not true?" Evelyn asked, her voice tight.

"No, not true. I seen enough killing in Nam. Too many dead. Too many," an agitated Albert murmured. His head whipped up. "You got any rum?"

"Olga, please bring a glass of rum for Señor Albert," said Evelyn with forced calmness.

With lightening speed, Olga delivered the rum and Albert gulped it down. Wiping his mouth with the back of his hand, he emitted a loud satisfied sigh.

The signs of posttraumatic stress were palpable. William Archibald had witnessed it in the young men returned from the war.

The disturbed man suddenly jumped to his feet. "They're out to get me, rev. I need to get away from here. I can go to Diriamba. It's nice there. They killed the forest though. Cut down all the trees. Maybe I'd like to live between Matagalpa and Jinotega, some of the most beautiful country in the world, even more beautiful than the Andes. But it wouldn't take them long to find out where I was and kill me." His voice cracked. "I didn't do it. They don't understand. I didn't do it!" he cried and shuddered.

Archibald placed a hand on Albert's shoulder. "Harry, you need help. We will call the US Embassy and get you help."

"No, no! They'll send me back" cried Albert swiveling away.

"Then how can we help?" asked Evelyn.

"Hide me."

"We can't do that."

"Then you, are of no help, ma'am," declared Albert, scornfully tossing his head in a derisive gesture. Placing his hands on his hips, he bent his torso backwards until his spine cracked. Straightening, he said in a lucid voice as though nothing strange had occurred, "I need to go." He headed toward the door, but halted to face them again and wag a forefinger in their direction. "It's a lie. Don't you believe what they say. It's a lie."

After he was gone, Evelyn locked the main wooden door, the screen door, and lastly the rod iron security door. Leaning her back against it, she looked as though she had just lifted a huge boulder.

"Is it true or is it in his imagination?" Anne asked.

"I don't know," responded Evelyn

"He is crazy," Archibald cautioned. "I offer my protection to you by remaining in your house tonight."

Evelyn was about to refuse the offer when she considered that Reverend Archibald may have wanted to stay for a reason beyond Harry Albert. The food was no doubt more plentiful than at Olga's.

"The murders of these women have been in the paper, but we don't know that the police suspect Albert. They must know where he is. If they really suspected him, they would have been here by now," Evelyn concluded.

"We should call the US Embassy," said Anne.

"It might be better to wait until tomorrow," commented Evelyn. "He may not be as delusional then. If we call them tonight, it will appear we feel threatened and they may treat him as dangerous when, in fact, he may only be sick."

"Good point," noted Anne, "but he's killed women."

"He may have in Vietnam," speculated Evelyn. "He may not have killed anyone in Nicaragua."

"I agree," said Archibald. "When they came back from war, they do not separate past from present, reality from things not real."

A fleeting thought of how Vietnam may have affected Ian whipped through Evelyn's mind. "Then it's decided. We'll wait until tomorrow and talk to him again," she said and they all went to bed.

Laying his weary body on a quickly assembled cot in the empty third bedroom, Archibald sighed deeply. Tiredness, the rare pleasure of a full stomach, and a bed on which he slept in silence and alone surrounded William Archibald like the arms of a loving mother. He drifted into a fuzzy haze, punctured by the dull throb of his grief over Patricia. At times he felt he was drowning in the circumstances of his daughter's destructive behavior, and he knew with pulse-pounding certainty after her abandonment of Raquel that he had lost her to Satan. Only God could save Patricia now, as God had saved them all from the pangs of hunger many times. God was the only solid reality in his shifting, unpredictable world.

Archibald had taken the small stipend offered by the FSLN for the trip to Managua and stretched it to include Patricia and Raquel. He had prayed that Renaldo Aguilar was not the drunken fool some claimed he was, but this opportunity for free passage to Managua would not come again, and he took the chance. He had sold everything he could, begged from everyone he dared to send the money for Patricia and Raquel to return to Bluefields from Managua six months ago, but the strain of having his wayward daughter in the house, coming and going at all hours to meet men for rum was distressing the family to the breaking point. He thought his idea of bringing her and Raquel to Managua might work, until he met Renaldo.

Although he was a gentle man steeped in the traditions of a culture that valued the dignity of each individual, he was enough of a pragmatist to believe Olga's kind steadiness might not be enough to counteract whatever grief Renaldo and his daughter brought upon her and Raquel. What a terrible dilemma he faced, but he was too drained to think another thought. Tomorrow he would decide.

Sonorous snoring reverberated through the Casa Sánchez like an intermittent drum roll as Archibald released his troubling thoughts into the darkness and entered into deep sleep. However, the women he had offered to protect slept raggedly, their minds refusing to cease wrestling with the challenges of a long and life-altering day.

CHAPTER TWENTY-TWO

Two days ago Anne had remained in bed awake, perspiring in heat and anxiety, her heart thumping, her mind racing, as she listened to Evelyn in the kitchen. She postponed what she thought would be a strained encounter following the barrage of anger aimed at Gregory, but she soon realized that Evelyn was too drained to engage her in any significant way; instead, her cousin had erected an opaque wall of silence between them. Anne felt as though she was sharing the house with a stranger and she struggled with how to approach Evelyn in a caring way, but the sudden arrival of Patricia and her daughter Raquel, Reverend Archibald, and Harry Albert presented the two of them with challenging distractions. A serious conversation about Gregory would have to wait. Gregory was "in the field," as he put it, and would not return for several days, so there was time.

This morning Anne tingled with a nervous energy that could not be contained. Evelyn's possible demise at the hands of marauding bandits quickened her heart whenever she thought of it, and the unsettling appearance of Harry Albert the evening before had jangled her nerves more than she wanted to admit. She felt shaky as she quietly slid into her slippers, first checking for snakes, and then tiptoed into the kitchen to make coffee. She settled into the rocker near the window that overlooked Sweetie Pie's perch, waiting for the coffee to perk.

The early rays of light illuminated the overhang where Sweetie Pie made its home, but the iguana was not there. Where was the creature she had declared her Nicaraguan pet soon after her arrival in Nicaragua: a creature, unchanging and ongoing, that for some inexplicable reason made her feel secure? Slipping out of the house, Anne walked slowly around its circumference looking for Sweetie Pie. She circled the house twice without success.

Although the temperature was nearing 77 F., Anne shivered. Was Sweetie Pie's disappearance an omen, like that of the coral snake invading her bedroom on the same evening as her frightening dream? Was she being prepared because something dreadful was about to befall her or Evelyn? "Silly," she chided herself aloud over her superstitious musings.

Reclaiming the rocker with coffee mug in hand, Anne tried to clear her mind without success. When Evelyn entered the kitchen, her face appearing almost bloodless, Anne wondered if she looked as wan and exhausted as her cousin.

"No sleep?" she asked.

"No sleep," Evelyn responded.

"Same here, but our 'protector' is still snoring."

Evelyn smiled. The wry comment punctured her careful reserve.

"I can't find the iguana," Anne said.

"Don't worry; it's around somewhere," assured Evelyn, as she poured herself a cup of coffee and sat at the table. "We have acquired a list of things to worry over, haven't we?" she commented taking a sip.

"A few," Anne agreed, joining her cousin.

Evelyn flashed a weak smile and said, "I'm sorry over my rude comments to Gregory."

"You're probably right about him, but I think I love him, and I don't know what to do."

"Whatever you decide, you have my support," whispered Evelyn. Anne sighed relieved they had, at least temporarily, negotiated the minefield of Gregory Garner.

"I have an idea about Raquel," Evelyn declared. Anne welcomed the change of subject. "I will commit to providing a small monthly sum for Raquel's support until she reaches eighteen, so even if Olga is not hired by the next people who occupy this house, she can afford to keep Raquel," Evelyn explained.

Taken aback Anne protested, "Evie, you don't even know the child. What about the children's home?"

"I want a refuge for lost children. Isn't this poor child, abandoned by her mother, lost? The love of her grandparents is probably the best thing in her life, but they are burdened with the care of their other children and grandchildren. And did you notice how ill Reverend Archibald looks? What would happen to Raquel should he die? I have been wrestling with this idea all night. Oh, Annie, Raquel is the same age as Jasmina was when…."

"This is for Jasmina?" Anne asked uneasily.

"It's the right thing to do," responded Evelyn.

Anne rose from her seat ostensibly to fill her coffee mug, but in reality to give herself a moment to digest the import of Evelyn's decision. Then placing her mug down, she wrapped her arms around the back of her still-seated cousin and gave her a kiss on the cheek.

When Raquel arrived that morning clinging to her Aunt Olga's hand, a still sleepy Archibald swooped his granddaughter into his arms. Like him, her skin was the color of black coffee. Loose ringlets of charcoal hair caped a round face that reflected innocent wonder. The child's bright wide eyes immediately fell upon Evelyn, poking through the warm current of Evelyn's memories of Jasmina.

"Hello, my name is Señora Evita. What is your name?" she asked the child, who was happy to be in the arms of her grandfather.

Raquel's lower lip quivered, her tiny voice responded shyly, "Raquel."

"Raquel. What a pretty name. You know, I have something you might like, Raquel, a Raggedy Anne doll my little girl Jasmina used to play with. Would you like to see it?"

The sweet child smell of the little girl's body consumed Evelyn as she stretched out her arms, and Raquel climbed into them without hesitation. Together they disappeared into the bedroom, emerging moments later with Raquel carrying a floppy Raggedy Anne doll and twirling its red braids.

"Grandpa, look," she cried happily, lifting the doll toward him. "Her name is Jasmina."

"Her name is Raggedy Anne," Evelyn corrected gently. "She used to belong to a little girl named Jasmina."

"Her name is Jasmina," insisted Raquel.

"Yes. She is Jasmina," Evelyn agreed, her voice wavering.

Moisture filled in the dark eyes of Archibald, who was aware of the fate of the Pastor Rudolfo Gutiérrez and his daughter. "We are honored," he said with deep humility.

They sat down to breakfast. Olga, at Evelyn's invitation, joined them along with Renaldo. After eating, Renaldo took his daughter outside, and the remaining four adults entered into discussion concerning Raquel's future.

"Señora Olga, you are a good woman, but your brother – I do not wish to be unkind – but your brother is not as capable as one would wish for a father," Archibald said honestly.

"Renaldo is my burden," Olga said. "I promised my parents to care for him, and I will care for his child."

"Who will watch the child when you and Renaldo work?" asked Archibald.

"I know a woman who will watch Raquel for a small sum," she answered. "She is a good friend who loves children."

Archibald frowned still uncertain. "I do not know what is best for Raquel," he bemoaned looking directly at the two American women for guidance.

"Reverend Archibald, I have an idea that may be of help." Evelyn spoke in English, as she wanted to get Archibald's agreement before she told Olga. In curious anticipation, Archibald widened his sad eyes and fastened them upon the kind face of the American woman sensing that if any way could be found to assure Raquel a happy future, Señora Gutiérrez would find it. "I will promise to provide a monthly sum for the care of Raquel," she was saying. "I will always live in Nicaragua, and I will monitor Raquel's care, if necessary. She will never be deprived as long as I am living. Will you accept my offer?"

A sudden illumination of unbridled joy flooded the pastor. Although she had no idea of what Evelyn had just said, Olga knew that it was good.

"Bless you, dear lady," Archibald gasped. "You have given us a miracle."

When Anne translated the reason for his sudden happiness, Olga clasped her hands and cried out, *"Gracias a Dios!"*

With the dignified reserve of his culture masking a great reservoir of feeling over this fortunate turn of events, Reverend Archibald said, "You will always be my sister in Christ." He took her hand and gave it a strong shake. It was unthinkable for him to hug this wonderful woman, the savior of his granddaughter, but it was appropriate to express the depth of his gratitude.

A tearful Olga rushed outside to tell Renaldo the good news, but before she could say a word, she heard the frightening pleas of Anita who was running toward the house, her arms pumping furiously. *"Señoras! Señoras! La policía están matando el hombre loco!"*

Evelyn, Anne, and Archibald immediately bolted from the house.

"Lo que pasó?" Evelyn called to Anita.

"El gordo Americano a la pulpería. Hurry!" cried Anita as she turned around and ran toward her store.

Fueled by the hard fist of an unknown fear, Evelyn, Anne, and Archibald bolted after her and as they neared the store, they saw Harry Albert's fat body spread against a police car while an enraged policeman viciously punched and kicked him. An older policeman was observing the spectacle, arms crossed, a satisfied expression on his face. Ernesto was in the doorway of the Pulpería Iván Guadalupe, holding the hand of a frightened Hernández while a wheezing Camilo clung to his body. Anita rushed to them and swooped the boys inside the store.

"Stop this at once!" demanded Evelyn. The attacker briefly looked at her, but he continued assaulting the fat man's body.

"Stop it!" screamed Evelyn. "I demand you to stop!"

The older policeman barked orders to his underling who reluctantly ceased the pummeling.

"They're killing me," Albert choked, coughing and wheezing as he clung to the vehicle to remain standing.

The offending policeman jerked nervously like a salivating dog baring its teeth at an enemy. Even though menace blazed in his eyes, Anne, too angry to be afraid, rushed to the heaving Albert to gently dab at the blood trickling from his mangled hair with her bandana.

"Why are you beating him?" Evelyn demanded of the policemen.

Archibald placed a warning hand on her arm. "Be careful," he said in English.

"Señora, this is not your concern," declared the older policeman, fiercely hooking his thumbs into his belt and glaring threateningly at her. "This man is a murderer of our women. Do you know him?"

"He is a neighbor," explained Archibald before Evelyn could speak.

"Who are you?" the policeman hissed looking at Archibald with impatient irritation.

"I am the Reverend William Archibald from Bluefields," Archibald answered.

The response was a sneer. "Bluefields? You are no neighbor."

"Albert is *my* neighbor," declared Evelyn.

"He is friend to you? You know of his brutality?" the policeman asked in an accusatory tone.

Ernesto stepped forward. "*Señor, soy Ernesto Flores.* My father is Mario Flores of Flores Bicycle Repair in Managua. He fought in Estelí."

The policeman's face softened. "I know of your father, but...."

Ernesto raised his hand in a friendly gesture. "*Momentito, Señor.* Please let me tell you that the *señora* is no friend to the bad man. She is a neighbor as am I." The policeman's ferocious scowl slowly began to fade. Ernesto continued. "The other *señora* is a *profesora* from America. They are kind to a neighbor. They are not his friend."

The policeman pondered the words of Flores. He knew Mario Flores and the son of Flores was telling him these things. Also, one of the women was American and maybe the other was too. Arresting three Americans could mean trouble for him. He drew back from Evelyn and Archibald and spoke in a less threatening tone.

"Your neighbor murdered five women," he said thinly.

Evelyn understood the politics of what had just occurred. She would thank Ernesto later. Now she had a little leverage to keep Albert from being murdered on the way to the police station.

"How do you know he murdered five women?" she asked.

"We were told to bring him in," was the response.

"On *suspicion* of murder, *verdad?*"

The policeman drew his lips tight and said nothing.

"Suspicion," she repeated forcefully. Turning her gaze to the more aggressive policeman she asked sarcastically, "Were you told to beat him lifeless?"

The man stared at her fuming, his fists curled by his side.

"We go," announced the older policeman gesturing to his subordinate to open the rear door of the vehicle. With a snarl, the younger policeman moved toward Albert, but when Anne positioned her body in front of Albert's, he stopped.

"He can get in by himself," Anne said fiercely. The policeman looked toward his companion who gestured for him to allow them to pass, and Albert with Anne by his side stumbled toward the open door. When he slid inside, he said a strangled, "Thank you."

Anne shivered at the sight of this human being that had fallen so far into a hell of his own making. Evelyn leaned into the window. "We'll get you help, Harry," she said.

Albert began to cry. "I won't be alive in the morning."

She stared at him with a mixture of antipathy and sympathy. "Yes, you will. Padre Douglas Michaels will visit you. He's Canadian. I don't know if you're Catholic, but say you are and ask to meet with him. We'll try to get you out of the country, perhaps to Canada, if the US decides to leave you to the mercy of the Nicaraguans."

Albert looked at her from a swollen, battered face. "Thank you," he wheezed. "I didn't kill those women. I did not."

Evelyn said, "I don't think you did. Otherwise I wouldn't help you." The older policeman started the car and Evelyn and Anne scuttled back.

"Will they kill him?" Anne asked.

"I doubt it," responded Evelyn, not as certain as she sounded.

"He has done terrible things. He is possessed by Satan," declared Archibald.

"He is sick," Evelyn commented with a tired sigh. "We don't know what he has done. We only know what others claim he has done."

"Yes, that is true," agreed Archibald. "But we do know he has sinned and we must pray for him."

When they arrived at the house, Evelyn dialed Padre Doug first and the US Embassy next.

***

After meeting with Harry Albert, a sobered Padre Doug trudged along the corridor from the cells to the exit, preoccupied with thoughts of what had just transpired. He had tried, but he was not much comfort to Albert. He could not breach the wall of terror imprisoning the distraught man's mind.

"Shit! I need a cigarette," Padre Doug mumbled to the empty corridor. As he fumbled in his pocket for his pack of smokes, he observed three men walking toward him, recognizing one of them as they neared. They were North Americans in beige pants, white shirts, and ties. The one carrying the briefcase was Gregory Garner. The men murmured their "good mornings" and walked on. Neither Garner nor Padre Doug acknowledged each other further, but when the priest entered the foyer leading to the main office, Garner was upon him.

"Where are your buddies?" asked Padre Doug.

"Waiting for me," was the answer. Garner's face betrayed the tension of secrets held rigidly under control. The first time Padre Doug had met him, when they had traveled to Los Ríos together, he had identified Garner's remoteness as a characteristic useful in his line of work.

"Are you the boss?" asked Padre Doug.

"Something like that. Evelyn tried to reach me. They called me back from the North when she told them Anne had witnessed the incident." Garner removed a pack of cigarettes and a lighter. He lit the cigarette dangling from Padre Doug's mouth, then lit his own.

Padre Doug wanted to ask why Garner had led Anne on when he had to know the outcome. As though he could read the priest's mind Garner said, "I will tell Anne as much about me as I can reveal." He took a long drag on his cigarette, expelling the smoke with slow deliberateness, holding this moment with a man he admired while thinking of a woman he loved and the emptiness of his life. He felt as though he, Gregory Garner, son of Lois and Howard Garner of Reeds Corners, Georgia, was of no use to anyone in this world, not even to himself.

"Tell her soon," demanded Padre Doug in a firm voice.

"I love her, Padre," Garner muttered barely audible.

Padre Doug waited for more. Garner stood taut, tall, and on guard, the usually unmanageable blond hair slicked back, controlled as his personage. "Then do the right thing, Greg, and do it kindly," said Padre Doug in a softer voice.

Garner nodded and inhaled before he spoke again, "What did Albert tell you?" he asked.

The question robbed Padre Doug of their fleeting moment of connection. "As a Canadian citizen, I do not have to disclose anything to you," he said ungraciously. "What I will tell you is that Albert did not commit murder. He's huddled in the cell, bulgy-eyed and terrified as a cornered fox after the hunt. He's one messed-up son-of-a-bitch, but he's no killer. He's convinced the Nicaraguans are going to kill him and begged me to give him the last rites. You Americans are always fucking up your own with your wars."

"Agree with you on that," Garner said gesturing with his cigarette.

"Get him out of here before they kill him."

"And if he is a murderer?" asked Garner.

"It is written, 'Vengeance is mine, I will repay, says the Lord', Romans, Chapter Twelve, Verse Nineteen," was the response. "Harry is in God's hands."

"I know you are a man of compassion, Doug, even for the despicable," Gregory Garner said before he walked away. Padre Doug never saw him again.

***

The morning after the terse parting note of her lover, Anne dragged herself from bed not bothering to check for snakes as she shuffled in bare feet toward the coffeepot.

"You slept late and you look terrible. Are you feeling well?" Evelyn noted.

"No. I drank too much wine last night and I feel worse than I look," Anne said. Jerking her head upward, she added in a mock cheerful voice, "Oh, well, on with life."

Although she felt sad for her cousin, Evelyn was relieved at Gregory Garner's departure. The relationship had to be terminated eventually, but what had possessed him to depart so suddenly leaving behind such a cold, cruel note for her cousin? *Anne, I have been assigned to another post. Goodbye. Gregory.* Anne deserved better. Observing Anne's jerky movements of cups and coffee pot, Evelyn placed a comforting hand on her arm. "You're sounding quite brave about this, *mi prima,*" she said.

Anne swung around to face her cousin, her eyes misty. "You told me when I was grieving over the pretzel boy at the airport – what choice do we have but to accept our losses and go on. But it's damned hard, isn't it?" she lamented.

"Yes, it's damned hard," Evelyn said softly.

Anne could not face work that day and called Dino, who willingly agreed to take her classes as he always did. She took a couple of aspirin and went back to bed, feeling slightly better when she awoke to Olga quietly humming as she mopped the floors. Evelyn had long since departed for Managua.

"Señora Ana, you look bad. I bring you some papaya and milk," Olga said.

Anne sank into the rocker mumbling her thanks automatically looking up toward Sweetie Pie's perch. "I have not seen the iguana for days," she mused not expecting an explanation.

"Hernández took the iguana with his sling. He was very proud," Olga said and related the story of how Renaldo had taught his son to use a slingshot.

"He killed the iguana?!" Anne cried, her face flushing.

A startled Olga tried to explain. "Señora Ana, the meat is good. The iguana is big. Four feet, Renaldo says. Renaldo let Hernández take it to Anita. And Anita gave us some of the meat. Not many get to eat iguana."

Anne moaned, "Dear God." Then turning her fury on Olga, she shouted in a mixture of Spanish and English, "What's wrong with you people! Iguanas are an endangered species!"

Olga realized her family had participated in something upsetting to her employer and felt terrible. "*Lo siento,*" she muttered forlornly. "I am sorry."

"I took pictures of Sweetie Pie. I loved seeing him. Anita knew that, why did you let Renaldo kill him, Olga? Why?" Anne sobbed, tears streaking down her cheeks. Anne had never understood the Nicaraguan attitude toward animals. As kind as Olga was, she did not flinch at the beating of oxen brought to their knees from pulling carts of wood too heavy for them. Skinny horses, their rib cages prominent, were whipped for balking at pulling a cartload of people, yet Olga was not disturbed at the sight. Olga seemed puzzled by Anne's reaction.

Olga believed God put animals on earth to help people live better and they had no value other than that. She had seen people in the American households she cleaned who treated their animals better than children. They had comfortable places to sleep and good food to eat. Cats and dogs even slept in the same beds as their owners. This was a strange thing to her. Cats were useful to keep rodents away, and they ate what they could find, not special food in fancy cans. And dogs were for protection. She was surprised when Señora Ana insisted she bring bones and other scraps to a place up the hill behind the Casa Sánchez where emaciated dogs soon learned to congregate. Why would the *señoras* want to encourage dangerous, half-starved animals to come to the property?

"I am sorry. I do not know the iguana is your – what do Americans say - pat."

"Pat?" Anne asked wiping her face with a tissue.

"A cat that sleeps in bed with people," explained Olga.

"Pet. You mean, pet."

"I am sorry*,*" Olga repeated, aware Señora Ana would not understand what a rare treat iguana was. She would not comprehend Hernández's pride in killing the creature for his family. She also knew that her mistress was mourning over the loss of her lover. The American was nice to Olga, often bringing her chocolate bars when he visited, but he was a man, and the specter of abandonment shadowed men. Olga had avoided the pain men were capable of inflicting, but others were not so lucky.

With a birdlike tremor, Anne said in a strangled voice, "I am sorry too, Olga. Forgive me." She fled into the bathroom. When Olga heard the shower run she prayed the water would cleanse Señora Ana's heart and make her happy again.

Weeping flooded Anne's lungs and pained her throat. She sobbed for the slaughtered iguana, for Raquel abandoned by her mother, for women brutally murdered, and for the asthmatic, struggling Camilo. She cried for her cousin's tragic losses, but most of all she wailed for Gregory until soreness closed her throat and raspy sounds filled the air. She had admired Evelyn's sense of adventure and longed to share in it, but her heart had not appreciated its cost. Shuddering and alone, she now longed for the familiar and the safe – her comfortable condo, the spirit-filled music of the church choir, the paper and book smell of her orderly classroom at Malden Community College. She had begun her good adventure intoxicated with the possibility of what lay ahead in this exotic country; seven months later, her energy swirled down a drain like the water in the shower. Still, in a few short months even though she had confronted the brutality of injustice and the grief that accompanies loss, she had to admit that her experience had also been a stimulating and hopeful celebration of the human spirit. Evie was the shining example of that spirit and Pastor Rafael and Marlene, Anita and Ernesto, Padre Doug, Dino, Pat and David, and even Olga had all demonstrated over and over again that life could be fully lived in the most adverse of circumstances.

As Anne lost herself in a willed and liberating sorrow, her lover was being driven to Augusto Sandino International Airport in Managua, his heart a rock, his mind a whirlpool of questions. Why had he pursued a relationship with Anne? What had he expected when he had pursued her? And after experiencing such soul nourishing moments in her presence, why had he walked away, leaving only a cold message of departure?

When Gregory's plane lifted into the air, he looked toward Lake Managua recalling the lake in the moonlight; Anne framed against the shimmering water in her stunning black dress. There they had first acknowledged the intensity of their mutual attraction. But now all hope of redemption with Anne was lost.

Feeling the tickle of tears in his eyes, Gregory wiped them away with his thumb and forefinger, an action that was observed by the Nicaraguan woman seated next to him in first class, her smooth face bearing no indication of a hard life in spite of its many years. Meticulously groomed, she was not of the class of Nicaraguan women Anne knew and Gregory immediately disliked her. He cranked his neck closer to the window and continued to look as Nicaragua faded from view.

Three weeks later, Padre Doug delivered a letter to Evelyn. "I think Anne would rather receive this from you. Garner mailed it to me at the church. Peter Hartwick claims he's in El Salvador."

When she handed Anne the envelope that evening, she said simply, "Peter thinks Gregory is in El Salvador."

Anne hesitantly accepted the envelope and extracted the letter.

Dear Anne,

How can I tell you the depth of my feeling when it is infinite? When I think of you, my spirit comes alive, my tempo quickens, my heart sings. You are the sweet tones of the flute, smooth and mellow. You warm my soul and call me forth.

I had to leave, my love. I think you know why. I don't know when I shall see you again, if ever. Know that you will always be in my heart. I thank the universe for having known you. – Greg

His poetic words hovered around her like a soft and radiant light. Anne carefully folded the letter and returned it to its envelope. "How I miss Sweetie Pie," she whispered in a small voice, pressing the envelope to her chest.

"I'm so sorry, *mi prima*," responded Evelyn. "Sometimes things you love just disappear."

CHAPTER TWENTY-THREE

September arrived quietly after four frenetic nights in August when Reverend William Archibald enthusiastically accepted Evelyn's invitation to sleep in their house while he attended the Atlantic Coast Autonomy Conference in Managua. As adopted aunt to his grandchild Raquel, Evelyn was now "family" with all the expectations of family hospitality, including vast quantities of food. Archibald chattered about the conference's daily accomplishments and Anne and Evelyn politely gave their attention to his updates.

But their main focus outside of their work was the children. They took Raquel and Anita's boys, Camilo and Hernández on outings to the beach, to a volcanic lake, and to festivals celebrating political and historical events, and saint festival days. Their hearts danced in the shimmering humid air no matter where they went, and when it rained they abandoned themselves to the freshness that wept on them in waves of choreographed water lifting their faces to the wetness.

"Pat left me a message yesterday that she had some good news to tell me in person," Evelyn said to Anne one morning as she nosed her truck through the gates of Managua University and parked.

"Let me know," said Anne.

Evelyn proceeded to Pat's office where Pat offered her a cheerful greeting. "It's official," she said. "Yesterday afternoon, we set the final details on the semester abroad program for Dr. Muriel Kent and her women's studies students. They're coming in March of next year for a term abroad."

"Thank you for making this happen," Evelyn declared. "I saw Muriel change, but I never expected her to go to such lengths to keep her connection with Nicaragua."

"It wouldn't have happened without you," Pat commented appreciatively.

Evelyn smiled over this positive result of her delegation work. A relationship between Managua University and a university in Boston was a definite plus for MU, no matter how tenuous. She felt lucky to work for La Esperanza. The loss of Rudy and Jasmina had created an angry stranger within her soul, but loving Raquel was slowly healing her, replacing bitterness with joy.

"As David says, the Kingdom of God is among us. We only need to manifest it," Pat declared and Evelyn smiled inside and out. With her elevated spirit, she bid Pat a good day and proceeded to the La Esperanza offices. She was humming a Nicaragua folk song when Pancho, the jaunty young guard, opened the gate with a bright *buenos dias*. Evelyn ascended sixteen concrete steps toward the office door and stepped into the tiny reception area. She greeted the receptionist, Julieta, then walked into a cavernous room where four carelessly crafted wooden desks rested awkwardly on a pitted tile floor.

Two smaller rooms had been carved from the larger one - the office of Alfonso Miranda and an all-purpose staff room. Waving to Miranda, Evelyn slid into her chair, unlocked the desk, and willed herself to tackle the paperwork essential to any non-profit financed by international donors.

A few moments later, Julieta bounced into the room, her frizzy hair sweeping the air like a broom, to announce a telephone call from America. Evelyn nodded and lifted the receiver.

"Hello, Evelyn? Señora Evelyn Gutiérrez?" said the disembodied voice.

"Yes, I am Evelyn Gutiérrez."

"Ah, my dear, how nice to hear your voice. Tom Shaw here. I have just listened to a recording of the Mormon Tabernacle Choir. My head is filled with music and I feel like singing. And, dear lady, you are a song to me. Forgive my indulgence."

Evelyn's smile curved into laughter. "Indulge all you want. It's wonderful to hear from you."

"I'm calling to report that I am well as is Shirley and, also, Ben. I called him yesterday and he tells me he wants to work in Central America when he graduates."

"What extraordinary news," Evelyn declared.

"He was quite impressed with the story of that young hero Benjamin Linder, especially to learn that he was Jewish. Ben's mother is Jewish, you know."

"I didn't know."

"That's only the beginning of my news. Before I tell you the rest, I want to thank you again on behalf of Shirley and myself. Your grace and courage under fire saved our lives."

"Others were involved as well," reminded Evelyn, visualizing Ian and feeling her heart warm as it always did when she thought of him.

"Oh, yes, Ian Campbell. A real take-charge fellow."

Evelyn wanted to ask Reverend Shaw if he had spoken to Ian, but the pastor's next sentence answered the unasked question. "I must give Ian and Rhoda a call some day."

Evelyn fell silent. "Are you managing, my dear?" Reverend Shaw asked carefully, and she understood the implied meaning.

"Yes, I'm fine," she responded in a whisper.

"I hope so," he said kindly. "You know, Evelyn, the tour was such an experience that I'm still digesting its meaning to my life. God is certainly at work in Nicaragua through people like you. The local media had a field day with the story of hometown clergy being attacked by bandits in Central America. We are a curiosity, great for church attendance, and we took advantage of all this publicity to organize several other churches in our community to hold a festival to raise funds for your children's home project. A large number turned out; some came as far as Minneapolis and the good news is that we raised fifteen thousand dollars."

Evelyn gasped, "Fifteen thousand dollars!" She sat erect and perfectly still, hearing the murmuring of voices around her responding to her sudden declaration.

"Yes, my dear, fifteen thousand dollars. We are sending you a check issued through my church. The United States Postal Service promises it will be hand-delivered to you at La Esperanza in four days."

"I can't believe it!" The office staff shuffled toward her desk and waited in curious anticipation for her exceptional news.

"Believe it. Accept it. And know that I will never forget the story you told me about your husband Rudolfo. It has inspired me to be a better preacher of the social gospel, even if I'm not always liked because of it."

"Thank you, thank you, Reverend Shaw," choked Evelyn.

"We thank *you*. Remember your promise to visit us in Minnesota. We have not had our little chat about God yet."

"Yes, I will keep my promise. I want to personally thank your congregation."

"We'll keep in touch, Evelyn."

"Oh, yes, please," she said, aware that her voice was cracking with emotion.

"God bless you," he concluded and hung up.

Evelyn surveyed the curious faces around her. When she blurted out an explanation, Alfonso Miranda remarked, "You can begin work on the children's home as soon as you find a building." He paused and added sadly. "We will miss you."

***

Rainy season was nearing an end, leaving behind a Nicaragua that shimmered in emerald green. Although Anne luxuriated in the verdancy of the natural world surrounding them, autumn in New England had always been her favorite season and she found herself missing it.

Returning from work on an auspicious day in mid-October, one that would be singed into their memories forever, she and Evelyn chatted about the brilliance of a foliage rich Massachusetts autumn, with its red and orange maples and fiery burning bushes. They lost themselves in wistful nostalgia remembering crisp nights, the smell of cider at orchard stands, the taste of cinnamon cider donuts, and the crunch of fallen leaves beneath their feet. Memories of Lynn and Danny hurling themselves into mounds of leaves, led Anne to imagine future days when she would welcome the little ones of her children. Anne knew her bonding with Raquel and Camilo and Hernández as pseudo grandchildren were fostering these memories.

As the women pulled the pick-up into San Linda, they spotted Renaldo standing in the middle of the road. Observing them, he turned away and jogged toward the Casa Sánchez. He held open the gate to the grounds of the house, appearing more dour than usual. Olga stood in the front yard, Raquel in her arms, Hernández clinging to her leg.

"Something's wrong," Anne remarked in alarm. Evelyn stopped the truck and the two women hopped out. Their presence unleashed a geyser of emotion in Olga who began to wail, "Camilo has gone to God!"

Dumbfounded, Anne knitted her brows and stared, certain she had misunderstood the Spanish until Olga repeated, "Camilo has gone to God!"

"No. Impossible," Anne protested refusing to believe it. She assured herself again that she had not understood the Spanish.

"Camilo has gone to God!" Olga groaned again, and Raquel burst into tears, telegraphing her terror at her aunt's lack of composure.

This is not true, Anne thought. *But Raquel is crying.* With an instinct to protect Raquel, Anne whisked the child into her arms and began to whisper gentle words of reassurance. Evelyn stood still, rooted in place and staring at Olga, her arms dangling by her sides. A stone-faced Renaldo approached Olga and jerked Hernández from her leg. Without uttering a word he walked off, pulling the protesting boy.

"The doctor say a scorpion stung him and made the asthma kill him," Olga wailed, looking at Evelyn who remained blank-eyed and straight as a soldier. *"Señora Evita! Escuche. Camilo está muerto. Por favor, Señora Evita!* Camilo has gone to God!*"*

"She is in shock," explained Anne, acknowledging that Olga's assaulting words were true and feeling the pain of them stab her heart. Had not Evelyn said the rainy season with its plethora of insects was the time when children die? Especially vulnerable children like Camilo. She squeezed the now whimpering Raquel to her as though protecting them both from the attack of an approaching enemy.

Olga wrapped her arms around Evelyn, repeating over and over, "Camilo has gone to God," until a guttural strangled sound emerged from Evelyn's throat, and she spoke in a strangely calm voice, "Who says this?"

"The doctor on the other side of the woods. Padre José went for him." Olga extracted a piece of paper from her apron pocket. It was a bill from the same physician to whom they had rushed Anita when she had suffered a miscarriage.

Looking at the paper Evelyn asked, "Camilo is dead?" The words from her own lips shattered the hastily erected shield of denial, allowing raw pain to surface like a malevolent shark. She began to totter. Olga grabbed her arm but Evelyn shook herself free, her arms flailing like the wings of a trapped bird, and she fell to her knees. Seeing her Aunt Evita fall, Raquel began to howl again. Anne handed her to Olga and went to her cousin.

"Evie, we'll get through this," she whispered softly, suppressing her own grief. A strange animal cry emerged from deep inside Evelyn who latched onto Anne's arm and pulled herself upright. Supported by Anne, she staggered across the road into the woods leading to the small house of Anita. The two women stumbled forward through the bush over the rocks and uneven earth, and when they reached the stark clearing, Evelyn's glazed eyes focused on the tiny dwelling.

Camilo lay on his bed, cold and white, a chaotic bouquet of wildflowers by his side. Anita was on her knees curving over him, gulping huge expansive breaths of air as though she needed a surplus of oxygen to survive. Standing next to her with a thin hand on her shoulder was the bent over elderly Catholic priest, Padre José of the Santa María Roman Catholic Church of Lower San Linda. When he realized the women were in the room, he gestured for them to approach. Evelyn sank to her knees to gather the distraught Anita into her arms and the padre stepped back.

"*Mi hijo! Mi hijo!*" Anita cried into Evelyn's chest.

"They will comfort each other," said the priest to Anne, his wrinkled face worn from a lifetime of ministering to his troubled flock. He took Anne's arm. "Come, we will talk outside." In the yard, he realized Anne's body was trembling and returned to the house for one of Renaldo's crooked wooden chairs. Insisting she sit, he remained standing, and taking her hand into his, he said, "God bless you, Señora. Your faith will support you in this tragedy."

Anne whispered, "Yes."

"Anita is a strong woman, Señora. She will overcome her sorrow."

"Yes."

"We must speak of the funeral. Anita was your employee*?*"

"Yes, before. She has the store now."

"I know. A good store." He paused. "I cannot talk to the mother. She is too upset, and the father is not here. We must pray he will not touch the rum." The priest made the sign of the cross. "We must decide when to say the funeral mass, and we must find a place of burial."

When she did not respond, the priest was unsure about how to speak to this American woman whom he did not know. "The sadness of the loss of a child is the worst, for when a child dies, we all die a little," he said softly and paused for her reaction.

The mix of sorrow and rage over the injustice of Camilo's death surging through Anne precluded comfort, yet she had sufficient presence of mind to respond, "Pray for us," she whispered.

"*Rezaré por vosotros y por la señora. Dios está con vosotros.* I will pray without ceasing," he assured Anne. She looked at him expectantly. "I do not wish to speak of the funeral at this time, yet it is necessary," he continued. "We are a small church and we have few resources."

Anne understood. "We will pay for the funeral," she promised.

***

Padre Doug arranged for Camilo to be buried in Managua's *Cementerio del Sagrado Corazón,* Cemetery of the Sacred Heart, near a section where he buried the bodies of abandoned children. The funeral was held in the Catholic

Church of San Juan el Bautista, not far from the cemetery, with Padre José officiating and Padre Doug assisting. Anita's extended family took a bus early that morning from Rivas in the south of Nicaragua.

Traffic stopped for the procession of people carrying flowers and walking behind the little bier carried by Renaldo and Esteban Guadeloupe, Anita's oldest brother. Under a heavy gray sky complementing the heaviness in their hearts, the mourners walked from the church to the cemetery. Camilo lay dressed in his best clothes, thin brown arms folded over his chest, cotton plugs in his ears and nostrils. The upper half of the coffin was open allowing everyone to see the child sleeping in eternal rest.

Padre José and Padre Doug led the procession, and a young Nicaraguan priest followed carrying a wooden cross taller than he was. Behind him, trudged Anita laboriously. Surrounded by her mother Lillian, her brothers, their families, aunts and uncles, and several cousins, she sobbed loudly, shoulders heaving as she walked. Evelyn, Anne and Pat Butler followed, Anne and Pat on either side of Evelyn, at the ready to catch her if she showed signs of collapse, but she was worrisomely calm. David did not feel well enough to attend. Olga followed behind, along with Anita's friends from Lower San Linda and Ernesto, Mario Flores, and his wife Rosita. Raquel and Hernández remained in San Linda with neighbor women who were preparing food at the Casa Sánchez for an after-funeral gathering.

The procession entered the cemetery under an arch carved with crosses. They passed a stone statue of the Virgin Mary, who showered them with her blessing, and proceeded solemnly to a small hole in the earth. Renaldo and Esteban laid the tiny coffin by the hole, and Padre José closed the open half of the coffin before he began to recite the ritualistic prayers that committed Camilo to the rich earth from whence he had come. One of Anita's sisters handed out daisies, and one by one the mourners stepped forward to lay a daisy upon the coffin. As Evelyn released her daisy, Padre Doug held her arm and whispered, "God is with you, my daughter."

When the coffin was covered with daisies, the gravediggers lowered it into the earth, and Anita Guadeloupe commenced to wail. "Come back. Just for a little while," she cried over and over as her brothers held her upright. Anne's thoughts were on Lynn and Danny and she yearned to tell them that she loved them deeply. As devastating as were the deaths of Jasmina and Rudolfo, she didn't know them well. Camilo, however, had captured her heart with his quiet curiosity during the last eight months. She grasped Evelyn's hand as Anita's excruciating wails for Camilo burned through them. Evelyn remained dry-eyed, but the expression on her face communicated her anguish over Anita's wailing.

Following the funeral, Anita's family piled into Evelyn's truck, driven by Ernesto, and the Jeep of Padre Doug; Pat Butler took a silent Evelyn, Anne, Anita and Renaldo in her car back to the village, and the Flores family took the bus. A meal of beans and rice, tortillas, yucca, and salad awaited them at the Casa Sánchez. When the crowd arrived, food was heaped onto plates and people ate and talked and reminisced. Anita, in the comforting bosom of her family, regained composure, talking with cousins, aunts, and uncles whom she seldom saw. Renaldo at the edge of the crowd, stared blankly, his fists curled, his complexion pallid. Hernández clung to his mother's hand until Anne took him and Raquel into her room where she sat on the bed with the two children as they snuggled into sleep, Raquel clutching her beloved Raggedy Ann doll.

Padre Doug, Pat, and Evelyn sat side-by-side in silence observing the mourners. Ernesto and his parents had retreated to a corner of the room, where they balanced plates of food on their laps. Evelyn pushed to her feet and approached them. "I know this is difficult for you, Ernesto. You loved little Camilo as did I," she said softly.

Ernesto nodded, his somber face twisted in an effort to keep from crying.

"You are a good man. You are good to Anita. You helped us with the police when they came for Harry Albert. I thank you." Ernesto, engaged in a struggle against tears, remained silent. He wanted to howl not only for the loss of Camilo, but for the loss of the brother he had never properly grieved, but he knew he had to remain strong and collected for his parents.

Mario, observing his son's distress spoke for him, "Thank you, Señora Gutiérrez, for your help to my son and Anita. You too are a good woman."

After the interchange, Evelyn returned to her seat next to Padre Doug, slipped her hand into his, and by that action she communicated her intention to recover her spirit.

The poignant reunion continued until six when the Rivas relatives needed to catch the last bus home. Padre Doug and Pat Butler squeezed them into their vehicles for the trip to the Managua bus station while Ernesto offered to take Lillian and her family, and his parents to their houses in Evelyn's truck.

"You stay with Anita, Ernesto. She needs you. I'll drive them home," said Evelyn.

"I wish I felt secure enough to drive," Anne lamented to her cousin. "You didn't cry during the funeral and you have been so quiet. Are you okay?"

Evelyn's skin lifted into tiny mounds on her forehead, yet she was calm. "No, I am not okay, Annie; my heart is wrenched," she said in a whisper that gained force as she spoke, "but I am grateful we had Camilo to love for a few months. I have been unwilling to accept tragedy with grace. No longer. I now accept that life is ephemeral. I will miss Camilo terribly, but my time with him was precious, as was my time with Jasmina. I am blessed with love and that has always been so."

A rush of compassion, mixed with a hopeful sense of liberation filled Anne. She remembered Evelyn's words when she had first arrived in Nicaragua and had dissolved into guilty tears over her reaction to the pretzel boy in Guatemala. *Annie, I'm not all that special. Anyone who refuses to be broken by tragedy can be inspiring.* Her cousin would overcome another of life's tragedies and go on, and so would she.

She would forgive herself for resenting Evelyn even as she admired her; she would forgive herself for her fear and revulsion over the pretzel boy, the beggars in the park, and the one-eyed beggar who showed up at their door in Lower San Linda. She would forgive herself for failing the poor children in the inner city school all those years ago, for not loving Keith enough to continue living with him, and for all the mistakes she had made as a mother. And she would not only forgive herself for loving Gregory, but be grateful for the happy moments she had shared with him. Like Evelyn, she would go on through whatever misery she had to endure and feel blessed for the love she received.

After everyone had departed, Olga started to wash dirty dishes, but Anne insisted she go home. "Renaldo needs you more than I do," she said.

"I will keep him from drinking," Olga promised. She gathered a sleepy Raquel into her arms and left to join Renaldo, who had retreated onto the patio where he had smoked his way through a pack of cigarettes.

Ernesto and Anita remained seated side-by-side on the hard backed dining chairs, Ernesto holding the grieving mother close, his hand curved protectively around her back. A sleepy Hernández was curled into her lap, his arms around her waist.

"Anita, do you want to take food home?" Anne asked softly. With a dull stare, Anita nodded, and Ernesto pressed his forehead to hers, whispering a few words before he joined Anne in the kitchen packaging the leftovers.

"Señora Ana," he said. "Anita will soon be happy again because she carries my child." Anne could not help but smile at this ray of sunshine poking through the gray gloom of the day.

"You will be a good father, Ernesto," she said sincerely.

When they were gone, Anne welcomed the work of scrubbing the dishes and mopping the floor. Afterwards she fell into a rocker and out of habit looked up toward the roof where Sweetie Pie had lived. For a fleeting moment, she saw Camilo with Sweetie Pie draped over his leg in his usual still repose. Camilo waved to her and she waved back.

***

The cousins jerked awake to a piercing animal shriek and the screeching of two human voices whipping toward them from Anita's house. They dashed across the street, in their night gowns hurtling through the brush and into the clearing where they saw Hernández, straddling the family pig that was shrieking in pain while Anita, red faced and furious, jabbed at its anus with a knife.

"She's castrating it," explained Evelyn, who jumped beside Anita to help with the wrenching task. She grasped the pig's hind legs allowing Anita to concentrate on cutting through its testicles. Anne had seen a villager in Los Ríos castrate a young pig claiming that with castration, the pig put on more fat and the meat did not have the strong piggy smell. The procedure was excruciating to watch. A boy as little as Hernández could not subdue the terrified animal that tossed the child like a rowboat in a storm.

"Where's Ernesto!" Evelyn shouted. Then she remembered this was his early morning at his father's bicycle shop. "Sit on the pig with Hernández!" she yelled to Anne.

Fearfully, Anne threw her long legs over the pig, its shrieks piercing her ears. She held on breathing through her mouth to lessen the stench. Her feet slid in a slop of blood, excrement and dirt. "Oh God! Oh God!" she cried, clinging to the pig's flailing torso.

With Evelyn's help, Anita severed the testicles and was dangling them like a victory prize when she lost her footing and tumbled into mud and pig slime. Evelyn reached down to help her and she too tumbled over as Anne and

Hernández catapulted off the pig landing in the same stench. For a moment they all sat stunned, spattered with filth. The traumatized pig relieved of the crushing pain bounded to its feet, grunting and swishing his ample body, flicking off more slime on everyone.

Such a bizarre scene struck Anne as hilarious and she started laughing. Anita and Evelyn soon joined in laughing wildly. Hernández thought the women crazy, but was relieved to see his mother laughing. The women laughed and laughed until they cried and their bodies ached.

That night Evelyn phoned Pat Butler and asked if she could have her portrait of Jasmina to hang in the Casa Sánchez. "Soon it will hang in the foyer of the Hogar Jasmina," she declared with certainty.

"Of course you may have the portrait, Evita," said Pat. "I've been waiting for you to ask."

EPILOG – 2003

Lynn Anne Scott stepped into the cool of the modern main terminal of the Aeropuerto Internacional Augusto Cesar Sandino, remembering her mother's stories of arriving to heat and chaos from Guatemala twelve years earlier.

"Don't be fooled by Managua," her mother warned referring to the vast amounts of money that had poured into Nicaragua from international banks to update the airport, build high-rise hotels, and repave roads throughout Managua and other sections of the country where tourism was important. "Nicaragua is still one of the poorest countries in Central America. Evelyn will show you the conditions in which most Nicaraguans live – over 60% of them according to the statistics I've read. The Hogar Jasmina is filled with kids abandoned by families too poor to keep them."

Lynn concluded Mom was appealing to Lynn's bleeding heart sensitivity by emphasizing the rightness of her decision to volunteer at Managua University. As owner of Harrison Intelligent Choice Computer Sales and Repair of Bishop, California, she had come at her Evelyn's request and Mom's not-so-subtle urging to dedicate four weeks of precious time toward rehabilitating Managua University's aging computers. She felt secure her business was in the capable hands of her employees back in California; nonetheless, she was uneasy over her departure from everyday management.

Twisting a strand of mousy brown hair back into the rubber band that secured a short ponytail, Lynn strode briskly toward the baggage carousel. She moved with an easy confidence, honed over six years as a small business owner dealing with demanding customers and erratic suppliers. At first glance, one would not think she was Anne Harrison's daughter. She had inherited her father's hazel eyes and brown hair. Like Anne, however, Lynn was tall and mimicked her mother's gestures unconsciously.

Collecting the two floppy brown cloth bags in which she had packed simple, practical clothes, lightweight jeans, T-shirts, and at her mother's suggestion, a couple of dresses, Lynn proceeded past a glass wall. On the other side, she recognized Evelyn, her black hair cut short and sprinkled with silver. She was talking to an older stocky man a few inches taller. When they spotted her, they both waved, Evelyn smiling, the man stony faced.

Must be Dr. Ramón Morales, the Rector of Managua University.

Mom told her he would probably be there. On the other side of Evelyn was easy-going Ian. Lynn was surprised when Evelyn had married him; not that she didn't think Evelyn would remarry, but she assumed any new husband would be Nicaraguan.

Evelyn had a talent for surprising people. Three years earlier, she had gone to Guatamala to visit an orphanage similar to Hogar Jasmina in Matagalpa, and there she met Ian Campbell working for an American non-profit on a solar energy project. He was divorced, and the rest was history.

"She's marrying the boy next door even though she left Stoneham at seventeen," Grandma Lynn declared at the wedding.

Evelyn's teen-aged adopted daughter, Raquel, was standing next to a tall man, all arms and legs. He had to be the man who had been in the same delegation trip as was Ian, the one wounded during the attack by bandits. Her mother had mentioned he was teaching anthropology at Managua University. Evelyn also spoke of him and her comments were glowing.

I hope my Evelyn isn't into matchmaking, thought Lynn remembering that she hadn't put on lipstick after lunch, her one concession to make-up. She rummaged inside her handbag, but she couldn't locate the tube. *Oh, well, it isn't like I'm trying to impress anyone.*

Lynn reluctantly admitted to herself that lately she was thinking more about men. With the birth of Annie, her niece, a yearning for motherhood had enveloped her. The child was so adorable that even her reserved brother, Danny, was reduced to babbling in his daughter's presence. Of course, since Danny's near miss during the terrorist attack of 9/11, his personality had warmed considerably. His cool cockiness was gone. He could have been killed had he not been out of town on a business trip that day. Within months, he had left New York to accept a job as comptroller at a university in Boston.

As satisfied as she was with owning a business, Lynn felt something was missing. During the four weeks in Nicaragua away from the distractions of the shop, she would reflect on her life. A bolt of revelation might strike her as it had her mother, who had returned from what she called her "good adventure" in Nicaragua more content, serene at times, and had become an anti-war activist. Lynn knew her mother possessed a social conscience but organizing vigils and marches and public displays of protest against war was something else. And even though Lynn respected her mother's dedication, she doubted it would do any good. When the politicos wanted war, war happened.

The important thing to Lynn was that she felt valued and respected by her mother and her brother. Even her father seemed interested in her these days, and he had also become quite chummy with her mother lately. Maybe they would get back together, in spite of Mom's protests to the contrary.

Shoving her bags through a cursory customs check, Lynn exited into the main terminal. She strode briskly toward Evelyn, surprised by her delight in seeing the woman whom she had once resented for stealing away her mother's affection. She first embraced Evelyn, then felt Ian's muscular arms around her. Released, she was introduced to Dr. Morales, who welcomed her to Nicaragua and Managua University with summary brusqueness before departing quickly.

"Typical," declared Evelyn, rolling her eyes as he strode off.

Lynn hugged Raquel, who planted a welcoming kiss on her cheek. As though they had a mind of their own, her eyes gravitated toward the man Evelyn introduced as Benjamin Conway. He winked at her, hazel eyes twinkling. Surprising herself, Lynn winked back.